The Murdered City

The Murdered City
and Other Stories

by
Fernand Mysor

Translated, annotated and introduced by
Brian Stableford

A Black Coat Press Book

TABLE OF CONTENTS

Introduction

La Ville assassinée by Fernand Mysor, here translated as "The Murdered City," was initially published by Librairie Baudinière in 1925. The second short novel included in the collection, *Par T.S.F.*, here translated as "By Wireless," was published by Bibliothèque-Charpentier in 1927. The short story completing the collection, "La Mort du soleil" (tr. here as "The Death of the Sun"), first appeared in the weekly literary supplement of the newspaper *Le Figaro* on 25 September 1926.

"Fernand Mysor" was the pseudonym of the poet apparently baptized Léonce-Marie-Fernand Fricou (1876-1931), who is most abundantly represented on the Bibliothèque Nationale's *gallica* website by those of his verses that were set to music by various composers, some of which became popular songs, many of them performed in the cabarets on Montmartre, where the author worked as a singer and musician while trying patiently to establish himself as a poet, playwright and journalist in early years of the century. His most notable compositions included "Aimons-nous toujours" [Will we love one another forever?] (1909) with music by Charles Bourgeois, and "L'Âme du vin" [The Soul of Wine] (1909) and "Ballade des pauvres gens" [Poor People's Ballad] (1910), both with music by Raphaël Wibier.

Almost nothing was recorded about the author prior to the Great War, and almost all of the details that subsequently reached reference sources appears to have been mistaken, in view of the scrupulous research recently carried out by Fabrice Mundzik and Jean-Luc Buard, reported in Mundzik's introduction to the collection *De la Terre d'autrefois à la Terre de demain* (2016), issued by his *Les Cahiers archéo-bibliographiques*. Mundzik and Buard have established that

Fricou was actually born in Espassel in Tarn-et-Garonne, in the home of his maternal grandmother, although he always claimed to have been born in Quercy, where he apparently lived before going to seek his fortune in Paris in the 1890s. His parents were both schoolteachers, and he married a schoolteacher, Jeanne Gimet, in 1910, shortly before he published his first volume of poetry, *Les Poèmes de la Belle Étreinte* (1911). He continued to publish poems during the Great War, almost all of them reflecting darkly on that "temps maudits" [accursed times], as one of his titles described it. He also published a few articles in newspapers, but appears to have had a very difficult time, and it was not until some years after the end of the war, by which time he was in his late forties, that he finally began to achieve a measurable success, as a journalist, a playwright and, most especially, as a novelist.

Mysor's first-published novel, *L'Âme ardente* [The Ardent Soul] (1922), a naturalistic but eccentric novel set in Paris and the environs of Quercy, was well-received, and laid the foundations for further critical success. His second novel *Les Semeurs d'épouvante* [The Sowers of Terror] (1923) was, however, a radical sidestep, a "Romance of the Jurassic Era" that attempted to renew the subgenre of prehistoric fiction pioneered in France by J.-H. Rosny *aîné* in a series of works begun with *Vamireh* (1892) and *Eyrimah* (1893)—both translated in *Vamireh and Other Prehistoric Fantasies*[1]—and Edmond Haraucourt's magisterial *Daâh, le premier homme* (1914; tr. as *Daah, the First Human*)[2]. Mysor's prehistoric romance was followed by another significant contribution to the same subgenre, *Va'Hour l'illuminé* [Va'Hour the Enlightened] (1924).

Mundzik quotes an article by Renée Dunan published in March 1923 in which Dunan claimed to have seen a manuscript by Mysor entitled *La Ville assassinée*, and gave a brief summation of its theme, and it appears that the novel was at

[1] Black Coat Press, ISBN 978-1-935558-38-5.
[2] Black Coat Press, ISBN 978-1-61227-355-6.

least partly, and probably mostly, written in 1919, in the immediate aftermath of the Great War; Mundzik also cites a letter written in that year in which Mysor reported that he was writing a novel entitled *La Cité des surhommes* [The City of the Superhumans], which is obviously the same story. The evidence of the text suggests that it might not have been concluded then, as the story undergoes a considerable metamorphosis in the course of its unfolding, but even though its rhetorical thrust is more than a trifle inconsistent, the entire exercise is very obviously a reaction to the bitter legacy of the war and its horrors.

Although the story obviously invites comparison with other speculative novels of the interbellum period in which modern science enables the fulfillment of the ancient alchemical dream of manufacturing gold, most notably *La Chasse aux chimères* (1932; tr. as *The Chimerical Quest*) by René Pujol,[3] *La Ville assassinée* is markedly different from stories that attempt to anticipate logically what the economic and social consequences of such a discovery might be; it is stylized almost to the point of surrealization. Gold effectively functions within the story as a symbol of modern civilization, facilitating the construction of a kind of ultimate city, and as an irresistible force of corruption; the plot of the story makes only the most tokenistic attempt at rational plausibility, aiming instead for a hectic melodramatic flamboyance that was rarely matched even in a post-war decade highly conducive to such passionate exercises.

La Ville assassinée has affinities with such pre-war accounts of island utopias gone wrong as André Couveur's *Caresco, surhomme* (1905; tr. as *Caresco, Superman*)[4] and also with such post-war accounts of doomed superscientific cities as Renée Dunan's *La Dernière jouissance* (1925; tr. as *The Ultimate Pleasure*),[5] but that kind of narrative schema has

---

[3] Black Coat Press, ISBN 978-1-61227-488-1.
[4] Black Coat Press, ISBN 978-1-61227-254-2.
[5] Black Coat Press, ISBN 978-1-61227-406-5.

abundant scope for variation, and Mysor's work only contains tenuous links with speculative fictions by his contemporaries—although it would not be surprising, if Dunan had actually read the manuscript to which she referred in 1923, if her own novel took some inspiration from it. As well as an exercise in speculative fiction, Mysor's novel is also an angry revenge fantasy and an extraordinary love story, in both of which respects it deliberately flies in the face of convention, aiming for an idiosyncratic cynicism. It intends to be deeply disturbing, and even at a safe historical distance of nearly a hundred years, it still makes for discomfiting reading.

As events transpired, *La Ville assassinée*, although undoubtedly the first of Mysor's books to be written, was the fifth to be published, 1924 also having seen the publication of *La Négresse dans la piscine* [The Negress in the Swimming-Bath], written with collaboration with his friend and fellow cabaret singer Vincent Hyspa (1865-1938), allegedly shortly before the latter's arrest on a charge of murder—although he later had a successful career as a movie actor—which shows a more evident association with the burgeoning ideology of surrealism. It was followed by *Par T.S.F.*, which had been advertized as forthcoming in 1925, which has definite affinities with it, in the marginally speculative elements of its plot, the strange character of its disfigured protagonist, and the bizarrerie of his hopeless and fatal amorous obsession.

Like its predecessor, *Par T.S.F.* seems to have been written in at least two separate periods of time, and it undergoes a similarly drastic metamorphosis of narrative focus. When the protagonist's enthusiasm for wireless technology and the science behind it is introduced, extravagant claims are made about the new equipment he has invented and his enthusiasm for science, including occult science, all of which seems to promise a fantastic story. When the protagonist finally gets around to deploying his equipment, however, he uses no devices that were not actually available at the time, and throughout the second half of the story there is not a shred of evidence of his interest or expertise in science; the marginal occult phenomena that occur within the story are all credited to other characters, to the utter bewilderment of the protagonist.

In respect of its featured technology, in fact, *Par T.S.F.* had the misfortune to be very rapidly outdated. Set in a time when the radio broadcasts made from the Eiffel Tower had relatively few listeners, who employed headphones rather than the kind of tabletop radio sets that soon became standard household items, its imagery became obsolete as soon as it was published—which must have frustrated the writer, who had probably begun it sometime before 1925, when its impending publication was first advertized, and perhaps in the same period, immediately after the war, when he began writing *La Ville assassinée*.

Close examination of the text of *Par T.S.F.* suggests that the phases of the story were probably not written in the order in which they appear, thus compounding the problems that arise from the complex admixture in the narrative of past and present tenses. It is not uncommon in French fiction for writers to move back and forth between past and present tenses, but Mysor's gradually-unfolding first-person narrative suffers from acute problems of temporal viewpoint as it interleaves adventurous stream-of-consciousness passages with the mapping of the sequence of events. Partly because of those problems, however, the text has a striking originality, and, seen as a melodramatic account of a doomed amour—of which there is certainly no scarcity in French literature—it is as remarkable in its peculiar idiosyncrasy as its predecessor.

Fabrice Mundzik reports that another Mysor title, *La Vie est douce* [Life is Sweet], has been cited as having been published in 1925, but that no copy of any such book is traceable; the list of the author's works included in *Par T.S.F.* credits its publication to the periodical *La Grande Revue*, so it is presumably a short story. The same list of the author's works includes *L'Étrange assassinat* [The Strange Murder], indicated as *en préparation*, which is presumably the novel that appeared as *Spasmes* (1929), an extremely difficult volume to find, on which I am not able to comment. A collection of the author's short stories, *Le Coeur blessé* (1922) is also extremely elusive; the short stories that remain traceable in their periodical publications are mostly whimsical *contes cruels*. Mundzik reprints a handful of them in *De la Terre d'autrefois à la Terre de demain*, but by far the most impressive piece in that collection is "La Mort du soleil." The tone and attitude of the story have a certain affinity with *La Ville assassinée*, although the bitter wrath of the novel has faded to an elegiac regret. The short story has affinities with other apocalyptic fantasies produced in the early twentieth century, most notably the striking *Le Triomphe de l'homme* [The Triumph of Humankind] (1911) by the Belgian writer François Léonard, but again, its tone is distinctive, marking the author out as the possessor of a highly unusual creative imagination.

As with many writers to whom a similar description can be applied, Fernand Mysor never achieved any considerable success with the reading public, and such critical praise as he received during the 1920s was rarely reiterated thereafter. He was almost completely forgotten for the remainder of the century, and had virtually vanished from the literary radar by the time that Fabrice Mundzik attempted a modest resurrection of his reputation. It is a great pity, but no cause for surprise, that a writer of such imaginative range found it so difficult to scrape a living; that was by no means unknown for imaginative writers in the period of his activity. Mundzik is, however, entirely correct in asserting that Mysor deserves to be better known in an era when more readers are capable of appreciating exotic artistry and interested in discovering unusual themes and philosophical viewpoints.

The translation of *La Ville assassinée* was made from a copy of the Librairie Baudinière edition. The copy in question is advertized on the cover as "tenth thousand," but that is probably not true, and the cover also has an overstamped price of two francs (it initially sold for seven francs fifty) suggesting that it was a remainder copy. The translation of "La Mort du soleil" was made from the version contained in the 2016 booklet published by Les Cahiers archéobibliographiques. The translation of *Par T.S.F.* was made from a copy of the Bibliothèque-Charpentier edition.

Brian Stableford

THE MURDERED CITY

I

As he was about to light his match, Blasius stopped.

He put it back in the box gently, placed the box on a dirty elm-wood table beside him, and sat down.

With a slow gaze he considered the small room with the low ceiling and the ragged wallpaper where he had dragged out his mediocre life for years.

Near the fireplace, on a cast iron stove three-quarters full of charcoal, two retorts displayed shiny bulbs. A thin glass tube linked their slender necks together. The one on the right was empty. The one on the left contained a red liquid, in which the setting sun caused occasional golden flecks to glimmer. On a small table near the stove, pewter crucibles, chipped trays and multiform test-tubes were heaped up in disorder.

On the shelves in a glass-fronted cupboard, flasks labeled with numbers and chemical formulae; jars with exaggerated curves, and green, yellow and blue bottles contained solutions, powders and mysterious mixtures.

On the walls, portraits of illustrious scientists were completing their gradual fading, They were facing portraits of musicians and poets, and even a few actors of quality, ostentatious between the black sticks of frames: glabrous profiles and arrogant muzzles.

No bed—but on four iron feet fitted with castors, a vast black bear skin stretched like a drumskin and laden with oval cushions.

A wicker armchair into which Blasius had just let himself fall and four disparate chairs completed the furniture of that monastic room.

Leaning his right arm on the chair, Blasius was pensive...

His gaze, with no precise objective, settled on the trees that were perceptible in the large park surrounding the solitary maisonette. It wandered furtively from crown to crown, lingered over box-trees, the acrid odors of which rose toward his nostrils through the open windows, and returned after that luminous voyage to the coupled retorts, the cast-iron stove and all the apparatus of his arduous research, ingrate and terrible labor in which he was at continual risk of leaving his life, after having left his youth therein.

He was very tall and very thin. His hooked nose, like an eagle's beak, and his prominent chin, gave him a hard and antipathetic appearance. The reflections of his steel-gray eyes penetrated the surroundings, seeming to dissect them like living scalpels, and his pale hands, as delicate as feminine hands, burned in places by mixtures concocted during quotidian experiments, appeared too weak to sustain his forehead, of a seeker and a visionary.

He did not wear the kind of smock usually worn by scientists, but his long fleshless body floated in a chocolate brown monastic habit attached at the waist by a knotted rope. The extremity of that rope hung down the left-hand upright of the armchair, and from time to time Blasius seized it with his unoccupied hand and swung it rhythmically around his legs.

He had arrived one morning, from no one knew where, in front of the abandoned maisonette. He had examined it carefully from every side and had left again, furnished with the information provided by the notice pinned to the entry door.

Then, after an interval of five days, the gate of the house had groaned under the pressure of a vigorous arm, tearing up the wild grass and gravel of the pathway; and through the gaping opening a vehicle covered by a tarpaulin had come, halting in front of the mossy stones of the perron.

Moving in, accomplished by Blasius without any external aid, had not taken long. No neighbor, in any case, was disturbed by the resurrection of those lethargic walls, for the dwelling least distant from the retreat was more than an hour's walk away.

The vehicle departed the same evening. The gate closed again, and silence extended its soft wings once again over the closed garden and the leafy hermitage.

Having organized his material life, choosing the suppliers who were to provide him with food and drink, Blasius installed his laboratory, and, deaf to the appeals of any ambient joy and splendor, he set to work.

Day and night, for years, he buried himself amid his retorts and crucibles. When his effort was crowned by a result, when another discovery was added to the previous discoveries, Blasius untied his belt of rope, took off his monk's habit, donned inelegant garments and took a train to the distant city. He stayed there for a week—rarely two—and then, still alone, still mute, he returned to his retreat and recommenced his labor.

He went back to it, driven by an invincible force, but with death in his soul. For, every time he departed for the somber city, taking with him the formula of a new discovery, he came back having been thrown out, demolished and soiled by the arbiters of renown and science, with such commentaries that be doubted himself for months.

During his tragic returns he dreamed of crazy vengeances. He extended his ascetic fists toward the abominable horde, and he wrapped in his hatred the most criminal, the purest and the most pitiful ideas.

Then the days went by, gray or blue. The peace of the next day attenuated the fury of the one before, and gradually, in slow animate undulations, serenity entered into him again. He found himself calm enough once again to reflect, to measure the vanity of his anger. And he continued his bitter route, without friends, without affection, alone in a insensible world, like an autumn leaf blown by the north wind in the middle of a forest.

Avenge oneself? On whom and on what? Does one avenge oneself on the world when one is, as he had been for forty years, a poor creature of impotence and obscurity? Does one avenge oneself on life when one has always vegetated on the margin of one's fellows, and when one does not even possess an exact notion of existence? Oh, yes! He would have avenged himself if he had been able to remain malevolent to the end. But to savor vengeances like those he desired, it is necessary to be rich and powerful, and he was, alas, neither powerful nor rich. Then again, it was better to resign oneself, to accept from life that which it wants to give, without extenuating oneself demanding the impossible.

And thus, he had come to bury himself in the depths of this valley, away from habitual routes, in an area similar to neighboring areas, but more deserted.

He had chosen this house, which the weight of ivy, wisteria and odorous foliage seemed to be crushing; this house, which gave him the impression of kneeling before the immense solitude. And little by little, after heart-rending dolors, the quietude of the surroundings submerged him. The charm of that adorable summer circled his scarred heart like a great veil of perfumes and harmonies; and in the pure air, in the healthy and limpid atmosphere, the creative force of his brain was multiplied tenfold.

Once again, after all, he became the visionary infatuated with the ungraspable. Tomorrow he would accomplish such prodigies that perhaps his enemies would finally recognize him as the foremost among sages. And before that contrition, before that reparation, he would forget everything; and nothing more would prevent him henceforth from arriving at the realization of the great work to which he consecrated all his genius, incessantly and without weakening. For, since the failure of his *Treatise on active and passive cerebral phenomena*, Blasius, who had sounded the arcana of chemistry, physics and occultism, had abandoned the elevated psychic, esoteric and spiritualist science in order to absorb himself uniquely in experiments in transmutation.

With an obstinate patience, in his rudimentary laboratory, he had studied the properties of radium. Progressively, in the course of dangerous trials, but from which he had always emerged without serious accidents, he had disintegrated that simple substance into a series of new elements.

And today, in the splendor of this regal dusk, he had prepared an experiment whose success would permit him, later, to regulate all the phases of the spontaneous transmutation.

He would triumph, he was certain of it. But a sudden anguish gripped him at the moment of action; and he, the audacious, the resolute, dared not even strike the match that would ignite his burner.

And then, what was the point? If he succeeded, did he imagine, perchance, that the masters would recognize his success? As from each of his journeys, he would come back from that one trailing his feet through the mud, defamed, more beaten down than ever by human stupidity and injustice.

Outside, night was falling gradually. The wind seemed to be expiring amid the foliage of the plane trees and the flowers on the bushes. The cries of birds could no longer be heard, and in the distance, on the slope of some fissured hill, two owls were launching nostalgic ululations into the star-spangled air. In the great nocturnal silence, compounded from a thousand imperceptible sonorities, the heart of the solitary individual constricted. He could not resolve to quit his armchair, approach the stove, heat the retorts and tempt God.

And yet he had to. He had to! He had to dare, under pain of failing in his own eyes.

And suddenly, he got up, determined.

He struck his match, first lit the incandescent lamp that he used for illumination, and then, with the same piece of ardent wood he set fire to the paper on which the charcoal was heaped.

The sheets twisted; with a dull growl the flame was engulfed in the sheet-metal flue, and the charcoal began to crackle with little dry sounds. Gradually, the entire hearth reddened, and, with a monotonous song, globules agitated in the bulb of frosted glass

Leaning over the stove, Blasius followed the progress of the heat with a passionate attention. A thermometer fixed to the interior wall of a retort indicated the exact temperature to him, and vapors were already flowing, in little spurts, through a hole pierced at the summit of the tube linking the two instruments.

Now the mixture was approaching boiling point. The vapor became denser and spread, whistling, into the laboratory. Large bubbles departed from the bottom of the retorts, traversing the liquid mass from bottom to top, and came to burst on the surface with the gurgles of a sick man choking on his own fluids.

The chemical compound gradually turned from red to blue, with glints of orange. Then the boiling was affirmed.

Blasius leaned toward the thermometer more attentively. At the same time he took out his watch, and placed it close to him on the stove, ready to remove the retorts when he judged the moment opportune.

He counted the seconds in a low voice, in order to operate with more certainty.

As he pronounced the number six, an explosion pulverized the receptacles, caused the chemical composition to spurt up to the ceiling in circles, jets and droplets, while the violence of the blast threw the experimenter backwards, and an unbearable acridity invaded the small room. Ruddy, heavy smoke, spread like a carpet over the floor by awkward hands, rolled around faded drapes, flattened beneath portraits, was incrusted in the interstices of frames, and gradually extinguished the fire. Mephitic odors spread through the laboratory, seizing Blasius by the throat, interposing themselves between the pure air and his nostrils. He struggled, trying to reach the exit, or to reopen the window, which he had carefully closed at the beginning of the experiment. It was in vain; asphyxia defeated him. The more he opened his mouth in order to gulp the salutary air, the more the nauseating gas plunged into his lungs.

Then he tried to call for help; but nothing emerged from his throat but muffled roans. And, more implacable from one second to the next, the mysterious poison paralyzed him. Like an inert mass, he collapsed next to the armchair; he stayed there for a long time, unconscious.

Meanwhile, the yellow vapors accomplished their slow ascensional labor. Having surpassed the top of the cupboard in which Blasius stacked his bottles and glassware, they stopped at the ceiling and maintained themselves there like miniature clouds beneath a sky of sorcery. They formed a compact layer, and from one minute to the next the particles of gas still lingering in the room came to add to that lake of moving smoke. By rising up in that fashion they cleared the atmosphere. And when there was no longer any noxious swirl in the laboratory, the salutary air returned to Blasius's nostrils.

First he agitated feebly and moaned. Then he tried to move, sensing his strength reborn. Painfully, he pushed himself up, supporting himself on his hands. His eyes, adapting to the obscurity, gradually distinguished objects and furniture. He dragged himself to the table, found a lighter in his pocket, and was able to light the stub of a candle picked up from underneath a chair. Once the candle was lit, a feeble gleam illuminated the room.

Then, hanging on to the edge of the rectangular table, Blasius got to his feet. Dazed, his eyes vague, he let himself fall on to a stool, with his head between his hands, and he strove to pull himself together. He cracked his knuckles, kneaded the muscles of his neck and stretched his thin legs. In the course of those gymnastics, he perceived the clouds heaped up against the ceiling.

Now he remembered! But before anything else, it was necessary to purify the atmosphere, to escape the poison whose origin he did not know, and which had nearly stifled him.

He went down on all fours again, and, crawling like a seal, he reached the door and opened it.

A wave of embalmed air invaded the laboratory; all the nocturnal effluvia rushed in, with a powerful surge, against the vapor accumulated under the ceiling.

Standing up, Blasius unfastened the window-catches, and it was no longer a mere gust of fresh air but an irresistible current that swept away all the smoke, expelling it into the splendor of the night like something hateful, and soon took possession again of the maisonette, to the song of toads and crickets intoxicated by the dew.

And when the last swirl of toxic substance had disappeared into the profound blue of the ether, Blasius sat down on an old bench facing the door. He seized an earthenware jug that he had filled from the well, drank a long draught of clear water, set the jug down at his feet, and sat there, motionless but resuscitated.

The breath of the rose bushes, the soul of wallflowers and magnolias, and the exhalations of honeysuckle and laburnum were mingled around his silvery hair. He did not feel sufficiently lucid, as yet, to analyze his adventure, to search for the causes of the explosion and the failure of his experiment, but he was alive! For the moment, he demanded nothing more.

In the distance, a monotonous cuckoo responded to the ululation of the owls.

Reassured, Blasius went back inside. With fearful precautions, he picked up the fragments of glass that littered the floor. Then, having cleared the parquet, he leaned over the stove, lamp in hand. No trace of liquid; here and there, a few scoria, reminiscent enough of clinker, and, on the edge of the extinct hearth, a morsel of lava twice the size of a walnut.

Blasius picked it up in his fingers, examined it attentively from every angle, and murmured: "That's prodigious! I expected lead, and this resembles pumice stone. Anyway, I'll see tomorrow what it is and I'll study the means of recommencing the experiment."

He opened a large drawer occupying the full length of the table, threw the stone into the midst of an accumulation of miscellaneous objects, and closed the drawer again with an abrupt movement. Then he lay down on his black bearskin couch, fully dressed, arranged a pile of cushions under his head, turned over on to his right side, and fell into a profound sleep.

II

Blasius had been born in a little village amid hills, which surrounded it, in radiant spring dawns, like a great blue girdle; on autumn evenings, like great sashes of crimson silk spangled with gold; and on winter afternoons, like huge opaque gray clouds.

His natal house, roughcast with limestone and decorated with red ornaments, was a little way outside the cluster of houses. A large rectangular garden, full of old trees, wild vines, nettles as tall as a man, climbing plants, glittering insects, hideous spiders and birds, isolated it from other habitations, and made it a sort of verdant oasis in which the curious child, amazed and delighted, took his first steps.

His entry into the world was, like most others, happy and banal. Exclusively delivered to the care of a grandmother, who pampered him, cherished him and heaped him with treats, his little soul lit up with joy. His little body expanded in the pure air. His little feet, uncertain and fragile at first, struck the grassy ground with an assurance that grew from day to day. His little hands, which brushed objects, flowers and people so gently to begin with that the flowers and the people quivered at the contact, grasped the same objects a little later with a surprising vigor, baking flowers and clawing faces instead of caressing them. And the inarticulate cries that emerged from his mouth during the first weeks became laughter so crystalline and so pretty that the old grandmother, in listening to it, mistook that laughter for celestial music.

At seven years of age, Blasius was overflowing with life. He ran barefoot and bare-legged along the paths that ended at the village, chased the geese and ducks that floundered with idiotic squawks in the mud of ditches, and wrestled with boys of his own age.

At nine he drove before him to the meadows herds of cattle that gazed at him fearlessly with their benevolent round eyes; knocked down apples, pears and walnuts with a stick, on which he gorged himself; amazed the peasants with his sallies and remarks; and, endowed with an uncommon musical instinct, intoned psalms and hymns in the church to which his grandmother took him every Sunday, in a voice that growth gradually rendered virile.

At ten, he was reputed to be the best raider of birds' nests in the region. No one knew as well as he did how to detect nestlings cowering in the shelter of foliage, and at the same time, no one was more interested in the books that an old master, chloroformed by thirty years of routine in the same school, tried to explain to him without always succeeding. There, more than anywhere else, in every regard, he triumphed over his comrades. Often, his questions embarrassed his rustic educator, and, forced to understand without his aid many things in which boys usually took no interest, he had gravitated toward the solitary meditations that are so harmful to the incomplete brains of children.

No anxiety however, darkened his radiant heart. He liked nothing so much as setting forth in company with his young neighbor Rose along the bushy paths, and considering beside her, with admiring exclamations, the comings and goings of all the mysterious population striping the country with a thousands of unexpected colors. Beetles of all kinds, caterpillars, warm emerald frogs that slipped with a nervous effort through his fingers to plunge into shiny water: he knew them all by their names. He described their habits to his wonderstruck friend, and never permitted her to kill them or inflict the slightest suffering on them, he already bore within him so much sensitivity and benevolence.

Having grown up in the midst of light, joy and happiness, he became himself, without being aware of it, a youthful joy, light and happiness. Since the first moments of his birth, he had never wept, except when someone told him a story that was too sad, or the old blacksmith in whose forge he spent most of his winter evenings, recounted his adventures in the distant lands to which the hazard of battles had taken him. To the entity of harmonious life that he was, death seemed inconceivable. At the most pathetic points of stories, he blocked his ears and forced the aged narrator to interrupt himself abruptly. And if the latter, wounded in his self-esteem, refused to continue, Blasius employed words so persuasive to convince him that the other felt his anger vanishing gradually, and changed the subject with a docility surprising in a man known to everyone for his stubbornness and brutality.

Oh, how happy he felt among those worthy people!

And suddenly, there was a different décor.

Successively, all the beings that he cherished disappeared. First, his little friend was extinguished in a matter of days by a devastating malady, and was carried away in a coffin draped in white to the end of a cemetery where hollyhocks flourished. After that, it was the turn of the woman of whom he was the only love, the only ecstasy: the poor grandmother who had guided him so tenderly and so nobly through all sorts of ambushes and perils, and made his soul exceptional, different from the rude and twisted souls that surrounded it.

When he accompanied her, next to a man whom he saw for about a week per year, whom he was obliged to call "Papa" and who had never shown him anything but indifference and hostility, to the dwelling of stone and clay where she would sleep henceforth without waking; when he found himself beside the old woman's empty bed, and heard sobbing around him those who had escorted her with him, and the certainty surged forth in his young intelligence that he would never see her again, he felt himself invaded by a frightful distress. He divined that the best of himself, the joy, the happiness, and everything that attached him to life, had just died with the poor old woman whose waxen hands still seemed to be telling the beads of her rosary after her last sigh; and, scarcely emerging from oblivion, but already terrified by what he would see and hear, he wanted to end it. He wanted to go and join her...

A few minutes later, he was pulled out, bloodless and stiff, from the pond into which he had hurled himself.

But death did not want him yet. He was saved.

And when the natal house and the familiar furniture were sold, he found himself in an unknown dwelling, with the man he had to call Father and the woman who demanded that he call her Mother without ever having done anything to merit it, Blasius had the very clear impression that his life was suddenly veiled in black and that he was going to march between the two beings from which he had emerged toward heartbreak and toward misery.

How many times, when he became a man, he remembered that dolorous past!

From the furthest distance that he evoked that period, he saw a quadragenarian with rugged features pursuing him, armed with an osier rod hardened by fire, and thrashing him until he bled for an imprudent word or the awkward gesture of a child. Next to that brutal father a poor wife, effaced and bleak, wept in vain; and that woman felt such a fear of her master that she dared not even come in secret to console the martyrized boy.

Under that ferocious regime he retreated into himself like a hunted animal. His heart, overflowing with tenderness and reckless with amour, he closed forever, as one locks a casket full of priceless objects, or hides a treasure in an obscure corner, sheltered from theft or profanation. The vibrant and impulsive scamp became a sly, crafty and grim individual. He only experienced wellbeing when he was isolated in some thicket in the paternal garden, lying down in the warm shade of acacias or lindens, contemplating the golden rings described by the sunlight of the fresh grass, the flight of bumble-bees and wasps drinking the life of sage, mint or berberis, or the fearful progress of shrew-mice fleeing among the rose-bushes at the approach of bloodthirsty cats or dogs.

After every flagellation he took refuge in the grain-loft and buried himself in the hay. He wept large tears there for hours, which he sometimes drank, and the taste of which he was astonished to find so bitter. Then, when the crisis eased, he wandered at random, his heart swollen with rage, seeking an object, a living being on which to inflict a little of what he had just suffered himself.

It was thus that he had taken possession one day of a brave tomcat purring around him confidently. Cautiously, after having caressed it for a long time, he had held it between his legs and had attached a tin can to its tail. Then he had carried it in his arms as far as the entry to the house, and, after having opened the door slightly, had launched it inside with a kick. Afterwards, he had returned to his shelter between two spindle-trees, and from there, solely by the tumult that was unleashed in the rooms, he evaluated with a hideous grimace the quality of his revenge.

Howling, clawing, leaping on to tables, armchairs and sideboards, that cat ran through the apartment. At each of its leaps the tin can collided with glasses, plates and art-works, and there were shards of broken glass and faience thrown to the floor, or pans rolling over the parquet with the sonority of clashing cymbals. And above all those diabolical sounds, dominating the mewling of the cat, passed his mother's squeals for fear and the oaths of the quadragenarian with the rugged features.

Oh, how he rejoiced in his hiding place, and with what a ferocious ardor he wished the worst things upon his persecutor! In a low voice, as if the demented cat were in front of him, he cited it and clapped his hands.

And after the unforgettable correction that his savage act earned him, he avenged himself again, but on a human this time, on a poor old woman who begged for her bread at the doors of houses, and whom everyone helped, as much because of her age as her debility; on a poor old woman, eighty years of age, in whose passage he extended a fox-trap in which her tottering foot had been caught as she emerged from the presbytery. Oh, with what intoxication he listened to the octogenarian's cries of pain, as weak as the cries of a child, and how he exulted when, mingling the curious crowd, he saw the poor leg emerging from the toothed semicircle, sectioned above the ankle all the way to the bone! Yes, that day his vengeance has been complete, for he had shown himself in front of the church, expressly, in the company of other good-for-nothings, immediately after his misdeed, and no one in the village could suspect him, thanks to that means. And he had laughed ferociously, hysterically, for more than half the night.

Later, his extraordinary height, his thinness and his timidity earned him the bullying and sarcasms of young people of his age. He ground his teeth thinking about his years at secondary school; he saw again the sinister courtyard, and its peeled trees, and his comrades who surrounded him, howling, and the bigger boys who gathered around him like crabs around a cadaver. He heard their gibes and their insults; he received, in memory, the punches and the kicks that the smaller ones dispensed, even more ferocious and pitiless because the strong urged them on and protected them. He saw them all again, darkened by their black smocks, delivering themselves to their repulsive orgies and trying to pervert him, and peppering him harder with epithets and blows when he refused.

He saw one, in particular, with a turgescent nose in the face of a cretin, one whose vigor and malevolence was feared by all the others, who seized him by the wrists immobilized him, and, in order to be appreciated by his junior masters, incited the headmaster's son to strike him mercilessly. All of that putrescence rose from his gut, and he felt hiccups of disgust stifling him merely at the evocation.

And the years went by.

He was now a young man. And as he had suffered at the hands his parents and his peers, he was to suffer even more from those he coveted recklessly. No more blows or malodorous insults, but nicknames, ironies sharper than stilettos, scorn from which he bled for entire nights, huddled in his bed, and from which he feared that he might die.

And yet, he was not dead—and that amazed him. And although he had reached his eighteenth year, he still let himself go, to savor the frightful joys of vengeance inflicted upon the innocent.

Every day at noon, a basset hound belonging to the concierge, which was almost blind, was allowed to enter a small yard behind the school kitchens, and the refectory boy would throw him heaps of detritus, which the starveling devoured effortfully with its unsteady teeth. By a frightful deviation of his imagination, the adolescent arrived at finding in that placid dog the features of his persecutor with the turgescent nose and the menacing fist, striking him and calling him, his mouth convulsed with rage, by the incomprehensible nickname of Crottmich, given to the cretin by one of his victims.

One morning, he encountered the basset in the depths of a first floor corridor. He encountered him after emerging from a rude ordeal in which, tied up by the athlete, he had received a monumental beating from the principal's offspring. And when he perceived the dog, humble, wheezy and defenseless, a monstrous idea germinated in his unhinged brain. Having muzzled him to prevent him from howling and biting, he laid him on his back, tied his hind legs together with a shoelace, and castrated him with a sweep of his pocket-knife.

A stifled groan shook the quivering body. The shamefully profaned thighs immediately became crimson. And before that spectacle of ignominy, he felt a sadistic sensual pleasure invade him. And he insulted the martyr, his bloody knife in his hand, as if he were speaking to the other.

The poor beast was found dead the next day, and no one ever knew what madman had been able to commit such a repulsive crime.

And for every one of his martyrizations, he inflicted torture around him, hidden in the shadows.

Another time, he tore in two, literally, taking it by the beak, a little canary that an unfortunate junior master was raising in his room with a paternal solicitude. He hid one of the fragments in his enemy's bed and the other under the teacher's pillow To each of those bloody shreds he pinned a piece of paper one which was legible, written in blood, the supposedly enigmatic words: *The Black Hand.*

But the most disconcerting and most grotesque of all his misdeeds was after emerging from a recreation during which his comrades had bullied, hit, jostled and insulted him for an interminable hour: the adventure of a bird belonging to the director's poultry-yard. Slowly, squeezing its beak with one clenched hand, he plucked it with the other, alive, from head to foot, and to each feather he ripped out he gave the name of one of his torturers. Then, when the horrible task was finished, as he left through a door opening into a deserted alleyway through which the other external pupils had already left, he threw the poor victim into the senior boys' study, where it started running around the immense rectangular room.

Stupor and panic, which he watched through a crack in a shutter! Hectic pursuit under tables, under benches, over geographical globes, bookshelves and easels supporting paintings!

God, how he had laughed at that satanic farce, and how he had felt his deranged heart beating with pride!

But now that he had reached old age, and he had endured all the insults and all the shame, a graver and more poignant dolor afflicted him, and a more precise and more formidable revolt was rumbling in the depths of his soul.

III

At about ten o'clock in the morning a ringing bell extracted Blasius from his bed. It was the baker from the nearby town who was bringing him, as he did every morning, the loaf of bread and the piece of cheese from which he almost invariably composed his meals.

Having greeted his food-supplier, Blasius closed the gate again, and went back to his laboratory, while the vehicle drew away with a clear tinkling of little bells.

All around him, the ravages of the explosion appeared in the raw morning light.

Under the corrosive action of the unknown gas, the ceiling had cracked all the way across, and above him, when Blasius raised his head, he could see all those streaks scattered like little black threads over the faded pallor of the plaster. The air pressure had shattered the glass front of the cupboard containing his bottles, and he was continually walking over shards of glass, which his wooden soles pulverized with little slight sounds, and shiny fragments of which were embedded in the fir-wood floorboards.

But it was the stove used in his experiments that had suffered the most. Its hearth had been literally torn apart by the explosion, and the cast iron tripod that sustained the two retorts lay at the foot of the apparatus, twisted like brass wire. The flue that carried emanations and smoke outside was cracked, dented and pierced with holes like a colander, and on the wall against which that mass of iron stood, large serpentine streaks could be seen, which broadened out toward the ceiling.

Without saying a word, Blasius considered the spectacle.

His arms folded over his breast, he scrutinized all the damage with his gaze, trying in vain to deduce its causes, dejected by the failure of an experiment that he had considered as the capital effort of his existence. From time to time, he twisted his faunesque beard with a mechanical movement.

After a long interval of meditation, he sketched a resigned gesture and we out.

Outside, there was an orgy of light.

The matutinal brightness bathed the house, playing over the plants that were climbing over the walls, festooning the columns of ivy that embraced the entry door like two great emerald arms and extended idly along the foot of the humble abode like a golden-haired cat at the feet of some fay.

A harmony compounded of murmurs, birdsong, the rustle of dead branches, the frisson of the wind in the long grass and unexpected whispers cradled the habitation. All the music of the air poured forth in sonorous waves over the mossy roof; but Blasius remained impassive before that magnificence.

He was not one of those who dream; the frightful life that he had led since his childhood had not prepared him for mollification or ecstasies. Lost in that dazzle, his soul only lingered over the positive, and at the present moment he was trying to figure out how he could resume he interrupted labor without wasting any time.

At first he racked his brains in order to arrive at precisions. Had his failure been caused by an insufficiency of the materials, or the precariousness of the means of investigation, which had afflicted him, but which, in spite of his efforts, he had been forced to admit that he was incapable of remedying? Was the formula that he had adopted as the best one, on the contrary, the only one that it was necessary to avoid? Were the aged balances on which he weighed his ingredients and mixtures functioning poorly? Or was it simply necessary to attribute the reason for the unexpected deflagration to the nature of the precipitate that had fallen to the bottom of the retort as soon as boiling point was reached? So many questions, which tormented him, stretching his will-power, his intelligence and his nerves toward a response that was stubborn in not coming, a solution impossible to find!

All day, Blasius was consumed by sterile research. When night enveloped the hermitage, he went back to bed, harassed and discouraged, without having been able to explain anything. His rage at feeling himself impotent to pierce such a mystery reached such a paroxysm that he got up again at midnight, and, his head burning, he went to sit down on the threshold, on the old bench where he liked to meditate for long hours in the coolness and the calm.

He stayed there until dawn, his head in his hands, as if crushed beneath the weight of that indecipherable enigma.

When the first stars began to pale, two or three blackbirds began to sing timidly in the depths of the bushes. Blasius raised his head slowly, his features hollowed out by the night of insomnia. He took a few steps along the central path that led to the well, the black stone rim of which was sparkling with dew. For a moment he peered into the dark depths, from which a damp current of air rose. Then, shrugging his shoulders at the stupid idea that had just crossed his mind, he drew away from the well with a firm tread and went back inside.

He marched directly toward the stove. Nothing had shifted since the previous day. The ashes were still smoldering, and they still formed their little gray heap in the middle of the hearth. On the edges, fragments of retorts were shining, stained with red, in bizarre attitudes; several of them resembled imaginary beasts that an invisible power had thrown down there, belly up.

With a thrust of his index finger, he moved aside the heap of ash and uncovered a fragment of lava similar to the one that he had put in the drawer of his rectangular table on the evening of the explosion. He picked it up and kept it in the palm of his left hand for a few seconds. Having turning it in all directions, he let it fall on the floor with a gesture of discouragement and lassitude.[6]

As the drawer of the large table was within arm's reach, impelled by the desire to see the first piece of stone again,

---

[6] This second fragment of the substance vital to the plot must have been introduced into the story at this point with a view to its subsequent recovery, but in fact it never reappears, the author having apparently forgotten it.

which seemed to him to be evidence of his ineptitude, he opened it

There was an inexpressible disorder within it of nails, screws, compasses, steel forces, sheets of blotched paper covered with annotations and symbols; amid that chaos he searched for the porous stone.

An extraordinary thing: he had the impression that all the objects contained in the drawer had acquired a brown tint, brightened here and there by green reflections; and although he searched attentively he could not succeed in distinguishing from one another those whose forms offered points of marked resemblance.

Carried away by a surge of fury, he took hold, at random, of a heap of charcoal-holders. One by one he examined them, comparing them with one another and with pencil-holders, recognizable by their ferruled tips. All the objects were now the same color.

"However," he murmured, I'm quite sure that yesterday, some were spotted with rust and others were colored with blue tints. None of them looked like this, and certainly didn't offer to the gaze those reflections that liken them to raw gold.

Having said that, Blasius let himself fall on to his furry couch, literally stunned by amazement.

After two or three minutes of silence, he stood up again. And as he stood up he repeated in a mechanical voice the last words he had pronounced:

"Raw gold! That hypothesis is so absurd that I wonder why it suddenly presented itself to my mind. No one, in scientific circles, and even in the circles where certain fools still believe in the possibility of transmuting substances at will, is unaware that the formula for which Flamel and his disciples searched for so long belongs to utopia. I, who am lingering over that stupidity, know very well that my experiment did not have any transmutation for its goal, but simply an effort toward the disintegration of an acid, with the effect of obtaining lead, which is its last period. And yet, all that gives the illusion of gold! And I remember that in the days when I was prospecting the gold-bearing terrains in the remote regions of California"—a sad smile twisted Blasius' downturned mouth—"the few nuggets extracted from the mountain resembled those objects closely. The same nuances, the same spotting…it's truly strange."

Blasius fell silent.

He was holding in his right hand the porous stone that he had just taken out of the drawer. Without noticing it, he had rested its summit on a sculpted copper ring circling his third finger, and as he hesitated, considering that inexplicable product, he perceived that the copper of the ring had turned a darker brown, and was dotted in places with green patches.

"That's impossible!" he murmured, at that vision. "Can the stone I'm holding at this moment have the virtue of inducing a sudden metamorphosis in anything it touches? One of two things must be true: either I'm dreaming—and I'm convinced that I'm not dreaming—or I'm in the presence of an even more hallucinatory discovery, of which I don't understand the first thing."

Suddenly, spotting a chipped and rusty iron spade on a bench, he drew it toward him and ran the stone that he was clutching in his right hand over the gardening implement.

"We'll soon see!" he said.

And as he touched the old spade, the same phenomenon of transmutation occurred. Almost instantaneously, every particle brushed was burnished, and in places, as on his ring and the implements in the drawer, dull emerald plaques appeared.

Blasius was breathless.

"This substance," he repeated, in a tremulous voice, "is really the one that comes from the retorts. And it transmutes. Into what? Why? And how? It's transmuting this spade. It's transmuting this copper bucket, and he chain in the well, and these fire irons, and the sheet metal of this stove."

And as he spoke, Blasius touched the objects he was listing.

And all of them, at the impact of the unknown substance, underwent metamorphosis.

"It's maddening!" Blasius exclaimed, galloping from one end of his house to the other. "I want to know what I've obtained. For until I have absolute certainty, I refuse to believe that this fragment of lava has the power to aurify metals.

With broad, disorderly gestures, he tore away his girdle of rope and his cenobyte's robe, threw it on to his bearskin, and put on his modern garments, with his large brodequins.

Then, filling two large pockets with the metal obtained by contact, and preciously stowing the transmuting stone in an interior pocket, he put on a felt hat, locked and bolted his gate, and set forth.

Taking huge strides, as if he were flying on stilts, along paths made by woodcutters and shepherds, without encountering a living soul, he reached the local railway station.

He leapt on to a train that was passing, and huddled in a corner of a compartment, eyeing his traveling companions grimly.

Eight hours later he disembarked in a sinister and tumultuous station in the capital.

In all haste, his long arms stuck to his sides for fear of sending his precious burden flying or letting it fall, Blasius strode along the avenues and slid across the boulevards, cleaving through the crowd, indifferent to the noises and pedestrians who surrounded him. Having crossed an iron bridge thrown over the troubled waters of the river, he went into a series of sordid streets swarming people and children, cluttered with trucks, drays and carts and reached a small square where ragged children were playing with feathers, with no concern for vehicles and the insults of passers-by. He turned left out of that square to go down a sandstone stairway from which most of the steps were missing, where he nearly broke his neck several times, and, after several minutes of that perilous exercise, he found himself in a sort of cul-de-sac, so narrow that one could give the accolade from one sidewalk to the other and so dirty that when he went into it he had to pinch his nose between the thumb and index finger of his left hand in order not to suffocate.

After a few meters he stopped in front of a basement boutique, at the back of which a faint light attested, against all expectation, the presence of living beings.

He grasped the door handle, turned it with a nervous movement, went down three sticky steps and found himself in an obscure and deserted shop. In the back room of the shop, by the tremulous light of a gas lamp, someone was working, leaning over a work-bench laden with microscopes, watches and rings, scattered without order or precaution.

At the noise made by the newcomer, the person in question calmly deserted the stool on which he was sitting like a parrot on a perch, and with slow steps, wiping his spectacles, headed toward Blasius. The latter saluted him with a curt "Bonsoir" and explained the objective of his visit in a few words.

⁕ According to all appearances, the two men knew one another, for they addressed one another with a one of familiarity, and even the least alert observer might have perceived a few ironic nuances, in the responses of the shopkeeper.

At the invitation of the master of the house, Blasius slipped into the back room with him. The old man offered him a stool similar to the one he employed himself, and when Blasius, having become taciturn and suspicious again, had sat down, his companion held out his dirty hands curiously.

"Let's see," he said.

Slowly, as if regretfully, Blasius removed from his pocket all the transmuted objects that he had stuffed into them at the time of his departure, handed them over, and waited while the other examined them.

"Damn!" said the goldsmith, softly, scanning the compasses, the forceps, the screws and the nuts with the microscope that he had wedged into the orbit of his eye as he sat down again. "That's extraordinary!"

"Am I mistaken?" asked Blasius.

"Not in the least," the goldsmith affirmed. "Either these objects must have been buried in the earth, or you discovered them many years ago, in order for them to be so dirty, but that's only a sight annoyance, and if you give me a few minutes I'll render them as neat and shiny as these watch-cases."

Having said that, he seized a brush with a supple whale-bone handle and started cleaning the first object, a pair of compasses. As he worked, Blasius, his eyes wide with amazement, saw the brown tint disappear, and the compasses, in the experienced hands of the goldsmith, become a glittering yellow.

"That's extremely curious," commented the artisan, brushing vigorously and polishing with a chamois leather to finish off. "One part of your find is composed of green gold and the other of red gold.[7] There's no doubt, by reason of the particular character of your discovery, that you haven't found them in the home of a boulevard antiquary or a high priced shop in the aristocratic quarters. I'd even add that if you know how to give your property a clever publicity, the collector would compete for them and bid enough in order to acquire them for you to be materially tranquil for the rest of your days."

"You're quite sure, then? It really is gold?" Blasius inter-rogated, in a dull voice, leaning over the work-bench.

"As sure as I am that you're talking. And if you'd care to permit me to negotiate the sale," he goldsmith insinuated, with and obsequious smile, "I'll gladly take charge of it, for an in-significant commission."

"No thank you," said Blasius, grimly. "I'll take care of it myself."

He paid the artisan, put all the objects examined back in his pocket, and departed with vast strides for the station. His teeth were chattering like those of a sick man attained by ma-

---

[7] Gold normally occurs naturally in mixtures with other met-als, usually silver and copper, which produce, in various pro-portions, alloys known as red, green, yellow and white gold. It is not obvious why gold produced by quasi-miraculous trans-mutation should be thus alloyed.

larial fever. And he, the meditative and mute, soliloquized as he marched, to the great bewilderment of strollers, who turned round, amused by that gangling and ridiculous silhouette.

As hunger was gnawing at him, Blasius bought a piece of bread and two apples for a few sous, and ate them voraciously while striding along the crowded sidewalks.

An hour later, he found himself at the railway station, climbed into an empty compartment and retraced in an inverse direction the route he had traveled the previous night. But he did not have the same state of mind during that return.

The goldsmith's revelation had bowled him over to the extent that he had lost the notion of reality and refused to believe in the veracity of his affirmations.

He could fabricate gold! Alone in the world, he found himself in possession of the secret of transmutation. A flame of triumph lit up in his eyes, encased under heavy russet eyebrows. A nervous tremor agitated him, His throat felt dry, and he would gladly have drunk long draughts of the refreshing water of his well from the round bucket that he had transformed into yellow gold before his departure.

An unaccustomed warmth rose to his temples, and his heart beat faster and more forcefully than in the most moving phases of his tortured life. It seemed to him that someone inside his breast was pounding that heart with a huge hammer, and that every blow of the hammer shook his entire being, to the point that he had the impression of hearing his bones crack, and he was afraid of dying of the emotion that invaded him and paralyzed his thought completely.

In that emotion of Blasius, there was not the slightest cupidity, or the least joy in sensing that he had become the master of wealth, but simply an infinite pride in finally having dominance over his rivals and curbing them this time, mercilessly, under the glare of his genius, the unexpectedness of his discovery, like a handful of termites crushed under a landslide illuminated by the sun.

With his nose stuck to the window he watched the telegraph poles fleeing before him with every rotation of the carriage wheels, and he thought, shivering, that soon, in an hour or two, he would have reached his house again, tidied up his laboratory, filled his retorts again, and that he would recommence—sure of success, this time—the decisive experiment.

Oh, how slowly the train was traveling, for him! Every quarter of an hour he consulted his watch, calculating in thought the distance that still separated him from his abode.

Finally, after numerous halts, he saw the bell-tower of the little town appear in the depths of the valley appear, all white in the resplendent moonlight.

Without even waiting for the train to come to a complete halt, he leapt on to the station platform, handed the stub of his ticket to the employee, and launched himself, as eleven o'clock chimed, into the great silence of the night.

Brutally, after having plunged his key into the ill-greased lock, he shoved the gate open, closed it again with a dry click, and rushed into his dwelling. He seized handfuls of the transmuted objects that were swelling his pockets, stuffed them in the drawer of the rectangular table and lay down fully dressed on the bearskin.

But sleep did not come.

Blasius turned over and over, placing his burning head under his folded arms, stretching out or drawing in his legs beneath the covers, placing himself by turns on his back, his side or his belly, but did not succeed, so exacerbated were his nerves, in remaining in the same position for five minutes.

And always, like an imperious leitmotiv, the triumphant words came back to his lips: "I am the man who can fabricate gold!"

Finally, dawn tinted the somber crack in the shutters pink. Through the rips in the wood and the oblong holes that the worms had gradually made under the catches and around the hinges, light penetrated. Like an arrow launched from outside by a invisible archer, it struck a corner of a wall, the edge of an item of furniture, the bulb of a retort or the neck of a bottle. And immediately, that corner, that edge, that bulb or that bottleneck became the color of silver. And as one of those shafts of daylight struck Blasius, huddled on his couch, full in the face, he got up with a bound. He pushed back the shutters, and the blinding light immediately irrupted into the room.

Then, bent over a dresser with drawers stuffed with papers, ledgers and files, Blasius started searching.

One by one he opened the files, and scanned them page by page; then he did the same with the ledgers, the papers and the scattered notes, and the hundreds of folders tied up with red string.

When he had searched for a very long time, a horrible anguish was suddenly painted on his desiccated face, and his thin hands clenched. He quit the dresser, opened the drawer in the table, and proceeded with further searches, shoving aside the various objects that cluttered it angrily. But he found nothing, and his hands clenched more forcefully, and his face, ravaged like old parchment, became utterly pale. He looked everywhere: under the furniture, under the chairs, in boxes, on the bread-board suspended from the ceiling by two thick cords; but, in spite of his efforts, he could not succeed in finding the formula that he thought he had put in a file at the moment of the experiment

And, having panted and tottered on the path like a drunkard at the idea of setting to work as soon as he returned, he gradually acquired the certainty that he had not put his formula in a safe place, as he had thought. He had left it close at hand, on the table or perhaps even on the stove. And the flame spreading over the cast iron plate had consumed it, to the last particle.

And in spite of his efforts to reconstitute it, he could not remember the exact quantities of the materials to mix, and, doubtless as a consequence of the cerebral upheaval caused by the commotion on one hand and the joy of his unlimited power on the other, even the names of some of those substances had escaped him completely.

All day long, disdaining to eat or drink, Blasius persisted in that labor devoid of result; but when night fell, and the house, like a grandparent weary of having been subjected to the cries and caresses of little children, went to sleep, exhausted by sunlight, perfumes and the song of the breeze, nothing precise came back to his poor memory. A few vague figures, a few equations, the strangeness of which alarmed him, a few names of ingredients of such inexactitude that he dared not settle on them—and nothing more! And although he continued searching obstinately, no scrap of paper brought him the miraculous formula

Then, when he was certain that the fire had devoured it, that he might never rediscover it, Blasius collapsed on a stool and, his head between his hands, started to sob. An immense dolor overwhelmed him, the reasons for which presented themselves one after another to his mind, multiplying it tenfold and rendering it even more frightful.

Never again would he become the master of matter. Never would he be able, as he had decreed on emerging from the goldsmith's shop, to gather around himself, in his place of exile where no one had set foot for twenty years, the infallible scientists and inventors who had depreciated him with their sarcasm every time he had presented them with a new work. He would never be able, now, to transmute vile matter before their dazzled eyes, show them with a magnificent gesture the ingots obtained, and finally convince them that he had surpassed them, in spite of their hatred, their jealousy and their baseness, with all the sublimity of his genius.

Oh yes! Until the last breath, he would remain infecund, able to conceive vast plans, to be sure, but incapable of carrying them through, of realizing them; and when he died he would leave nothing behind, nothing but the memory of an abnormal being, a disequilibrated and hypochondriac seeker. And his eyes would never see the resplendent day on which he would finally be avenged on all those who martyrized him, at present morally, as they had once martyrized his poor debilitated body.

Suddenly, however, at the shock of a sudden idea, he stopped weeping. Since he still had the stone, why be obstinate in searching for anything else? Was not the essential thing, rather than knowing exactly how, merely to have the power of transmutation?

Then he touched, successively, the keys to the dresser and the locks on the doors, and all of that, in the space of a few seconds, became red gold! Then he tapped, with a right hand that was now firm, the pots and the old pewter trays that ornamented the rustic shelves where he kept his kitchen equipment, and the pewter became green gold. All the nickel and aluminum utensils that were within reach, Blasius transmuted as well, and all the nickel and aluminum became yellow gold, the color of autumn leaves. The bronze of the tall pendulum clock took on yellow reflections, like everything else; and in less than half an hour, Blasius had a prodigious quantity of the precious metal before him. As those miracles were operated, by a simple contact, Blasius' heart swelled with an untranslatable delight, and he murmured inconsequential phrases, incoherent words...

Now he felt sure of himself. He had the proof that the porous block would give him all the wealth he wanted, and by means of that wealth he could obtain power, and then he would employ that power...

But there, a confusion stopped him.

He searched hard, but he did not know how he would employ that superhuman power.

Very often, in the course of his labors, he had allowed himself to be carried away by his imagination. He had elaborated fantastic plans, each more unrealizable and more absurd than the last, and now, he felt, what he could realize, thanks to that unexpected gold, ought to be so great, so magnificent and so formidable that the entire world would be amazed,

Then he started searching; and when he had found it, his nostrils quivered with pride. As a sign of victory, he intoned strange strophes that made the fragile house vibrate from top to bottom.

While he was bringing his conceptions to completion, he made several journeys by day and night, after which heavy trucks were seen arriving at his abode laden with blocks of tin, enormous and massive iron bars, bronze pipes sparkling in the regal June sun, and copper ingots of all weights and all dimensions. The carters deposited that merchandise on the gilded sand of the courtyard, received the price immediately, and departed, wondering what purpose all of that could serve. They asked in the surrounding houses and the town what kind of living man was mad enough to come and bury himself in this remote region and devote himself to such enigmatic labors, but the people of the town and the local peasants admitted that they were unable to inform the conveyors, because they did not possess sufficient information themselves. And all of them, no matter how avid they were to know, were obliged to limit themselves to conjectures.

Left alone, Blasius dragged, rolled or carried all the blocks or ingots into a cellar hollowed out beneath the house, and after having transmuted them, he locked the door to the garden and departed for the city, until the arrival of a new cargo.

Prudently, in order not to awaken suspicions, he exchanged his nuggets and ingots in the establishments of the multitudes of goldsmiths, artisans and jewelers prevalent in all the quarters of the city. He heaped up gold coins and banknotes in an old chest hidden under his couch, and those gold coins and notes gradually piled up, forming the basis of a fortune that no one could evaluate subsequently.

That clandestine traffic lasted for an entire year.

When he estimated that he had a sufficient provision, Blasius spent several consecutive days nailing his coin and paper into crates that he circled with steel himself. When that operation was complete, he had eight of the heavy trucks that had transported iron, copper and bronze to his retreat twelve months earlier return from the city, and, assisted by the haulers, he heaped up along with the inestimable packages a few wooden boxes containing his clothes, his instruments and other objects that he wanted to take with him.

Then he embraced with a long bewildered gaze the solitude that he loved with an amour as fervent and profound as death, and which he would doubtless never see again.

Two tears ran slowly down his cheeks. With an abrupt movement, however, ashamed of that weakness, unworthy of him, he wiped them away. He took his dogwood stick in his right hand, put his black felt hat on his head, and made a sign.

The haulers pulled away under the effort of robust Percherons. The wheels bit into the damp sand of the pathways, and the caravan set forth into the constellated night. Blasius allowed it to travel a hundred meters before emerging from the garden. Motionless on the threshold, he seemed to be unable to tear himself away from that peaceful place. Everything around him retained him: the familiar trees, the atmosphere charged with summery odors, the harmonious syringas, and the earth above all, the earth whose mysterious voice he heard and every mound of which, every clod and every bank seemed to be murmuring in his fearful ear: "Why are you quitting us like this? Where are you going? What are you going to do?"

But Blasius shook his head in response to those appeals. With a determined gesture, he closed the gate behind him and locked it with a ripple turn of the key. Then, bending down, with the tinder wick of his lighter he lit a gray fuse emerging from a clump of geraniums near the entrance, which extended invisibly through the bushes toward the house.

The fuse was consumed slowly, crackling; and Blasius, sure that the irreparable action would be accomplished at the precise moment he desired, drew away without looking back, and caught up with the haulers.

After traveling for an hour the caravan stopped at the top of a long hill. The Percherons where panting noisily, and the carters, mute before the impressive man, sat down on the edge of a ditch. One of them turned toward the plain, which was visible through the ocher of the night, and uttered an exclamation.

"Fire!" he said.

With his finger, he indicated to his companions a long ruddy flame that was ascending, bordered by smoke, into the nocturnal limpidity. The flame was springing from three very distinct nuclei, and they appeared more luminous and intense with every passing minute. Thousands of sparks were fusing from their incandescence, and with their reflection, the surrounding woods became momentarily resplendent, like golden tresses, and a second later became black and confused masses, blacker and more confused than nature.

Blasius also looked.

That fire, he had lit. For he wanted, at the moment of quitting his dwelling, that no one after him would be able to penetrate it, that no one would be able to discover there, at the hazard of digging or unhealthy curiosity, vestiges of his presence, his labors and his efforts.

Sure now that nothing would subsist the following day of his retreat except a heap of smoking debris and charred beams, he turned to the haulers.

In a halting voice, as muted as the groan of a wounded man, he gave the signal for departure. And the caravan moved off again, without a word, without the crack of a whip, along the road bordered by gorse and elders.

IV

At the hour when the reflections of dawn extended their silver sheet over the blue waves, when the fishermen raised anchor and headed out to sea in order to devote themselves to their quotidian labors, a boat that had arrived several days before in a little solitary port cast off its moorings silently.

Leaning sideways like an idle swimmer, it cleaved through the waves discolored by the marvelous dawn, and while its prow cut through the calm water, a harmonious splashing could be heard to either side of its flanks.

Painted bright gray, fully decked, it measured about fifty meters from stem to stern and fifteen from port to starboard. It was not impelled by sail, although it was rigged as a sloop and possessed a full set of sails in case of an unexpected accident. A powerful electric motor activated its propeller, and in that peaceful morning, the boat seemed to be skimming the sea rather than cutting it, so rapid and regular was its progress.

No flag was flapping at the extremity of its mast; no name was legible on its sonorous hull.

The interior of the nameless vessel had been fitted out with an evident care for comfort and elegance. The corridors, decorated by an artist smitten with the never-seen, were ornamented with bold designs and friezes in which the most violent and unusual colors collided under the reflection of the sunlight piercing the glass of portholes with its golden lances. The commandant's cabin, the cabin that lodged the two officers, and even the crew's quarters, testified to the unusual will of the master of the establishment, and also testified to his desire to provide his traveling companions with a mobile abode as agreeable as possible

The commandant's cabin, painted bright mauve and blue, contained no other furniture than a large armchair, a table, a couchette made of a black bearskin stretched tautly over four low feet, and an item of furniture half-cupboard and half-chest of drawers, carefully locked. On a small table between that cabinet and the couchette, were a map of the world and several precision instruments. On the walls there was not the smallest painting or other work of art. On the couchette, a Siamese cat was asleep, purring softly, curled up in a ball with its delicate little head on its gray-haired hindquarters, indifferent to the tumult of the large boots that the crewmen were dragging back and forth on the deck above the cabin.

In one corner, stuffed in a rotating bookcase, the gilded bindings of books shone, mute and faithful companions of long crossings.

The boat glided over the presently green-tinted foam of the ocean, and the pilot manning the helm, in his glass cage, was singing a nostalgic ballad in a low voice. The sailors, without saying a word, were rolling ironbound crates and stout barrels between the decks, in response to signals from the duty officer. The watchman, perched aloft on the main mast, was inspecting the immense shiny and deserted watery plain with his telescope.

And alone, utterly alone, sitting at the prow, gazing with his profound eyes at the violet-tinted land that was gradually fading away into the morning mist, Blasius was dreaming.

The mysterious slender boat traveled for entire weeks without any other sound being heard aboard than the melancholy song of the pilot, the splash of the water against the sides of the hull, brief words of command and the strident whistles ordering maneuvers in bad weather. It seemed to be avoiding the habitual routes of navigation, and, in fact, during its interminable journey, the mute crew did not encounter any steamship, motor-boat or fishing boat.

They skirted vast sandy terrains where palm-trees, date palms and orange trees flourished in blazing sunlight and brown men dressed in burnooses, carrying rifles with flared barrels, raised themselves up on fast sinewy horses and watched them pass from the shore, anxiously. Always heading southwards, they lingered on the edge of tropical forests, in the estuaries of great rivers where semi-naked human beings maneuvered bark pirogues, uttering hoarse and muted fearful clamors as they approached.

Ever avid for the unknown, always mute, the explorers allowed themselves to drift in the great sub-equatorial currents, along fertile coasts, perceiving in the grasslands herds of buffalo, striped zebras and placid onagers guarded by black men; who lived there under furry tents with their wives, and often, because of amorous rivalries or questions of interest, fought one another until the weaker combatants fled before the victors, when they did not show mercy.

They doubled an immense cape, and, still borne by the sub-equatorial currents that circled untiringly around the torrid continent, they traversed an ocean deeper and vaster than the sea from which they had emerged. They passed between legendary islands where the most exuberant vegetation vibrated like instruments of dream to the impact of the trade winds, pursued during their landings by undulating panthers, monstrous pythons and apes similar to primitive humans.

They turned northwards again through the meanders of archipelagoes, amid enchantments of light and flora, toward even stranger countries, and they traversed an ocean even vaster than the other two, where no tempest assailed them.

They sat down before sumptuous pagodas, before palaces of precious wood, marble and gold, at inconceivable ceremonies. In forests of bamboo, magnolias and cedars, they saw men coiffed in turbans, clad in scintillating tunics, armed with scimitars encrusted with gems, brandished by compact troops; and steering their heavy elephants caparisoned in brocade with the aid of sharpened hooks, those men hunted cruel wolves in the jungle, heavy bears and scaly crocodiles somnolent on the orange mud of rivers, and tigers with striped pelts that sometimes fell upon them and crushed their skulls with a single movement of heir powerful muzzles.

And always mute, always mysterious, always anonymous, the navigators headed toward unexplored lands.

They visited shores where men with yellow complexions and hooded eyes offered them, with confident smiles, porcelain jars full of rice, the thighs of leopards, swallows' nests and other foodstuffs more succulent and more precious.

Then the temperature dropped again.

Instead of prodigious forests with frightening and tumultuous fauna there were desert places, immeasurable mountains, grasslands that extended as far as the eye could see from one end of the horizon to the other. And in those grasslands, red men clad in gaudy rags, coiffed with feathers, armed with short spears and arrows, rode vertiginous stallions, and, while uttering guttural clamors, pursued herds of bison and wild horses. Then, when the hunt was over, the red men went back to their villages, crouched on their heels in groups in front of their animal-hide dwellings and smoked long clay calumets decorated with symbols, which they passed from hand to hand without exchanging a word.

Then came regions where, poring over yellow sands that they extracted from river beds, hirsute men, naked to the waist, armed with revolvers of which they made use at the slightest alarm, searched for flecks of gold for months on end and often died of privations or fatigue and the very moment when the desired seam glittered before their mad eyes.

And when they had gone along shores where gigantic trees grew; had camped at the mouths of rivers so broad that they took on the appearance of seas in places; dropped anchor on the edges of impenetrable forests as vast as entire countries; contemplated with amazement eucalypti and baobabs hundreds of years old; had seen balsamic resin flowing along the damascened trunks of trees, with the oil of which the sorcerers of the region rubbed women in labor; had admired the robust guayacan whose wood offers such resistance that the iron of the most trenchant axes is blunted and broken by it, the laurel with the intoxicating emanations, the cinchona whose pulverized bark renders virility to the sickly and the debilitated, the ebony with golden yellow reflection and the divi divi, whose bark boiled in water serves to color leather brown; fished in torrential rivers full of extraordinary and dangerous fish; had seen passing overhead in bloody dusks the maleficent

51

flight of condors and lammergeiers; watched the sun die like an immense wounded beast behind inaccessible peaks whose height defied all human imagination; had drunk the milk of sheep and yaks in clay spoons outside the pastor's tent; eaten Tibetan tsamba in the vaulted halls of lamaseries; hunted wild asses along riverbanks; and had collected on the slopes of mountains the rarest of their amazing flora, they set forth to go even further in their bright silent boat.

Again they went along shores, inspected expanses, visited profound gorges from top to bottom, valleys covered in verdure and woods, and encountered populations sometimes civilized and at other times vegetating in barbarity and the most pitiful poverty.

At each of those halts, and each of those discoveries, Blasius frowned; his forehead was barred by a harsh furrow, and with a word he gave the order to depart. And the seven taciturn men who made up his crew returned to the vessel, and the vessel, with slight sighs of lassitude, resumed cleaving the water.

And one day, extenuated, unable to stand any more bitterness and discouragement, Blasius said: "No."

That morning, a great conflagration the color of beryl set the inviolate cloud of the Cordillera ablaze. And, docile to the man in command, the sailors steered away in silence.

For weeks they retraced, in an inverse direction the, route they had taken in coming. And one evening, during which Blasius, his forehead inclined over his two hands, rolled secret thoughts around his brain, the little ship reentered the solitary port from which it had departed months before. The men loaded the ironbound crates and barrels on to their shoulders and descended to the land.

And Blasius followed them, his arms dangling, but his gaze illuminated with a grim resolution.

A month later, at daybreak, a caravan composed of three spacious vehicles drawn by strong horses was traveling along a broad road bordered by elms and plane trees.

Sitting at the front of the first vehicle, buried in his monastic habit as if in a brown shroud, Blasius guided his companions. They were all there, the discoverers of the gray vessel, and all of them, those who went on foot, those who marched alongside the horses and those who were perched on the footsteps of the vehicles, remained mute, somber and resigned.

And when they had traveled the mining regions, the agricultural lands, the desolate steppes, the polluted infertile plains of pestilential marshland, the fecund hills where plum trees, almond trees and peach trees caused the perfumed rain of their petals to pour forth amid the crystal of the morning, the deserted calcareous plateaux where the blood-colored earth refused to produce nourishing wheat and barley, the villages where blind old men sing the praises of the heroic deeds of their ancestors while accompanying themselves on the guzla, the ports and sunlit towns where women gaze though the insurmountable bars of harems at the comings and goings of strollers and merchants; when they had seen warriors armed with improved engines attacking one another under the pretexts of liberation and law, they stopped. That morning, a great conflagration crimsoned the summits of hills crowned with vines and fruit trees.

And Blasius shook his head again, and said: "No."

Docile to the man in command, the nomads seized the Percherons by the bridle, and for weeks, the caravan followed in an inverse direction the outward route.

Then, all alone this time, confined within the walls of an aircraft that droned at the impacts of the air like a fantastic wasp, Blasius took flight.

He saw, far below, as tiny as ants, people busy with their sordid tasks. He considered with a pitying gaze the proud Pyramids, launched forth into the desert, whose waves of sand accumulated, pitched and collided under the formidable assault of the simoom. He landed in the virgin regions of great lakes; visited the most perilous corners of limitless forests;

flew over the huts of mud and branches of naked races crouched in abjection; flew vainly for hours toward an enchanted city that he perceived in the distance, in the wonder of the dazzling horizon, and which drew away from the airplane as its velocity accelerated; traversed a sea the color of locusts; flew over capitals with golden roofs, walls of jasper and sardonyx; alighted like a prodigious raptor on the highest peaks; scythed with his propeller through flocks of eagles and vultures that swooped upon him as on a fabulous prey; passed over icebergs and ice-sheets; skimmed the hyperborean countries where herds of seals frolicked among mosses and lichens; witnessed polar labors and hunts; saw fur-seals harpooned as they came to the surface to breathe through holes in the ice, and their bloody corpses carried away on sledges drawn by dogs to the thresholds of igloos; and when he had seen all that, abruptly, at the risk of breaking his neck, Blasius executed an abrupt turn and departed southwards at top speed.

But, having undertaken a long reconnaissance above islands florid with lemon trees, banana trees and orange trees, where life seems so amiable that one would like to live there when one knows them, until the last minute, Blasius smiled for the first time. And, as if he were giving orders to his companions, he cried through the sonorous space: "It's here!"

And then a great softness rose from the ground, and air the color of iris surrounded Blasius and his airplane with a transparent aureole. And in successive bounds, leaving houses, woods and valleys behind him, Blasius returned to the haven where the solitaries were waiting for him.

When he had communicated the result of his voyage to them; when he had made them party to the decision he had made, all of them inclined before the master, and prepared for the magnificent labor with which he had resolved to associate them.

One afternoon, the inhabitants, animals, trees and flowers of the island, somnolent beneath the solar sumptuousness, like kings and their retinues asleep under vermilion tents, the nameless little ship entered the shelter of the port.

Blasius and his companions descended to land, and Blasius had himself taken to the islanders' headman. And at the end of their discussion, the islanders, with great marks of respect and deference, escorted the stranger who had just visited them back to his vessel. The next day, mounted on rapid ponies, guided by a bronzed horseman in a jacket spotted with black and blue, the companions traveled the island in all directions. And Blasius smiled. He patted the neck of his mount with his ascetic hand as a sign of contentment, and flattered it with fraternal words.

After long hours of cavalcade the troop reached the edge of an immense circular arena, in the middle of which the glaucous waters of a river flowed slowly. In all directions, mountains the color of lapis, agate and aquamarine surrounded that river. On either bank grew a profusion of reeds as straight as lances, willows with gray foliage, and a multitude of other aquatic trees, the low branches of which dipped into the cool water like pilgrims of dream bathing foreheads soiled by opprobrium in the purifying water of some new Jordan.

The arena seemed so vast, and so many perfumes swirled there hectically, that Blasius and the seven taciturn men sensed a kind of intoxication rising to their heads. And when, with the aid of ingenious calculations, they had measured the surface area of that surprising Eden, the master sat down on the bank between a clump of buttercups and other flowers with voluptuous emanations, of which he did not know the names. He made a sign to the bronzed guide, and the latter, in a harsh and singsong language, recounted the origin of his people to the strangers.

They were descended from a handful of sailors whom a tempest had thrown up on the coast one equinoctial evening, and who, immediately vanquished by the mildness of the climate, by the beauty of the luminous landscapes, by all those scents, all that grace and all that harmony unknown in their own land of fog and nostalgia, had refused to return to their natal soil.

On that desert island they had built a little village, and a small boat with rounded flanks had departed toward an island similar to theirs, which was perceptible amid the mists of dawn and the translucence of the sunset. They had found young women there with supple bodies and amber skin, like the bark of lemon trees; at first those young women had laughed at the strangers so blond and so grave, but amour had come into their souls like a flock of turtle-doves into the warmth of a walled garden, and they had united in a long kiss their ardent lips with the mute mouths of the men of the north. And on the small boat rocked by the whim of the violet waves, they had departed with them two days later.

And children were born to the young women with the somber eyes and the mariners with the blue eyes more limpid than the sea. And those children, having grown up in their turn, had, like their fathers, in boats of oak or elm, brought other young women to their perfumed shores.

And thus at the end of a century, a little colony had been constituted of free men, living outside laws, outside the world, a primitive and delightful existence. The fertile soil and the fecund trees willingly gave them the barley, wheat, buckwheat and fruits necessary to their subsistence. And in the river that rejoined the sea at the foot of their village, and in the musical sea, they found fish and shellfish without effort. The vines on the hillsides, swelled with sap by the sun and velveted paternally by its rays, gave them a lavish provision of thick and generous wine. The sirocco and the cold winds of winter never blew in that region, sheltered by the high surrounding mountains. The fleeces of sheep, the skins of goats and the tanned leather of cattle served to fabricate tunics and light sandals. And they lived there, peacefully, without ambition, without jealousy, and without baseness.

And Blasius, on listening to the guide speak, shivered.

He thought of the life that he might have been able to lead if destiny, instead of the man who had hated and beaten him, had given him one of these sages for a father, happy with his rustic house and his fishing boat. And when they had visited the verdant and fresh arena thoroughly, when they had drunk the dark wine in large draughts from the guide's bulging goatskin, the taciturn men remounted their ponies and went back to the village.

Then they visited other corners, other hills, other woods and other valleys. And while his comrades relaxed from their fatigues on beds covered with coarse fabrics, Blasius conversed with the headman, and gradually succeeded in convincing him.

One evening, after a longer and more animated discussion than the previous ones, the chief of the islanders extended to Blasius his broad hand, bronzed by the sun and the sea air, and shook it forcefully for a long time, as a sign of solemn accord.

Then the blond men and the golden-skinned women loaded their furniture, their clothing, their utensils and their weapons on to numerous boats that arrived from neighboring islands, and a propitious wind carried the flotilla toward an unknown destination, far from the shores where they had been born which they would never see again.

The children wept with chagrin, and held out their little arms, like pink snowy stems, toward the florid land. The women veiled their eyes with their brown hands, and large tears flowed down their cheeks illumining their splendid upper torsos with a shiny glimmer, and they murmured words of despair in very low voices, in their rude and singsong language. But the men imposed silence on them with a word, and they showed them with their gaze, without quitting the oar or the tiller, the barrels and crates circled with iron that Blasius had given them as the price of their renunciation of their exile.

Then the sobs of the women stopped. A furtive smile lit up their large eyes misted by tears; and they thought about all the jewels, all the bracelets and all the precious fabrics that they would be able to acquire thanks to those riches, when they arrived in the City to which Blasius and his companions guided them, like guards taking to a prison camp a convoy of convicts ignorant of the vicissitudes that await them.

After weeks of absence, Blasius and his companions returned, remaining on the island alone.

For days on end they prospected the terrain, sounding the rocks, analyzing the clay, and determining the nature of the soil stratified by the slow work of the centuries.

After that arduous labor, Blasius summoned to his island bridge-builders and constructors of monuments and palaces, architects and edifiers of astonishing works, and the chiefs of titans who transformed before furnaces, at will, blocks of cast iron and long bars of steel.

And all of them hastened to his appeal, avid for renown and money, and they inclined their lowly foreheads before the man who possessed the great mystery, with slavish platitudes.

Among them there were counterfeiters, corrupt officials, embezzlers, traitors and very few honest men. Some, in the course of homicidal wars, in exchange for fabulous sums of money, had delivered defective arms and projectiles to governments whose representatives pocketed large shares of the money in return for their complicity. Others had edified, for individuals or collectives, houses, temples or barracks with such inferior materials that the houses, temples or barracks cracked or crumbled the day after their completion or their inauguration. Other, thanks to the lure of illusory profits, had gleaned the last penny from the humble, extorting the savings of the needy. Others had overtly trafficked with the enemy, and it was known that their ships, laden with nickel, aluminum and prohibited materials had furrowed the sea, coming under the protection of highly-placed officials to unload their cargoes into the hands to secret or known agents of the adversary.

But as the majority of those rich men were shareholders in the newspapers charged with keeping the people informed of their disinterest and their sacrifices, as they received at their table the most powerful ministers and steeped their slavering lips humbly in the bidets of courtesans, their sins were secret or unpunished. And if by chance a revolted scribe took it into his head to want to divulge some story and demand justice, he was incontinently locked in prison, where he was guarded day and night, or, weary of enduring woes of all kinds, he promised to shut up, or even to swell the ranks of the eulogists.

Some of them smoked odorous Havana cigars in gold and diamond cigar-holders, and those Havanas bore on paper rings the effigies of emperors and the profiles of generals or tsarinas. Others exhibited on their sausage-like fingers rings heightened by precious stones. Several were obese, gelatinous and rheumatic. Some offered to the gaze cheeks as plump as the fattest of pigs, so shiny that one might have thought them illuminated by a painter of dolls or marionettes. Others, by contrast, resembled living skeletons and marched with curbed backs, necks extended as if they were already prepared for the guillotine. Others agitated their bulbous posteriors as they advanced, and seemed by that instinctive mime to be overtly inviting ephebes to unnatural amours.

And all of them, without distinction of thinness, fatness or height, sported innumerable decorations in their button-holes. There were red ones, ornamenting the collars of traitors like drops of blood. There were yellow ones, blue ones, green ones, tricolors, bicolors and multicolors, orange and goose-shit ribbons. Some affected triangular forms; others were knotted backwards like the belts of dwarfs, others attained a breadth of several centimeters; others, finally, were deployed in fans, according to importance, and sprang from buttonholes like rockets of glory and certificates of honor.

When Blasius had seen that reptilian multitude pressing around him, he gave them his instructions curtly, with a scornful smile. And all the embezzlers, all the corrupt officials, all the traitors and all the counterfeiters, dazzled by the magnificence of his project, breathless with rapacity on calculating the incredible profits that the labor of their slaves would bring them, acclaimed that sumptuous stranger. And as they flowed like a stream of living mud through the myrtle-perfumed paths, those potentates with putrefied consciences manifested their astonishment in fearful words. On luggers, automotive launches and pleasure yachts, that horde quit the port, and for some time the island recovered its initial mildness, purity and beauty.

One morning, however, at the hour when all the roses of the heavens were scattered over the horizon, perching on the summits of hills and posing in delicate cascades of the softness of the lilac waves, dark forms were seen to appear in that festival of hues, and those dark forms cleaved the sea rapidly.

From the shore Blasius and the seven taciturn men were looking out for their approach, and joy inundated the master's face. Leaning toward his companions, he murmured: "It's them."

Immediately, a delight similar to that of Blasius illuminated the suntanned faces of the adventurers.

For days and nights, tugs spitting jets of black smoke brought pinnaces laden with serfs and materials into the harbor. The overseers on the quay supervised that disembarkation, and heaped insults and threats on the subcontractors and manual laborers who were exhausting themselves manipulating the stone and iron. Soon, throughout the island, there was a tumult of trucks and wagons transporting toward the circular valley all the accumulations destined for the superhuman task. Along with the tugs and the mariners and the workmen, citizens with illuminated faces and vast paunches disembarked, and those citizens erected canvas tents and wooden shacks around the construction yards. They equipped those shacks and tents with barrels full of wine, and tables larded with victuals and thick glass cups, in order that he subcontractors and manual workers could, during hours of rest—and, clandestinely, during working hours—come to nourish themselves or get drunk, and thus drop into the coffers of the taverners the brightest part of their savings and their salary.

And with the taverners, troops of high-class courtesans and prostitutes of base extraction also arrived in pointed pinnaces, destined for the sexual relief and debauchery of the serfs, overseers and boatmen. The courtesans and the whores installed themselves in rectangular shacks that were separated into cells by partitions of planks, and the hardest of hearing could perceive through those walls the blasphemies, the groans of sadism, the insults and the cries of lust uttered by the rutting men and the women fainting under the hectic emprise of the males.

Busy and prolix, architects consulting blueprints were flying and fluttering in all directions. Those architects argued with the directors of the construction yards clad in velvet and plum overalls, from the large pockets of which emerged compasses, yellow meter rules and pencils with bulbous ends.

And army of grunting diggers in shirtsleeves and large boots caked with dirt were hollowing out prodigious foundations relentlessly; and woodcutters, in order to fray a passage for them, felled centenarian trees with great blows of their axes, which groaned like human beings as they fell. Sawyers with long blades reduced those trees to planks, and other sawyers armed with more robust instruments squared off the blocks of stone that haulers bracing themselves with levers precipitated from their tumbrels.

All languages, dialects and patois could be heard in speech.

Workers came running from all over the world, and in the enchantment of that privileged nature, under the soft warm light that bathed the atmosphere and the fields, the most contrasting and the most curious specimens were encountered. There were giants with bronzed torsos, dwarfs with hooded eyes and shiny hair, individuals of bestial appearance and others who remained, in spite of the debilitating labor to which they devoted themselves, as young and handsome as gods.

Disputes often flared up, or battles, between those mercenaries of such varied races. Then blood flowed, and the overseers, impotent to separate the antagonists, carried the defeated and the wounded to the infirmary, where women in white blouses and headgear bandaged them with a maternal solicitude, and closed their eyes when they had rendered the last sigh.

Every day, Blasius, escorted by the taciturn men, visited the construction yards and informed himself of the progress of the works. He harassed the builders and architects mercilessly, and those arrogant individuals, instantly discarding their vanity, curbed their heads silently before that man, more opulent alone than all kings and financiers combined. He stayed for entire hours on the bank of the river, which the builders were spanning with a bridge with a single arch, made entirely of wrought iron, and the sculptors charged with ornamenting the marble parapets came to solicit his advice humbly.

Gradually, the City was born and rose up; and after a year of gigantic labor, during which it had absorbed thousands of lives and taken over the thought of hundreds of brains, it was displayed to the fulgurant gaze of Blasius, as noble and pure as a virgin, under the flavescence of dusk.

On every roof, on every dome, at the summit of every palace and every tower, immense black flags fluttered.

The serfs, on seeing those flags hoisted by the carpenters above all that resplendent whiteness, had taken refuge in the taverners' tents or the prostitutes' shacks, and by means of drunkenness or lubricity they were striving to forget the anguish that apparition caused them.

Now, caravans of painters, gilders, ornamenters and decorators were arriving without discontinuity on the odorous island. They replaced the artisans and the workers, who, having collected their salary, were packing up the implements of their labor, loading them on to their robust shoulders with an effort and heading slowly for the boats ready to depart for the continents inhabited by modern men.

The tugs, cables taut, cleaving the citrine waves, drew away from the city those who had built it and who would never know, their efforts and their curiosity notwithstanding, with what objective and for what inhabitants the master of wealth had ordered its construction.

And when the subcontractors, the manual workers, the masons and the carpenters had disappeared, the artists, perched in groups on scaffolding, clung like swarms of bees to the walls of temples and the vaults of palaces, or climbed with the aid of flexible ladders along the columns supporting the concave walls of museums, music halls and laboratories.

One crew, more skilled and more talented than the others, assumed the redoubtable task of decorating the immense theater in which plays and concerts were to be staged. They were seen coming and going along aerial planks, carefully carrying jars filled with paint, and coating the stone, wood and marble with sweeps of the arm. The entire troop was singing, whirling, calling to one another, trading gibes and witticisms, mischievous remarks and invective, and one sensed that those creators were overflowing with life and enthusiasm.

An old man, whose white smock, snowy hair and long beard gave him an apostolic appearance, was censuring and guiding that exuberant and tumultuous youth. But many a time, instead of obeying him, several of his pupils yielded to their inspiration and replaced the sketches designed by the master with subjects or motifs issued from their feverish brains; and when the master passed close to them and perceived those acts of indiscipline, he reprimanded the disciples in sensate and measured terms, unless he recognized, being impregnated with justice, the superiority of their work over the project that he had charged them with realizing.

Thus, during those works of nobility and beauty, he discovered a few artists whose talents equaled the most famous, and he identified them to Blasius, who came immediately to admire their friezes, their frescoes or their ornaments, and recompensed them with a regal generosity

Alongside the painters, the sculptors chiseled bas-reliefs, hollowed out bands, and caused bezants, billets and checkerboards to spring from the Paros marble with blows of mallets, or graved entrelacs, festoons and gadroons while singing old songs and smoking enormous pipes. Some stretched waves to the height of the human breast, as sinuous as interminable serpents. Others rounded out moldings in the form on ovals and pearls, posed grooves at the summit of walls, or surmounted doors with vermiculations or tresses, which the decorators emphasized or enveloped with subtle colors. And on the sides of the spacious bridge linking the two parts of the City together, other sculptors incrusted nautical scenes or reproduced with fervor scenes of life or amour; and other painters, hirsute or glabrous, colored the great wrought iron arch.

Artisans skilled in giving wood subtle forms, curving planks and directing in unexpected and disconcerting fashions the arms of armchairs and the backs of cathedra, twisting the feet of sofas and chaise-longues into abnormal torsades, were fabricating amazing items of furniture; and upholsterers were pinning up ancient drapes or tapestries of an outrageous modernism with golden nails and clasps inlaid with diamonds in the halls.

Engineers planning the play of lights suspended globes of opaque crystal or sandstone from ceilings with silken cables from, surveyed the hanging of enormous chandeliers whose facets ought to diffuse light in all directions and render it more ardent than a fire, and studied the emplacements for the installation of the mirrors and looking-glasses that would arrive from the most celebrated manufacturers, on vessels specially equipped for that purpose.

And on all sides, at all hours, there was a hive of human activity, such a swarm that it became impossible to fray a passage through the unfinished streets.

Meanwhile, the founders and the gilders finished putting tons of yellow, red and brown gold to melt in crucibles as profound and gulfs. When the liquefaction appeared to them to be complete, they spread the hot metal by means of a special apparatus over the domes and roofs of monuments and palaces. Other apparatus leveled it while extracting the smallest scoria; and gradually, the City, under the flux of the solar rays that collides with it like luminous lances, became a light-source itself.

When dawn broke, shedding over the golden roofs its stamens of ruby, beryl and chrysoprase, the City appeared the gaze like a hallucinatory tree-stump on which morels and orange agarics and mushrooms of every species were displaying their fleshy cupolas, rounding out the gigantic parasols of their heads protectively against the assaults of the star.

The mists of the dawn attenuated the brutality of the light, and those mists settled around the domes like multitudes of white doves, curled around columns like impalpable cashmere scarves, hung on to the angles of roofs or the asperities of balustrades, and tore apart, falling back like princely tatters along the sides of the palaces until the moment when a warmer ray than the previous ones sucked them up, drank them and incorporated them into the azure of infinity.

When one gazed at the City from a distance, at those matutinal hours, all the hues were confounded in a single one, in which sparkling rose was dominant; and the City then because a vast prodigious flower, ready to bloom between the masses of the mountains and forests that surrounded it.

At noon, when the rockets of the sun struck its bright domes with rude jets, without respite, the City appeared to the eyes as an immense flamboyant jewel-case; and before that resplendence, human eyes closed, dazzled.

And in the evening, when everything in nature went to sleep, from the smallest insect to the proudest and most vivacious tree, when the murmur of springs and the twittering of birds were gradually extinguished; when the jagged ridges of rocks stood out in the crepuscular warmth, when the violet, turquoise, jade and amethyst reflections of the sky were effaced in the breath of the air, at the caprice of the clouds, which mutated them into crimson, emerald or sapphire; then the light projected toward the zenith by the City gradually faded away; and human gazes could admire in their multiple aspects, in all their grace, and all their majesty, the sculptures, the bas-reliefs and the masterpieces that glorified it, and made it the unique marvel of the world.

After many months of labor, everything in the City was finished.

The broad avenues, paved with scented wood, interleaved with harmonious mosaics, awaited the passers-by and strollers who were to tread them. The spacious squares, shaded by trees belonging to the rarest species, were decorated with gardens in which the exhalations of the most unexpected flowers were combined; the streets, which were not dishonored by trams or taxis, seemed somnolent under the magnificence of the sun.

There was no trace of men or women anywhere, except for one house of marble and porphyry situated at the extremity of the principal avenue, and dominating, by virtue of its placement and its proportions, all the surrounding houses and palaces.

There, in high and sonorous halls, of architectures still unknown to modern people, Blasius and the seven taciturn men were resident. Each of them occupied a private room fitted out with a sobriety that contrasted with the luxury and sumptuousness of the surrounding dwellings. Neither Blasius nor his companions employed serfs to serve or flatter them.

Blasius' room, rather narrow, was as simple as the room in which, in the house crowned with foliage and flowers, he had once devoted himself to his research; it was oval in form. The ceiling, devoid of ornaments, was as low as the ceiling of a cell, and the furniture was only distinguished from ordinary furniture by the strangeness of its curves and torsions. As before, in the time of poverty and struggles, Blasius slept on his black bearskin, and it was the same monk's habit that surrounded his body and the same leather sandals that shod him. As before, he ate on a corner of the table, from terra cotta bowls, the frugal broth prepared for him by the taciturn man in charge of meals. But a complex and improved chemical apparatus occupying the greater part of the room replaced the rudimentary charcoal-burning stove with which the indefatigable researcher had discovered the terrible secret, one evening when the sky was tremulous above him with all its stars and constellations.

In the fireproof earthenware furnace that now served for his experiments, there was a mercury thermostat, a burner, a magnesia crucible into which Blasius poured material for disintegration, and, in the middle, like two black index fingers pointing at one another, the carbon electrodes by means of which Blasius could obtain temperatures superior to five hundred degrees.

The cells of the taciturn men contained a few items of furniture as curious as the master's; and in each wall, invisible doors leading to subterrains opened by means of electric buttons.

Those subterrains, whose extent surpassed all imagination, went from one end of the city to the other, and contained in their tenebrous depths the blocks of metal and ingots that Blasius transmuted indefatigably with a light contact. There was the wherewithal there to pay out unimaginable sums, and the most prodigious fortunes were nonexistent compared with the contents of any one of the compartments. Those ingots and masses were awaiting the advent of goldsmiths and coiners who were due to strike them with numbers and multiple effigies, in workshops prepared with that intention.

Arenas with perimeters of jasper and steps of chalcedony, onyx and lazulite were gleaming at the extremity of the City, projecting incredible hues over the surrounding meadows and bushes. Thus denatured by reflections, the meadows appeared sky blue, and the tree trunks bright yellow or cobalt, the branches burnt opal and the foliage mauve or crimson. And because no one, except for Blasius and the seven taciturn men had yet penetrated into that enclosure, those dead arenas took on a appearance of infinite desolation under the crepuscular resplendence.

At sunrise one morning, however, Blasius and the seven taciturn men quit the perfumed island and crossed the sea, whose white waves foamed beneath them, in airplanes, like a flock of demented eagles. The island remained completely deserted for a week. Then, in a dawn as blonde and charming as the dawn of their departure, the aerial navigators reappeared high in the hyaline sky, and disembarked on the aerodrome whose sand, stirred up by the wind of the propellers, had golden sparkles.

When they had disembarked and put their inert birds away under hangars with polished roofs, a great rumor was born on the horizon, and Blasius and the seven taciturn men ran to the marble jetty on the edge of the harbor, from which the eye could see the entire ocean without any obstacle.

From the depths of the distant waves, forming a clear line that separated the sky from the water, myriads of dark dots—a fleet—emerged.

As the vessels comprising it drew nearer to the island, the great rumor became more distinct; and that rumor was a slow and grave hymn sung by the invisible sailors and passengers.

At the spectacle of that surge of ships, Blasius trembled like a child frightened by a nursery tale, and his eyes, framed by their profound orbits and shaded by the gray bushes of his eyebrows, blazed. But no one could have discerned whether the gleam that set his eyes ablaze was a glimmer of joy or anger.

Gradually, as the vessels accosted the quay, the mysterious navigators disembarked on to firm ground. Under the conduct of chiefs and guides recognizable by particular signs they formed groups in the four corners of the landing-stage, and Blasius, in the middle of those groups, gave orders.

The groups to the left were composed of venerable old men with pensive foreheads and long beards; they assembled silently, clutching to their breasts boxes or leather bags swollen like balloons.

The group to the right was composed of young men with sharp gazes and harmonious bodies; those, deaf to the injunctions of their guides, translated into bold and expressive words their joy in having escaped the marine perils and finding themselves on that amiable and cheerful island.

The group facing Blasius was the least numerous. One could see people therein of all ages and appearances, who remained as mute as the austere old men of the first group, and their gazes were lost in all the profusion of light, foliage and fabulous monuments, resembling the naïve gazes of the saints who ornament the stained glass windows in village churches.

The last group, the most compact and the most surprising, consisted entirely of men clad in red tunics, shod in cothurnes with wooden sandals. The oldest of them could not have surpassed twenty-five years. All of them, without exception, were holding elegant musical instruments in their hands, with vibrant strings and cornets curved like the orifices of amphorae, invented by the most famous instrument-makers in the world.

When the groups were complete, at a sign from Blasius, the musicians started walking toward the City; and while marching in rows of a hundred, they sang the slow and grave hymn that Blasius and the seven taciturn men had perceived several hours before from the harbor. The instruments underscored the modulations and the outbursts of that solemn choir. The instrumentalists and the cantors surpassed the number of ten thousand, and the power of their harmony was such that the entire island vibrated like an immense organ.

Behind them went the men of the first group. Less numerous than the musicians, they advanced, heads bowed, plunged in their meditations, as if indifferent to the musical magnificence that surrounded them.

Next, separated from the scholars by an interval of some forty meters, came the men with keen gazes of the second group. They walked with a light step, and at times they took up the sublime chorus intoned by the ten thousand musicians with their clear and ardent voices.

The group of poets and dreamers closed the splendid cortege; and on hearing the celestial soul of the instruments weep, their souls of vibrations and sensibility also quivered, and tears were seen trickling slowly from their eyes.

Now, those thousands of superhumans arrived in the heart of the City, and, still under the conduct of their chiefs, they separated in order to go to the dwellings that the will of Blasius assigned to them.

Those of the scientists were in the direction of the dawn. Blasius had placed them thus because science is still in its first stammers; because it ought to turn toward the future as a virgin turns toward the lover she desires; because it will require many centuries to emerge from the dolorous penumbra in which it is trailing, and truly to become the agent of salvation at which the generations of the future will marvel.

Those of the artists were in the center of the City. Blasius had placed them thus because art is the culminating point of human perfection; because it is inseparable from humanity itself; because it dominates and illuminates it as a star at its zenith dominates the universe; because without it, humans would perish gradually like an earth devoid of sunlight; and above all because it will remain the immortal testament of centuries and races, the formal attestation that people have veritably been that which they evoke; and because, in radiating from all directions over elites, over the ignorant and the vulgar, they oblige them occasionally, in spite of themselves, to forget the ignominy of existence.

Those of the poets were toward the sunset. Blasius had placed them thus because the death of the dream is approaching; the young people of today tend uniquely to brutal action; literature appears to their mechanical, positivistic and sportive souls to be an insane and ridiculous thing, and they deny all poetry and all intellectual culture by virtue of theories that do not conceal their ignorance and stupidity.

And when those thousands of souls, intelligences and bodies had organized their lives, regulated their time, ordered their labor, their amusements and their repose in accordance with a code drawn up by Blasius and the most perfect of each group, in the port, where the waves can to expire with old nursery songs, ships appeared bearing pennants that fluttered in the light wind, garlanded with flowers from stem to stern. The decks of the ships disappeared under cassolettes and perfume-burners, and odors of incense, of myrrh, amber and cinnamon, arrived from the sea in the nostrils of men who had run to watch the disembarkation of unexpected navigators.

When the ships were lined up along the quays, a clamor of admiration emerged from all mouths. The vessels only contained women; and Blasius had summoned them expressly, in thousands, from the four corners of the world, in order to unite them with the inhabitants of the resplendent City.

They passed like living glories along the avenues where the scientists, the poets and the artists acclaimed them with gestures of desire.

And the musicians preceded them; but instead of the slow and grave hymn that they had played on the day of their advent, a triumphant chorus sprang from their fervent lips, and for the first time, affirmed by those vibrant bodies, those marmoreal throats and those breasts rearing up on torsos like gazelles on virginal mountain slopes, Harmony saluted Amour.

And Blasius, leaning on the high terrace of his dwelling, considered that luminous procession without saying a word. And his eyes, even more than at the disembarkation of the thousands of males, were flamboyant between their long lashes; but no one would have been able to discern, on looking at him, whether the gleam that set his eyes ablaze was a glimmer of joy or anger.

All the women who had just disembarked in the City attained inconceivable degrees of perfection. Incomparably beautiful, they left behind them a wake of perfumes and lust. Some boldly unveiled flesh as nacreous as seashells. Others walked with a feline suppleness, and their undulating rumps ignited flashes of covetousness in the gazes of the most austere. Some of them were as svelte as the lianas of the equatorial forests, others as slender as statuettes and as frail as dolls. They were encountered at every hour of the day in the gardens, at the corners of avenues or under the porticos of monuments. The men, thirsty for kisses and embraces, followed those who charmed them, and gradually, all the scientists, all the thinkers and all the artists found companions in accordance with their flesh and their ideal.

And when all the people of the City, with the exception of Blasius and the seven taciturn men had taken the women they had chosen into their dwellings, Blasius had a great nuptial feast announced in the streets and crossroads, by means of electrical loudhailers and voice-transmitters.

V

The celebration began at dawn.

From every threshold, at a signal launched by alarms and sirens specially constructed to assemble the multitudes, groups of women clad in their finest tunics sprang forth like moving brightness.

Around their foreheads they wore golden diadems, crowns of violets, chaplets of roses or strips formed of plaques of diamonds as large as orange blossom, heightened by heavy polished turquoises. Ivory bracelets, all of the same form and the same dimensions, dispended by the artisans and goldsmiths of the City in accordance with Blasius' instructions, rattled on their arms; those trinkets composed the ritual ornamentation of the solemn ceremonies.

The whiteness of those ivories was supposed to symbolize the purity of soul and the nobility of spirit of all those who had landed, from the vessels decked with fabrics and embalmed by cassolettes, on the island where they were awaited by the quivering masters to whom Blasius nourished the design of giving them now. For all those who volunteered for the mysterious voyage had been required to prove that they were above the common run morally and physically, and that they were worthy to prolong, beyond the centuries and above the moribund races of the two continents, the generation of superhumans that the Master had just gathered together, at the price of incredible efforts, in the City that he had created.

Behind the women, draped in ample and loose linen garments, the seekers of formulae advanced, the sculptors of words and the inventors of rhythms. They each held in the right hand a long silver cane, and, avid for the beauty that the best of them were about to assume the redoubtable mission of unveiling, they were heading toward the arenas of marble and gold opening in the matutinal splendor the bloody petals of their awnings and their porticos.

Without precipitation, at the signal of the taciturn men who were guarding the entrances to the vomitoria, men and women invaded the steps of chalcedony, onyx and lazulite. They sat down on cushions of byssus cloth, and, mutely, their hearts oppressed by the majestic grandeur of the monument, into which they were penetrating for the first time, considered the stage that an immense dark blue curtain protected from the curiosity of spectators.

Already, muted plaints, like extrahuman voices, were reaching them in gusts of phrases, snatches and arpeggios of wind instruments and the vibration of drums.

From time to time, stifling that musical hum, the grim throb of an aircraft passed overhead. Those who were waiting on the steps knew that particular sound well. They understood that Blasius was watching from above, and that in a little while, when he judged it appropriate, he would give the signal and would come to sit down behind them, in the retreat accommodated in the back of the arena, between two columns.

When the chief of the actors and singers had received the electrical signal, the immense blue curtain gradually drew aide, uncovering a proscenium illuminated by green and violet lamps, full of musicians, Between the stringed instruments and the instruments of harmony, upright on a platform, with a slender lemon-wood baton in his hand, stood the conductor of the orchestra.

As on the day of their arrival in the City, the musicians formed a compact troop, which extended into the depths of the stage, and it would not have been presumptuous to estimate their number at ten thousand. As on the day of their arrival, they wore red tunics, tightened at the waist by massive golden chains; and all their instruments, with the exception of the violins and cellos, affected unusual proportions. In low voices the men and women on the steps described them, trying in vain to put names to them; all of them were waiting for the magisterial gesture that would cause the ensemble of those previously-unheard sonorities to resound under the concave vaults of the great hall.

And when the conductor had raised his hand to command attention, and the artistes had raised their instruments to their lips, fitted them to their shoulders or between their legs, the frail lemon-wood baton cleaved the air, and with a deafening clamor, then ten thousand attacked their symphony.

First there was a slow and pathetic unison. The melodic phrase departed from the depths where the ebony shafts of a thousand bordicors twice as tall and twice as broad as double basses growled under the obstinate bows of virtuosos. Then that phrase spread to the right, propagated in the multitude of major basses tuned two octaves lower than the violin, rose as high as the cellos, as taken up by the host of baritones, tenors and haut-contres, which were playing an octave above the violins, and suddenly stopped at an injunction of the baton.

Then, to the left, the wind instruments responded to the strings.

Mysteriously, like a whisper of goat-foots in a thicket, the muted flutes sang the intoxication of bright mornings, underlining the gray chords of altos and mezzo violin; transmitted they motif, in the course of a reprise, to the long clarinets with mouths turned back on themselves, like double saxophones; and fell silent, while the soprano and treble violins, like a crystalline twitter of birdsong, strung out the trills, arpeggios and cadences of a radiant and light scherzo.

And when the strings had chirped the wellbeing of living, the joy of the sun sprinkling the bushes, the flowers and everything with its dazzling rain, there was, in a sudden, formidable apotheosis, the explosion of three thousand trumpets.

Then the choristers, hidden until that moment in the interior passages, advanced in groups of three hundred, and sustained by the prodigious phalanx of the orchestra, they intoned the Hymn to Amour.

And that music, the moaning of strings under bows, the fanfares, the rumbles of bordicors and the enthusiasm of trumpets, was so powerful and so moving that the thinks, the scientists, the esthetes and the women began to weep large hectic tears.

Blasius, his elbows on the black balustrade of his retreat, leaned over silently between the columns, and his narrow chest, at that unleashing of magnificence and passion, was as breathless as the agonized chest of a dying man.

When the symphony had finished, when nothing could any longer be heard in the painful silence but the sobbing of women and the rustle of fabrics that the men were twisting in their feverish fingers, Blasius aimed a thin index finger, corroded by acids, at the conductor. Like an emperor summoning gladiators and andabatae from the depths of his crimson-clad box, he gave the order to recommence the work of genus. And again, in the midst of the stupefied meditation and tears, the slender lemon-wood baton caused the ten thousand marvelous instruments to moan.

Then the immense stage was slowly depopulated of all its musicians. And serfs, at the command of their chief, came to lay out on the shiny floor esparto mats the color of sunlight. When the entire plateau had been covered, they threw on to the mats a profusion of fennel and wild mint, which suddenly perfumed the warm air.

With a quiver of their nostrils, the women inhaled those emanations, and as the odorant carpet thickened, a vivifying freshness enveloped the audience.

The serfs disappeared, and a great silence was established in the hall; very softly, mutedly, the now invisible and distant orchestra attacked the prelude of a transcaucasian dance. And while the nostalgic appeals of major basses and the velvety undulations of muted flutes wound around the foreheads of the audience like sonorous scarves, groups of young women appeared through all the openings in the wings and curtains of the stage.

The impact of their white feet in the emerald carpet was so light that one might have thought it a distant purring of lovers; only the click of bracelets around their delicate ankles put a slightly brutal note into that atmosphere of pace and delight.

The groups succeeded one another, and soon the spectators, hallucinated by the unexpected vision, were able to count hundreds. The plateau constructed by the architects on the indications of Blasius was so broad and so deep that all the white forms, spinning and leaping at the whim of the mysterious music, resembled tiny things lost in the vast silence of some haunted manor.

Their number was increasing by the minute. When there were more than a thousand, at the signal of the two protagonists who were guiding them, they all began to mime in unison the action invented for that prodigious fête by the most powerful dramatists and the most moving musician in the city.

At first, to the sound of the treble violins and muted horns, their hands, raised toward the heavens, translated the harmonious awakening of great plains, the quivering of foliage shaking off the brown rags of the dead night in the pallor of dawn. Then, their parted lips, as moist as nacreous shells, imitated the rippling of limpid water flowing over a bed of gravel, and an unison, the young women leaned over toward the fennel and the mint, pretending to mirror in some hallucinatory stream the delicate slenderness of their features. After having simulated ablutions in an imaginary mirror of wavelets, twisted and dried their long tresses, they pinned them up over the napes of their necks with enormous golden combs; and to the punctuated rhythm of tambourines, their fingers interlaced for a capricious round-dance.

Sometimes their living circle stretched like a circle of light, sometimes it shrank to the extent of becoming a simple snowy line; and in that vehement play the breasts of the young women swelled, their loins were elevated by lassitude and gaiety; and suddenly, under the impulsion of one of their number, more intrepid than her companions, they set off again around the verdant track, uttering joyous laughter.

From the depths of the stage, meanwhile, rose an Amboise prelude,[8] as thin and charming as the song of a robin,

---

[8] The town of Amboise was famous in France as a source of brass instruments made by the Courtois family, but it is un-

Then the round was suddenly interrupted, and the young women, gripped by fear, ran to hide behind the silvery trunks of birches forming the principal part of the décor. From the shelter of those illusory retreats, they watched. And through the opening in the middle of the stage, crowned with saffron, his torso naked and his pelvis braced beneath a girdle of frosted cotton cloth, the leader of the dance appeared.

He drew plaintive, slightly nasal sounds from his Amboise, and the musical phrases that he modulated, exclusively constructed of four notes and in a minor key, became because of its strangeness and monotony a nostalgic and sad appeal. And from all directions, at each repetition of the Amboise, other men were seen to appear, half-naked like the leading player, whose eyes were flamboyant in the gloom, like the eyes of lynxes.

Now the troop of young women took refuge in the left-hand corner of the stage; and, huddling together, shivering with dread, they waited for the rush of the dominators who were bringing them amour. The latter, massed in the opposite corner, were motionless, ready to leap forward at the command uttered by the invisible cymbals. That order rang out like a savage cry, and immediately, the thousand male dancers charged the fearful young women and dragged them away, with an irresistible surge, in a new bacchanal more hectic and more vertiginous than the round that had just extenuated their youthful vigor.

The music growled; the sobs of the cellos and the pedal-notes of the contrabassoons deafened the surroundings; and to those insane harmonies, the male dancers enlaced the females; their loins collides; their supple legs intertwined like vines in the warm breath of the autumn wind; and, more drowned by desire with every passing second, the eyes of the young women closed.

---

clear exactly which instrument is being indicated here by the term.

All the men and all the women, carried away by that diabolical music, by the dances in the course of which the two thousand seemed to be writing with their bodies the poem of lust and sensuality, were standing up on the steps. They clapped their hands together to the rhythm of the reed-trumpets and the bellowing of sarrusophones. Maddened by that mime and that lubricity, the men sought beneath the tunics of their companions for the splendid florescence of the breasts and the blossoming of the loins, and already, more than one woman, at that contact, those odors, and those instrumental explosions, fell inert, her eyes closed, ruddy foam on her lips. And those thousands upon thousands of spectators awaited the ultimate embrace that would lay the female lovers down on the fennel and the mint, finally curbed by the males.

And when the dark blue curtain closed again on the two thousand confounded youths, a long acclamation made the awnings and the walls of the enclosure tremble. The serfs had to part the heavy curtain several times in order to permit the inhabitants of the City to contemplate again and applaud that unprecedented spectacle. And, hidden in the friezes, while the male and female dancers, exhausted by their superhuman effort, got up again, a chorus of poets chanted in slow voices an ardent and luminous hymn to the glory of the man whose genius had realized so many incredible marvels. The members of the audience, nonplussed by the new magnificence, interrogated one another with their gazes, and wondered whether they ought to admire more the enchantment of that evocative music or the magic of the words, which summarized not only all harmony but also all nobility, all color, all amour and all passion.

Blasius watched, impassive this time, the apotheoses of which he was the director; and when he had understood that all that quivering flesh and all those unhinged brains had attained the paroxysm of enervation and dementia, he had the order cried to the members of the audience by means of public address systems and loudhailers, to make their way to the enclosure where the feast awaited them.

The multitude, still dazed by that vision, still mollified by all the music, all the verses and all the songs, headed slowly toward the arenas situated some distance from the city, near Blasius' dwelling.

The lovers, male or female, did not speak.

They were thinking about what they had just seen and heard; and, remembering with amazement their past existence, they wondered how they had been able to live until that day in modern cities, killers of fervor and dreams; and they tried to divine the new enchantments that waited them between the walls where the communion was to be held.

From time to time, cleaving through the silent groups, vast carts passed along the marble-paved avenue. Those carts were transporting the musicians' large instruments, for the elite of virtuosos was to be heard again, hidden behind brocade curtains, at the beginning and end of the repast. The guests, avid for reiterated sensations, rejoiced in thinking that, to the intoxication of vintage wines and the savor of the princely dishes that would be served to them, the intoxication of all those distant sonorities would be added for hours on end.

They went through the immense porticos giving access to the arena, and all of them, on setting foot on the sand that dusted it, recoiled, not daring to believe what they saw.

That sand, billons of grains of which were scattered under their prodigious footfalls, was not sand but pulverized gold. In the warm light falling from the vaults, that gold mutated into a carpet seemed to quiver like a living thing. When the comings and goings of men and woman had disturbed its evenness, servants armed with silver rakes slipped between the groups and repaired the damage in a matter of seconds.

The banquet was to be served on little tables seating four at the most, in order to permit everyone to choose their places and companions freely. Those small rectangular tables in ebony and sandalwood did not bar any incrustation, ornament or sculpture, but the sumptuousness of the place-settings, cups and accessories that garnished them corrected that deliberate simplicity. The large crimson couches with four twisted feet that were to serve the diners as seats denounced, at the same time as the magnificence of Blasius, his desire to remain, in spite of everything and forever, the incomparable magician dominating lamentable humankind with his genius.

The guests, becoming loquacious again before the dazzling organization of the feast, gradually installed themselves as they wished

Women full of aversion and scorn for men gathered around a few separate tables, while poets and artists incapable of imagining that anyone could testify amour and affection to such superficial and frivolous individuals isolated themselves on the other side of the arena, and, before tasting the succulent dishes, lingered over subtle controversies, agitating the vastest problems that had ever tormented the brains of thinkers and philosophers. But the majority of the others, finding an indescribable charm in the company of their elect, invited unknown and handsome couples to sit down with them, fraternally, and by that means knotted improvised amities that only death would sever subsequently.

The women extended themselves on the cushions, tasting with fearful and curious expressions the delicate dishes that were presented to them; the men, more inclined to libations, reserved their solicitude for the wines sparkling like jewels through the limpid crustal of amphorae. All the wines went gradually to their heads, giving them an unexpected strength, eloquence and presumption, and the serfs responsible for the beverages had difficulty replacing from silver decanters filled to the brim the empty receptacles that fell incessantly on to the gold of the arena and strewed it like bandaged victims.

In honor of the nuptial day, the masters of the culinary arts had surpassed themselves. Disdainful of the age-old formulae and bleak menus familiar on the continents, they had invented new things recklessly. They had adapted, ground and metamorphosed into amazing dishes the plants, flowers and animals that seemed most inappropriate to serve as human prey.

Over the sandalwood tables, to the exclamations of the surprised diners, filed in turn crowns of violets coated in an unctuous and sugary cream; otters and ermines spiked with lilies and vervain, presented with their immaculate skins on ruby dishes sculpted by means of a mysterious artifice; swarms of bees captured alive and cooked in their own honey; candied onagers in magnolia leaves and flowers; Tibetan yaks, monstrous and hairy, impaled on skewers as thick as beams and roasted over braziers of box-wood and cedar, which communicated an astonishing odor to their flesh; stews of grass snakes and water snakes; little white mice whose delicate muzzles emerged from the gilded crusts of pastries and seemed to be gazing with their pink eyes at the thousands of tumultuous and disorderly guests; and other dishes even rarer, spicier and tastier...

Minds and senses were heated more than reasonably by the fire of those aliments and wines. Couples enlaced one another, kissing one another on the lips without restraint and without shame; and in the distance, in the part of the arena chosen by the lesbians, arms could be seen seeking one another above the profound beds, bodies undulating, and groups rising up in prolonged and convulsive spasms, while the major basses and the clarinets deployed over all those desires the supernatural sensuality of their sobs and their rhythms...

Already, several couples, incapable of containing themselves any longer, had quit the banqueting hall and, their eyes drowned with desire, hastened toward the high-ceilinged and spacious bedrooms.

In the corner opposite the lesbians, ephebes crowned with ivy and saffron offered themselves with ardent words to the contact of their over-excited male lovers. Even the serfs sometimes slipped away into deserted corners and reappeared shortly afterwards, their eyelids darkly circled, their legs unsteady, carrying large silver trays or jade urns awkwardly in their weary hands.

Blasius, sitting all alone at a table in the remotest corner of the arena, contemplated the formidable orgy, of which he was the promoter, without saying a word. His eyes blazing, his mouth twisted into a formidable rictus, he made uninterrupted signals to the chief of the serfs and wine-waiters, and flagon succeeded flagon. Wines aged for several centuries disappeared into the insatiable gullets of drinkers, and the drunkenness of all those men and women increased vertiginously.

Suddenly, a great tumult became audible outside the hall.

The disheveled guests, intoxicated by wine and lust, raised themselves up on their ebony and onyx couches, and turned their vitreous eyes in the direction of the portico. And like the dull rumble of a rising flood, a long murmur of admiration and dread mingled its pedal-note with the vibrations of the symphony. And the music, as soon as the first murmurs were born, gradually died down. And in the silence, now absolute, a woman appeared on the highest of the three red-gold steps dominating the arena.

She was completely naked. And the immense awning decorating the vault, the rubescence of the walls and the columns, the capitals and the large slabs on which heaps of tuberoses, tulips and poppies were dying, formed a royal purple backcloth for her splendid body. Her hair, lifted up by the wind of ventilators, spread out around her ivory shoulders like blonde wings. Her hips were rounded like the curves of a bow tightened by the robust hands of a hunter; each of her breasts stood out from her torso like the bulbous dome of a Turkish cymbal, and their proud nipples seemed to be palpitating under the jets of light that streamed from the stained glass windows. Her hands were crossed being her hips, and blue, black and yellow rings around her ankles were tinkling, as brightly as the sound of little bells. Her slightly swollen abdomen had the appearance of a pink and fleshy petal, and a gilded down was stamped beneath it like quivering pollen thrown upon that flower by another invisible and fecundating flower.

Beside the woman, its head resting on her thighs, its almond eyes raised toward her throat through the somber filter of eyelashes, its long tail wound like a serpent around her left leg, its two forepaws widely splayed, its rump quivering at the contact of the hair that brushed it at every breath of air, a gray leopard spotted with brown was purring softly.

And behind the sculptural group, like repellers, the serfs guarding the exits were gasping with fright.

The woman scanned the stupefied audience with a luminous gaze; in a grave vice, raising her hands, palms joined as if for an offering, toward the golden vault, she spoke.

"Hear me! I have been told that in your city, those who bear within them the pride of generous thoughts that tend to other amours, rare and more elevated than customary amours, who aspire to the total liberation of bodies and sexes, who dream of a new life, freer and more harmonious than the life of the deliquescent peoples and races of the Occident, find a definitive and sumptuous refuge. And I, who have touched human abjection with my finger, who have searched in vain from one end of the earth to the other for what the so-called civilized call amour; who have exhausted, as one exhausts the contents of a precious vase, all sensations, from the most banal to the most insensate, have deplored the vanity of my search. I departed on a sonorous ship, from island to island, and from continent to continent. And then, on an island even more beautiful than yours, I saw coming toward me, laughing with all his bloodthirsty fangs, quivering throughout his elastic and cunning body, ripping the burning arena with his sharp claws, beating the lianas and young bamboos with his flexible tail, the male that was to tame me forever...

"I renounced the pollution of men; and beside him I have commenced a new existence, purer and more adorable than all sublunar existences combined. And everywhere I have passed, men and women have shamed and calumniated me, and they have tried to kill the male that I have chosen freely as a lover. Then we both fled, and we sailed for long days, and this morning we disembarked on this island, about which the whole world talks in low voices, as the most incredible of marvels. And because I believe that the man who rules you is just and honest, I ask him before all of you: 'Welcome us, and let me savor in company with the male that dominates me, the incomparable joys of this abnormal amour!'"

When the woman had spoken, the guests looked at one another, stupefied. And from the height of the cathedra from which he was regulating the feast, the man replied to her:

"In truth, unknown woman, your words astonish my soul, and your voice resonates in my ear like an accursed music, but because you have come to us with confidence and you have unveiled our soul to us without guile, you merit being one of us. Advance, come take your place on this bed of silver and cedar, and in your honor, strange guests, let the plaintive strings of instruments vibrate..."

Immediately, four serfs, overcoming their terror, guided the woman winged with blonde hair and the undulating, softly-purring leopard to an unoccupied bed in the middle of the banqueting hall. She extended herself on the byssus cushions, and her entire body was incrusted there like a precious stone in a regal jewel-case. She passed the bright stems of her arms around the nape of her neck, and stretched out idly in the light flooding from the awning like a golden cataract. In executing that harmonious gesture she was reminiscent of some great lily opening its petals under the first rays of dawn. Then she made a sign; the leopard got up with a bound, leapt on to the bed, lay down beside her and, placing its hairy muzzle on her blue-veined neck, started to play with the nipples of her breasts like a child radiant with life amusing himself with a marvelous toy.

Meanwhile, two bronzed serfs clad in Egyptian calisiris, coiffed with grooved pschents, whose long beards hung down from either side of their ears, hastened toward the woman. They deposited crystal amphorae in front of her, sandstone flagons decorated by the flames of ovens, silver and gold bowls, and trays containing unusual dishes. They filled the receptacles with limpid wines, sparkling or dark.

The leopard shared the food with the woman, like a human, and drank while closing its eyes from the flagons and bowls cluttering the little table. It lapped with clicks of the tongue, and droplets of wine pearled around its mouth; and as it drank, and intoxication invaded its brain, all the droplets and the foam spread over its pelt, and gave it the appearance of a precious Oriental carpet glistening under summer rain.

The woman considered it with submissive eyes, and from time to time she passed a hand over its ocellated coat, the mere touch of which made the feline shudder, like an electric shock. Although they were both the focal point of general curiosity, they did not appear to perceive the existence of other humans around them. They were isolated in that atmosphere of stupor and lust, which surrounded them with its unhealthy halo; they no longer saw anything but the quiver of their bodies; they no longer heard anything but the appeal to orgasm moaned by thousands of invisible instruments.

Gradually, the woman's fingers forgot themselves in the fur of the leopard. At that contact, so gentle that it became as dolorous as a wound, the feline stiffened, flattening itself upon the cushions, its ears lowered, and its tail lashing the air.

And as if the guests were only waiting for that signal from another race, there was a sudden release of lubricity, a bewildered melee of hands, lips and bodies.

The ephebes abandoned themselves to their masters with languorous plaints. The hands of the lesbians and their ardent mouths strayed over the marble of hips and the burning snow of foreheads. In the penumbra of larders and the corners of vast kitchens, the serfs knocked over the negresses and oriental women charged with the preparation and coking of the feast. And everywhere, there was an immense rumor of amour, which swirled, spread out, sobbed and came to die at the feet of the impassive and mute Blasius.

The orgy lasted two entire days and two entire nights.

When all the participants, stunned by debauchery, extenuated by the wines that never ceased to flow over the tables, stuffed with the dishes that succeeded one another, increasingly disturbing and increasingly copious, had fallen down on the gold of the arena and fallen asleep in the midst of the followers and fabrics, ignominiously polluted by their excrements, the serfs invaded the hall. And as if they were getting rid of filth, turning their nostrils and gazes away, they loaded those inert bodies on to carts, and the coachmen took them away, in a tumultuous coming-and-going, back to their porphyry dwellings.

For three days, not a living soul was to be seen in the avenues of the city. It seemed that all the thinkers, all the scientists and all the artists, frightened by the degradation into which they had fallen, no longer dared appear in daylight, and remained inconsolable for having participated in that profanation of beauty.

But while the master continued to bury himself in his cell amid his retorts, his crucibles and his alembics, assurance gradually returned to them. The most audacious risked themselves on the threshold of their terraces, soon followed by their neighbors. The women paraded their bodies, rested from the struggles of amour and more tempting than ever, along the streets and in the gardens. And gradually, as on the day after a banal event, the city resumed its accustomed physiognomy.

VI

Because no material worry haunted the inhabitants of the city, because they were sated by the most charming, the most novel and the most harmonious spectacles between the sonorous walls of theaters and concert halls, and because they possessed the most perfect lovers, and could, in consequence, attain the maximum of amour and sensuality, they led an existence of delights in the palaces.

In that quietude, propitious to mediation and dreams, the poets wrote the most beautiful and the most sublime works that had ever made humanity illustrious; the painters and the sculptors exhibited splendid paintings and powerful groups in the halls of museums, in the public squares and on the facades of dwellings. The scientists and seekers, disdainful of those realizations unnecessary to the wellbeing and progress of their fellows, considered them with pity, and instead of lingering before the bas-reliefs and the statues, as the women did, they hastened to their laboratories, in which audacious preparations and salutary discoveries were amalgamated at the whim of their genius.

Every evening, during the hour when the gold of the sunlight mutated progressively into mauve or vermilion fragrances, in order to arrive at gladiolus red or wild duck silk, the ten thousand musicians assembled on their platform, and there, at the command of the conductor, they executed the symphonies and cantatas of the most divine harmonists of the City. Everyone hastened to the chalcedony steps in order to forget the physical or intellectual labors of their day in that intoxication of rhythms and chords. Sometimes the naked dancers and the actors crowned with ivy mimed hallucinatory or marvelous actions, as on the unforgettable day of the great nuptial feast.

And time flowed by in complete forgetfulness of the paltry preoccupations that desolated, out there, in the distance, far away, the populations of the civilized continents. Everyone experienced the sensation of living in a prodigious paradise, and they did not suppose that their existence could ever be troubled by any of the terrestrial miseries to which they had become unaccustomed since the years that had become immemorial for their metamorphosed brains.

None of them, during the frightful orgy that mingled their bodies and their souls, had heard emerging from the mouth of Blasius, leaning over the edge of his box, the enigmatic words with which he had closed that unprecedented manifestation. In any case, those words would not have indicated anything or caused them or foresee anything, since Blasius had simply murmured, as he quit the arena: "Yes, that's exactly as I wanted them..."

And when he wandered through the streets, bare-headed, swathed in his monastic habit, closely followed by the taciturn men clad in dark gray mantles, he remained impassive and grim; and if he sometimes admired the masterpieces conceived by the artists, he often manifested to them, by contrast, his disapproval or his discontent.

Gradually, children were born in the vast dwellings; now, to the sound of hammers, mallets and gravers subjugating stone or marble; to the psalmody of poets reciting to their companions or their close friends the stanzas and epodes they had just conceived; to the songs of the painters spreading on bleak canvas the victorious dazzle of hues and colors; to the gurgle of the liquids boiling in the urns of inventors; to the crystalline whisper of feminine voices chatting or laughing on odorous terraces, was added the thin wailing and shrill screams of new-born babies. Sometimes, women appeared on the gleaming thresholds of palaces with noble breasts swollen with nourishing milk, carrying moving and delicate little objects in a swathe of muslin. With pride, they held them up to the gazes of strollers; and the majority of them who remained inexorably sterile felt, at that adorable vision, their hearts constricted by an inexplicable jealousy.

Because Blasius alone possessed all the treasures of the subterrains, the provenance and value of which were unknown to anyone else, and he regulated as he wished the supplies of food, clothing and everything related to the material organization of the City, gold was something unknown to everyone.

In the morning, in immense halls, the inhabitants hastened around the serfs, and the latter, in response to a simple desire, dispensed to them luscious and sugary fruits; savory meats; fish with a thousand reflections and a thousand forms, which lay still alive on beds of mint or nenuphar leaves; doves with plumage scarcely tarnished by death, which still seemed ready to palpitate at the slightest movement and dart a plaintive gaze at their murderers; hinds with bloodstained pelts and eyelids drawn back fearfully; and even rarer victuals than the dishes revealed by Blasius to the gluttons at the dishonorable orgy.

One saw jewel beetles there accommodated in black figs; moles in redcurrant sauce; hairy caterpillars assembled in the form of vol-au-vents and sprinkled with caramel; and a whole series of nocturnal raptors whose firm and gamy flesh excited the enthusiasm of gourmets. Some took away long-eared owls as tall as little boys on silver platters that the serfs came to collect the same evening, in order to use them again for various purposes. Others loaded on to the shoulders of their domestics vast green gold cauldrons in which badgers, blue teal, bats or crocodile legs were simmering in the midst of fuming sauces. Others heaped enormous emerald jars, red marble amphorae or goatskins swelled to bursting point, in which a variety of incalculable wines were sparkling, on to carts pulled by zebras or onagers. Huge bottles full of violet, indigo or sorb liqueurs completed those cargoes; and everyone, having made his choice, went back to his lodgings without worrying about giving the dispensers the slightest gratuity.

When men or women wanted to choose garments they went into the public warehouses where artisans habituated to handling fabrics and discerning what suited everyone, in accordance with their rank or bearing, gave them warm and supple tunics to try on, and made sparkling brocades and voluptuous silks flutter before their eyes. The men and women took what they pleased, and servants perched on electric vehicles that ran through the streets at vertiginous sped deposited the carved wooden boxes containing the tunics or robes in front of each dwelling.

The most perfect concord reigned in the bosom of the City. No rivalry and no dispute had tarnished that superhuman fraternity, in which all those people liberated from modern societies blossomed. Even women, although more inclined to slander and envy than men, never pronounced bitter or sarcastic words regarding their companions.

When two men loved the same woman, or two women had an irresistible penchant for the same man, they gladly shared the object of their covetousness, and it often transpired that the prolonged commerce in question was confounded in a single amour that abolished the law of sexes and the delimitation of desire. It appeared quite natural that an adolescent copulated with a matron, or that a scarcely pubertal virgin manifested an inclination for a scientist or artist whose talent made her forget his maturity, so true is it that matrons, in no matter what part of the world, exercise a insurmountable fascination on adolescents, and that girls have always conceived an undeniable pride being distinguished by venerable citizens scarcely designated in appearance for inspiring such an amour.

Blasius, whose designs still remained impenetrable, conferred frequently with the taciturn men. From time to time, one of the master's disciples went to a distant dwelling, and there he talked to his host in a low and confidential tone. After an hour of dialogue, sometimes less, they were seen to emerge together. They went to the cell cluttered with retorts, where the Siamese cat was purring, and when the disciple left, he hid heavy and voluminous objects in the folds of his garments.

At first, the people who lived in the neighboring dwellings did not pay any attention to that, but at length, as the mysterious expeditions of the unknown individuals were renewed with an increasingly inexplicable frequency, the men and women sensed a curiosity appear in their inner depths from which they had thought they had been liberated forever a long time ago; and, secretly, the watched the coming and goings.

One day, a woman more audacious than the others followed the man who came out of Blasius' abode and questioned him. But the man refused point blank to respond, alleging for his excuse that he had received formal orders from the master not to reveal anything. And when the curious woman persisted a little too much, the man took flight, like a pursued thief, clutching to his abdomen the invisible package that he was transporting, and, outdistancing the bewildered gazes of the multitude, he disappeared around the corner of an avenue.

It did not require any more to create an indescribable nervous excitement among the avid individuals who were awaiting the return of the enquirer. The event soon made a tour of the palaces, and all those who heard it did not fail to comment on it in pointed and disobliging terms. That bitterness and resentment increased in direct proportion to the ever greater number of visitors. And Blasius' neighbors did not fail to emphasize, in addition, that only the artists and scientists most distant from the cell were summoned to meet him, while all those of the great square remained systematically excluded.

Before that inequality of treatment and that unfathomable mystery, the curiosity soon became jealousy. In the warmth of cubicles; in the freshness of bathrooms; in the shadow of porticos where essence of roses flowed into marble basins, and a mixture derived from the juice of lilies and violets was crushed without respite in silver mortars; behind the heavy curtains of workshops and studios; in the propitious shelter of larders and kitchens, an entire quarter was now inveighing, calculating, vaticinating and vilifying. Women needled the men hypocritically with their bilious insinuations, and the most audacious talked about stopping the favored few as they emerged from the magisterial dwelling and stealing from them whatever they were hiding with so much care.

No one dared risk such ill-treatment, however, and it all remained talk.

One day, a white-bearded scientist insisted more than was reasonable in demanding of a poet overflowing with youth and beauty to know the motive for his visit to the master's house, but the poet, rendered impatient by the old man's aggressive tone, responded without reverence, and his imprudent words unleashed such a tumult at the corner of the principal street that Blasius suddenly erupted on to his terrace. He had the argument and the dispute explained to him; but as the actors excused themselves in confused voices for having allowed themselves to be carried away in that fashion, he started to laugh, and sent them away without condemning the incident.

All those who saw that raised their heads again after his departure, and some of them, the first to have praised initially the restraint and monastic austerity of the master of the City, spread the rumor through the streets and crossroads that the virtuous man certainly disdained women, and summoned ephebes of quality and the most passionate esthetes of the city to his abode, in order to satisfy his base instincts.

Those slanders soon reached Blasius' ears. Far from getting irritated, he smiled even more mildly than on the day of the dispute, and continued to receive, to the increasingly viperish irritation of the neglected, visitors who were invariably provided with an invisible burden at the moment of their emerged from his abode.

A little later, however, Blasius had it announced by the public address systems and loudhailers that he was instituting a hymn competition between the poets, the winner of which would receive a royal recompense. That news stirred up such emotion that for weeks, from dawn to dusk, nothing was seen but groups whispering on doorsteps, gesticulating on the lapis and jasper benches of bright gardens, and manifesting in tortuous phrases their disapproval of such a measure. That disapproval emanated above all from painters, musicians, scientists and philosophers, who could not participate in that joust and could not explain the reasons for an ostracism prejudicial to their interests.

However, the poets rejoiced, and each of them strove to create works of a lyricism that would surpass those of their rivals.

When the day of the competition arrived, and the poets, accompanied by clarinets, muted flutes and stringed instruments with heart-ending vibrations, had come one after another to recite their splendid rhythms before a quivering public, whose unanimous acclamations had designated the winner, Blasius appeared.

With words as stinging as whiplashes, he declared that the man who had united all the suffrages did not merit being the elect; and, with a provocative hand, he handed the purse containing the inestimable prize to the competitor who had, in the general opinion, given the most complete impression of mediocrity and platitude.

At that vision, a clamor of reprobation rose up from the steps toward his emaciated and balding figure. No one in the audience could conceive of such an injustice, and the dispossessed poet disappeared during that protest, sobbing with indignation and anger.

But Blasius remained impassive on his cathedra, his arms folded. Everyone could understand perfectly well that he held their miserable destinies in his hands, and they went home in silence, hearts constricted by such an anguish that they almost lost the faculty of respiration.

The day after that scandalous scene, Blasius summoned to his cell the man who, in the opinion of everyone, seemed worthy of the recompense. The poet approached him, his features ravaged and his eyes swollen, for having wept all night, and waited.

Looking at him with eyes as piercing as lightning, Blasius spoke.

"I know," he said, "that you are the most perfect and the greatest of all the sculptors of rhymes, and no one professes more admiration than me for the incomparable hymn that you sang in the arena yesterday. But I also know that you are fiercely proud, and that you put nothing above independence and liberty, and it is for that reason that I gave the prize to the man who merited it least of all. That one, I know to be submissive to my will, and I would only have to make a sign for him immediately to praise the most abject people and things in terms more enthusiastic than sublime, for him to burn what he had adored until that moment, and for him to have no other will, no other dignity and no other dream than whatever I pleased to leave to him. Would you, whose pride is well-known, lend yourself to such an abdication if I ordered it? Would you consent to celebrate what you scorn, or put your genius at the service of my arbitrary whim and my arrogance?"

At those words, the poet raised his head; and, looking his interlocutor full in the face, he replied: "No."

"I foresaw that response," said Blasius. "Now you know the reasons for my conduct and you understand why I refused you the laurel. For reasons that I do not care to explain at the moment, I have resolved to metamorphose the soul of the city and break all those who resist me. That is why I demand of you, in spite of your negation and your resistance, that you magnify shame, slavery, degradation and abasement with the same flame that you put into glorifying liberty yesterday."

"Don't count on me," replied the poet. "I'd rather die."

"Remember," Blasius insinuated, with a frightful smile, "that the abdication in question would be worth insensate honors and riches to you. If you wanted to obey me I would let you choose in my subterrains the most precious ingots and the most resplendent gems."

"Above basely acquired treasures," cried the poet, "I put human dignity; and if it pleases you to kill it in others, you shall not murder it in me."

"That's good," said Blasius, in a dull voice. "From this moment on, you no longer belong to the city. You will leave here tomorrow, staff in hand and a beggar's wallet over our shoulder, dressed in rags like a vagabond. You will quit your dwelling under the jeers of your companions and the serfs, and you will resume, in the sordid quarters of capitals, your existence of famine and struggle."

"I will go!" declared the poet, in a vibrant voice.

"I will, however, make the remark to you that if you change our mind at the last moment, and wish to accord me what I demand, and which appears to you to be impossible today, you will only have to retrace your steps, throw away your staff and your wallet, and return to the shelter where you have savored unhoped-for joys for years."

And with an index finger as twisted as the branch of an arbutus, Blasius dismissed the poet.

The next day, a turbulent and compact crowd had gathered along the avenues, on the sidewalks and in the crowns of the trees shading crossroads and squares, to see the departure of the man who preferred exile and misery to degradation and dishonor.

He appeared, as Blasius had ordered, in rags and bareheaded; and when he appeared, an unspeakable sadness gripped the hearts of the watchers. And all of them, far from jeering him, took their hats off to him.

But while they bared their heads as he passed, as if at the passage of a martyr, they remarked with surprise that the poet lowered his head shamefully instead of manifesting, in accordance with his promise of the day before, an immense pride in his action. Young and resplendent with strength, he gave the impression of an old man suddenly broken in two, and in order to advance over the marble and gold paving slabs, he had to lean on his knotty staff, which now constituted his sole wealth, along with his beggar's wallet. And when he arrived at the gates of the city, he turned round.

He embraced with his gaze all that elegance, all that glory and all that opulence, in which he had lived for so long, and where he was leaving thousands of brains that would lose the memory of him in a matter of days. He saw, on the resplendent blue of a terrace, a woman who was carrying a newborn child in her arms, and who was considering him at length and profoundly, as if she wanted to engrave his features and his attitudes within her memory forever; and that woman was weeping large silent tears. He evoked the luxury of his palace, the softness of the carpet into which his crimson sandals sank, and the ivory table where, with a golden pen, he sculpted incomparable poetry and prose. And before him, he saw space, the unknown, struggle and hunger...

Blasius, who was standing next to the great golden gate with his arms folded, scrutinized him.

And suddenly, the heart of the insurgent broke. All his arrogance, all his dignity, all the pride of which he had made such a parade the day before, vanished like smoke in the evening. With an effort, he threw away his knotty staff, his beggar's wallet and his tattered mantle. He fell to his knees before Blasius, and, his head in his hands, as if crushed by the weight of his denial, he murmured:

"I'll stay."

Then a smile of triumph illuminated Blasius' face. And, leaning toward the taciturn man who accompanied him, he said to him: "My vengeance will surpass my hope."

The day after that symptomatic abdication, it seemed that a wind of abjection suddenly blew over the city. A thirst for lucre and servility took possession of the inhabitants, and without interruption, the serfs introduced solicitors to Blasius' presence avid to anticipate his will and to provoke proofs. He greeted them all with a glacial arrogance, and when he had heard them out he ordered each of them to execute what appeared to him to be the most painful and the most degrading task. And consciences did not revolt; all of them carried away the gold ingots that formed the price of their palinode and their cowardice, rejoicing in acceding to a fortune without having to sacrifice anything but the nobility of their souls.

And when jealousy, slander and calumny had corrupted the entire City, Blasius stirred up tragic rivalries between the scientists, the artists and the thinkers. That jealousy, which had no other motive to begin with than considerations of a general order, became a paltry, personal and professional jealousy. The writers who had thus far recognized honestly the value of their companions, began to denigrate one another. Sculptors and painters reproached one another mutually for their technical ignorance and their lack of inspiration; and those reproaches, which would have made the least of them smile in ordinary times, became, because of the bad faith of the provocateurs, subjects of ferocious quarrels.

Even the scientists accused one another reciprocally of plagiarism or the theft of formulae; they were seen on the perfumed terraces threatening one another with retorts or test tubes, and would have come to blows if the serfs had not interposed themselves in order to separate them.

And it became worse still in regard to the women. All the lovers and all the wives, whose breadth of mind and elevation of character had won the admiration of their elect, descended to the vainest and most stupid gossip, the most dangerous slanders and the most implausible anecdotes. Like the housewives of sub-prefectures, they devoted themselves to the criticism of garments and hairstyles, worried about the comings and goings of their friends and neighbors, and lay in wait, hidden behind heavy curtains for passers-by and strollers of either sex.

Under imbecilic or mediocre pretexts, brothers quarreled inexorably after painful disputes in which they displayed their irritations, their pettiness and the vices before the indifferent or the hostile.

Soon there were bloody brawls in the streets, and Blasius had to organize patrols of serfs, with the mission to reestablish order and to punish delinquents mercilessly. Then, seeing that it was becoming impossible for them to settle their quarrels publicly, enemies and rivals set ambushes for one another, and drew one another into traps. One evening, at the corner of the most beautiful avenue and the most spacious, the serfs charged with security discovered the cadavers of two of the most famous artists bathed in their blood with multiple stab-wounds.

When Blasius as informed of that first murder, his eyes were flamboyant with a demonic gleam, and instead of searching for the guilty parties or punishing them, he said: "It is thus because it must be thus."

Gradually, the City of perfection and beauty descended to the rank of the most disqualified cities of the continents. Unconsciously despoiling their culture, dominated by imperious atavisms, the inhabitants sensed hermetic partitions rising between them. As everywhere, there were depths and dens of vice where unspeakable orgies unfurled. And because those dens conserved their magnificence and noble lines, in spite of the decadence of those who haunted them, those orgies appeared in the light of those enclosures more repulsive and more crapulent.

Women who had been held up as exemplars and who had descended without being aware of it to the most depraved and most venal of whores, gathered in houses that became brothels, and welcomed in preference to others the serfs and the rabble. Scientists renowned for their disinterest, their intransigence and their probity suddenly became cut-throats, pimps and thieves.

And as the putrefaction of all those souls accelerated, Blasius rejoiced, and searched for means of increasing to the utmost limits the debasement of the thousands of decadent individuals who surrounded him.

One morning, when the clouds covered like blue wings the cell in which he lived, grim and peevish, he decided to send emissaries to the world charged with unleashing revolutions and wars, disaggregating hearths and carrying abomination and ruin from North to South in every country. When those emissaries learned what the Master expected of them, they all recoiled before the enormity of the task and refused that excessively infamous task in spite of threats and punishments.

Then Blasius recalled that in a famous capital an old man existed renowned for his intelligence and his ferocity, and he resolved to obtain his collaboration, no matter what the cost. He summoned him by airplane, promising him, if he accepted, the most fabulous prebends. The old man's name was Rudolph.

The messenger was away for a week, and when he came back, instead of exhaling in truculent terms his pride in having concluded his mission successfully, the taciturn man inclined, mute, before Blasius, and seemed to be begging him to pardon his defeat.

When Blasius interrogated the taciturn man, who was paralyzed by emotion, regret and fear, he was only able to articulate one sentence: "The old man threw me out."

Then a fearful anger overwhelmed Blasius. One after another he summoned the taciturn men, stuck them to the seats of airplanes, and designated the Occident. And all of them, after the long voyage, returned contrite and heartbroken, and all of them repeated to Blasius what their companions had said.

Only the last one, who was more persuasive than the others, succeeded in vanquishing the old man's resistance. He painted him such a picture of the City, its beauties and its delights, that the other sensed his resistance weakening, because he carried within him, as well as cruelty, an invincible liking for the strange, the paradoxical and the marvelous.

"Go back," he said to the taciturn man," and announce my arrival to your master."

And, eager to see the man who held the fate of the world in his omnipotent hands, Rudolph embarked on a ship. A few days later, he landed. Two taciturn men were waiting for him when he disembarked. They took him to the Corrupter, and Blasius received Rudolph in his small bare room.

When they were face to face, the two men looked at one another for a long time.

Large white bushy eyebrows shaded Rudolph's eyes. Those eyebrows further emphasized the expression of intelligence and malevolence in his hooded eyes, giving him a false resemblance to a Mongol or a Manchurian. A round hat, tilted over the right ear, coiffed Rudolph, and as the hat was rather narrow for his vast head, it made him look more like a clown than a Statesman. A pot belly, as round as a geographical globe, surmounted the arched colonnettes of his legs, and when he advanced, his hands in his trouser pockets, his nose in the air, one expected to see him skip, and remained surprised that the illustrious man walked in a posed and regular fashion, like a vulgar taxpayer.

Finding that Blasius was keeping silent for too long, Rudolph spoke.

"You summoned me," he said to him. "Here I am."

But the Corrupter did not reply. He was thinking.

He was thinking that he had before him one of those who had the fate of millions of vigorous men in his vacillating hands. He was thinking that this homunculus knew an incomparable glory, and that only a famous assassin, a pugilist successively acclaimed by kings, ministers and billionaires, and a cinema clown celebrated for his semi-moustache and his oversized shoes enjoyed a renown equal to his in the two continents.

He remembered the history of that adventurous life, all the hypocrisy and the compromises, and remained stupefied that a creature so insignificant in appearance had been able to cause so much damage to his fellows.

He knew that Rudolph, endowed with a bitter eloquence and a verve that rendered him redoubtable to his adversaries, had spent his life smearing, soiling and demolishing what his fellows had striven painfully to edify, that his work was purely evil, that its brought nothing to the common edifice and would leave nothing behind but the memory of a octogenarian so transported by his rancor that he had often, without perceiving it, been the accomplice of his country's enemies.

He rejoiced in having been able to recruit him, to bring such an acolyte to his terrible and magnificent project; and his eyes shone with a joy so horrible that Rudolph, gripped by fear, recoiled. But with an irresistible sign, Blasius made him take his place again facing his chair; and the homunculus obeyed.

When he had come back to stand before him, as when he had entered the room, the Corrupter spoke to him.

"Here it is. I summoned you in order for you to become my liege-man in an adventure so colossal that it will secure us not only an imperishable glory but also, and above all, universal malediction.

"I won't say no to that," said the homunculus, smiling, tipping his bowler hat a little more toward the left ear with a flick of a finger. "I love a battle more than anything else, especially when it's a matter of nothing more than pitting adversaries against one another, and I esteem maledictions and insults more than a royal crown."

"I affirm," Blasius continued, "that the result will surpass all imagination."

"Nothing would please me more," riposted the octogenarian, sketching a slight pirouette. "Of what does it consist?"

The Corrupter lowered his voice.

"It consists of debasing peoples and races as I have debased the inhabitants of my City, of disorganizing them, of setting them against one another in bloodthirsty hordes, and arriving at such rivalries, such conflicts and such massacres that the world will be awash with blood for months, that no hearth will be exempt from dolor and despair, and that the flower of youth, in all the inhabited continents, will disappear n the midst of frightful ordeals. Do you have sufficient cruelty, the necessary insensibility and the abjection indispensable to that diabolical labor? If my proposition makes you pale, return immediately to the ship that brought you all the way to these walls, and return in haste to your homeland without looking back. But if you truly feel sufficiently formidable to second me, if nothing moves you to pity, choose the noblest and most sumptuous among all these dream palaces. Tell me how many serfs, courtesans and ephebes you desire. Fix yourself the sum that my treasurer will pay you every month, and when that is settled, set to work right away."

A frisson of pride shook Rudolph. He raised himself up on tiptoe and grew by mean of the subterfuge by six millimeters or so. He replied to the Corrupter, addressing in familiarly in his turn

"It seems to me, in fact, that we ought to understand one another. Not only do I promise to carry out your instructions to the letter, but while you were talking, I sensed grandiose ideas rising within me like a vertiginous tide. I can imagine projects such that, if you allow me to realize them, your sadism will become puerile by comparison, and not one city, not one throne, not one State will escape being dragged into the cataclysm of which I am nourishing the design. With regard to your palace and your subsidies, they don't tempt me, and you'll permit me to decline your princely offer. No recompense could equal the joy that I shall experience in doing evil."

The physiognomy of the Corrupter brightened at that response. With a convulsive gesture he drew the stupefied homunculus to his heart, and embraced him tenderly, as a younger brother embraces an ender brother vanished many years before on his return to the natal abode.

When they had hugged one another frenetically, Rudolph installed himself on a stool, facing Blasius, and asked him, in a jovial tone: "May I know the motive that drives you to accomplish such exploits?"

"Yes," replied Blasius. "Because I have been accursed since birth, because I have been subjected to all insults, all dolors, all ordeals, and because one day, hazard put me in possession of a prodigious secret, I resolved to avenge myself on the entire world for the ill-treatment inflicted on me by some. For years I have been preparing that vengeance; and now that I am ready, I intend to savor all its sensual pleasure, thanks to your aid, before dying."

"But since you have under your hand," Rudolph objected, "thousands of citizens on whom you can experiment at leisure, why the devil do you want to seek other subjects outside your domain? Does the assassination of this magnificent City not seem sufficient to you?"

"My dolor and my gehenna have surpassed the frame of human dolors. I deem it necessary that humankind entire endure the same evil as my City. And, I repeat, I am counting on you to accomplish that epic labor."

"It's going to be fun," remarked the homunculus, in a profound voice.

And the very next day, without losing a minute, he buckled down to his diabolical work.

VII

Thanks to his perfect knowledge of men and his innumerable connections in all milieux, Rudolph had soon unleashed the first disasters.

Every morning, when he got up, special couriers arrived from the four corners of the world and informed him of the results that had been obtained. As soon as he was in possession of certainties, he ran to Blasius' palace, penetrated without being announced into the cell that always remained open to him, and brought him up to date with events.

"Yesterday," he said to him by way of preamble, "our emissaries were able to persuade the entire mining population of the great centers of coal production to stop work. In conformity with their indications, collisions were produced between soldiers and the people. There is talk of hundreds dead and thousands wounded. In addition, for it is necessary that the vengeance attains the two enemy castes equally, the strikers have flooded the mines, extinguished the blast furnaces and set fire to the palaces of the kings of steel, coal and minerals, whom they accuse of exploiting them. It is unemployment and poverty for the workers, but it is also ruination for all the great industrialists."

"And?" interrogated the Corrupter, avidly.

"And," Rudolph continued, "we have unleashed a war between the Orient and the Occident: questions of oil, armaments and railways. At the present moment, ten million men are preparing to confront one another, and I can affirm that all the wars in history will seem to have been child's play by comparison with this one, which will depopulate but the victors and the vanquished. I won't mention the bombardments that will pulverize innocent populations, the plague, and all the other evils called to crown the enterprise splendidly."

"And?" repeated Blasius, his elbows on the arms of his cathedra and his palms beneath his chin.

"And we have fraudulent bankruptcies, murders, adulteries and thefts without number. My orders are being carried out in such a way that within two months, I swear on all I hold most dear in the world, there will not be a single country, a single hearth or a single human being who will not be bowled over, destroyed or corrupted by my efforts.

"Truly," exclaimed Blasius, seized by a delirium of dementia, "you've kept your word. I don't know how to recompense you for your ferocity."

"Oh," riposted Rudolph, modestly, "It's not worth the trouble of mentioning it. In any case, I told you that it would be fun." And to underline that funereal pleasantry, the homunculus gave the Corrupter an affectionate tap on the fleshless shoulder."

Often, when they were together, in recompense for their magnificent labor, they set forth, chatting about the noblest subjects, through the orange and lemon groves that ringed the city like clusters of emeralds mounted in heavy golden necklaces. They loved to wander in the lost pathways; and Rudolph, whose sapience seemed to be unlimited, revealed philosophers to him, cited poets and annotated historians, while springs murmured around them and the dazzling roofs of the City dispersed the fireworks of their multicolored radiance in the blonde morning light.

Sometimes, as they walked toward the gates that opened to the countryside, they crossed the paths of men and women who had once had noble souls within them, but who only possessed at present reptilian souls; and those men and women bowed down before them, almost touching the ground. Rudolph, who always kept a supply of gold nuggets and fragments of precious stone in his jacket pocket, amused himself by throwing them handfuls. All those debased individuals hurled themselves against one another, insulting one another, clawing one another and striking one another, until the most audacious or the most rapacious had taken possession of the gold or precious stones and fled at top speed in the direction of their homes, unless the serfs changed with breaking up mobs dispersed them by striking their arms with flexible rods made from the dorsal spines of sharks.

Before those spectacles, Blasius and the homunculus expanded in sonorous laughter, and when they sat down in the shade of pomegranate trees or myrtles, the odors of which filled their nostrils and lungs, they evoked the macabre melee, and recounted, in order to increase their hilarity further, the most sinister and the most repulsive stories.

One morning, when they had just learned via special telephones of a conflagration in a city of which nothing remained but ashes, no inhabitant of which had survived, the Corrupter and his henchman were walking along a path. The whispering grass came up to their knees; they plunged into that freshness as if into a fount of youth, and after having walked for more than an hour they arrived in a clearing carpeted with moss and sage. Heavy acacias deployed their white clusters above them, and bitter scents fell from every tree that they were not accustomed to respiring in the course of their habitual strolls.

In the distance, at the back of that alluring and tempting clearing, leaning against a centenarian baobab like a newborn against the breast of his nurse, a little cabin was hidden under the somber foliage; and, issuing from a hole pierced in the roof, smoke was bounding toward the sky in bright gray spirals. The two wanderers stopped, amazed by that discovery and fascinated by that evidence of existences they did not suspect, about which they knew nothing.

And Rudolph said to Blasius: "It's necessary to know!"

Their footfalls muffled by the moss and the sage, the emanations of which swirled around them, they advanced. As they arrived at the threshold of the cabin, they found themselves face to face with a woman, who stared at them fearlessly.

She was coiffed in a blue headscarf garnished with coins that rang like little bells as she moved. Locks of hair, dark blue in color, emerged from that blue headscarf, which seemed to prolong the coiffure. The nape of her neck and her cleavage, as brown as the sorbs of the forest, sprang from a garish green silk scarf, holed in places and ragged at the edges. She was resting her arms, as supple as rustic branches, on her slim hips, and her bare feet were digging into the black soil on the threshold. Under the resplendence of the sunlight, which licked her in slow floods through the foliage, she gave the impression of a living bronze statue.

Seeing that the two of them remained immobile, she asked them, in an irritated voice: "What do you want with me?"

Surprised by that irritation, Blasius replied, arrogantly: "We're the masters of the island, and it's for us, not for you, to ask why you're hidden here."

Then the woman in the headscarf started laughing. Twisting her upper body, closing her fists on her hips, she looked him up and down. Then, slowly, she riposted: "Yes, I know. Although I don't know the runt who's with you, I'm not unaware, on the other hand, of all your ignominies. I saw you arrive on this island a long time ago with your gang of pirates. At that time I was scarcely as tall as that sprig of mint, and when I saw your accursed horde for the first time I took refuge, shivering with repulsion, in my mother's arms. But with all the other women and all the men of the tribe, my mother allowed herself to be won over by the gold you spread with full hands, and she departed for the unknown with her companions in the boats with the sharp prows. But I wanted to stay on my island, and I succeeded in escaping in the company of a small boy of my own age, who already loved me and had promised to defend me. The others left us. And while you were building your damned city, we lived in the woods of oranges, lemons and wild fruits. We had grown up together without your people ever discovering us. Amour came into our hearts, and now I belong to him, and all your riches can't compare with the happiness that a single one of his embraces gives me."

While she articulated those words, her eyes flashed, and Blasius, amazed by such audacity, remained silent.

"Go away," the woman went on. "Because we disdained your gold, this clearing, which belonged to us before you came, still belongs to us. Only we can live here, sleep here and die here, and I forbid you access to it from now on. And I'll add that if you value your life and that of the moribund with you, avoid finding yourself in these parts when my lover comes back from the forest, because he hates you as much as I do, and if he sees you, it will be all over for the two of you."

And turning on her heels, she went back into the cabin, singing a joyful refrain loudly.

Blasius and Rudolph, more profoundly impressed by that defiance and those threats than they would have liked to appear, retraced their steps. While darting searching glances around them, all the way to the gates of the City, they went back to their dwellings. Neither of them breathed a word during the journey. Blasius seemed to be plunged in profound meditations, and the homunculus was whistling, as if to give an appearance of carelessness, a fashionable tune as stupid as the man who had composed it and those who had rendered it popular.

On the parvis of the palace, as he separated from the Corrupter, he spoke. "That," he said, "is a happy and rebellious couple. It's appropriate that they don't escape the common rule and they incline before our power, under penalty of worse torments."

But Blasius was not listening to him. Instead of responding to his bilious invective, he murmured: "That woman is beautiful."

"No," protested Rudolph, who had heard. "On the contrary, that woman is ugly. Her hips are thin, her breasts as pointed as little pink figs, her eyes so large that their clarity seems to absorb her whole face, and her skin, as dark as Cordovan leather, exhales an odor of damp earth. In truth, I don't know what beauty you can find in such disharmony."

But Blasius repeated, in a peremptory fashion: "That woman is beautiful." And without giving his acolyte the customary accolade, he disappeared through the coral penumbra of the corridors.

The next day, at dawn, he set forth again for the forest. This time, he was alone. All night long he had seen before his eyes, like an apparition, the woman in the green silk scarf, and he had sensed a bewildered desire to see her again welling up within him.

A power from which he could not escape forbade him any other thought, and while he was striding along the paths he was breathless, as if he were exhausted.

When he reached the cabin he put his hands to his breast in order to try to calm the disordered beating of his heart. Then he let himself fall back against the trunk of a beech tree that must have served the inhabitants of the wood as a seat, and without foreseeing anything, without understanding anything, of his solitary journey, he waited.

After a few moments, the woman came out of the cabin, carrying a pitcher.

She headed in the direction where Blasius was, and the latter, on perceiving her, put his hands together; and he remained there, in that ecstatic posture, until the woman had filled her pitcher from a spring that rippled through reeds at the foot of a bitter osier, turned back to her retreat and found him in front of her.

Hr beautiful nocturnal eyebrows frowned, and. marching toward Blasius, she said to him angrily: "I forbade you to profane this refuge. Why, then, have you come back?"

And Blasius replied, very simply and very humbly: "I came back because I love you."

At those words, the woman placed her pitcher on the ground. She burst into prolonged laughter, as musical as the cooing of a dove and more mocking than the divagation of a curlew on the edge of a pool. Then, picking up her pitcher, she poured its contents into an earthenware bowl, seized the bowl in both hands and, presenting it to Blasius' stupefied eyes, forced him to look into that improvised mirror.

At the same time she heaped him with sarcasms. "You love me?" she mocked. "But consider your wrinkled temples, let your gaze linger upon your thin face, your white hair, your fleshless skeletal body, your hideous hands, your fingernails bitten to the quick, and tell me whether you can inspire anything but laughter or pity?"

Blasius repeated, like a plaint: "I came because I love you."

The woman stopped laughing at those words.

"There's room in your heart, then, for a sentiment other than ferocity? You'll suddenly forget all your misdeeds and crimes? You want to redeem yourself in the fire of my large eyes? You think, then, that it's possible for someone to love you?"

For the third time, Blasius repeated: "I came because I love you." And he added: "It's true. My crimes are more numerous than the pebbles of the sea. I've committed all sins; I've swallowed all shame; I've sown malediction and opprobrium around me. But I did that because my life has been nothing but a lamentable Calvary, because everyone hated me, tortured me and martyrized me. But now that I've seen you, it seems to me that a dawn has just risen within me. I disdained women; and I remain dazzled by bearing you in my desires and in my dreams. What is your name?"

"Helia," the woman replied.

"Helia, repeated Blasius. "That name is both as soft as a fruits and as limped as a ray of twilight." He fell silent, but, having contemplated her for a few seconds, he went on: "Helia, I am the master of fortune and life; and I ask you at what price you want to belong to me."

On hearing that proposition, the woman went pale. "Belong to you? Deliver my youth and my liberty to you, when I vibrate under the caresses of a lover more handsome than the day and more regal than light? You don't know what possession is, then. You don't know what delight is, to speak thus?"

"No," Blasius confessed.

"Then what's the point of replying to you, since you haven't sensed life escaping you at the contact of a beloved mouth, since your entire body hasn't stiffened with desire at the approach of your elect, since you don't know that love is more powerful and greater than death itself? And you come to propose a shameful bargain to me because, out there, in your City, everyone kneels before you? Know that I'll never belong to you, in spite of your treasures, in spite of your power, and that I'll never belong to anyone except my lover, who is a poor, famished outcast, like me..."

Then two large tears pearled in Blasius' eyelids, trickled slowly down his cheeks and caught on the asperities of his beard. But that dolor did not move Helia at all. In a hissing voice, she went on:

"Truly, there's something disconcerting in your conduct. You are the man who can do anything, you affirm. The power of your gold causes everything that breathes and everything that thinks to bow down before you. You have only to choose among the most beautiful women of the City, and they would come running at a gesture from you, trembling with pride at seeing themselves distinguished in the midst of the others. And it's to me, who possesses neither beauty, nor intelligence, nor elegance, that you bring your demented covetousness...?"

"Shut up!" said Blasius, interrupting. "Your eyes have more brightness than the headlights of the great monsters that travel the routes with long formidable rumbles and pierce the thickest obscurity. The sway of your hips is so soft that one would like to incline one's head over your loins in order to be rocked there incessantly like a sick child; and in the marvelous nest of your thighs I would like to bury my face in order to hide from everyone until death my fear of the execrable passion that is roaring within me like a torrent. Know, you who dominate my poor grieving weakness, that there is no woman in the world more perfect and more enviable than you."

"I'm glad of that praise," replied Helia. "Glad because it gives me the exact measure of your passion, because it reveals to me all that you're suffering, because it prophesies to me all that you're going to suffer, and above all because I can repeat it in a little while to my lover. And I know that his joy will be tenfold, and the nape of my neck will tip back under the bite of his teeth, and my shoulders will be marbled by his slow perverse suctions, and my body will open up beneath him while he penetrates me completely with dominating words."

"Shut up!" begged Blasius, again. "While you talk, I experience a torture as frightful as if my flesh were being torn by red hot pincers, and I can't bear your words any longer. If you refuse again, my serfs will come to snatch you from your solitude, from your happiness. They'll take you into my blackest subterrain, and you'll stay there, without seeing anything and without hearing anything until the moment when your inanimate corpse falls on the porphyry paving stones."

"I'm not afraid of you!" Helia declared. "In order for your serfs to reach me, they will have to pass over the body of my protector, and he is strong enough and brave enough to hold at bay for months the eunuchs and degenerates that populate your putrid City."

Blasius, having heard those words, returned to his cell, head bowed. But every day, he reappeared in the clearing, and every day, Helia's sarcasms and insults became more violent and more provocative. Always, she gave him evidence of more aversion and repulsion, and always, she put more morbid coquetry into showing herself to him with new charms. Once, she crowned herself with leaves and flowers, and she seemed under that adornment as odorous as a woodland nymph awaited the brutal embrace of a goat-foot. Another time, she abandoned her green silk scarf and naked to the waist, simply enveloped in a leather loincloth, she presented the pure curve of her breasts to Blasius' impotent desire. At other times she lay down on the moss, pretending finally to soften and yield, but when Blasius approached his ardent hands, she fled with a bound and spat in his face.

One morning, she presented herself to him completely naked, without a scrap of cloth to hide the swelling of her snowy belly and the pink slenderness of her limbs. She offered herself, like a great fruit burnished by the light and velveted by the violet air, her arms wide, her lips parted, laughing with all her teeth and all her young strength. Blasius, seized by folly this time, tried to throw himself upon her...but at the contact of his fleshless fingers Helia uttered a long, savage cry, and with her sharp fingernails she scratched his face and forehead.

Blood ran from his wounds; he persisted in trying to possess her, and each of his efforts multiplied the woman's rage tenfold. Vanquished by that indomitable energy, by the ever-increasing pain occasioned by his wounds, Blasius collapsed on the beaten earth of the threshold, while the victorious woman shut the little door of her cabin with hysterical clamors.

And Blasius' Calvary became more and more atrocious.

He no longer slept. He spent his nights lying on the black bearskin, writhing with concupiscence, imploring the woman with words alternately chaste and hideous, who refused him disdainfully and, with a gesture, could have made him commit the vilest or the most generous actions.

He had frightful moments, and for him, whose entire life had passed in ignorance of women and scorn for lust, those moments of physical overexcitement constituted an inconceivable torture.

The taciturn men, whom he loved to the exception of all others, and for whom he testified a paternal affection, no longer dared speak to him. Saddened and stupefied by his enigmatic attitude and his unaccustomed rudeness, they avoided him at the corners of galleries and in the vestibules.

Even Rudolph was fearful of penetrating his lair, and, one day when he risked lifting, with a thousand precautions, the red curtain with broad black stripes that served as a door to his cell, he perceived Blasius lying face down on the bearskin, holding his head convulsively between his clenched hands, stammering inconsequential words. Frightened by that vision, he departed on tiptoe, and, having returned to his room, he spent all morning reflecting on the omnipotence of the passion that put a prodigious individual like the Corrupter at the mercy of a girl of the woods, devoid of charm and intelligence.

However, just as he was leaving the dining room to return to the studio in the gloom of which he spent the greater part of his nights framing his schemes and his Machiavellian plans, a taciturn man came to tell him that Blasius wanted to see him.

When he found himself before him, and he saw his hollow features, his eyelids swollen by tears and his mouth twisted by groans of despair, Rudolph felt a twinge of pity for the first time in his life.

Blasius, who had understood that movement, made him a sign to sit down next to him in an armchair with twisted arms in the form of serpents, and in a voice punctuated by plaints he confessed all the phases of his lamentable Calvary.

The homunculus listened in silence. When he had finished his story, the Corrupter looked at him.

"Now that you know," he implored, "advise me. You, who have put the world to fire and blood, whose power of corruption surpasses mine, enlighten my poor reason, which I can feel sinking with every second. Find a means to break the revolt of that woman and bring her to this palace. I will follow your advice blindly, but I sense clearly that if she persists in her refusal, in standing up to me and toying with my pusillanimous soul, I shall die of chagrin like the least of the serfs of my city."

At that heart-rending appeal, Rudolph reflected for a few minutes.

"Evidently," he replied to the Corrupter, "the problem isn't easy to resolve. However, I think I can glimpse a possible solution. And after all, it will cost nothing to try it..."

"You going to save me, aren't you?" moaned the Corrupter.

"I'll do my best, at least," Rudolph promised, "But I warn you, honestly, that I can't guarantee success. In any case, this is how I see the matter..."

There was a pause; then the homunculus went on: "This woman with whom you're infatuated, with a puerile imprudence, has a lover she adores?"

"Yes."

"That's where the obstacle lies. Before anything else, we must take care to get rid of him."

"You want me to order his death?" asked the Corrupter.

"Refrain from that carefully. Nothing would compromise your cause so irremediably. There are a thousand ways of reducing the most stubborn energies, and the example of this City, which you have murdered slowly and guided to an incomparable degree of putrescence, proves that you dispose of arguments more persuasive and less murderous. In your place, I'd disappear from the clearing..."

"Not see her again!"

"If you don't feel capable of obeying me and persist in your deplorable childishness, I shall declare frankly that you can no longer count on me."

On hearing those rude words, Blasius put his hands together and replied, very softly: "I'll do whatever you wish."

"I would disappear from the clearing," Rudolph continued, "in order that peace and serenity can flourish again in the woman's soul. In the meantime, I shall try to get to know the master of her flesh and her thought, to gain his confidence, to draw him here gradually, and reveal marvels and comforts to him that the rusticity of his cabin can only give him, I'm convinced, very vague image."

"Yes, that's it! I'll go to see him; I'll talk to him!"

"Would you like us to go together," proposed the homunculus, "to the forest where he accomplishes his daily labor? The sky is pure; soothing aromas are fluttering in the air, and a walk can't fail to lessen your dolor?"

The two men seized their gold-pummeled canes and went out by the gate opening on to the path to the woods. They took a direction opposite to that of the clearing, and the Corrupter turned his head at every step toward the place where the woman dwelt who abolished everything else in his gaze. A severe admonition from Rudolph, however soon brought him back to the true path.

After an hour's march, the forest loomed up before them.

It was the end of autumn, and all the leaves were reddening like blood in the bright sunlight. They were trembling around the branches like old women already decrepit and marked by the inexorable finger of time. Often, several of them were detached from the natal branch, and after swirling for a few seconds, fell with a tiny sound on the ground covered with moss and twigs. Some trees were already denuded, and on those no birds perched any longer. An ineffable peace rose from the horizon, and nothing could be heard, from the place where Blasius and the homunculus had just stopped, except the ax of a distant woodcutter mutilating the forest with regular blows.

On perceiving those impacts, muffled by distance, Rudolph raised his hand.

"That's where it's necessary to go," he advised. "The unknown woodcutter can only be the man by virtue of whom you're suffering."

They resumed their march, breaking branches and bushes, and the blows of the ax became increasingly distinct.

At the corner of a goat-path that faded away between two rows of sycamores, they perceived the solitary individual. Bent double, at odds with a maple, the base of which was split by a huge wound, he lifted the ax above his head, paused momentarily, and brought its shining blade down against the maple, grunting. The cutting edge of the steel whistled and bit into the wood; and chips steeped in white sap flew around his head.

Entirely devoted to his labor, he did not hear the two men approaching, and it was necessary, in order to reveal their presence to him, for Rudolph to touch him on the shoulder with his finger at the precise moment when he raised his powerful weapon above him.

He interrupted himself suddenly, let the ax fall, and leaning on the handle polished by the friction and sweat of his rough hands, he considered the intruders.

Before the debility of Blasius and the antiquity of the homunculus, he felt the mistrust that had initially made him stiffen himself easing. He did not know either one of the newcomers, but he was sure of having nothing to fear, and, with a smile uncovering his white teeth of young faun, he saluted them.

At that mark of deference, Blasius did not budge. As for Rudolph, he seized the brim of his round hat between his thumb and his index finger, swiveled it twice like a teetotum on its double pivot, and replaced it briskly, jamming the concave felt against his cranium. Proud of the bell-like sound that he had just imitated, he launched into conversation. The woodcutter replied to him with a naïve abandonment.

Blasius, torn by jealousy, studied the broad shoulders, the jutting breast, the knotty arms, he flat abdomen, the curly hair and the muscular thighs of the elect. And mentally—for he was just—he compared them to his own imperfect torso, bow-legs, interminable simian arms and his long head, pointed and bony at the back like that of a Belgian hare.

He understood now, in a despair more dolorous than a crucifixion, all the disdain, all the irony and all the hatred of the woman he was stupidly obstinate in coveting.

Meanwhile, Rudolph interrogated the woodcutter.

With oblique phrases and insidious words, he caused him to reveal his name and place of habitation, led him to talk about his cabin, the companion with whom he had lived since childhood and whom he loved more than anything; got him to confess his ignorance of the City, and learned with a joyful stupefaction that his interlocutor did not know anything about the exterior world.

He and she lived in their forest full of sounds and perfumes, and they found everything necessary to their subsistence there: the mushroom growing at the foot of the cedar, the orange, the lemon and the citron; the turtle-doves that one catches in sticky traps; the fish that one catches from the edge of limpid streams; and the clumps of new-born herbs, dandelion and wild chicory, that one collects on the edge of ditches or amid the quivering swell of the grasslands.

He marveled at that sagacity as much as the curly-haired rustic marveled at the description of the City, the prestigious depiction that Rudolph made for him of the fêtes, feasts and spectacles to which the munificence of Blasius, always impenetrable and mute, had invited his thousand of inhabitants for years. And gradually, he seduced him; he enveloped him in his persuasive speech with the dexterity of a retiarius deploying his net over a gladiator, and when the three of them separated, Yann went to sit on the weeping trunk of a fig tree, and, his head between his hands, he reflected on everything that he had just been told by the little man with the sonorous hat and he wrinkled face.

For their part, the Corrupter and his accomplice went back lightly to the golden gates of the City. And while making his cane pass though the braced fingers of his right hand with a gyratory movement, Rudolph said to the master: "Have confidence."

The two continued their evil work for a week.

Now, the simple soul of the woodcutter opened completely, and he dreamed about the City with the brilliant roofs and the jasper steps, which it was sufficient to enter in order to savor immediately the greatest pleasures and the most unsuspected delights. And when the homunculus estimated that the moment had come, he had the Corrupter, tremulous that he might see his sinister offer refused, propose to him that he come with them into the sumptuous dwellings and direct, in exchange for a royal salary, the groups of serfs armed with billhooks, rakes and secateurs who maintained the gardens in which poets, seekers and lovers idled and chatted.

In order not to alarm him, however, and to distance him from scenting the slightest trap, they made him promise to conceal all that from his lover, and assured him that he would return every evening, if he so desired, to his cabin of foliage and planks, where the person whose sole ecstasy he was awaited him.

The next day, Yann left the clearing as soon as he had gone into the forest, arrived at the path that his two friends took to come and see him, hid his ax and his knapsack in a thicket, and with long strides, turning round to make sure that the woman was not following him, headed for the crossroads where Blasius and the homunculus were waiting for him.

Utterly ecstatic, clapping his hands like a child, he climbed into the electric carriage with lace and down cushions; at every slightly abrupt jolt his muscular body sank into the soft springs, and his face was wonderstruck as he saw filing past the windows of the carriage, in a dazzling phantasmagoria, the avenues, the boulevards, the symmetrical parks and the gardens where, by the will of Blasius, he would soon be the absolute master.

When they had made him traverse the City they took him to the arena, where lubricious dances were being performed that day. And he, who had not suspected lust, sensed in that revelation of vice unknown desires germinating within his flesh. Suddenly forgetting his oaths and the caresses with which he had vibrated a few hours before in his cabin, he desired those supple women and envied those ephebes and those actors clad in red tunics, and the arena sanded with gold, into which his bare feet sank up to the ankles. And he also envied the harmonious garments of the spectators, and as everyone stared, with eyes that were simultaneously curious and submissive, at the stranger who was watching the entertainments in the company of the Corrupter and his auxiliary, Yann sensed a flood of pride rising to his forehead.

And when the moment came to return to his humble abode, when he found himself again, alone and wretched, at the edge of the wood where nothing vibrated except birdsong, where nothing scintillated but the droplets of springs; when he considered his cotton shirt soiled by sweat and torn by the thorns of the thickets, the faded silk kerchief that covered his head and was knotted behind his neck, and he measured al his embarrassment and humility, he sensed shame penetrating him and curbing him.

And suddenly, he denied his entire past. He blushed at his ignorance, and he also blushed at the woman who had appeared to him as the sweetest and the most beautiful and the most perfect. He blushed at her green scarf, her hands tanned by the wind and torn by the ingrate labors to which destiny constrains the poor; and he compared his lover with all the women he had just seen in the City, ornamented in brocade and hyacinth, ringed with gems, diamonds and chalcedonies, crowned with roses, saffron and tuberoses, with all those who had contemplated him with languid eyes because he seemed to them to enjoy the master's amity.

He came back for several days in succession to the murderous City, and was gradually initiated into all its customs, all its perversities and all its concupiscences. Before those reiterated temptations, his purity, his candor and his grandeur of soul crumbled like a wall obstinately scraped by the mason, and nothing remained within him but thirst for lucre, covetousness for one of the beryl palaces where men and women on rectangular terraces absorbed beverages with strange hues, without any other labor than watching the time flow in blue crystal sand-glasses, making love to one another immodestly, calumniating their fellows and accomplishing in idleness the most insipid of the petty things of life.

One evening, a few hours before his departure, Blasius and Rudolph took him to the subterrains.

When they arrived on the threshold, Blasius activated a hidden mechanism and a heavy steel door as thick as the wall of a feudal castle rotated slowly on invisible hinges. And before the inconceivable vision, Yann uttered a cry of admiration and put his hands together. Glistening in the blaze of colored electric bulbs, there were heaps of green gold, pyramids of yellow gold and cones of red gold rising all the way to the vaulted ceilings.

Some of those heaps, pyramids and cones were composed of ingots. Others were composed of douros, sequins, crowns, rubles or gold coins struck with the effigies of sanguinary kings or pot-bellied princes. And next to that gold, sheathing it with resplendence, surrounding it with violet luminosities, heaps of diamonds, turquoises, rubies, amethysts and other stones, all rarer and more precious than the last, gave the impression of mounting guard around those fabulous treasures like sentinels decked in magical uniforms.

Along the mosaic of the halls and through the labyrinth of corridors, golden rails ran like interminable serpents, on which serfs pushed small gold wagons destined to transport from one end of the subterrains to the other the multitudes of ingots and gems that arrived continuously from the laboratories. The walls themselves were of gold, and the columns that sustained the ceilings were gold; and all that splendor struck the gaze, forcing the most audacious eyes to close at intervals, and became, after a prolonged sojourn, a hallucinatory vision.

The forest woodcutter, his throat constricted, had let himself fall on a heap of stones that were raw beryl, and, his head between his hands, he gasped with fear and admiration.

And when Blasius and the homunculus had left him to recover from his surprise and emotion at his leisure, Blasius touched him with his finger and said: "Choose!"

The rustic shuddered, and his hands rose in a gesture of amazement and apprehension. He dared not believe in the veracity of such a proposition, and he interrogated Blasius and Rudolph, who stood before him impassively, with his gaze.

Conscious of the disturbance into which his incredible word had just plunged him, Blasius repeated "Choose!"

But just as Yann was about to throw himself on the treasures as a feline exasperated by hunger pounces on a prey, the homunculus stopped him with a gesture and went on: "You can, in fact, choose whatever pleases you in this confusion of rutilance and wealth, and you can, with the collaboration of the serfs that we will attach to your service, take it all to the abode that awaits you at our will. However, we put one essential condition on that, easy of execution, to which you will yield without a murmur, I am certain, as soon as we have exposed it to you. It is simply a matter of engaging, once you have become the master of that fortune, not to return again to the forest where you have only known difficulty and labor..."

"I have known amour there," Yann interrupted, in an ardent voice."

"...Not to reappear in your cabin of branches, and to recommence another existence with us."

"Could I," ventured the young man, "have the woman I love, and who would die of my absence, come with me?"

"No," decreed Rudolph. "The renunciation of your past life also implies the renunciation of past amour."

"My God!" groaned the workman.

"And I will add, to leave you free to fix your choice, than nothing obliges you to rally to our opinion. If you prefer to take up your good ax again, and exhaust yourself combating the forests, that is up to you. We have simply wanted, out of sympathy for you, to reveal to you the envied pleasures of all those who know the reputation of the City, and to permit you to finish your days in charming idleness. Go back, reflect, and decide. But it remains understood that if you leave, you lose the right to take away an ounce of that gold and the smallest parcel of those precious stones."

At those words, Yann's heart broke.

He saw the cabin again with the cracked sandstone pots and the red clay bowls, where he had savored since infancy the joys of tenderness and liberty. He saw the bed of fern leaves where, in the arms of the woman to whom he had promised all his youth and all his grace, and had experienced joys the day before, the mere memory of which made him shiver. At the thought of abandoning all those customary things, of renouncing that ecstasy, a frightful sadness gripped him.

Large tears slid along his dark eyes, and he did not try to retain them. But when his tear-misted eyes posed on that resplendence and those treasures, it seemed to him that the sadness was attenuated, gradually fading away and giving way to magnificent hopes, to mad projects...

Blasius and Rudolph watched those interior combats, and an indescribable fear of seeing Yann leave clawed Blasius.

But the struggle soon ended; and the woodcutter, vanquished by cupidity, in a frenzied and fervent thirst for enjoyments, collapsed on the pyramid of green gold. And in a hoarse voice, his eyes drowned by that new sensuality, he gasped: "I accept."

Immediately, Blasius placed his middle finger on a bell-push. From all directions, carrying profound sacks and baskets as large as vats, serfs came running in response to that summons. And at the injunction of the rustic, who ran like a madman through the midst of gold, diamonds, pearls and chrysoprases, they filed the sacks and loaded them on to golden wagons.

When the rustic had a fortune before him of whose like the most opulent kings would never have dared to dream, he cried: "Let's go!" And in carriages with soft cushions, Blasius and Rudolph accompanied him to the palace they had reserved for him.

Servants welcomed him on the rosy threshold where turtle-doves were cooing on the corbels of colonnettes, and, bowing very low before him, they guided him as far as the bedroom prepared with his intention since the moment when the homunculus, alerted by his infallible prescience, had sniffed the defeat of the solitary.

That bedroom, hung with crimson and black, overlooked the river whose waters snaked through the middle of the city. Moored to the pillars of the terrace, a boat was bobbing in accordance with the movement of the waves. An immense bed curtained by Oriental tapestries occupied the center of the room, and all along the walls, low divans, seats espousing the forms of bodies and double-backed chairs formed a furniture of unusual richness.

To either side of the bed, eucalyptus-wood tables supported accessories of distraction and toilette, and a hookah as stout as a lawyer seemed to be offering via its invisible beak and its curved pipe the most ecstatic perfumes to the woodcutter, bewildered by all that unexpected luxury.

Yann passed, fearfully, from one object to the next. With childish words he interrogated Blasius and Rudolph about their utility, their fabrication and their usage; and after each of his explanations, in order to entangle him further, to take away any desire to return to the clearing, Blasius added: "This belongs to you."

When they had visited the dwelling, from the bathrooms were improved apparatus waited to project an odorous rain of regenerative essences banishing lassitude over the trembling body of the rustic, to the harmony rooms where electric organs interpreted themselves at the flick of a switch the works of the musicians of the city and illustrious composers from all over the world, Rudolph invited Yann to pass into a vestry with a silver ceiling.

There, serfs were waiting, charged with dressing him in an indigo tunic knotted with a yellow gold belt, circling his dark hair with a headband encrusted with diamonds, and encasing his feet in embroidered leather sandals. When he looked at himself in a looking-glass as high as a wall and saw himself thus metamorphosed, he uttered a sort of joyous roar.

Afterwards, his two guides introduced him into a room of more restricted dimensions than the preceding ones, where he would take his meals. When he was installed in front of a table covered in dishes, decanters and carafes full of wines and liqueurs, and a servant docile to his orders was posted behind him, Blasius and Rudolph disappeared through a lateral door.

As Yann hesitated to eat those meats and fruits disposed in symmetrical rows on platters and in baskets, and looked around him, uncertain whether he was dreaming or whether what he saw really existed, the curtain dissimulating the main entrance of the room, facing him, was slowly lifted, and before his eyes dilated by surprise, a woman appeared.

She formed the most complete contrast with the woman he had abandoned in the woods. Whereas the other was small and thin, tanned by the sun and the pure air, the one who had just appeared was tall, buxom and blonde. She was wearing a clinging dress that molded her upper body perfectly, through which the flavorsome curve of her breasts could be divined. Her plump arms were hollowed by pink dimples, and her cerulean eyes had the transparency of springs spilling in cascades from a mountain. Her hair, the color of sunlight, formed an aureole around the warm snow of her forehead, and her imperious chin attained the perfection of an antique statue.

At the sight of her, the young man got up, suddenly seized by an inexplicable dread; but she reassured him with a tender movement.

"Have no fear," she said, in a harmonious and grave voice. "I have come here because I am to be henceforth, if you find me beautiful and desirable, the companion of your youth. I'm not unaware that you have loved before knowing me, and that the woman who has remained out there equals me in grace, but I believe that before long, I shall be able to make you forget her."

She sat down at his feet on a round cushion, and having taken that posture of humility, she continued: "Yes, I'm certain that my image will gradually expel the other, and that my caresses will surpass in sensual pleasure those that enchanted you before. For the moment, I only ask that you allow me to come back to see you often, in order to hear me and get to know me, and when you judge that the time has come, to cherish me—if you judge it—it will be sufficient to give me a sign. I will belong to you for as long and as completely as you order.

And Yann, charmed by the music of those confessions, by the emanations of that splendid flesh, had her sit beside him on the ebony bed, and he shared with her the crisp bread and the delicate dishes, and the fruits, each of which delighted him more than the one he had just tasted.

Together they drank wines as blonde as the woman's hair and as brown as the skin of the beloved. The warmth of those wines went to their heads; and desire gradually set them ablaze, led them astray, impelled them to approach one another more closely. And truly they formed on the princely bed the most beautiful couple imaginable; and the woman's speech enveloped the forest woodcutter like irresistible arms; and the laughter that flowed from her sharp teeth stunned him to the extent of casing him to lose the notion of the place where they both were.

Sometimes between two draughts of golden wine, he sensed a memory rising within him, a remorse seizing his throat. Then he leaned his head toward the table and remained silent for a moment. But the woman immediately perceived that melancholy; quickly, she pressed herself against him more tightly, with seductive whispers; and the young man shuddered at the appeal of that flesh, already braced for the embrace, enlacing him with a passionate movement; and he kissed, voraciously, the pale nape over which the tresses of the solar hair gradually collapsed.

Insensibly, by means of an exterior mechanism, the blinding glare of the electric lamps and lanterns was attenuated. By the time the meal neared its end, all that was any longer scintillating beneath the silken shade was a veiled light as soft as evening twilight, and that light designed around the closely associated heads of the two diners a halo the color of dead leaves. The larger lantern behind the dazed duo projected on the wall in front of them the shadow of two tightly enlaced bodies, and two mouths welded together by an interminable kiss.

Now desire curbed them completely. The rustic's forearm, as brutal and powerful as a vice, squeezed the body of the woman as if to break it, and under that fervent pressure the latter abandoned herself. She had unfastened her robe and through the gap in the light silk, the perfect globes of her breasts offered themselves to Yann's avidity. Her legs parted with a slow but uninterrupted movement, and her lips, under the moist tongue of the lover, parted like two perfumed valves. And with a long cry of savage passion, his hands clenched behind his companion's shoulders, the man possessed her.

And as he fell back, breathless, on his crimson cushions, taking from the fingers of his elect am amphora full to the brim with black wine, another cry, even more savage than his own, ripped through the calm of the vast dwelling—the cry of a wounded beast, a beast at bay, an adieu of a moribund to life, to light, to the surrounding things, to flowers, to amour, to joy—which caused the two lovers to sit up, their fists clutching the uprights of the sculptural bed, their necks taut and their mouths anxiously open.

And almost immediately after that scream, there was the soft sound of a fall on the other side of the heavy curtain, and muffled whispering, and an imprecise movement—as if serfs had loaded an inert body on to a stretcher in order to carry it away from the depths of the palace.

VIII

Very gently, with paternal precautions, Blasius and the three serfs who were helping him in the delicate task deposited the inanimate Helia on a low bed in a chamber adjacent to the Corrupter's cell.

Beneath her silk kerchief, her hair flowed in broad sheets, invading the discolored cheeks, the motionless throat, and the shoulders chilled by the cataleptic state into which she was plunged.

Hr hands, like those of a dying woman, clung obstinately to her green scarf above her breasts, and from time to time a nervous spasm shook her from head to toe.

Blasius leaned over her, took her wrist, and felt her scarcely perceptible pulse beating. After a few seconds, his gaze illuminated.

"She's alive," he murmured.

Then one of the City's scientists, who had entered the room behind the tragic group, approached Helia, unclenched her teeth by means of a golden spatula, and introduced a few drops of a brick red liquid into her unclosed mouth.

Under the energetic action of the cordial, the blood rose again to Helia's cheeks and lips, and her eyelids quivered. For a moment, her long eyelashes fluttered like the elytra of a marvelous insect about to take flight; then they parted, and the whites of the eyes appeared, still a little jaundiced by the shock that had left her half-dead. Haggard and devoid of expression, her gaze swerved from right to left, posing on the scientist, the serfs and examining Blasius before a long sigh caused her to shudder from head to toe.

After that attempt at mute resurrection, her head fell back on the cushion, and like an exhausted child, Helia fell asleep.

At a sign from Blasius, the serfs and the scientists left the room, and the man remained alone at the sleeper's bedside. He sat on a stool very close to her, and, holding his breath in order not to wake her, he put his meager fingers in front of her mouth. And while she slept, he watched her.

Before that poor weakness, which had curbed, broken and enslaved him for so long, and over which he was not yet certain of triumphing, he sensed his heart melting; a surge of intoxication invaded him; invisible hands seized him and lifted him from the ground; and under that mysterious force he began to tremble in all his limbs, and while trembling, he wept silently. It seemed to him that something new was hatching within him, gently closing his wounds, embalming him and regenerating him; and as he knew nothing of human metamorphoses, he could not understand that that upheaval, terrible and delectable at the same time, was happiness.

After a slumber that lasted for two hours, however, in the course of which Blasius, sitting by the bedside, did not make a movement, Helia opened her eyes.

This time she recognized the man who was keeping vigil next to her, and with a cry of repulsion, she recoiled. With a brutal gesture she pushed away the blue woolen blanket that was keeping her chilled body warm and wanted to flee. But she was still so weak that she fell back on the bed at the first effort; then she started to sob, convulsively In a poor small voice she murmured, between two gasps of chagrin: "I'd like to die!"

Blasius replied to her, very softly: "It's not a matter of dying, but, on the contrary, of reviving. You're at home here in this palace; you have only to command. Everything belongs to you, from the richest rooms filled with works of art and precious furniture, to the serfs committed to the care of looking after and protecting you. Speak! What do you want?"

"To return to the forest," Helia groaned

"And what will you do there, abandoned and desolate as you are?"

"I'll die there. Since you have not hesitated to impose the formidable ordeal upon me in which my understanding has perished along with my youth, I no longer have anything to do down here."

While the rustic was feasting in the company of his new elect, one of the taciturn men had come to the cabin where Helia was waiting for the infidel, weeping. He had persuaded her to come into the city, where she would find the one whom she sought. Scarcely having entered, she had been hidden behind the heavy curtain that had been lifted two hours earlier to let the sorceress pass, and from there, her clenched fingernails digging into her rigid flesh, she had witnessed all the phases of the treason. And at the moment when the lovers' cry of pleasure had erupted into the silence, she had responded, falling backwards into the arms of the taciturn men who were watching her, with a long, hoarse, desperate, inhuman cry.

Now she no longer felt anything within her but a great lassitude, a great emptiness. She was no longer able to think, no longer able to speak; she abandoned herself to the nonexistence from which death might emerge, for which she wished with all that remained of her strength.

But Blasius, measuring her collapse, had started speaking.

"Yes," he said to her, dully, "I've committed a frightful action, and doubtless you will never forgive me. But I knew that the master of your flesh and your heart did not love you as you merited being adored. I knew that his passion would weaken at the spectacle of my wealth, and that his desire for you would suddenly be extinguished at the spectacle of the rival that I caused to surge forth before him. Everything that I prophesied has been accomplished. Everything that I wanted has happened. And I, who love you with an amour that is simultaneously frightful and sublime, am the only one who can give you that which you dream, and that is why you will love me."

"I hate you!" growled the woman.

"You hate me today, I know, but tomorrow you'll be calmer. You'll reflect. You'll compare your past life with the existence that I offer you..."

"You horrify me!"

"That's true; you're as beautiful as the light of a spring day, and I'm as ugly as the sinister shadow of a stormy evening. But amour realizes miracles. And in the same way that your lover, on the contact of new flesh, has forgotten your splendor and your fidelity, you will gradually forget my ugliness, my grotesque body, my gummy eyes, my hairy torso and my fleshless arms; gradually, you will be able to tolerate the sight of it; and when you are accustomed to me, I swear to you that you will be very close to loving me."

"I will always hate you."

"You will hate me for a long time. But in this atmosphere of luxury, harmony and appeasement, the best tempered characters soften. You will hate me for a long time, perhaps for weeks, or months, or even years. But that hatred will not be eternal, because in this world there is only one thing that is truly eternal: amour."

"You're lying, you who have just killed it in the man for whom I lived."

"That man was a primitive being, devoid of culture, delicacy and intelligence. For that reason, his love could not last. But mine will last, because I bear within me all power and all genius, because I have grown old in the scorn of those incomparable women, one alone of whom has sufficed to defeat your beloved, and because I am one of those who are confined within a single amour. I frighten you? What does that matter to me? Tomorrow, I shall be the one who curbs you, the one for whose kisses you will beg.

"You sicken me!" Helia replied. "In listening to you I measured the stupid vanity of your heart and your brain, and now you have spoken, I'm wondering which you merit more, being pitied or being scorned."

"You can insult me as much as you please," said Blasius. "I've decided to tolerate everything from you, from the cruelest words to the worst ill-treatment, if it suits you one day to strike me. To suffer at your hands would be an indescribable joy for me, and besides, it's necessary for me to suffer in order to deserve you."

"Don't deceive yourself to that extent. I'll never have anything for you but aversion."

"I'll wait. But for now, stay here and command. Do as you wish. No one has the right to impede your actions, and I want to dazzle you with the magnificence of my tenderness."

And the implacable duel commenced.

To begin with, Helia enclosed herself in a grim isolation.

She had Blasius forbidden access to her dwelling, and Blasius submitted without a murmur to her decision. She spent entire days lying on the cushions of her chamber or plunged in an onyx bathtub. In vain, the servants and the serfs that the Corrupter had attached to her service attempted to distract her. The most sensual music irritated her, and the sound of the human voice made her enter into mad rages. When dusk fell, clad in a long red silk tunic, with a comb as sharp as a dagger in her black hair, she went up on to her terrace, leaned on the polished balustrade and, with her head between her hands, lingered in her reveries until the cool of the night made her shiver and obliged her to return to her apartments.

Sometimes she got up at dawn and departed, straight ahead, along the deserted avenues, through streets where nothing resonated but the noise of her sandals on the large gold-encrusted porphyry paving slabs.

Then, one morning, she manifested abruptly the desire to see the Corrupter; and in answer to her appeal, the other hastened.

He bowed before her, profoundly, and waited.

"I had you summoned," Helia said in a grave voice, "to repeat to you that I still hate you as much."

At that abuse, Blasius smiled.

"You hate me less," he replied, "since you are tolerating my presence, and even desired it. As for winning you, I know how hard the task will be, and I think it wiser at first to wait until you no longer detest me. But since you seem to have been reborn to life—for which I rejoice—permit me to give in honor of your resurrection a fête of song and dance. If you do not wish to watch it all the way through, I will not oppose your withdrawal at the moment that suits you."

Helia nodded her head in acquiescence.

She appeared at the fête, strange and pale. All the inhabitants, knowing by virtue of the indiscretion of the serfs, the extraordinary adventure that had brought her into the city, considered her avidly, but she opposed a disdainful indifference to their unhealthy curiosity, and, as if to stand up to it, remained until the end in the box that Blasius had ceded to her.

The next day, he presented himself before Helia, and although she had not summoned him, she received him; and curiously enough, in the course of their brief conversation, she did not mention her hatred once.

That welcome emboldened the Corrupter, and having visited her several times in succession, he proposed one day to take her in one of the electric carriages whose velocity had ecstasized her beloved a few weeks before; and she accepted his proposition.

They departed through the spacious avenues and went through the gates of the city. When they were on the threshold of open country, Helia placed her hand gently on the arm of the silent Blasius, and said to him "I'd like to ask you for a favor."

Blasius looked at her for a long time.

"Yes," he said, "I can guess. That desire is the only one I had sworn not to grant, but today, I can't refuse you anything. We'll go."

With a brief order, he orientated the vibrant carriage toward the forest. After a short lapse of time, the driver stopped the monster. Holding Helia's hand, Blasius helped her to descend; but as he prepared to accompany her, she immobilized him with an imperious gesture.

"Leave me alone!"

Docile, Blasius inclined his head.

Slender and supple in her red silk tunic, she walked at a rapid pace, and beneath her nervous feet, twigs and branches broke with a light sound. And when she arrived at the cabin that had sheltered her happiness and her confidence or so many years, she knelt down,

Already, inexorable time had done its work.

In the same way that the scars of amour had gradually closed in Helia's bruised heart, nature seemed to have wanted to close with leaves and flowers the refuge that had sheltered her for such a long time. Along the walls, little branches were sprouting from the trunks planted in series, and on the roof there was a veritable bouquet of buds and nascent stems undulating in the warm breeze.

On every side, everywhere, life was erupting in the midst of that abandonment, and as she tried, having approached, to penetrate into the verdant dwelling, Helia recoiled.

A tangle of brambles, creepers, clematis, ivy and campanula obstructed the entrance. There was a barrier of flowers and leaves prohibiting the revenant access to the miserably deserted abode.

Yes, all that vegetation, all those flowers and herbs had formed a coalition against the fugitive, forbidding that adorable retreat to her. Now, it was no longer a quiver of foliage trembling in the wind; it was the voice of the bushes, the ivy and the campanula repeating obstinately: "You shall not enter!"

The woman understood that voice. And before that pitiful death of the past, she lowered her head in shame. And with steps as slow as they were in haste to go, she rejoined the carriage where the Corrupter was waiting for her.

He did not saying anything to her; but he guessed, and a triumphant gleam set his ardent eyes ablaze.

Then they departed with a bound toward the City, and the woman went back to her dwelling silently, the yellow gold roof of which launched myriads of silvery darts at the midday sun.

And life continued for her and for him with alternatives of calm and overexcitement. Sometimes, when Blasius appeared, Helia sent him away with a sign of the head, as she would have sent away a serf; sometimes, on the contrary, she summoned him. Sometimes she laughed, dementedly, without a motive; sometimes she threw herself on to her cushions, prey to a crisis of sobs and despair that lasted for hours.

But Blasius did not weary.

He allowed the crises of tears and the fits of mad laughter to pass with the same firmness. He heaped Helia with presents. Several times he offered her splendid fêtes; but, faithful to a rigorously studied plan, not once did he attempt either a touch or a word of tenderness.

One might have thought that that impassivity, at length, frightened the woman. Gradually, she remarked changes in the Corrupter that did not fail to surprise her, and even, deep down, to charm her. One morning he presented himself before her clad in a black woolen robe spangled with silver, and as she was mentally astonished by that unexpected elegance, she perceived that Blasius was no longer wearing his flowing, impetuous and unkempt beard, but that skillful scissors had disciplined it. She was convinced by that spectacle the Blasius' physiognomy had gained in softness and mobility.

One evening, when he solicited from her, as he had done in vain for many days, the favor of sharing her meal, she accepted the proposition. They ate facing one another in the great sonorous hall; and that evening, Blasius spoke for several consecutive minutes, contrary to his habit. When he wanted to withdraw, bowing before her, she retained him momentarily. The next day, she declined briefly the further offer he made her of his company; but as he went away, she called him back, and retained him until midnight.

It was believable, now, that hatred had been abolished in Helia's heart. The cruel words became rarer, and it even happened, after vesperal feasts, that she abandoned her fingers to Blasius' quivering hands. But that contact only lasted for a few seconds, and when he tried to renew it an instant later, she snatched herself away from his emprise nervously.

That bizarre game went on for months, but Blasius' patience remained untiring, for he knew that victory would crown his tenacity. Gradually, the fingers were no longer re-fused, and one evening, drawing them toward him slowly, he even deposited a kiss on the fingernails the color of rose and henna.

From that evening on, Helia's attitude changed.

She gradually abdicated rancor and arrogance, and her insensible heart grew accustomed to that respectful and passionate worship. The novelty of the contest, in which Blasius deployed treasures of patience and subtlety in order to defeat her, disconcerted her. And the moment came when she felt without revolt Blasius' lips brushing the somber azure of her hair; and from the hair those lips descended toward the eyes, which closed, palpitating, under that caress; and one day, at the emergence from the long kiss that seemed to stir her completely, she abandoned her mouth to him.

Their embrace was so ardent that Blasius, bowled over by emotion, joy and desire, fell beside her, his cheeks inundated by cold sweat. He appeared to have lost consciousness, and Helia, mute beside him was panting. Then the embrace was renewed; and another evening, at the end of the most magnificent feast, Helia gave herself completely.

After that possession, a frightful passion was released in Blasius. Having remained until then on the threshold of old age, he suddenly discovered unimaginable refinements of lust. His frenzied perversities left the woman inert and devoid of force on the golden cushions of the big bed. And that depravity, that sensuality, was exacerbated as the possession became total and free.

Helia surrendered to Blasius' whim. She did not refuse him anything, neither the most chaste caresses nor the most abnormal and most unexpected contacts. She made her body an amorous urn in which the crazed Blasius tried in vain to sate his incessantly increasing desire for enjoyment and lubricity. And when she had led him to the paroxysm of passion and dementia, by virtue of an inexplicable caprice, she suddenly refused herself.

Then there were atrocious hours, horrible nights when Blasius rolled at her feet, but the golden fringes of her tunic, tried to enlace her muscular legs, to draw toward him that mouth sugared like a ripe fruit. But his efforts remained vain and his passion broke against Helia's inflexible obstinacy.

That gehenna lasted for two entire weeks; then, one evening when he begged her, when he attained an insupportable degree of exasperation, she took off her tunic, seized the tremulous Blasius by the shoulders, and fell back beneath him on to her cushions, dragging him down. The act lasted all night, and from that moment on it seemed to Blasius that the woman had veritably become his companion and his mistress.

In the course of their craziest previous embraces, insensate confessions and incoherent words had escaped Blasius in uninterrupted floods, stimulating his amour and his thirst for possession, but Helia, by contrast, had remained mute. Not once, while she abandoned herself, had she every murmured: "I love you..."

Now she no longer remained silent. After intercourse, when they separated, exhausted, unable to do any more, she interrogated him about his past life and his family, provoking confidences. And Blasius, recklessly happy to have finally found someone worthy and capable of understanding him, poured forth long narratives. He told her about his childhood, the solitude that dragged him like a chain for more than forty years, and the dazzle that had left him haggard and soulless before her when he had perceived her on the threshold of her cabin.

But when she tried to interrogate him about his discoveries, Blasius suddenly enclosed himself in a grim mutism; and that day, it was impossible for Helia to get another word out of him. As if she had lost interest in it, she ceased to talk to him about that subject, and then confidence returned progressively to Blasius' soul. Meanwhile, Helia made herself more and more seductive and lascivious, and after a considerable lapse of time, she risked once again asking him one of the questions that had irritated him so much the first time.

But Blasius' eyebrows frowned, and, prey to an anger that he did not seek to dissimulate, he said to her: "What does the secret of which I am the master matter to you, since it serves me to render you as fortunate as you were once unfortunate, to surround you with a luxury and a beauty compared with which all royal riches pale? Allow yourself to be loved, enjoy all my treasures, and don't seek to concern yourself with their provenance."

And once again, the woman avoided for weeks any conversation relating to the secret, and redoubled her sensuality toward Blasius.

The latter, entirely devoted his passion, was neglecting his labors. Over the retorts, the test tubes and the bronze tables of the laboratory, a white dust settled, and along the walls, no longer surveyed by the serf who performed the functions of laboratory assistant, minuscule spiders began to weave silky webs.

Avid to know in depth the history of all erotic monstrosities, he had had Rudolph buy rare books in the continental cities, which recounted in incredible detail all the aberrations of sodomites, tribades and erotomaniacs. He read descriptions of orgies, flagellations and pederasty so horrible that his hair stood on end and bristled all over his body as if on contact with an electric pile. Then he rushed into the room where Helia was sleeping, and both of them, avidly poring over the obscene narratives, savored that putrescence; and when they had arrived at a degree of irresistible overexcitement, they had intercourse, mingled with obscene verbiage. Or the Corrupter, unable to resist a moment longer the deadly influence of those accounts, lay down on his black bearskin, and there, summoning Helia with diabolical mimes, whom distance prevented from hearing and coming running, he possessed her in thought for hours.

Gradually, he arrived at demanding things of her the mere idea of which would have made him recoil in disgust a few months earlier.

One day he demanded that she flagellate him with a supple hazel rod. And the more pleasure Helia seemed to take in that perverse game, the more pleasure Blasius experienced in the suffering that reduced him to the level of insanity. And when the blood spurted from his concave ribs and meager back, from his pointed and vaulted shoulders, he uttered a series of gasps and rolled on the ground, belching like a vulgar drunkard.

Helia, who sensed her power over him increasing by the day, gradually enveloped him in the toils of his vices and his lust, as if in the mesh of an unbreakable net. When she was certain of dominating him, of having in her hands a flaccid object, devoid of will, incapable of further resistance, she spoke to him.

"Why do you refuse so brutally to reveal your secret to me? Am I not your companion in the most complete sense of the word, and do you think that I could not second you, also, in your sinister designs? I'm a woman; I attain degrees of refinement and cruelty that you can't suspect. I too have suffered; and I would like to make others suffer; and I would not want to see around me, since I love you, anything but dolors; and I would only like to hear, outside of your indecent words, the vociferations and maledictions of my victims. And then, think! If you were to disappear, if death, stronger than anything, laid you low and stiff between the planks of a coffin, what would become of your work of genus?

"What would become of your city? Is it the homunculus who could regulate it in accordance with your plans, or that avaricious and reptilian horde who only think of devouring one another, harming one another and killing one another? You know better than I do, and you have said it to me many times: not one of them is capable of an elevated thought, and I do not know any of them worthy to receive the torch from your trembling hands when the hour of the great departure sounds for you.

"Have confidence! Tell yourself that I am the prolongation of all your rancor, all your debauchery, all your superhuman malevolence, and make me your redoubtable heir! On your lips, which I kiss recklessly and for which I have as much thirst as you have for mine, I swear to you that I will accomplish all your orders scrupulously and inexorably; and thanks to me, your city will remain what you have made of it; and throughout the entire world I will continue your work of degradation, ruination and murder!"

She fell silent; and, exhausted by the emotion of that long confession, let her head fall back on Blasius' breast.

He, feeling the desire for that young body seize him again, caressed her blue tresses chastely, and she, anticipating an amorous assault more violent than she had ever sustained before, braced herself, while pressing herself against him more tightly. Blasius hesitated for a long time before responding. He kissed Helia's eyes and murmured: "Later..."

"Why later?" she said, enlacing his legs already quivering, with hers. "Is it necessary, then, for me to prove that I am truly worthy of you, that you will not find a similar accomplice anywhere?"

Her impatient hands palpated Blasius; and when she judged that the decisive moment had arrived, instead of granting herself, she got up with a great leap, and started to flee around the room, provoking him.

He pursued her, her hair undone and her robe parted, without being able to catch her. And to each of his supplications, Helia replied, with a scornful laugh: "When I know..."

And suddenly, like a wounded tigress, she leapt upon him, raked his face and body with her fingernails, and bit him so cruelly that blood spurted from the wound and Blasius uttered a scream of pain.

But Helia continued; and Blasius sensed his inflexible resistance slowly melting away. And when he was extenuated by suffering and lust, he got up and said: Come!"

And, vacillating on his tibias, as exhausted as a moribund, he dragged himself to his laboratory, followed by the triumphant woman.

But at the moment when he drew near to the hybrid item of furniture in which he hid the transmuting stone, he hesitated. It was necessary for Helia to push him gently toward the drawer on which no external trace of any lock was visible. And as she pushed him gently she exhorted him:

"Go on! Have no fear...I'll keep your secret with the same prudence as you, and I promise you never to make use of it without your authorization."

Vanquished, Blasius touched the small cabinet with his fingertip, and a door suddenly opened. And in the middle of the drawer, a stone scarcely larger than a fist brightened with its pale hue the garnet velvet cushion on which it was set.

The woman approached, curiously.

When she perceived the stone she uttered a sardonic laugh and looked at Blasius. "You're joking, of course?" she asked. "That stone has sufficient virtue, according to you, that it has sufficed to render you master of the world? In truth, I don't know what's stopping me from leaving here and never coming back..."

But Blasius seed the flap of her tunic and replied: "No! I'm not joking. Know that that stone contains more power than the most numerous and the most invincible armies. I'll prove it to you."

He seized the pebble with one hand, and with the other he drew toward him a small block of cast iron placed on a marble table next to an electric furnace.

"This is iron," he explained to Helia. And having touched it with the stone, he added: "Now that iron is becoming gold..."

Indeed, on contact with the transmuting stone, the block of iron had taken on a reed hue.

Bewildered, Helia considered the spectacle.

"Gold!" she said

"Yes, gold!" replied Blasius, triumphantly. "And I am the only person in the world who can obtain that gold at will, with a simple contact. Do you understand now why I am the most powerful man on earth?"

Crushed by that revelation, the woman replied: "Yes." Then she added, as if talking to herself: "You can fabricate gold with that stone!"

"That stone," Blasius confessed, "I obtained one evening when I undertook an experiment that did not have the objective of discovering it. But the explosion that destroyed my retorts and my apparatus also destroyed the formula whose power I did not know. You understand now why I hesitated to show you the transmuting stone."

"With the consequence," said Helia, thoughtfully, "that if you lost this, you would also lose the faculty of transmutation?"

"Naturally."

"And you'd become a man like any other?"

"Inferior to others, since I would no longer have, as before, the means of defending myself against them."

"Ah!" murmured Helia.

Blasius replaced the stone on its garnet cushion, and they went back to the room where the royal feast awaited them.

Exhausted by the afternoon's embraces and the emotion that they had both felt in the course of Blasius' revelations, they guzzled the food and liquids to the point that the Corrupter, for the first time in his life, found himself completely drunk at the end of the supper.

Although she had arrived at the utmost limit of enervation, however, Helia had conserved all her lucidity, and it was her who guided the tottering Blasius to his cell, and laid him down on the bearskin, after having removed his monastic robe and his leather sandals.

Then, when the Corrupter appealed to her in a thick voice, she lay down next to him, and, by means of the most expert and the most irresistible artifices, she awakened his concupiscence.

That evening, they possessed one another abominably until a very advanced hour of the night, and the Corrupter, his strength exhausted, fell back on his side, and, his mouth agape in order better to draw in air, he fell asleep.

Then Helia raised herself up on her hands and gazed at him.

A little saliva was hanging from the corners of his mouth; through the opening of the mouth the man's teeth were visible, long and yellow, poorly planted, corroded by decay, and at intervals, a large gap marked places where they were missing.

At that sight, a shudder of repulsion shook her; but she reacted immediately, and with serpentine suppleness she emerged from the couch.

She put on her hyacinth tunic and Cordovan blue slippers lined with swansdown, and she slid through the deserted corridors, stopping at the slighted creak of her feet on the marble, listening for the alarming sounds of the night, ready to go back, at the first alert, to the bedroom where the Corrupter was now snoring incessantly.

She advanced for minutes that seemed to her to be interminable under the indecisive light that the moon was pouring through the frosted windows of the vaults; and when she had walked in that anguished silence she arrived at the laboratory where Blasius had revealed his secret.

Slowly, scrutinizing the penumbra around her and holding her breath, she moved aside the curtain, let it fall back behind her heels, and found herself in the solitary little room.

She turned a commutator; immediately, the filtered light of a jade ceiling lamp encrusted with sapphires revealed the corners and the furniture.

Spectral, trembling like a leaf in the wind, she palpated all the faces of the cabinet with her finger, and suddenly stiffened, her hand on her heart. The little door had just opened, and the transmuting stone was there before hr, dull and ragged with asperities, on its garnet velvet cushion.

She seized it, closed the little door with the same precautions that she had put into opening it, and, with the prize clenched in her fingers, she returned via the same corridors, almost fainting with the same emotions as in going, and found herself back in the cell.

Blasius was still snoring, and his respiration, now regular, revealed that he was plunged in an invincible sleep.

The Helia, clutching the miraculous stone in her hands, quit the dwelling again by a cedar door opening over the river, which served for the access of the serfs and merchants. There was no one in the avenues, or along the quays disciplining the green-tinted water. The whole city was sleeping, like Blasius, the heavy slumber that follows hideous debauches; and in the distance, festooning the parapet of a massive bridge with pallor, dawn was breaking.

With hasty strides, Helia headed for the bank. She descended, holding on to plants and stray stems, all the way to the water, silently flowing its strange and profound mystery; and with a convulsive movement, with all her might, she threw the stone into the middle of the river.

There was a small splash, very slight, a hole instantly closed…gray foam…an eddy…and that was all.

Helia departed at a run; her breast heaving with a hoarse sound. When she reached the terrace of polished slabs, she fell unconscious.

She remained there for nearly an hour.

When she recovered her senses, the sun was rising above the domes of the city, shaking millions of gems over the golden roofs. She got up slowly, bewildered; staggering she went to lean on a wrought iron balustrade representing dragons and nuns frozen in incredible postures. There, her hair scattered over her bare shoulders, her teeth chattering feverishly, she let her mind wander.

Meanwhile, Blasius had woken up in the cell. Surprised no longer to find her by his side, he set out in search of her. He made a tour of the rooms, scrutinized the coverts of the corridors and discovered her, motionless, in the place where she had leaned after getting up.

He advanced toward her and touched her with his finger.

"I was looking for you," he murmured

Helia turned round, and on recognizing him, shuddered.

"I was looking for you," Blasius repeated. "Come into the cell; I'm thirsty for your body."

But he woman pulled away with an abrupt movement, and in a dull voice, with a flame of mysticism in her eyes, she replied to him: "Times have changed. What I wanted has arrived. And I won't go with you, because you're no longer anything now but weakness and poverty."

"What do you mean?" asked Blasius.

"You shall know. Months ago, I lived, placid and joyful, in a cabin of branches, with my lover. We had no other ambition than to cherish one another, no other dream than to go abroad beside one another, and when the great moment came, to sleep together in the same grave, to the song of the flowers, the insects and the branches. But you surged forth, and with you, misfortune fell upon us. You stole that lover from me; you drew me into the putrescent city, and you made of me, who was nothing but candor and simplicity, a creature of lust and depravity."

"I loved you!" Blasius interjected.

"I went with you. I yielded to all your caprices, all your whims; and I was able, thanks to a superhuman effort of energy, to submit to you and to make you believe that I also loved you."

Blasius started.

"For I had my plan!" Helia went on. "I wanted to render you a hundredfold the suffering that I owed to you, to make you expiate your double sin in an infernal vengeance. But for that it was necessary for me to know. It was necessary for me to know where you obtained that power. It was necessary for me to know the fantastic secret that rendered you master of the world. And, by means of hypocrisy, cunning and shrewdness, I've succeeded in that. Now you're no longer anything. You can no longer do anything."

"The transmuting stone!" Blasius articulated, in a voice strangled by fear.

"It's out there, somewhere, at the bottom of the river. And I defy your scientists and your servants to recover it."

"You're lying! You haven't done that!" he cried.

"You doubt it? Go to your laboratory and see for yourself whether I'm lying."

Like a madman, Blasius ran.

Helia marched behind him, supple and victorious; and when she went into the laboratory she saw the Corrupter kneeling in front of the empty drawer, wringing his hands in despair. And when he stood up, he saw her in front of him, defying him.

But his distress was such that he did not roar any word of revolt, did not sketch any gesture of menace, and only said, plaintively: "You've done that!"

"Yes, I've done it. And my pride is formidable in having vanquished you. Now I can finally take off the mask. I can tell you that I hate you, that I've always hated you, that you are the being that I hate most in the world. I hate you because you murdered my life, but I also hate you, and more, because you've murdered this city, depraved the most beautiful and noblest souls that inhabited it, and because, from one end of the earth to the other, because of you, women and children are weeping, old men are praying before tombs, and millions of innocent people have perished. And I hate you, above all, because you're evil."

"I've suffered!" repeated Blasius, his head in his hands.

"You've suffered? And haven't all of them suffered, and weren't they as innocent as you? And yet, if you had wanted, you would have been able to accomplish such things that the entire world would have cherished and venerated you! Think of what you could have done if you had employed for good all the treasures what you have utilized for your homicidal designs! Think that, at this moment, thanks to you, instead of desolation and misery, there might have been ecstasy in the four corners of the continents! There might be no more poor people; there might be no more wretched people, no more starvelings. You might have been the new messiah before whom races would have prostrated themselves, and you might have savored the most complete and the most noble sensuality: that which comes from benevolence."

"Benevolence!" said Blasius, on his knees on the cold flagstones. "No one ever taught me that."

"You could have learned it for yourself. Then you would have seen, and then you would have understood, that nothing is durable without it, that nothing is true and nothing is just."

"I was unworthy to raise myself so high," murmured Blasius.

"You've never tried!"

"I grew up in humiliation and hatred."

"You could have escaped from it. But you preferred to spend your entire life wallowing in your turpitude like a wild boar in the depths of its den. And now the hour of expiation has chimed. Like Ahasuerus, you will be accursed among the accursed; men will spit in our face and cover you with filth, and little children and virgins will turn away from you. Yes, you will be cursed, and henceforth, you will truly know what dolor is. And it will be thanks to me, whose heart you murdered, as you have murdered everything around you, that you will endure the cruelest torture that a human being can support: remorse."

"I repent!" moaned Blasius, wringing his hands.

"It's too late!"

The corrupter raised wild eyes toward Helia.

"Too late? Yes, you're doubtless right. That's why I ought to die. Take this dagger and strike me."

"Death would be insufficient to punish you. Another chastisement is required for your unspeakable crimes."

"Order," murmured Blasius, annihilated. "I'll obey, because I love you."

"You will live," decreed the woman. "You will live until the day when you fall by the roadside, of privation and weakness, where the cockroaches and the ants will devour your decomposing cadaver to the last particle of flesh, where animals and humans will avoid your skeleton, abandoned without a sepulcher, with a hiccup of repugnance."

"I'll live, since you wish it," promised the Corrupter.

"Go back to your cell," Helia continued. "Put on your pauper's clothes., and, covered with your sordid rags of old, lean on your staff like the least of beggars and quit this City. Quit it, before your victims have learned the incredible news; for they would bar your path and stone you, and I want you to live in order to suffer and to expiate."

"I will obey," Blasius stammered.

"You will go, without looking back, as far as the harbor where the departing ships are bobbing gently in the morning wind. You will embark on one of them. You will talk to the captain and you will ask him to fulfill, under his orders, one of the vilest and most onerous employments. And you will return to the continents. You will find all my brothers there, all those you snatched from the pleasant life of this island and condemned to mortal exile. But they will drive you away, and you will drag yourself along, miserable and alone, until the last day of your life..."

"Leave!" sobbed Blasius, wringing his hands. "But if I leave, if I execute the frightful order that you have just given me in the name of I know not what divine justice; if I accept this definitive exile and this return among the civilized from whom I escaped so many years ago, I'll never see you again! I'll no longer have before my eyes the languor of your eyelashes, the brightness of your hips, the warmth of your belly, which I feel palpitating after every embrace as the flanks of a hind palpitate after a long flight from hunters. I'll no longer feel the warmth of your elbows trembling around my shoulders; the marmoreal pallor of your throat; the scattered waves of your hair quivering like the feathers of a stray sparrow between my hands. If I leave I'll no longer hear your gasps of amour! I'll no longer hear your voice when we pored over accursed books, detailing me, more loudly as the indecency was augmented, the precepts of sadism and vice in which we both learned the artistry of lust!"

"You'll never hear it again," decreed Helia.

"And you believe," proffered Blasius, dementedly, "that I'm going to push madness as far as obeying you? Rather than lose you, understand me well, I'd a hundred times rather kill you."

"You wouldn't dare!" Helia hurled at him, folding her arms over her breast and defying him.

And Blasius, who had coiled himself up like a feline, pounced on the woman, extending his fingers toward her, hooked like claws.

But she evaded him with a sidestep; and while he got to his feet—for the violence of his miscalculated leap had projected him, sprawling, on to the paving stones—and rubbed his bruised forearms mechanically, she resumed her attitude of provocation, undaunted and grim.

Blasius considered her, an immense stupefaction in his gaze. For a long moment they remained face to face without speaking. And during that exceedingly long moment of mutism, it seemed to Blasius that something mysterious gradually broke within him; that all his fury died, to make way for a pitiable desolation.

He was there, devoid of thought, before the woman who had escaped him forever. And what he sensed dying in his poor fleshless carcass, in his poor demented head, was his pride, his happiness, his hope, his genius, his joy and his strength. Nothing of that remained to him now, he understood, after that definitive exchange of words. He no longer had enough energy to punish her, to dominate her or to defeat her. Nor did he have enough energy to beg her, to convince her and to keep her. There was nothing around him but impotence and annihilation.

And he sensed that the great moment was approaching when he would finally be delivered from all his terrestrial dolors, when the soul and his body were about to return, one to infinity and the other to the maternal earth. Then his hoarse voice became very soft, gradually, and, sitting on a sandal-wood stool incrusted with nacre, he spoke.

He spoke like a moribund man dictating his last will to those around him, and Helia, nonplussed, listened to him, moved in spite of herself by what that voice had of the heart-rending and the *already dead.*

"Have no more fear of anything," he said to her. "In a few moments, I will no longer be anything for you but a miserable thing, and you will look at me without hatred, because you will no longer fear me. I have done you harm, as I have done harm to all those who have approached me. But I have done much more to you than to the others, for they descended deliberately to the degree of degradation to which I wanted to reduce them, without sacrificing anything of myself, and I killed nothing in them but arrogance, whereas I had to kill in you, in order to slake my reckless desire for your flesh, hope, confidence, youth and fervor. And yet, I committed those sins because I loved you, whereas all my previous sins I had committed because I hated their victims unspeakably.

"Today I can measure my ignominy and my baseness; and I agree that I have merited losing a power that I held unduly, and of which I have only ever made use for evil. I agree that I merit the punishment that you have inflicted upon me, and of which I shall shortly die. And I understand that, when your voice will announce my miserable end at the crossroads, those I have degraded will feel suddenly resuscitated; and it is necessary that they should be resuscitated. It is necessary that their souls become noble and bright souls again, and that they curse my memory as that of the most dishonest of their enemies.

"It is necessary that you, whom I love to such a degree that my life only truly commenced on the day when I found you, should return with the man whom you cherish, who will soon recognize his execrable error, to the cabin of foliage where you lived humbly and peacefully. And it is necessary that this city is demolished from top to bottom, and that not the slightest vestige of it any longer remains either on the ground or in the depths of human memory. Obey me when I'm no longer here, since I'm only asking things, this time, that you can grant me."

"I'll grant your wish," promised Helia, in a voice as faint as a breath.

"I loved you," murmured Blasius, in response to that supreme promise. "I loved you more than anything in the world; and I have never loved anyone but you; and now you no longer have the slightest anger against me. Perhaps you will think of me later, in the forest; and perhaps you will sense within you, at those moments, a few tears of absolution and regret welling up within you."

He lay down on the marble slabs and implored her: "Go away. Leave me alone. When the sun strikes the blue-tinted corner of the terrace with its golden blades, you can return to my cell. The one who made you suffer so much will have ended his life."

"What are you going to do, then?" asked Helia, seized by a sudden inexplicable terror.

"Leave me alone," Blasius repeated. "What I'm going to do won't harm anyone, for I've finished henceforth with making tears flow, breaking hearts and degrading souls."

The woman left at those words, her hands joined together, her head bowed, quavering a prayer that she had learned once, long before Blasius and his seven taciturn men had disembarked on the rosy island. While praying, she felt a great sadness added to the terror that already enveloped her

And when the sun had struck the blue-tinted corner of the terrace with its golden blades, she went back into the room, as the Corrupter had decided.

She saw him, his eyes closed, his hands crossed, in a posture of meditation and repose, calm and mild, transfigured like a saint in a chapel.

The she knelt down beside his body and considered it.

His colored face was now as white as magnolia petals, and all the wrinkles creasing his face, previously ravaged by suffering and passions, had disappeared. His physiognomy reflected a profound quietude; and Helia, leaning over the breast of the man, prey to an increasing anxiety, watched for a back-and-forth movement attesting that the Master was still alive.

But the body remained as rigid as the face, and when she posed a fearful finger on the hand that was beside her, Helia perceived that the hand was gradually growing cold.

Yes, the man she had before her was dead.

And death, which divinizes everything, had evened out his angular features, made his jutting cheekbones diaphanous, put a nacreous sheen on his dull and bitten fingernails; placed a slight shadow on his eyelids, closed forever, and had made of that ugly, disgraceful and unharmonious being an imposing and majestic individual. With her funereal hands, Death had spread over him, in abundance, a supernatural beauty by which Helia was presently moved, frightened to find herself alone with that cadaver.

She let her mind drift.

She remembered the whole adventure that had transported her from her cabin of branches to this resplendent palace, and the hours of criminal sensuality in which she had vibrated in Blasius' arms like a satanic instrument in the hands of a hallucinated artiste; and at the thought that all that was finished, that the being powerful enough to reveal those enjoyments to her, that princely luxury and that sumptuousness, would never wake up again from the great black slumber to which he had condemned himself voluntarily; that she would never again hear his harsh voice begging her or insulting her; that she would not feel against her supple body the warmth of that knotty and brutal body, a sob suddenly shook her from head to foot, and, her forehead curbed between her desperate fingers, *she understood*!

That man, whom she believed she had hated with all the force of her soul, she had loved without knowing it.

And she would weep for him for weeks, or months, perhaps for years; and the man for whom she had nearly died of dolor, no longer appeared to her, at present, as anything but a vile and vulgar individual; and she asked herself why death had not chosen him, in spite of his youth and strength, in the place of the great vanquished solitary.

But while she passed over all that again, her flesh, pricked by the memory of the rustic, woke up again, and some of the words once pronounced, while their bodies were mingled on the couch of leaves in their shelter, came back to her, as an odor of fresh earth and flowers rises to the head of that traveler who rediscovers familiar landscapes after years of exile and mourning.

She felt caught between those two passions, between those two cruel dolors; and she panted with anguish at the thought that neither of her lovers would ever possess her again!

But yes! Since Blasius was dead, would not the accursed charm fall of its own accord? Would there not, by the very force of things, be an end to that horrible nightmare, that horrible bewitchment into which he beloved had sunk? What would prevent her, now that the irreparable had just been accomplished, from running to Yann, from unbewitching him, from curing him, from taking him back? And in so doing, would she not be obeying the will of the disappeared? What had he ordered her to do, if not to depart again with the reconquered adored toward the musician wood, and to recommence there, as if it had only been interrupted for a few hours, the old life, in the fullness of joy?

And her thoughts, tumultuous at first, became ordered, and lucid.

For the master, she experienced nothing but pity. And the man she truly loved was the friend of her youth, and by him alone she could live, she was certain of it. And since she knew where to find him, since she knew the dwelling of marble and jasper where he was spending charming hours next to her rival with the blue eyes, she only had to present herself, boldly, and say to him, with her arms open in an irresistible appeal:

"I've come to fetch you!"

And, as if seized by dementia, she launched herself toward the exit.

But as she passed before the post that was manned night and day by the serfs appointed as voice-transmitters and broadcasters, she suddenly stopped.

An insurmountable desire to announce to the entire City her incredible victory over Blasius, to howl its liberation and its redemption, had just assailed her. And, relegating her emotions to the background, dominated by a female vanity stronger than dolor or hope, she evaluated the prestige that her grandiose action would confer on her, in the eyes of everyone, and the gratitude and confusion that would curb the infidel when she declared to him, with her lips close to his: "See what I have done for you!"

And, seizing with a feverish hand, the mouthpiece of the principal loudhailer. Helia began to cry: "The Corrupter is dead! The City is liberated!"

The serfs listened, fearfully.

Two taciturn men who happened to be on the terrace at the moment when she clamored the terrible news launched themselves into the palace, pressing the switches that were needed to trigger the alarm signals, and, soon followed by a troop of servants, invaded Blasius' apartments.

Gradually, from one end of the city to the other, an immense rumor was born.

Men and women, snatched from the warmth of beds, hastened on to the terraces, formed groups at crossroads, and interrogated one another anxiously. And when thousands had gathered around the large serial station that overhung the blue square, Helia spoke.

In a few curt sentences she revealed to them, from its origin to its success, the plan of liberation that she had conceived. She told them about the theft of the transmuting stone, and how she had thrown it into the river, about the Corrupter's remorse and his suicide. And when she had said all that, her arms spread out in the form of a cross to either side of her body, she went on:

"Now the murdered City will revive. Now, all of us will be able to rediscover our hearts, our intelligence, our will, our nobility and our liberty. All together, let us go to the great arena, and let a sublime choir celebrate and carry to the skies the joy of our deliverance!"

When she had finished, all of them looked at one another, confused, their hearts constricted and their faces distorted,

But suddenly, from a compact group, as imperious as a clarion call, a voice rang out:

"That woman is lying! The man who was able to conceive and build such a City, the man who commanded wealth, power and humanity entire, could not have killed himself! He could not have committed suicide, because he was overflowing with life and love and magnificence, and he was Life itself. Do not believe these insidious declarations, for I tell you that, in truth, it is her who killed him!"

And Helia, suddenly becoming livid, twisted her fingers; she had just recognized, in the man who spoke and accused her, the beloved individual for whom she had accomplished the formidable theft.

"No!" she cried. "I have not killed him! I swear to you on our love, you who know me, since we lived the same existence of privation and poverty together for long years I swear to you that Blasius really has killed himself, and that before dying he gave me an order to leave him alone in his cell..."

"Don't believe any of it!" roared the voice. "That woman bears within her all hypocrisy and all lies, and I can attest to it, since I have lived with her, as she told you, for years. Her duplicity and her cruelty are unfathomable, and I do not recall owing a single moment of real happiness to her."

On hearing those abominable words, Helia put her hands to her heart. A long groan emerged from her breast, and in order not to fall she was obliged to lean on the iron balustrade that surrounded the terrace with a brown circle.

At the same moment, before she had articulated a syllable of protest, dolorous appeals sprang from the dwelling, passing over her unkempt head like a flock of bloody birds, and made the multitude shiver.

"On your knees!" ordered the invisible weepers. "You are going to see, for the last time, the man you loved."

And through the great bay, both battens of which opened, porters clad in black appeared.

They held on their robust shoulders a platform of sandalwood covered by a violet colored carpet. And, very white, his hands crossed, his eyes closed, clad in his humble monastic robe and shod in his red leather sandals, Blasius was sleeping the eternal slumber on that platform.

At that apparition, a vast sob as profound as the plaint of the ocean whipped by winter winds rose from the crowd. The men bared their heads; the women veiled their faces with their multicolored mantles; and while the taciturn men deposited their funereal burden on the paving stones of the terrace, the hundred thousand watchers bowed, their foreheads in the golden dust of the avenue. A prodigiously moving silence now succeeded the moans of grief floating over the city. And next to Blasius, in a posture of despair, Helia sobbed silently.

And, more vibrant than a funeral hymn, in the midst of that meditation and that anguish, Yann's voice vibrated again.

"We were trailing in poverty and waiting, like beasts, for the end of a life without hope; and a man came who extracted us from adversity, who gave us in this incomparable city a peace, a wealth and a happiness such that none among us had ever dared to one imagine one so great. And in exchange, that man only asked us to recognize his power and render homage to his heart, and not, as that prostitute pretends, to abdicate all independence, all dignity and all pride.

"By virtue of the crime of that woman, avid to avenge herself on a lover who did not love her, since he abandoned her without regret, the Master is dead, and we shall never see him again."

"You're lying!" moaned Helia.

But the other, seeing the effect that his accusations had produced on the audience, continued in a voice that became louder and louder:

"Yes! That woman has caused our ruination, as she has caused the death of the man who was our father; and because of her we will have to leave here tomorrow, resume our terrestrial chains, to recommence the ingrate and degrading labor from which we were in the process of dying when he came to find us; to become similar again to those who sleep in hovels, heaped up pell-mell; who live on scraps and spoiled meat, who dress in ragged and discolored clothes, and who only know, instead of joys, uncertainty and terror of the future."

At those words the woman uttered shrill clamors and the men hid their tear-bathed faces in their hands.

"In truth," Yann proclaimed, "that woman has committed a terrible sin, and I attest that she must die. And it is necessary that you, who are listening to me, attest it with me."

And with a single voice, like the roar of a tempest, the crowd repeated: "We attest it! That woman must die!"

"But she must not die," the judge concluded, "like an ordinary criminal, who is hanged high and short, or guillotined. She must pass through our midst; the young women, the children and the old men must stone her, and she must go to die in her clearing beside her cabin, as a rabbit struck by the hunter dies at the foot of its burrow."

And, bounding all the way to Helia, who gazed at him, bewildered, her eyelids swollen, he dragged her by the hair to the bottom of the steps of the terrace, while the multitude opened up before him in two waves. And when the inhabitants of the city had drawn aside, leaving the spacious avenue free, the renegade shoved the condemned woman along it, who was now plastering her hands and forearms over her face in order to protect herself.

Suddenly, a stone departing from that fratricidal swell hit her shoulder. She uttered a howl; and, like a poor hind fleeing before a pack of hounds, she started running straight ahead toward the gates of the city.

And other stones hit her legs and her arms, which were bloodied, and tore the divine curve of her breast, bit into her rounded loins, and punctured her abdomen. And behind her, a long trail of blood soiled the parvis.

Some, finding a simple lapidation insufficient for such a sin, covered her with excrement as she passed; and over her pure forehead and along her shoulders the color of bronze and sunlight, the faeces trickled in noxious stripes.

She groaned as she advanced, and the stones continued to rain down upon her; and her groans became weaker and weaker, and more heart-rending. And behind her, forcing her to advance in spite of her suffering and her debility, Yann harassed her from a distance with the aid of a long spike, the extremity of which penetrated by degrees into her back, causing her intolerable wounds.

That ignoble lapidation lasted for two hours.

When Helia had gone through the gates of the city, dragging herself on the stump of a leg—for a young woman had broken the ankle with the impact of a stone—they immediately closed behind her. Deafened by the maledictions of the serfs and the inhabitants, wounded again by the last projectiles thrown at her through the bards by the most furious of the lapidators, she found herself alone in the open country.

She fell on the edge of a ditch; iridescent flies and sumptuous scarabs settled or crawled over her wounds, and their bites were so painful that she was obliged to get up again.

She set forth again along the path, making extraordinary efforts to reach the clearing where the renegade had prophesied that she would finish her life, for she wanted to render her last sigh before the cabin of branches that had been witness for many years to her delight and her ecstasy.

The sunlight played in the foliage and peppered the mint of the woods with gold coins.

Dragonflies fluttered with a silky rustle around her forehead and her shoulders soiled with ordure, and amid the branches amorous doves were cooing. Everything smelled good. The joy of living burst forth in the smallest stem, the thinnest trunk of a lemon tree or a birch, and the dying woman, clutching at bushes that bent under her bloody fragility, advanced at the price of unspeakable suffering.

As she sensed life escaping her, she perceived, some fifteen paces away, shining in the sunlight, he clearing and the cabin, on the roof of which young buds were agitating gently. Aiding herself which her hands, from the torn fingers of which the nails were hanging like shreds of bloody nacre, dragging her poor broken leg behind her, she crawled; and that reptilian slither required more than an hour, so paralyzed was she by her weakness.

And when she had reached the threshold of the hut, she contemplated with the already vitreous eye that remained to her—a stone had put out the other before her emergence from the city—the accumulation of leaves and branches, and all the glare that was about to become for her, in an instant, the great endless obscurity...

Her head fell back on the foot of a sage which ants were running, like little black dots. A sigh as faint as the breath of a new-born child exhaled from her toothless mouth and her martyrized lips.

Her hands scratched the gilded sand for a couple of seconds, and she died.

IX

While the little soul of the lapidated woman, delivered from its terrestrial torments, mingled with the aerial turbulence, flew among the perfumes and the breezes toward the ineffable regions, the multitude rushed to assault the subterrains where Blasius' treasures lay, after having massacred Rudolph and the seven taciturn men, who tried in vain to resist them.

At the contact of the human claws, the heaps of gold and the piles of precious stones collapsed with the sound of a cascade.

Each of the serfs, having filled his tunic and stuffed the canvas sacks of which he had gone in search hastily in his dwelling, fled, clutching to his breast the precious treasure that nothing henceforth would increase, and barricaded himself in his cellar or his bedroom.

The subterrains contained so much gold and so many jewels that the execrable pillage went on for five days and five nights.

When the last arrivals perceived that the galleries were empty, they precipitated themselves, guided by Yann, into Blasius' palace and the one that had been Helia's abode.

They carried away the hangings, the works of art, the gold frames of mirrors, glass cases and windows; and as the fruits of that rapine seemed insufficient to them, they gathered in a horde and marched against their more favored companions. They broke down their doors, killed them all, set fire to their apartments, and finally threw themselves on one another, making use, in order to cut one another's throats or bludgeon one another to death, both the most advanced and the most rudimentary weapons.

The abject melee was prolonged or five days and five nights, exactly the same time as the pillage.

The streets, the crossroads and the terraces were strewn with cadavers, still clutching between their stiffened phalanges fragment of rubies, amethysts, sapphires and large gold nuggets.

The rare survivors embarked, revolvers in hand, on luggers and yachts, and, watching one another grimly, like wild beasts lying in ambush, they resumed across the glaucous ocean, under scarlet clouds, the road to the civilized continents.

And the twice murdered city, the city dead forever, remained alone, with its thousands of victims, on the edge of the river, alone and deserted and silent, like a great marble coffin, amid the heavy odor of orange trees and the warmth of dusks...

THE DEATH OF THE SUN

And the sun itself will be extinguished.

Millions of years ago the last man and the last woman had rendered their souls after frightful death-throes.

Grotesque survivors, pitiful debris of a humankind whose decline had accelerated from one generation to the next, they had died lying full length in some shelter from the ice, and the great wild beasts that appeared from time to time on the desolate shores where the hairy bimanes had taken refuge had carried away their shriveled cadavers, roaring, in order to feed on them.

Now, nothing more remained of what had once been thought: architecture, poetry and science. The monuments erected by the peoples of Europe had slowly turned to dust under the continuous effort of the centuries.

The cities where multitudes had gathered; the countryside over which the laborers had driven their electric tractors from dawn to dusk, and where the artisans manipulated their tools and their improved machines; the oceans where ships vaster than villages had raced, cleaving the waters with their sharpened prows; the air, where the airbuses, aviettes, monoplanes, hydroplanes and flying trucks throbbed to the impact of the winds, had all become an immense desert.

Nothing in the fields once so fertile, nothing on the banks of rivers and streams, once so verdant, nothing on the once-wooded mountainsides, the slopes of undulating hills and the hollows of valleys.

Not one plant, not one tree, not one flower. No birdsong. No animal cry. Only the moaning of a wind, growing colder and colder as the years went by, troubled at times the white silence of the world devoid of inhabitants and frontiers. It passed by, attaching its plaint to the asperities of ravines, rebounding from peak to peak, and went to die away, swirling, in some unknown location, only to return, more funereal and more violent than ever, after a fantastic voyage around the world.

Several times, civilization and progress, obedient to some immutable ad prodigious law, had endowed human races by turns with their benefits and their deadly improvements. One after another, the white, black, yellow, olive or brick-colored peoples had murdered one another mercilessly in order to steal power, wealth and authority.

The vanquished gradually fell back into primitive barbarity, vegetating for a more or less long time in misery and opprobrium. Then, insensibly, they recommenced their formidable endeavor of renascence, invented new things, underwent physical and mental metamorphoses; and, after millennia, resumed the foremost rank among humans, until the moment when other hands, having accomplished the same labor as them, dispossessed them and reduced them again to their former degradation and abjection.

In the world, which had now become a vast extent of snow and ice, kings, emperors, empresses and courtiers had seen the tremulous crowds prostrating themselves before their scepters and helmets. Prophets, usurpers, adventurers, illuminati and madmen had electrified those crowds with their eloquence and their promises, and, with bloody cries, the masses in revolt had rushes to assault thrones.

Believing that they were inaugurating the triumph of justice and goodness they had favored the designs of those who made fools of them or harmed them unconsciously, until the day when, weary of suffering under a master, they had got rid of one and given themselves another, almost always crueler and more malevolent than the previous one.

And thus the great cycle of earthly dolors and joys had terminated. The last tribes, returned to the same degree of brutality and ugliness as the first humans, had gradually become extinct. Domestic animals, returned to the wild state, had served as pretty for carnivores; and the carnivores themselves, no longer finding the wherewithal to live when the last livestock escaped from byres and meadows had been immolated and torn apart, and disappeared with vertiginous rapidity.

The cycle of the seasons had slowed down.

The warmth that had bathed and fecundated central Europe had declined rapidly, disorganized, and drawing the order of natural things toward the equator. And all the way to the southern extremity of the word there was no longer anything now but cold and tempests. Moonlight no longer struck the mute plains with its yellow fingers.

And the sun itself, which had created so many forests, so much moss, so much superb vegetation, grew paler from one year to the next. Instead of the dazzling and generous flame of old, it only poured over the globe a wan light, scarcely stronger than the extinct light of the moon; and if living beings had wanted to warm themselves therein, they would have remained vainly beneath its rays for hours on end without feeling any warmth.

Nothing any longer remained of the Earth, in that moribund era, but an old white bear, bicentenarian, as thin as a rock, as jagged as a ridge, from which the dirty skin was falling off in lumps, and whose teeth, by dint of gnawing the mosses and lichens that had been its only nourishment since birth, were being gradually worn away.

When it agitated its pear-shaped head and rummaged with its pointed muzzle in the fissures of the hills, it resembled a mobile block of ice; it had lived so long in solitude that it had never been able to growl. When it was exhausted by fatigue, it lay down no matter where, got up again at daybreak, and went on, thoughtless and devoid of a goal, moving straight ahead until the following night.

Wandering and grazing thus, it had traveled almost all regions, crossing the beds of dried up rivers, lakes and dreams—for water had withdrawn from the earth a long time ago. It drank snow, peeled an excrescence of russet lichen from the ground with the underside of its tongue, raised its crimson eyes toward the wan sky, and sometimes crawled in the manner of a snake between two masses of hardened snow in order to shelter from the wind that bit it hatefully.

That morning, it had slept beneath a granite shelter, and, poorly rested from its travels of the previous day, its sides hollowed out by hunger, it had raised itself up on its paws with difficulty.

Extraordinarily, however, day did not dawn, and, in that quasi-obscurity, the old solitary sniffed around in vain, without being able to rediscover its route.

On the horizon, instead of the roseate line usually bordering the denuded mountains, of the pale light that did not warm and did not dazzle, it saw nothing but a gray veil extending from one end of the distance to the other, scarcely brighter than the night. One might have thought that obstinate clouds were hiding the sun, at which it was accustomed to stare without lowering its eyes. Over the entire Earth, the same gray veil extended.

The great wind that had been blowing for days and nights over the immense steppe had gradually eased. And there was silence everywhere: an anguishing silence through which none of the sonorities that had once composed it passed, which were life, joy and freshness, and which had seemed to give a soul to the beautiful dawns of olden times.

The bear advanced, and as it advanced, it had the confused impression that the obscurity through which it was walking was gradually becoming denser. A rigorous and terrible cold enveloped the expanse. It became more and more intense, and the old solitary, whose jaws were grinding together with dolor, could scarcely drag itself along.

It browsed effortfully on a patch of shriveled moss and, with its desperately wide eyes, tried to see into the distance.

In the distance, there was a great shadow departing from the line of the horizon, gradually extinguishing the blue edge that bordered the mountains. That great shadow rose toward the zenith, extended to the left and the right, and covered everything, mountains, plains and valleys.

It effaced the silhouette of dead trees that had remained upright for centuries, coated with a layer of shiny icy, fossilized by time. It blurred the curve of promontories, the tapering of estuaries, the undulation of hillocks, and the indentation of rocky crests.

In that increasingly profound night, long yellow flashes of lightning suddenly sprang forth, designing a corner of a valley or the outline of a branch, and vanishing as quickly as they had linked up.

Then there was nothing but blackness: a more profound blackness than nocturnal darkness.

Horrified, the solitary stopped.

A cold more intense that the cold that it was attempting to escape by advancing gripped its flanks; and as that cold cut off its respiration, the old plantigrade panted and vacillated at every step, like a drunken animal.

Long hours went by, and when the blackness had become so profound that it fell upon things and the last being with the weight of a leaden mantle, a prodigious phenomenon was suddenly produced.

From all the corners of the horizon, turquoise, orange, lapis-lazuli, ocher and ruby gleams were born. Those gleams rose toward the zenith like immense dazzling plumes; and, having arrived at their apogee, were soldered to one another with a silent sizzle. One might have thought it an aurora borealis of unimaginable proportions, beneath which the entire Earth was illuminated and ablaze, but which did not emit any warmth.

At the impact of those millions of colored lances, the ground underwent a metamorphosis. The slightest details of landscapes, the slightest curves of dried up river beds and desiccated lakes, took on a gripping relief, and after an interval of time equivalent to a day of old, the entire terrestrial globe was nothing but an incandescence.

Dazzled and hallucinated by all the colors, the bear wandered over plains and hills, stumbling here and getting up again there, snapping things up as if it wanted to steal from the meager vegetation that still covered the terrestrial crust everything that it found before it.

Suddenly, a formidable conflagration was produced. While a rumble reverberated throughout the illimitable solitudes like a superhuman thunder, the luminous mass disintegrated, and dispersed under the gusts that had begun to blow. And again there was night, a night more terrifying than the previous obscurities. It was the definitive night

And, lying on a wide granite ledge, the bear waited, roaring in terror, for the first time in its existence, at the end of the world.

Frightfully contracted, the rocky walls cracked at every increase in the lethal cold. And the hoarse growls of the plantigrade, punctuated the horror of that monstrous agony, like a funereal appeal, like a supreme adieu uttered by the moribund creature to the sun, which had just been extinguished forever.

BY WIRELESS

I

To come one morning, when one's name is Patrice-Hector-Hugues de Beaumont and one has had "a very Parisian physiognomy" for years, and bury oneself in the sinister gorge of Lagarde-Viaur in Aveyron, and to lead the existence of a recluse there, with one's older sister Alexandrine-Ysolde and three wolfhounds, would have seemed paradoxical to anyone who had known me before.

And yet, it will be six years ago this evening that two heavy trucks brought my furniture to this manor, hanging like an eagle's nest on the flank of the red mountain.

This is where I have lived since then. This is where all my memories have been progressively effaced, all the one-familiar faces and all the details of my first life. It is here that all terrestrial images will suddenly be effaced for me on the day when the great Architect judges it good to extinguish with a breath the light of my eyes. And it is here that I shall sleep the ineffable black slumber, here that I shall sleep, finally delivered from all dolor, all remorse and all revolt; and I shall sleep forever in the rocky hollow of which I have resolved to make my tomb.

My life?

It resembles that of all rich men.

My ancestors—for I have multiple blazoned ancestors—were, by turns, crusaders, navigators, gentlemen of the plow, idlers and warriors.

My father, dead at forty as a consequence of his excessive debauchery, left my sister and myself in the power of a mother who was to die some years after him and a copious fortune. In addition to the ancestral domain situated four leagues from Tours, we possessed hunting land in Sologne, a town house in the Avenue de la Bois and a plush villa in Deauville. Our annual income counted among the largest in France. A multimillionaire, young, becoming, intelligent enough and cultivated enough to appreciate at their true value the stupidity and vacuity of people in the milieu in which destiny forced me to move, I could satisfy without merit the costliest and craziest caprices.

I maintained notorious prostitutes. Like everyone else, I seduced, in order to abandon them subsequently, shop-girls, milliners and poor girls. I lingered over the commerce of several ladies of mature age, who initiated me into high quality libertinage. I had the normal adventures with many demoiselles of the bourgeoisie, business and the nobility. I was a member of the Jockey Club, and my mail-coach, in the defunct days of Drags, was immutable classified among the most sensational and the most perfect.

Like the majority of men of my age and status, I acquired a reckless passion for automobiles. I participated personally in several famous races, and, if I did not come back covered in laurels, I nevertheless conquered a rank that won me the esteem of true sportsmen and a certain reputation in the corporative periodicals. I was familiar, along white highways, with the intoxication of speed, the insensate pride of burning rubber to the roar of my engine, drunk on gasoline, through villages and hamlets, over hills and across plains; the dazzle of sunrises and sunsets bathing with gold and blood the polished flanks of my Voisin; and the joy of acclamations howled by crowds; and the glory of arrivals in the outskirts of the capital, between hedges of gigolos, cooking pots and drunken workers; and bilious compliments of aces of the wheel; and banquets with speeches; and horrible accidents from which people emerged crippled, disfigured, finished...

Oh, that April morning when, amid the streaming spring, we flew over the road to Ventimiglia at more than a hundred and fifty an hour, and where my competitor Henry Beckett, the English champion, in order to overtake me, gave the steering-wheel the misfortunate wrench that hurled him upon me! How and why did I not die immediately in that terrible impact? What vital energies, what instincts of conservation did I carry within me to have resisted the extraordinary violence of the collision, the suffering of my entire, atrociously broken body? How was I able to wake up from that cataleptic sleep in which I was plunged for more than forty-eight hours, and support the surgical intervention, which, the Art affirmed, I ought not to have survived, and to languish for six whole months in that sanitarium, the atmosphere of which sickened me and depressed me as much as my injuries themselves?

How was I able, how did I dare, on the day of my release, to retake my place in my home, to reappear before my friends, to speak to them, to shake their hands? How was I able, how did I dare, to present myself at the home of my mistress, the abject and splendid Madeleine de Vinci, and not kill her, and not kill myself, on hearing her scream of terror, and not kill them all—all the others—on seeing the movements of repulsion and disgust with which they underlined my horrific appearance?

I don't know.

I only know one thing, which is that I went away again, from them, from her, sticking my handkerchief over my face to stifle my sobs and to hide my face from passers-by; that I went back to my town house, coiled up like a wild beast at bay in a corner of the car; and that I lived, in the week that followed those superhuman ordeals, the most heart-rending hours of my youth.

For an entire month I was cloistered in my bedroom, deaf to the bewildered exhortations of my sister, the poignant consolations of Justin, my aged manservant, the caresses of my dogs; and I did not want to leave the house, or take my meals in the dining room, or receive the man who had been my inseparable companion-in-arms, my beloved friend, the man for whom nothing that frightened the others existed, who always

171

maintained the same fraternal tenderness for me in spite of the frightful catastrophe, and who begged me so sadly and so softly to open my door to him—the great musician Antoine Lux.

For an entire month I envisaged the most demented and the most absurd hypotheses in order to discover a means of suffering less. One after another I summoned to my home the most illustrious reconstructors of faces, the most adroit and most audacious experts in rhinoplasty. I promised them half my fortune if they contrived to correct, to some extent, the repulsive deformation of my face, to render me, not—alas!— as agreeable as I might have been before my fall, but acceptable, supportable, in the eyes of those who shuddered and turned away on seeing me. All of them, after having palpated, examined and poked me from every angle, shook their heads in a melancholy fashion. Nothing was possible. I was physically irreparable. Even those who had accomplished surgical miracles during the war confessed their impotence to diminish or attenuate my disfigurement in the feeblest measure. I was condemned without appeal.

To begin with, I resolved to commit suicide. But, too cowardly or too fond of life to settle on that extreme solution, I orientated myself in another direction. There, I would certainly find what I sought: burial; darkness—living death, if I might express it thus.

It was a Sunday morning, a bright and joyous Sunday in August, when my decision was made.

I had spent the whole of the previous night in reflection. I had interrogated myself without weakness. I had weighed with equal impartiality the motives that impelled me to the tragic resolution, and those that might deflect me from it. Those interior conflicts had only confirmed me in my initial design, exacerbating my frantic desire to go, to efface myself, to disappear as quickly as possible, to disappear forever.

Over breakfast, my mind as calm as if it were a matter of a banal affair, I exposed my project to my sister. I explained at length the increasing acuity of my suffering, the certainty, more profoundly anchored within me every day, that those immolated in my fashion ought to break in a definitive fashion with society, to create another existence on the margin of their fellows, to seek, in retreats that rumors, passions and quotidian torments never reached, the peace that I could not discover anywhere else.

I described to her the appeasements that would descend gradually into my soul, the resignation to which the pitiless regulation of the household would lead me insensibly; the consolations that incessant contact with those with whom I had lived until the last minute, and the knowledge of their infinite celestial pity, could not bring me. Certainly, I would doubtless regret, at first, all those I loved today. I would only accept reluctantly humility, poverty, mortification, abnegation and the total renunciation of all worldly things. But those would only be temporary annoyances, and I would soon be able to discipline myself, like all the others, and practice the regulation penitence and privations without a murmur.

I did not dissimulate from my dear Alexandrine-Ysolde that my chagrin in quitting her without any hope of seeing her again would be profound and ineffaceable, dominating all the others, For her part, I knew her well enough to know that her dolor would only equal mine; and it required a considerable energy for me not to cry: "I'll stay!" on seeing her bosom, in the course of my poignant revelation, lifted by sobs, and her eyes inundated by tears that, poor soul, she did not try to hide or hold back.

But anything! Anything rather than suffer as I was suffering.

Those into whose company I wanted to go did not bear within them any of the common faults. They did not know cruelty, mockery, dissimulation or perfidy. They knew that ugliness, that physical imperfection, is trivial, and that all that counts with the divine Judge are moral ulcers, degradations of the spirit and the soul. A cell in which to meditate at my ease, a meager bed on which to rest for a few hours a night my definitively tamed flesh; rough garments, invariable for the most rigorous cold and the most excessive heat; rope sandals in which winter could freely bite my reddened feet; and, above all, the shadow of the cloister, the long corridors in which I could circulate soundlessly, while telling my rosary and chanting, with my entire being extended toward redemptive Heaven, words of renunciation and forgetfulness.

Tomorrow, before noon, I shall knock on the door of the monastery.

This is the last day that Alexandrine-Ysolde and I shall spend together in that sumptuous house. And, surrounding her fragile head with my two hands, I swear to forgive myself for the harm that I am doing her.

She lets me finish, shaken by a new crisis of sobs. Then she wipes her eyes, draws me toward her tenderly, considers me for a long moment, and, in a low voice, asks me: "Do you have faith?"

Nonplussed by that question, so simple and so unexpected, I remain silent at first. Then, as if I were certain of what I was proposing, I reply: "I'll acquire it."

"I hope so," she moans. "But what tortures I, who have none, will endure far away from you!"

"Don't talk to me about that, I beg you. I need all my courage; and it's necessary, whatever the torture of your soul, that you help me to conserve it, instead of seeking to diminish or extinguish it."

"I'll do as you ask, my poor Patrice," Alexandrine-Ysolde replies, "but I didn't suppose that you could resolve yourself to such a harsh and vain extremity. I thought that you would have pity for me."

None of my sister's supplications succeed in undermining my energy. Very calmly, in the blue-black silence of the night, I make my last will known to her. Together, we make our dispositions to leave to others whom we cherish and who, alone, will remain faithful to us and strong in adversity, all of that which, if we neglected the necessary formalities would revert by law—rightfully!—to distant relatives, people we had neither seen nor known, and who would bless our death while pocketing the windfall that had suddenly fallen upon them.

Those who will receive our fortune will, I am certain, weep for us even in the utmost depths of their heart, and I know them to be worthy of the ultimate proof of affection that we are giving them.

The task accomplished, we hug one another for a long time, my sister and I, and I retire to my room.

I was received yesterday by the superior.

After a rather long wait, in the course of which I got up several times to flee, without being able to break the occult force that imprisoned me in the parloir, the doorkeeper monk came to fetch me. He introduced me into a room of medium proportions, with whitewashed walls, completely devoid of the pious images and simulacra that I expected to encounter here.

The superior is a man of about sixty, tall, thin and ascetic, and crowned with gray hair. Beneath the habit of coarse cloth tightened at the waist by a hempen cord, one divines a body obliged to the fasting, mortification and discipline by means of which the savior's elect arrive, it is affirmed in the abode of the Innocent and the Blessed. His bony fingers, posed one upon another, seem to be searching along the coarse fabric of the long sleeves for some illusory mud, in order to cling on to it with an obstinate scratching, like shipwreck victims to the side of a dismasted vessel.

I know nothing about him except that his name is Athanase and that he imposes a pitiless rule on his subordinates and his novices. It is said that his speech is magnetic; it is claimed that he gives an example to those around him of all the virtues that the recluses committed to his authority must practice; and it is whispered, in a locale neighboring the somber retreat, that he has been living for more than thirty years, buried between these walls, in the wake of an adventure involving a woman in which his best friend found death.

I gaze at those prominent cheekbones, and those eyes sunk in their orbits like nocturnal raptors in the hollow of a rock; those eyes from which a radiance so sharp flows that they become, after two or three seconds, insupportable to those who receive it; those eyes, which inspect me from head to toe, with the intention of penetrating and chilling me.

Father Athanase has spoken.

In curt sentences, he interrogates me about my past life. I tell him in detail about the horrible catastrophe in consequence of which I have come to seek shelter under the vaults of this convent from disenchantment and despair. I confess my secret dolors to him, my rancor and my revolts, my nights of insomnia and the reasons that are impelling me to beg him to grant me a place in the midst of his brethren, in order that I can forget, regather courage, and be reborn.

While I am imploring him he listens to me impassively. Not one muscle in his face quivers at the spectacle of my suffering. Not one word of consolation, affection or encouragement emerges from his shaven lips; and still his fingers are scratching the coarse cloth of his habit, and still his eyes are spearing me with the same radiation, under the persistence of which my eyelids gradually close. I am literally hypnotized by the monk.

And when I have finished the narration of my Calvary, I remain there, in front of him, trembling with anguish; and I murmur, in bewildered supplication:

"Welcome me, Father. I no longer have any salvation except in you.

Only then did the mute skeleton steer slowly toward me. His hooked fingers gripped my shoulders and, in a voice as low and as grave as the pedal note of a harmonium, he replied to me:

"God's mercy in infinite, my son; and if he orders us to open our refuge to you, believe that we will obey him. But have you reflected, before coming to find me, on everything that that a life that you want to enter in consequence of a simple disappointment involves of sacrifice and ordeals?"

"I have reflected on that, Father. Those ordeals, those sacrifices, I accept in advance, without a murmur."

"Have you thought hard about what you are leaving behind you, the heartbreak of those who will weep for you until their last breath, and who will perhaps learn of your agony or your death one day without it being possible to run to you to see you again, to speak to you and embrace you, before the great final departure?"

"I have thought about that, Father. Those who love me and whom I shall leave behind have been informed of my resolution, and, not having been able to deflect me from it, they have accepted all its consequences, with a desolate but resigned heart."

"Them, perhaps—but you, my son? You, young, rich, accustomed to the most entire independence? You who have grown up in the wake of Satan, and who suddenly claim to be touched by grace, are you certain of bearing within you the irresistible vocation without which one cannot become, as it is necessary that one sometimes becomes among us, either a martyr or an apostle?"

"I am certain of it, Father. What you order me to do, I will do without argument. Where you tell me to go, I will go without looking back, even if I must find death at the end of my route."

"The road that you want to follow is difficult, and many men who believed they had the strength to travel it have abandoned it at the first obstacles. The man who does not carry the divine spirit within him is not veritably elected. Reflect carefully."

"I ask to don the habit, Father. Neither the monastic rule not the cilice frightens me."

"If you can answer for yourself, my son, we will be glad to welcome you and to love you. Get up, then, and follow me. I will show you the dwelling that will be yours, provisionally, and will become so definitively if Providence suggests to you the supraterrestrial courage to pronounce your vows at the expiration of your novitiate.

And, under the conduct of Père Athanase, I visited the convent from top to bottom.

No one along the oozing corridors. No one in the opening of the capitulary halls, the chapel, the refectory or the cells. One might think that this house is a house of the dead. And it is here that I'm going to stay? It is here, on these cracked flagstones, under these arches covered in Latin dicta, in these moldy courtyards where the sun never drinks the damp, under these yews, these cypresses, these lindens, where not the smallest bird every twitters, where the only perceptible rustle of wings is that of the last leaves swirling over the soft ground in the autumnal wind? It is here, next to this monk with the desiccated hands, that I must henceforth spend my days, in close company with strangers who will be my improvised brethren and with whom I shall rub shoulders without being able or being obliged to learn anything of their souls, their past, their memories, their joys or their sadness?

It's impossible! I'll never be able to accept that. I'm going to leave. I'm going to return to Alexandrine-Ysolde, throw myself into her arms, as of old, when I was small, when I was mischievous, and cry to her, between two sobs: "Protect me!"

Go back!

But to go back would be to run toward further affronts, further shames, further torments. No! It's necessary that I stay here, whatever the cost. It's necessary that I succeed in killing that which is killing me, destroying that which is breaking me, in rejecting by means of a superhuman effort everything that I can no longer do, everything that I can no longer bear, all the dolor that, at least, will not follow me in this place.

And when the lugubrious tour is finished, when I find myself again, forehead moist and heart beating forcefully, in the whitewashed cell of Père Athanase; when, after a truce of a few minutes at the end of which I am able to recover my spirits, the voice of the superior asks me the terrible question:

"Well, my son, what have you decided?"

All my will, all my muscles contract in a dolorous effort; and, in a sort of croak, I reply:

"I'm ready. I desire more ardently than ever to become one of you."

"May your prayers by granted," the superior concludes, sketching in flight in the direction of my forehead a sign of the cross as angular as a threat. "You shall enter tomorrow."

For twenty-four hours I have been wearing the robe of a novice.

I have renounced my aristocratic name, and the forename of Patrice that Alexandrine-Ysolde took so much pleasure repeating, and which she chose herself. For those who surround me, since I no longer exist for the others, I call myself Irmin-Anaclet: Irmin-Anaclet, novice. I occupy, at the end of a secluded gallery, cell number 20, the narrowest, the most sordid and the most dismal. Others, I know, look out upon corners where a few trees are finishing their depletion, and from which one can perceive a patch of sky. For me, nothing. Not a scrap of azure. No courtyard. An immense wall that looms up directly in front of the loophole through which, logically, daylight ought to reach me, but which forbids that clarity with all of its unhealthy extent. I can see nothing but that wall, green-tinted by the centuries; and so long as this cell remains mine—which is to say, until the hour of my vows—I shall be condemned to this gloom...what am I saying? to this uninterrupted darkness, for daylight never enters my abode in the morning or the afternoon, nor in the resplendent minutes of sunset.

And why should I complain, in any case, of this burial? Have I not demanded, myself, in entering here, the most rigorous treatment, the most bitter fate? I have demanded it not only in the name of the humility in which I nourish the design of living henceforth, but also and above all because, having made at the outset a princely donation to the community, I understand that the obol in question does not exempt me from any of the ennuis, any of the chores, or any of the tasks devolved to those who surround me My desire, in any case, have been granted in the fullest measure. There is no base work, no odious labor, to which I am not constrained. Since my arrival here, all the monks, obedient to a mysterious order, have joined forces in order to make my life, already tenebrous and

179

lugubrious, an existence even more painful that the one for which Père Athanase's discourse had brutally prepared me.

And, evening having come, when I fall back into solitude after an irritating commerce with all those wearers of habits and hoods, when I review, with my head between my hands, the events of the day, I wonder whether these men are not veritably exceeding their rights, and whether the novitiate that is being rendered so harsh for me is not a novitiate instituted specifically for me, outside the rule and the discipline of this grim abode.

I have searched in vain among them for the slightest sign of sympathy, the slightest hint of benevolence. There is nothing confronting me but closed mouths, frowning eyebrows and hostile gazes. Is that how the forbearance and fraternity, in the name of which the son of the Virgin and the carpenter of Nazareth accepted to be crucified, are construed in these holy houses? Is it thus that the words of the gospel are translated in these refuges forbidden to outsiders? Is it thus that one applies to one's neighbor the adorable precept to the illuminate of genius: "Love one another!"

I have lost myself in conjectures in order to explain to myself their attitude, their physiognomy, their conduct. All of it surpasses my understanding. The subtlety that was once lent to me, when it was a matter of analyzing and judging my entourage, has become insufficient in this retreat. And, without grasping anything, I submit to the insults, the offences and the quotidian knocks.

It is in the refectory, above all, that the antipathy of the members of the community in my regard is manifest. The tonsured individuals who hazard places alongside me during the brief midday and evening meals pass me the tinplate dishes with such discourtesy that a mad desire takes hold of me, almost every time, to grab them by the throat, tip them back over the oak table, worn away by the friction of elbows and blackened by the drops of gruel gradually incrusted there, and cry out to them, eyeball to eyeball: "Why do you detest me? What have I done to you?"

But I do not have the courage. And, although my dolor at sensing myself hated and vilified by these false elect, by these cheapjack saints, increases from day to day, I submit to all that as a merited punishment. On high, I am sure, the One who can do anything will take account of these injustices. It is in his presence that I will forget the harsh terrestrial proofs, and in his name, in the name of his divine orders, I pardon those who offend me, as he pardoned those who made him perish igno-miniously.

It is when my crises of despair reach their paroxysm that the memory of possessions voluntarily abandoned and wellbe-ing voluntarily sacrificed haunts me with an extraordinary violence.

I see again my house in Avenue du Bois, its magnificent perron, its three marble stairways on which the richest and most perfect Oriental carpets muffle the sound of footsteps I see again my ceilings decorated by the greatest painters, and all the old furniture that Alexandrine-Ysolde and I collected devotedly; and the vast rooms in which everything that the capital counts of the most noble, the most ardent, the most cultivated and the most sensible was gathered. I remember the Sunday mornings when, leaning voluptuously on my wrought iron balustrades, I watched the ebb and flow along the avenue, like a noisy and colorful tide, of all that idle and pretentious Paris, condemned by snobbery and amour to appear and circu-late at fixed hours on thoroughfares reeking of gasoline, bitu-men and human odors. Oh, they had made no vow of chastity, nor of kindness, nor of pity, nor of frankness! Among them there was debauchery, depravity, hypocrisy, pederasty and tribadism, circulating ostentatiously beneath my gaze. Among those people there was wickedness, cruelty, sadism, envy, slander, jealousy and abjection!

But those wicked individuals, in sum, were worth more than my companions of the present moment, since they prac-ticed all their vices overtly, proudly contaminated, whereas the monks, my brethren, have solemnly renounced all those accursed things and have engaged to consecrate themselves without return, without afterthought and without restriction to generosity, sanctity and love of their fellows.

And, more imperious than ever, the desire to decipher the enigma of their aversion, impenetrable thus far, haunted me. I tried, but without ever succeeding, to surprise at the corners of corridors and doors standing ajar, the secret of that hostility, which I sensed progressively driving me mad.

Even Père Athanase, to whom I would have liked to get closer, as an orphan wants to get closer to the charitable soul who has taken him in, to whom I would have liked to confess my distress, and whose strict, inexorable duty would have been to console me and fort me, testified to me even more coldness and more aversion than his monks. Strangely enough, the more distant and unfriendly I sensed him to be, the more I desired to go and knock on his door, to throw myself at his knees, to confess my tortures to him and to ask him, while gripping his waxy hands:

"Why does everyone here hate me?"

Twenty times, while everyone was asleep in the monastery, I left my cell silently, and, walking on the tips of my sandals in order not to make any noise, I traveled the long distance separating my plastered tomb from that of the superior. I arrived outside the little door, hermetically sealed, through which only a single luminous line filleted; and there, seized by an inexplicable fear, I turned back, and returned to my cell.

How did he surprise my conduct? Why was he stationed on the threshold of his room on the evening when, more bruised than usual, I had retraced my nocturnal route, holding my breath? I don't know. I found myself in his cell, where the flickering flame of a candle made our black shadows tremble on the walls. I found myself before him, kneeling in a posture of supplication and anguish. And as long as I live, I shall hear his voice unleashing upon me, like a mortal blow launched by an implacable enemy, the sentence that revealed and explained everything to me.

Oh, those disciples of Christ, how much crueler and viler they are than the others, and how I hate them for having veiled their turpitude and their hypocrisy from me for such a long time!

"Since you have been here, my son, you have given all our brethren the most edifying and most laudable example. But those brothers you take for saints are only human. They retain all the weaknesses, all the faults of humanity. That is why that which caused fear and alarm outside, also causes it in the refuge of God. Mortal imperfections are trivial in the eyes of our unction, but certain physical imperfections are as insupportable to the immured, like us, as they are to the profane."

"What are you trying to say, Father?" I demanded, fearful of understanding.

"Can't you see, my son?" the superior replied. "Evoke the motives that brought you here. They are the same ones that raise up—quite involuntarily, I swear to you—the animosity and aversion of those with whom you are living."

The horror!

There it is, the key to the frightful enigma. There it is, the reason for the oblique glances, the whispers interrupted as I passed by, that hostility, that scorn, that hatred. I horrify all those monks just as I horrified all the men, all the women and all the children that happened to be in my path, the day after my atrocious disfigurement. Now I know. I know!

And, downcast by that revelation, I collapse on the floor of the cell, face in the dust, uttering desperate groans.

Père Athanase considers me without saying a word. He remains as impassive and as impenetrable as the day when he perceived me for the first time. And when, getting up after hard efforts, tottering like a drunkard, I murmur to him in a moribund voice: "What should I do now?" the representative of Christ on earth turns his eyes away from mine, silently.

I have understood.

I shall leave these simulated saints the money that I brought them. I shall parcel up my novice's robe. Clad, as before, in my ordinary garments, hiding myself as before from the indiscreet, I shall return tomorrow to the house where my older sister Alexandrine-Ysolde is weeping. And then...

And then?

My decision is made.

Eight o'clock was chiming on the clock of the Gare Saint-Lazare when I disembarked from the train that brought me back to the capital.

Swallowed up in the swarm of the hasty multitude going up and down the steps of the waiting room, I reached the Cour de Rome without attracting any attention, where I found a taxi easily. Half a hour later, I arrived home.

I opened the little iron gate giving access to the perron of my dwelling, and, having stopped before the deserted threshold, the threshold that was no longer illuminated by the electric lamp of happy days, I placed the extremity of my index finger on the bell push. A crystalline trill ran along the mute corridors. I heard muffled footsteps on the tiles; and, always impeccable in the livery waistcoat with the black sleeves that he wore inside the house, stuck in the regulation manner against the beaten that he had just opened, Justin appeared.

At first, in that obscurity, he did not recognize me; but when he had switched on the light, and the dazzle of the arc-lamps had spread as far as the highest corners of the ceilings, all the way among the walls, as far as the corners of ancient pieces of furniture whose copper gleamed like golden branches, in myriads of rays, the poor fellow, at the sight of me, became pale with astonishment. And in a stifled, scarcely perceptible one he said: "Monsieur!"

"Yes," I replied. "It's me, back for good."

On hearing that voice vibrate in his ear—that voice with the already distant timbre, that bleak voice that he had never expected to hear again—and on seeing, looming up before him, the silhouette of the master of whom he was fond, whom he had seen grow up, blossom like a robust plant, overflowing with wellbeing, and all of whose misfortunes and despairs he knew, the old man put his hands together. Two large tears slid along his wrinkled cheeks. Unable to pronounce any other words than his initial exclamation, he stood aside in order to let me go past him, closed the heavy door, and, after having relieved me of the valise into which I had crammed my monastic robe, walked behind me to the dining room.

As I advanced through the various parts of the immense dwelling, I had the impression of respiring an unknown atmosphere. I was like a drowned man, gradually resuscitated after the slow efforts of rescuers and sending the vivifying air penetrating the depths of his lungs, the air vanquishing the asphyxia of which those surrounding him all thought that he was about to perish. The emanations of the flowers encumbering the dining room table, as usual; the indeterminable odors that fell from caskets, curtains, wall-hangings, bulging amphorae—the very soul of the house, more subtle than crepuscular effluvia, more enveloping than recklessly cherished hands—were all mingled, melting as I passed into an ensemble simultaneously so violent and so gentle that I experienced a veritable intoxication, tottering as I advanced, and, three times, I had to lean on the wall of the corridor in order not to fall.

I stiffened myself, like a wounded man forbidding himself to faint, wanting to hold firm in spite of his increasing weakness. But it was impossible for me to surpass the drawing rom. I collapsed in a wing-chair, and made a sign with my hand to Justin, to go and inform my beloved sister of my return.

Nearly ten minutes went by between the servant's exit and the apparition of Alexandrine-Ysolde.

Until the hour of my death I shall see that livid complexion, those features decomposed by emotion; that face, once so pure, now emaciated, like the mask of an old woman; and those bloodless fingers, those fingers joined over the flat bosom, those fingers interlaced in a convulsive crispation.

She looked at me, from the threshold, as if she dared not believe what Justin had just announced to her. She looked at me, and, while looking at me thus, she strove to recognize me, to recover in my face, rendered even more hideous than before by the new ordeals from which I had scarcely escaped, the features of the person she cherished more than any other in the world, and for whose heart-rending disappearance she had been weeping a few minutes earlier, I sensed.

We stayed there, confronting one another, without daring to break the silence. My heart was beating so forcefully that it seemed to me to be rushing like a ball at each of its palpitations all the way to the hollow of my throat, and I experienced a choking sensation. I dared not stand up, nor hold out my arms to my sister, or speak to hr. Paralyzed as much as I was by that surge of joy, Alexandrine-Ysolde conserved, in front of the armchair in which I remained engulfed, an immobility similar to mine. Stronger than me beneath her debilitated appearance, however, she succeeded in overcoming her disturbance, and with a great cry in which palpitated, simultaneously, her delight, her surprise and fear of learning the reasons or my unexpected return, she called me: "Patrice!"

I stayed in her arms for a long time.

And when, with her diaphanous hands, she had unfastened my embrace, drawn me to sit next to her on a sofa and caressed my forehead several times, as she was accustomed to do every time she found me sadder or more bruised than usual, she stated to interrogate me.

Reticent at first, I gradually abandoned myself to the horrible delight of confidences. As I narrated, I saw her shiver. During my final remarks, I saw her mouth twist, in a preamble to sobs about which I was never mistaken. I had hardly finished when she inclined my head upon her shoulder and murmured to me, while caressing me with an infinite tenderness:

"All that is nothing, my poor boy. I knew that you were not made for such renunciations, and I bore within me the certainty that you would soon come back to me. Oh, Patrice, what does the antipathy of those saintly men matter, and their hypocrisies, and their baseness, since you're here and you're going to stay with me until the end."

I felt so well on the support of those frail shoulders that my eyes closed involuntarily, and I allowed myself to become drowsy without thinking about anything, and without suffering. All evil fate was abolished before that feminine voice; all rancor was appeased on the contact of those pale hands, and I arrived at imagining that I was a man similar to all men, forgetting that I had been obliged to quit the convent, to renounce the world, to desert vibrant life because I had become an object of horror.

Thanks to the enchantment that Alexandrine-Ysolde poured over me, I was able to sit down facing her, at the table florid with gladioli and irises. I was able to reply to her, to converse with her without bitterness, and devour with an appetite that stupefied me the delicate and flavorsome dinner that she had ordered the cook to prepare in my honor.

Oh, the ineffable evening that I spent there, in the vast room that none of the exterior noises reached! The good and maternal kiss that my sister posed over my eyes when she escorted me to the threshold of my bedroom! And the exquisite sensation of wellbeing that I experienced in lying down on the low bed from which I had exiled myself voluntarily for seven weeks!

Oh, yes, she had known very well that I would return to that bedroom. And that was why, far from wrapping them up or removing them, she had left in place all the familiar objects that decorated it and enlivened it. With child-like eyes I looked at them all, one after another, and instantaneously, merely by seeing them, the thousand memories that they evoked were replaced in my memory in good order. With the soul of a child, a soul unsuspected by me, naïve and primal and chimerical, I sensed such a state of rebirth and happiness that, without astonishing myself or turning away, I began to make the most absurd and unrealizable plans.

Gradually, the past gripped me again. I remembered, with a sensual thrill, defunct amours and vanished pleasures, all the enchantment of my dead youth. That past, which haunted me in the calm of that sumptuous room, I sensed myself gradually becoming something present, incorporated into my dreams of the moment to the point of absorbing them and no longer leaving any room in my soul for the slightest logic or reasoning. Yes, I would revive from now on. I would revive in a total fashion, more ardent, nobler and more harmonious than I had ever lived.

My existence? Certainly, I would not recommence it, but I would orientate it toward new goals, new enjoyments and new realizations, compared with which the old ones would be nothing but platitude and puerility. And immediately, since the glad days are brief, and one arrives at the terminus of the voyage without having had the leisure or the possibility to pause in all the havens where one had dreamed of disembarking!

Yes, from tomorrow onwards, Patrice-Hector-Hugues de Beaumont, descendant of one of the most ancient families in France, would resume among his peers the privileged place to which he had a right. From tomorrow onwards, the man of all audacities and all intrepidities would affirm publicly his firm determination to reappear in the stet, and show that, in spite of his ennui, his ill luck and his lamentable vicissitudes, he still possessed the impetus and impassivity that had so often designated him to the admiration of his friends and the indifferent, not to say the hostile.

Oh, how slowly the hands of that clock advanced! How I longed to see the dawn filter through the steel Venetian blinds of my chamber, to see the first light of morning strike my bedhead with its impalpable fingers and invite me to get up! Quickly, a few minutes of exercise to put everything back in place, as my doctor put it. Quickly, quickly, a renovating bath, from which one emerges as if one were emerging from a fount of youth. Quickly, Justin, ring for my chauffeur. Let him bring my shiny Voisin to the perron, my tumultuous and wild Voisin, the beast of aluminum and copper, in which I want to devour space again, and retrace, for myself, the magnificent journeys whose grandeur still intoxicates me tonight after so many years.

But those journeys, those voyages, those excursions, I shall not accomplish alone, this time. Quickly, someone go in quest of, and bring here, one of those beautiful women who once sought me out, even more for my elegance than for my wealth, and let her prepare to depart with me. One of those beautiful daughters of Paris, the most adorable and most exquisite of all! I know where to find her, and I won't accept any, if she isn't worthy of exciting my admiration and emotion as well as my desire. It's next to her that I want to launch myself over the swollen roads. It's her cry of fright, her cry of amour that I want to hear at each of those perilous swerves, the boldness of which makes me burst out laughing, and the risks of which my skill in manipulating the steering-wheel annihilates instantaneously. Oh, those swerves, those demented brakings that sometimes determine head-to-tails in which nine out of ten pilots would have left their skin, flesh and bones, how clearly I see them, while the bell of my clock chimes eleven.

All of them, the one at Clermont-Ferrand, the one at Simplon, the one on the Corniche, and the bend at Remouchamp in the Belgian Ardennes, and the crash at Ventimiglia...

God, what am I thinking now!

Why that one, among all the others? Why not all the others except that one? Is it to remind me how I came out of it, to intimate to myself not to form the slightest project, since I cannot, since I must not re-enter life? The most beautiful woman in Paris with me—what derision! What would she think, what would she say, on seeing me, that harmony, that perfection, when hideous men, priests in monkish habits, armored by oaths against all deformities, all vices and all human ugliness, have held me as an object of repulsion for seven weeks and had me summoned by their ruler and ordered to quit their holy monastery without delay?

A truce on hollow dreams! A truce on insanities, Patrice de Beaumont! You are not and never will be anything but a monster. To hope to make those you invite to look at it forget the ugliness of your face would be to testify with regard to your contemporaries an unconsciousness devoid of any parallel. Suppress your sterile impulses, and without jabbering, envisage the reality coldly.

Since sacred cells have not succeeded for you, there remains your profane cell, until the end of your days. Since you do not bear within you either religious wisdom or faith, immure yourself in this opulent dwelling. Try to organize a supportable existence for yourself here, and don't seek outside what you can't discover there. You hate sarcasm? The affection of your aged sister will avoid its venom for you. You fear the horror that is painted on all faces at the sight of you? The respect of the man who has served you and loved you since your childhood will spare you that. And you can go white, between the two of them, until the last breath. With a better share than the anchorites whom history filled with so much admiration, you will know neither cabins of branches not garments of bark, nor the bite of horns along your thin legs, nor the fury of wild beasts intent on devouring, tearing apart and massacring.

Install yourself in isolation. Limit your ambitions to reading, to music, to the company of Alexandrine-Ysolde, to the unbreakable amity of Antoine Lux. How many people, if they knew you, would envy your fate, in spite in spite of everything? How many wretched people would accept the disfiguration that desolates you in order to taste the refined joys that your fortune permits you to savor?

How many wretches? Not one, I swear it. Not one would exchange my sumptuous prison for the starveling and debilitating existence that ruins people before old age, and brings nothing but privations, pain and anger! What vagrant truly worthy of the name would not prefer death a thousand times to the voluntary reclusion to which adversity is condemning me? To live thus? To grow old thus? Never! Better to finish it right away. That would be so simple for me! I would only have to quit the bed in which, immobile and chilled by fear, I'm turning over all these heart-rending thoughts, and go to my table.

In front of me I see paper, pens and ink. And here, in the drawer, the little instrument of death, which it's sufficient to put to one's temple to enter instantaneously into eternity. A simple pressure of the finger on the trigger, and the monster's suffering will be over.

I hold the ebony butt between my hands, I caress it. It's curious; I don't sense any fear at the idea that I'm about to accomplish! I don't tremble in writing the letter of adieu destined for my dear Alexandrine-Ysolde. I know she won't forget me. But I also know that after having wept for me copiously, she'll end up understanding that I was right, that I've adopted the only possible solution, that it was necessary that it was thus because...

Now, a hand has slid gently between the paper that I have just finished blackening and the weapon that I put down beside me on the jacaranda table: a thin hand, the color of ivory, with almond-shaped nails tarnished by debility. That hand takes away the pistol ready to function, while another hand, as icy as marble, is placed on my forehead and lifts up the inclined head, with an effort.

"You here? You knew, then...you understood, then?"

"Yes, Patrice. You know full well that telepathic mysteries are sometimes established between us, and that I can divine at those moments all your intentions and all your thoughts. Since you quit the dining room to come here, I've known everything that you've dreamed, everything you've suffered, everything you've wanted. At the precise moment when you leapt out of your bed, I leapt out of mine. I came to join you, certain of arriving in time, certain of seeing you write that letter, certain of persuading you how blameworthy your resolution was; certain, in sum, of reasoning with you, of converting you with my arguments, of bringing you to the pity that you owe me, and which you'll grant me, when I've spoken, my Patrice, because you love me as much as I love myself. Throw away this weapon. Put your forehead on my knees, let me cradle your dolor, so I can send it to sleep."

Curbed by the irresistible charm of that voice, I obey; and it is in that posture of a child listening to his mother telling him a marvelous story, that I hear Alexandrine-Ysolde speaking.

"Why do you want to add this new folly to so many others?" she said to me. "I've been mourning you for seven weeks as one mourns a beloved death. And it's just at the moment when you reappear, when you're resuscitated for me, when my entire being is overflowing with an inexpressible joy at seeing you again, when I'm telling myself that I'll finally be able to keep you forever, to cure you by means of tenderness and attentions, that you want to go away again? You think it's insufficient, then to have inflicted such pain on me, that you've been able to nurture the design of reopening my atrocious wound and leaving me alone with my regrets and my tears?"

"Life exceeds me. I can no longer support it."

"It's necessary to support it, for love of me, my boy; for love of what I've given you, what I've sacrificed for you, since your birth. It's necessary to pay the debt that you've contracted toward me, and that you couldn't acquit if you go away in a moment of madness. Remember, Patrice; recall your childhood in our dear natal house; recall how I pampered you, how I strove to smooth all the obstacles in your path, to prepare a luminous and privileged route for you, while my heart was breaking in the shadows.

"If you knew how often my eyes, which smiled at you at every hour of the day, wept! If you knew how many times, in the course of my poor sleepless nights, sobs stifled me! But I suppressed them, out of tenderness for you. And I appeared, in the morning, as calm and as attentive as if nothing had happened in my heart.

"You're suffering from your abandonment, from your misfortunes? What about me? Haven't I suffered as much as and more than you from the renunciations that you know, the renunciations decided because I swore to our mother to replace her, without egotism and without weakness? Do you think, then, that the burial of my youth wasn't as dolorous as that of your ambitions and your dreams?

"Patrice, my dear child, recover your consciousness. You don't have the right to desert the arena into which I descended in order to protect you, under the pretext that adversity has defeated you. It's beside me that you have to continue to travel the route, no matter how painful it appears to you, and I demand it of you in the name of the charity that you want refuse me. If you don't want me to die, Patrice, stay with me."

"I'm suffering too much!"

"Why do you always talk about your suffering, and never pause on that of others?"

"You don't understand, then, that I can't master myself, that the thirst for life will prevail one morning over all surrounding considerations, and that I'll throw myself back into the melee, and, mortally wounded this time by human wickedness, I won't have the energy to get past it? Would you rather I killed myself in front of you, or that someone brings me back to you some day, crushed by the truck or other vehicle under the wheels of which I'll have thrown myself voluntarily?"

"I'd rather, on the whole, that the two of us departed into exile. The evil attraction that you fear not being able to resist is the attraction of Paris? Well, follow me. Let's quit this city. Let's go live elsewhere. At that price, I swear to save you, to cure you. Would you like to try? Would you like to travel?"

"Travel? Which is to say, to encounter more people who would turn away from me in my passage? Never."

"Would you like to seek with me a solitary corner in one of the landscapes you love, in a region that you can choose for yourself, and where we can install ourselves definitively?"

"All regions are inhabited. All regions contain people, and everywhere that they live, humans are wicked."

"What obliges you to approach them? Aren't you rich enough to organize your existence in such a fashion as to have no need of anyone, not to entertain relations with anyone, not to see anyone except me, Antoine and our worthy Justin?"

"I don't feel capable of organizing anything whatsoever. I have no more strength, no more energy, no more will-power."

"Let me act alone. Only tell me what country tempts you the most."

"Do I know myself? If I renounce this gesture, from which I expected the great repose, if I consent to bury myself alive, let it be in a desert. Let it be in one of those sad and somber places through which no one passes, one of those regions unknown to snobs, tourists and the curious, a region such as we saw five years ago in the course of our excursion in Rouergue, and of which we've retained, as you know, an ineffaceable memory. I'd like...well, an old house with vast rooms, overhanging a river or a stream., surrounded by centenarian trees, and completely isolated, completely lost in the middle of its immense park. There, but there alone, it seems to me, I might consent to live, if you promise never to abandon me."

"I promise you that, Patrice. And what you wish for, at this moment, I swear to discover."

Four months later, we left Paris, never to return. Accompanied by Justin, who was not frightened by the prospect of inhabiting these lugubrious rocks, and a restricted domesticity hired by my faithful valet de chambre, we disembarked one October morning at Lagarde-Viaur. My determination not to see anyone was so clear that I had refused to take the train, and we went in an automobile that my sister had bought and fitted out with my intention.

In accordance with my desires, a large park enclosed by high walls surrounded it on every side, and no one could penetrate it either by day or by night. The servants, brought by Justin, had received strict orders, under pain of immediate dismissal, never to find themselves in my presence, and to draw away in haste as soon as they perceived me. I did not go out. When the desire took me to go for a walk, I descended along a broad avenue bordered by chestnut trees, yews and walnut trees as far as the bank of the Viaur. I sat down on the water's edge, and if I did not want to fish I stayed there for long hours, until Alexandrine-Ysolde, anxious because of my long absence, sent Justin in quest of me, or came to look for me herself.

For six years I have had no other horizon than the hamlet suspended on the mountain-side facing me. Neither the river-dwellers of the Viaur nor the villagers have ever perceived me, have ever spoken to me. The only items of mail that I open are letters from my dear Antoine. The only labor of the pen that I accomplish is to reply to him, to keep him up to date with my life, to interrogate him in regard to his efforts and his triumphs. The only sadness that I experience is that of seeing him depart when he spends a few weeks with us. And that voluntary isolation, in which I am content, confers an impassivity that nothing, according all appearance, will ever trouble.

Nothing.

For I am now certain of not weeping any longer. By virtue of shedding tears, their source has dried up irremediably. My jealousies, my anger and my bitterness have gradually calmed. The wounds of my heart have closed, like those of my lacerated flesh. A strange peace has descended within me. From the long meditations in which I am plunged in his hermitage, an incredible metamorphosis has resulted. I have become, without perceiving the transformation, the opposite of what I was before my fall. My previous soul has given way to a new soul. And, driven by an invincible power, I have begun to love what I disdained, to disdain what I loved, and to live a life as interior and profound as my previous life was superficial and vain.

I once scorned books, but I now have around me all that human thought has conceived of the purest and most subtle.

Music once exasperated me, but I do not cease, when my dear Antoine comes to see me, to ask him to sit down at the piano and play to me without stopping, after his own works, the compositions of masters who translate into rhythms, palpitations and sonorities as enveloping as dreams, as impalpable as crepuscular magnificence, amour, joy, sadness, hope and pity.

I once smiled at the spectacle of a work of art, but my galleries are full of paintings, busts and bas-reliefs.

The mere mention of the discovery of a scientist once unleashed my sarcasm, but now I read for entire nights the relations of voyages, researches and inventions; I quiver with anguish as I run through the long martyrology of souls more elevated than the souls of their fellows, and I sense that I would be disposed to sacrifice without egret my entire fortune in order to facilitate for those superhumans the titanic labors from which they draw, nine times out of ten, nothing but ingratitude, opprobrium and poverty.

Science! That, above all, is what fascinates me. I find more delight therein than in poetry, music and the art of colors. How was I able to waste so much time in odious occupations, when I could have employed my leisure and wealth so beautifully and so nobly? And, all things considered, the tragic adventure that eliminated me from the number of the living, is it not, on the contrary, necessary for me to bless it, since I owe to it having penetrated realms forbidden to so many of the mediocre, the good-for-nothing and the indifferent?

Yes, it is by means of science that I have succeeded in forgetting everything. And as I advance in age and in experience, I have a better understanding of the prize with which the master of All is recompensing my past horrors and lacerations.

And here I am, in my immense study, in this October dusk. At my feet, César, Brutus and Sahib, my wolfhounds, are sleeping peacefully. As the air is infinitely mild, the two large bay windows are pouring dazzling light into the furthest corners of the room are open. And near one of them, inclined over her embroidery, wrinkled like a fay of legend, delicate beneath her silvery tresses, my sister, my cherished sister Alexandrine-Ysolde, is silently plying her needle.

Three hundred meters below us, the frozen beryl of the Viaur's waters is flowing soundlessly. To either side of the mountain, the great somber curtains of chestnut trees and walnut trees that make up the exclusive vegetation of this corner of the Rouergue, rustle and sing in the warm wind. And facing me, leprous, tortuous and pitiful, is the little hamlet in which half the houses no longer count any inhabitants, displays the gray alopecia of its rooftops in the presently-crimson sunlight.

This afternoon, I have read successively Berthelot's *Origines de l'alchimie* and *Le Problème de l'Être et de la Destinée* by Léon Denis. More than any others, the occult sciences solicit me, and I sometimes spend entire nights deciphering the mysterious works devoted to them. I receive all the journals of esoteric spiritism and theosophy here, and if I am neither a theosophist, nor a spiritist, nor a magician, it is because nothing that those so-called new theories bring me satisfies me, and because, a dreamer all the more passionate because my dreams are of recent date, I always want to search further and to search higher.

And now, everything around us is gradually becoming blurred. The branches of the chestnut trees and walnut trees seem, like immeasurable arms, to be drawing the shadows of the nascent night toward them and to envelop them, in order to wait beneath their shelter for the next dawn. The cries of a few nocturnal raptors can be heard, and already, outside my windows, mute flocks of bats are undulating.

Alexandrine-Ysolde has just put down her embroidery. I have replaced the book that it is now impossible to read on my table. And my sister approaches me slowly. She places her pale and delicate hand on my head, where hollows in the skin conceal poorly the absence of a section of the frontal bone. Her fingers, the gentleness of which makes me tremble, brush the mask of black cloth that dissimulates the left side of my face from gazes, the mask of black cloth that hides my toothless mouth, my crushed nose, and my shredded ear. They put their incomparable freshness there, the freshness that was for me, in the cruelest hours, more salutary than all the surgical operations.

I allow myself to be stroked, the nape of my neck titled back on the back of my armchair. I no longer desire anything.

I no longer see anything. I am no longer thinking about anything. I am happy, as happy as the monster that evil fate has made of me can be.

And now my eyes suddenly focus on the large portrait hanging above the Louis XVI mirror exactly in the middle of the chimney-breast: a portrait of a man, a young man of remarkable beauty. A sportsman, no doubt, but who offers nothing in common with the grotesque academies of balloon-launchers, boxers and followers of pistes claiming—O irony!—to be regenerating our race and giving our moribund country a new luster. His bulging pectorals project beneath the blazer like a living breastplate. From his bare arms biceps spring knottier than the branches of a fully-grown oak tree; and his physiognomy seems to be illuminated by good will, intelligence and finesse. His fleshy mouth opens over the nacre of the teeth like a nectarine slit in two by a laborer's knife; and his unfastened shirt projects the slender and sinewy neck like a flexible stem above vast shoulders.

Oh, how many women have loved that man! How many have begged him, how many have shuddered at this pleas, wept at his abandonments, quivered under his kisses, groaned in his voluptuous emprise! What must his pride be when he remembers the arms clasped around his back, the lips extended toward his, the eyes imploring those overturning words that penetrate you more profoundly and more completely than a possession! How many names has it whispered, stammered and cried, that mouth from which nothing bursts but the joy of living and the satisfaction of dominating!

How many names! How many women!

Boyish haircuts; long tresses employed like wings; cleavages as smooth as the breasts of ephebes; regal forms, in the center of which triumph, like two incandescent globes over the translucency of a warm complexion, the milky heaviness of breasts; bodies undulating over the softness of profound beds with feline suppleness; hips braced in a splendid revolt; fingernails encrusted in flesh at the supraterrestrial moment of orgasm!

All of them! Marcelle, Marie, Claire, Huguette, Hélène, Emilienne, Tita, Germaine, Madeleine! All the names that come back, the purest as well as the most ridiculous, so magnificently divinized by amour! What a past! What ecstasy! What memories!

Come on, miserable carcass! Come on, incorrigible brain! Would you care to descend again as far as the frightful reality, to forget all those lovers, all those vanished charms? Nothing of that subsists any longer. It's all over! And nothing remains, nothing ought to remain of those unhealthy evocations, but a disfigured man sitting near an old spinster, in a curved wicker armchair.

The old spinster knows them well, those mad flights. She is not unaware of any of the malaises, or any of the crises that follow those excursions toward the impossible; and she understands, by my silence and the trembling of my hand, that it is necessary to come to my aid.

"Wake up, Patrice!" she orders, in her low, slightly masculine voice. "The time for wandering is past."

"You're right, my sister. Let's not look at this sunset any longer. Let's not admire these leaves with reflections of hematite and lacquer. There's mildness everywhere. So it's necessary, isn't it, that it should be in our souls too?"

"Yes, Patrice. In any case, six o'clock is about to chime. Do you want your headset?"

"Give it to me. Give it to me, quickly! Let me think about something other than that heart-rending long-ago."

Alexandrine-Ysolde brings me the little table around which the receivers are hung, and in the nocturnal calm we listen to the unknown voices that reach us from all the European regions.

I have constructed my wireless apparatus myself, after years of furious study. It's me who installed it, regulated and perfected it, as a result of my personal discoveries, which have given it a power that the most recent apparatus in the capitals will probably never attain. Curbed over my electrodes, condensers and armatures for months on end, I've brought to completion something so marvelous that I could, if I wished, not only capture at will the sonorous waves emitted by broadcasting stations, but also penetrate into dwellings, palaces, hovels and prisons, and hear without quitting the grim place where I have gone to earth everything that is said and everything that is murmured anywhere in the world.

An impossible miracle, some claim.

Why?

Has not modern science, which has tamed electric force, which has created the steel hippogriffs whose revolt cost me my life, which has realized prodigious aircraft, submarines and express trains, accomplished gigantic works? Can one know where it will stop? Can one suspect what the feverish brains of scientists and inventors will engender in twenty years, in fifty years, in a hundred years? Are we not living in an era of enchantment that is only dishonored by the discordance of our costumes and our ferocious mentality? Everything is admissible today, and if someone affirmed to me that a maleficent necromancer had found a means, if not of vanquishing death, at least of prolonging life to incredible limits, I would welcome the news without derision or incredulity.

Sometimes, dominated by an irresistible desire to hear harmonious voices vibrating in my ear, to mingle in the vital swarm, to know what is happening in the depths of hearts, in the depths of minds, I make the gesture of directing my apparatus at the region that momentary caprice suggests. But that inopportune gesture I immediately suppress. What's the point?

Whether I surprise the secrets of the rich, the poor, gypsies heaped up like vermin in their repulsive caravans, laborers, young women with bright faces, moralists, artisans or proletarians, I am always sickened. Hatred everywhere, calumny everywhere, slander, malevolence, envy and abjection everywhere. And everywhere, more than any other vice, an intellectual baseness to which I shall never succeed in acclimatizing myself. Can it be that stupidity dominates our contemporaries with such intensity?

How much poverty, stupidity, nonsense and idiocy I have swallowed while I listened to princely celebrations! And how much I have captured in the course of political games, in which illustrious pirates perched on platforms by a panurgian crowd slice up, recast and reorganize States, armies and industrial finances at the whim of their criminal nullity and their personal interests; pressure imbecile conscripts to the point of agony; and as soon as they have pillaged, betrayed, stolen and prevaricated sufficiently, disappear, extracting a sinister reverence from their dupes, having abandoned scepters or portfolios to successors who will perpetuate the tradition worthily!

How much asininity I have overheard in bourgeois drawing rooms where good manners, good virtues and common ideas are conserved with an austere rigidity like canned truffles! How much pitiful rubbish I have overheard in artistic milieux, those of manual and agricultural laborers, in all milieux without exception!

Oh, I'm no longer astonished now, on rereading the history of their frightful Calvaries, that the great inventors, the great poets, the great scientists and the great apostles—all those who rose above the general shriveled mediocrity—have been jeered, abused, exploited, misunderstood, insulted and mocked, that the best and purest of them have ended up in need and famine. What did they come among us to do? By what right did they aspire to improve us, to refine us, to enlighten us, to render us worthy of the title of human beings, in which we dress ourselves up as a fairground acrobat dressed himself up in gaudy finery, beneath which the chronic dirt appears in spite of his efforts. And yet, all those popinjays, all those hypocrites, want to live, want to enjoy, want to appear!

And I, who does not surpass their level, who is made of the same clay, I cling on like the least of them to this existence that crushes me and which I do not want to quit, in spite of my frustrations, my revolts and my disappointments...

And gradually, lulled by the murmurs that the ebonite and steel-encircled headphones pour forth, I forget the banality of the whispered words, the stupidity of the poems ejected at speed by actors of the lowest grade and the vulgarity of dances that are trumpeted, bellowed and brayed by the hammy front men of celebrated jazz bands. Saxophones, muted trumpets and trombones, what cacophonies are you feeding us? We must be avid, in this retreat, for any human noises whatsoever to be able to support without hanging up the receivers these quotidian insults to poetry, to harmony and grace!

Since I have been in communication with the Eiffel Tower, Radio Toulouse, Radio Lyon, Radio Paris, Radio London and other similar enterprises, I do not recall having heard a single artiste truly worthy of the name, a single genuinely musical and charming piece not signed by an old master, a single authentically moving and poignant cantatrice. To profane the miraculous grandeur of such an invention thus! Have the civilized nothing to reveal but fox-blues, lectures on loans or Montmartrean songs, and gavottes hammered out by the deformed fingers of old frumps heavier than their pianos?

But what am I saying?

That voice that has just risen after the brief ritornelle; has not that female voice intoning with an accuracy, a sensitivity and an unusual perfection my favorite Schumann Lied suddenly inflicted on all my bitter pessimism the most striking denial? The marvelous sensation that I no longer hoped to experience, the rhythmic envelopment from which I have been separated since the departure of my dear Antoine…all of that curbs me suddenly, and it is while shivering that I listen to the incomparable artiste whose name I do not know. A glory? A contralto applauded frantically on the great ages and coveted like a rare prey by some lord, some baronet, some master of the tango? What is her name, the woman who possesses such a voice? Her name, I want to know it right away! And with spasmodic gestures, I riffle through the pages of the newspaper that brings me details every morning of all the concerts and all the performances...

Ah! Here it is! A poor, unknown name; a poor, ridiculous name, swallowed up between the pseudonyms of two gamy stars: Claudia Pichet.

Claudia Pichet!

And, penetrated by a sudden melancholy, I begin to dream about her, to imagine her. Claudia Pichet! Is she the daughter of a concierge? A thin and ugly mistress of song, hidden away, finishing on a metro banquette the hunk of bread and piece of chocolate that comprise her daily breakfast? A mistress of song clad in a dirty dress, coiffed with and obsolete hat, brought to the Eiffel tower by some manager after interminable stations in the antechambers of agencies? Trembling with fear, has she come to sing into the microphone for twenty francs, for ten...? And yet, I dream about her, I listen to her.

Roses, lilies...you are like a flower...moonlight...the lotus flower...

The phrases rise, limpid, nuanced with mastery, with an incredible artistry, toward my solitude. At intervals, Alexandrine-Ysolde, sitting facing me, also wearing black and white headphones, looks at me. And as the last note of the final melody expires on the invisible lips of Claudia Pichet, two large tears trickle slowly down my aged sister's cheeks and fall on to the table on which we are both leaning.

It's over.

We remain silent. And with a common accord, refusing to submit after that incomparable song to the star that is to warble a fashionable one-step, we remove the receivers from our ears and sit there, both incapable of finding words adequate to translate our surprise and our emotion

Our surprise, our emotion—and our regret, I ought to add. For shall we ever hear again that obscure cantatrice come from who knows where? Probably not. Unless, perhaps, listeners transported with enthusiasm by the genius of the interpreter implore the organizers to enable her to feature on future programs, and the organizers are kind enough to consent to that.

Throughout the meal, we talk about her. In my humble opinion, she surpasses the most renowned virtuosos, and her debut on a Parisian stage would except frenetic acclamations.

But is she numbered among the favorites whose ascension to glory and fortune fate facilitates in a hundred different ways? Does she have a rich lover, sufficient connections, a Maecenas? All that isn't found frequently. And then, after all, why interest myself so much in that unknown woman? Because she fascinated me for thirty minutes and, making use of imagination, I immediately concocted an idiotic romance in her regard? Will I always be the same? Will the discipline of my past life, so positive and so brutal, never teach me anything?

Alexandrine-Ysolde, who likes hearing absurdities recounted even more than I do, seeing me embark for the distant realms where shipwreck is, all things considered, less dolorous than my returns to the past, listens to me with an indulgent smile. She responds to my hypotheses with other hypotheses, more sensate and more reasonable than mine, but she is so happy to sense me vibrant and alive that she prolongs the conversation deliberately until it is time for bed.

Dear big sister! How sweet and tender she is to me? I owe her the brightest hours of my childhood, and, no matter how far back I look, I see her, already grave, already matured by ordeals, already prepared to assume the heavy responsibilities that have aged her, curbed and wrinkled before her time. It's because of me that she set aside from her route the joys to which every woman aspires. It's for me alone that she renounced them, I know, although she forbids any mention of that dolorous subject in our conversation. It was to consecrate herself to me, to conserve all her affection for me, that she eliminated from her heart any passion, any amour and any desire that was not me. It is to be my sister-mama until the end, without weakening, without afterthought and without regret of any kind that she remained deaf to the ardent words of the man who only wanted to live for her, and sacrificed resolutely a happiness that might have been immense and complete.

Oh, how she loves me, and how I love her! She was the confidante and the healer of my chagrins, of all my chagrins. It was in her arms that I took refuge when I had a heavy heart, when one of those unmotivated and heart-rending infantile dolors shook my body as if to break it. It was in her arms that I took refuge later, when, shaken too violently by the ferocity of the adolescents in whose midst I grew up, I fled toward her as a panicked goat-kid flees before the threat of a storm rumbling overhead. It was in her arms that I sought refuge when, my heart broken by the first treasons, the first disappointments and the first rancors of amour, I could no longer bear them, and, an unconscious force launched through life, I already thought without paling of disappearing from a world in which someone dared to resist me, to mock me and afflict me.

I listened to her speaking to me, her arms extended over my desk, her head raised toward the sky, where flocks of pigeons punctured in a flurry of wings the ultramarine of the afternoon, her eyes lost in that blue void in which, I was assured when I was a little child, the Dispenser of consolations, peace and mercy was enthroned. And, as in the somber hours of old, I sensed descending upon me, flowing over me like a vivifying wave, all the benevolence and all the pity that overflowed from the adorable soul of my sister.

Sometimes, when we are sitting together in this room, as we are this evening, I consider her slightly stooped shoulders, her slightly sagging mouth, her entire fragile body that old age has already touched with its finger, and I wonder, fearfully, what will become of me when I have laid her down, eyes closed and limbs stiff, in the red rock dwelling we have chosen, with a common accord, for us to repose together definitively.

Will I be able to continue one my own? Will the burden of my isolation not be too heavy for me? This refuge that we love so much today, which we would not want to desert under any pretext, will I find in myself the strength to continue living in it alone, not to hold it in aversion, not to escape it in order to return to the city where I suffered and wept so much? By what right does the occult power that dominates us separate us thus, in a matter of days, hours and seconds, from beings that are cherished tenderly, who only experience happiness in living in company, and whose neuroses, whose fits of ill-temper and imperfections disappear at the first alarm to make way for the most entre and absolute tenderness? By what right does the occult power that dominates us scatter to the wind of eternity that which was beauty, genius, clairvoyance and amour, does it break the mainspring that causes the machine of our heart to beat, does it deliberately permit the forces of destruction to prevail over all the others?

Of what are we made, that the petty trigger of a petty gesture, a suffering that vanishes as soon as it is born, is sufficient to extinguish everything that was light and flame? What malevolent spirit invested with the mission to undermine everything, to shake everything, to ruin everything that palpitates, the acts and thinks, is stationed within us? What is it, then? Of what is it composed, that accursed power that no one can tame, annihilate or destroy? Death, the absolute finality of everything, the invincible sovereign of the material, the vegetal and the human, you of whom I spoke until this minute with a disdainful smile, now I am beginning to hate you, to fear you, not became you will soon chill my vertebrae but because you will come one day, insensible to my supplications and my sobs, to close the eyes the person without whom everything in this world will be abolished, will vanish, for me.

And, at the same time as those sad thoughts assail me, I hear resonating within a secret corner of myself the divine harmonies of Schumann. Even more dominating than death and distress, that music inundates me with such clarity that the evil imagines gradually evaporate, that the immense room in which we are sitting together seems to be progressively irradiated, and I forget everything in evoking the voice of Claudia— everything, even the person for whom I was suffering so horribly a moment ago!

A week has gone by.

A week, during which I have scanned all the schedules in vain, have captured all the broadcasts from Paris in vain. Nowhere have I seen her name; nowhere have I heard her voice.

And, with a great surge of energy I decide to efface the mysterious cantatrice from my memory and never think about her again. I know that there is, in the City of Bluff, in some modest apartment in Batignolles, Montmartre or Montparnasse, a woman whose genius surpasses everything that can be imagined. And that ought to be sufficient for me. A furtive apparition of an unknown artiste, followed by a definitive disappearance, a vertiginous eclipse—what could astonish me about that? Am I not informed enough about people and things to be fortified by that history in the conviction that in this world, ninety per cent of the time, only the mediocre triumph? To suppose that an audition of thirty minutes might give even a shadow of renown to a woman of talent, does that not imply in me a cerebral infirmity at which I ought to blush or smile? Poor Claudia Pichet, I shall never hear you again! Instead of your divine contralto, the managers will pour over me the acidic timbres of the ejaculators of serenades, Javas or ragtimes! And could I, in truth, demand more?

But what? That ballad by Reynaldo Hahn, who would be able to sing it thus, if not her? Has she come back, then? And while the accompaniment flutters around the melodic line on arpeggios more delicate than birdsong, the voice rises, the voice is amplified, the voice grips me again and curbs me as it did the first time. If my verses had wings…! Oh, Claudia, poignant interpreter, distant masseuse, for the frissons that you cause to run through his being, the exile blesses you!

And I listen! We listen, elbows on the little rectangular table, hand stuck to the receivers in order to isolate ourselves more fully from ambient noises, in order no longer to exist with anything but you. Now it is *La Coupe du Roi de Thulé*, by Berlioz, that is vibrating in our ears; and the strange sonority of the alto strings, so particular, so different from that of the other instruments of the quartet, sculpts a voluptuous and moving pedestal for it. Then two habaneras by Granados; and to conclude, *Lohengrin*.

Certainly, I do not recover the joy of the initial surprise today; and yet, the pleasure I have just experienced, seems infinitely superior to the enjoyment of the debut. It is increased by the satisfaction one has in finally seeing the accomplishment of a desire nourished anxiously for a long time; and, I don't know why, I find in Claudia's voice a seduction and a charm that the first hearing did not reveal to me. Is it because the woman is already no longer unknown to me that my curiosity and my sympathy are going toward her, and because, in this deserted quarter where we live without emotion and without any other human contact than the Rouergats of Lagarde-Viaur, everything that emerges from the habitual frame of our existence becomes a sensational event for us? Is it because my heart, weaned for so long...?

No! I don't want that! It's necessary that this heart remains placid. It's necessary that everything around me, a man who has suffered so much, remains as calm as an expanse of water sheltered by formidable rocks against surrounding storms and squalls.

And I gaze, through the open bay window, at the nocturnal landscape, into the blackness of which our dwelling insinuates the glimmer of its massive grayness. The rocks, I have all around me here, as I wish. Nothing will break them. They loom up on either side of the Viaur, as cold as incorruptible guardians. It is to them that I have come, in the extremity of my misery, and I want them still to protect me.

Nothing! No passion in my soul! I forbid it. Nothing but a reckless love of music; nothing but a reckless love of her voice. Let everything else become silence, calm, nothingness.

And while the chimes of my tall clock reminds me that it is eleven o'clock, that I ought to go to bed, as I do every evening, until the first light of dawn, my unconscious pen traces a letter: the letter that I would write to her if I dared to reveal to her everything that I bear within me of the vibrant, the spontaneous and the veridical. After all, can I not write it, and write it without reticence, since no one will read it? I shall tear it up as soon as I have finished it, and I shall only have created, in sum, one petty pain more, scarcely sharper than the sting of a lancet on an old, ill-closed abscess. And I won't think about it anymore when I wake up.

But how many things I would have to tell her if I didn't hold back my unleashed imagination! I could tell her how I imagine her, how I see her, how I see her soul; and how I quiver when, poring over the transmitting wires, I receive, as one receives a royal present, the magnificent offering of her song. I could tell her about our reclusive life, voluntarily restricted, voluntarily monotonous, in which nothing but her has happened for six years, and which she has just illuminated suddenly, solely by means of the irradiation of her genius. I could tell her how much I would like to know her, to approach her, to hear her speak.

Is she tall, as flexible as one of the melodies she causes to undulate at the whim of her inspiration and her will? Is she slender, frail and as pale as one of those apparitions of the church, one of these virgins in the strained glass or the apse, which enabled me so often to dream and pray? Where does she live? In what milieu? Have my prognostications of the first day deceived me? Was I, on the contrary, completely accurate? Does she have beside her a guide with a profound heart and a lucid brain, a guide whose decisive hand removes all the obstacles from her path with which she might collide with too much brutality? Or, in accordance with my generous hypothesis, does she live all alone, in penury, sadness and desolation? How far do her ambitions go? Toward what do her enthusiasms rise? Would it not be pleasant for her to confide in someone who could understand her, who would admire her, who could discern her incomparable merit better than any of her other listeners or her friends?

A correspondence such as is rarely exchanged: not regular, on fixed days, at equal intervals, but a commerce of ideas, sensations, confidences and advice; an intermittent correspondence commanded by the fluctuations of characters, the conditions of souls and the dispositions of the moment; today a note, ten lines, tomorrow a voluminous journal; the day after, annotations. To know what each of them is doing, what one bears within oneself; all the bitterness, all the pain, all the contentments, all the excitements and all the depressions of the mind and body—oh, what letters they would be! And what ineffable joys those who were capable of writing them would savor!

And then, to let oneself yield gradually to the inclination that bears one toward a perfect knowledge of two sister-mentalities, the inclination from which a happiness sometimes emerges such as one dares not dream without closing one's eyes and putting one's hands together fervently!

How did I do it?

How was such a letter able to depart from my home, to depart unknown to Alexandrine-Ysolde, to depart at hazard, with no other indication, no other address, than the name of the intended recipient at that of the Eiffel Tower? I wrote it in secret—me, who has never had anything secret from my sister!—and I was careful, as I handed the daily correspondence to my domestic, to make sure that it was dissimulated among other letters, and that no one could read the address.

And now it is en route, I wonder by virtue of what aberration I was able to confess like that, to open to a stranger the garden jealously forbidden to everyone. With what laughter will she welcome those vibrant pages? With what sarcasm will she underline, not what I wrote about her—for what woman cam remain insensible to praise?—but what I told her about myself? And I pushed unconsciousness so far as to reveal my domicile to her! A double stupidity for which I shall probably pay in disappointment and confusion.

Then, suddenly, the regret I had regarding my thoughtless action disappeared. What was done was done. Nothing would come of it. I was only risking, in sum, receiving no response to my letter. And the harm, in that case, would not be great. As for the commentaries with which Claudia Pichet would not fail to frame it, that was not of the slightest importance. Thus, let us not deplore anything and let us not breathe a word to my sister about that slightly risible childishness.

That night, I slept heavily. Was that the enervation into which my imprudence had plunged me, involuntarily? Was it the stormy warmth that was penetrating into the bedroom, in suffocating gusts, through the windows, which remained open in all weathers while I slept?

I don't seek to explain it, but, after breakfast, avid for fresh air and movement, I whistled to my dogs, I took my rod and line and I went down the abrupt goat-path, so slippery and dangerous in winter, all the way to the river bank.

I sit down in the usual spot, a little below the mill. When I look up, I perceived rocks, woods and fallow land everywhere. The scrofulous vegetation on those steep slopes forbids me a sight of the whole of the amethyst and lapis sky, drowned in places by salmon-pink mist. A long aerial sash, successively indigo, jade and crimson is all I can perceive along the Viaur. The rest is hidden from me by the curve of the mountain, and I think that the landscape, inexorably narrowed for my gaze, ought also to determine an inexorable narrowing of my aspirations and my dreams, which can no longer extend any further than the end of their verdant valley, and not higher than those twisted and bloody peaks. Of what would my imaginative debility go in search in that infinity? Is it not sufficient for me to see that limpid water flowing at my feet, in which gilded gudgeon and moustached barbels are circling, rising and falling.

Hey! A bite. A large chub that has just greedily bitten into the grape pip with which I garnished the hook, and which is struggling with all its might at the end of my line, poor thing!

On seeing it thus, lamentable and martyrized, a bitter disgust invades me for the cruel sport I which I am indulging. I unhook the captive, and, after having made sure that the wound in its gullet is benign, I put it back with a tender gentleness into the icy wavelets that are trembling in front of me. No more suffering by my fault! From today on I shall put my rod away in a corner of the shed, and, I promise myself, I shall never touch it again.

Now the wind is getting up.

A morning wind, amiable and cheerful, brings me the scents of wild plants and the odors of dried plums and the flames of the ovens up in the village, three-quarters deserted by the younger generations. The odor of plums, both perfumed and sweet, embalm me delightfully and give me an irrational desire to go and eat them immediately, while chatting with the sages shrewd enough to grow old in their dusty huts. But I soon suppress that desire. Neither the people of the village nor those of the city!

And, folding up my fishing tackle, I climb back to the manor, where Justin is waiting for me, in order to hand me a large envelope, on the back of which is the address of my friend Antoine Lux.

Where is the fellow? What is he doing? When shall I see him again? I know that he has just completed a stay of several months in Turkey. Has he returned to France? Has he gone on to other unfamiliar regions? Yes! He's back, there's the return address.

Oh, the good letter, the fine, fraternal letter, all of the pages of which I read with a quiver of pleasure! The good letter that brings me the announcement of his imminent arrival here, which confirms his decision, so long deferred, to become my guest for the greater part of the winter!

If you want me, he writes, *I'll disembark next Tuesday. Send Justin to Najac with the car. The Opéra is pressing me to deliver the score for my latest work by the beginning of spring, and, as you know, I don't work well in Paris. But out there, with you and Alexandrine, that refuge where the old solitary that I am finds tenderness, the pampering and the order that he lacks at home, I sense that I shall accomplish prodigies, and that my lyrical drama will be finished in the indispensable conditions of silence and peace.*

Antoine in my house!

Quickly, quickly, let's run to announce that major event to my dear Alexandrine-Ysolde. Have the bedroom that he loves prepared without delay. Send someone to Villefranche-de-Rouergue immediately in quest of the customary tuner of my old piano. It's necessary that, as soon as he enters the house, Antoine can get to work, and entertain me every evening with all the tunes at which the entire house seems to tremble as soon as he touches the keyboard, all those tunes that bring tears to my sister's eyes and catch my throat to the extent of stopping my breath.

Someone take my vertiginous sports car out of the garage where it has been reposing for week, have it cleaned from top to bottom, and have all the springs greased. Next Tuesday, it's me, and me alone, who will fly to the little station of Najac to meet the man who is much more to me than a relative, much more than a brother, the man who is my best, my only, friend.

A friend!

Something simultaneously moving and pleasant! A being that one has known so longer that one cannot recall where and when, or in what circumstances, the first meeting took place, and to whom one has drawn closer, spontaneously or gradually, without even perceiving it. Fortunate is the man who, broken by the most terrible ordeals, abandoned by everyone, abused by everyone, can perhaps take refuge in the arms of someone he loves and say to him, assured of a response: "Console me! Illuminate me! Show me how to support adversity. Hold out your hand to me, in order to help me get over this redoubtable blow of misfortune, since only you, of all those who watch me struggling without pity, are my friend!"

Antoine's room has been ready since yesterday.

Alexandrine-Ysolde has promised me to go into the park an hour before Antoine arrives, to cut a few of the enormous autumn roses whose perfume in so penetrating, those flowers of the after-season whose melancholy tints and scents still continue, as if to prolong the disenchantment and agony of everything, and to use them to garnish the Sèvres of her man-

telpiece, the amphorae of the table, the flame-colored sandstone of her bookshelves and he crystals of her lectern.

Justin has exhumed from the cupboard where Antoine
keeps his manuscripts, the old seasoned pipes that he adores
finding again at every visit. He has cleaned them with jealous
care, and arranged them in a row on the rack overlooking Antoine's desk. He has stuffed the bowl of a blue-tinted Nevers
with a Maryland as blond as amber; and while carrying out
these preparations he has announced to Sahib, his favorite dog
the imminent arrival in the dwelling of the illustrious and familiar maestro. Sahib, who understands human speech mar-
velously, has responded with delighted barks to Justin's discourse. He knows that he will accompany me in the auto, and
will be there beside me to welcome his companion in excursions, his dispenser of caresses, the man who is his master by
the same entitlement as myself, and with whom, unlike all the
others, I would allow to depart, in spite of my chagrin, if he
asked it of me.

Oh, the delightful moment when the train will stop in
front of me in a tumult of metal, vomiting soot and smoke, and
when I see Antoine Lux leaning out of the carriage window,
his arms extended toward his ardently-awaited friend, making
me a sign to hurry toward him.

And, my head seething with enthusiasm, I imagine and
set, minute by minute, for myself alone, the adorable scene of
the arrival.

To begin with, there will be a moment of expectation, in
the course of which, not perceiving him anywhere, I wonder
whether Antoine, as is his habit, might have forgotten the time
of departure, or changed his mind at the last moment. But no!
I recognize immediately that vibrant "baryton-Martin" voice,
as it is called by virtue of some theatrical tradition.[9] It's him
who is hailing me. It's him who passes me, while giving me a
sonorous "Bonjour!" his yellow valise, his overnight bag and

---

[9] So-called after the singer Jean-Blaise Martin 1768-1837),
sometimes known as "light baritone."

the scrolls of lined paper composing his entire luggage. And when I've collected it, and deposited my light burden on the platform, Antoine leaps upon me with a single bound.

A long, affectionate embrace; the usual interrogations. "Have you had a good journey? You're not too tired? How are you?" A few affectionate pats for Sahib, who barks contentedly in the back seat of the car on recognizing the person he loves so much, and we pull away.

At top speed we'll swallow up the sinuous road clinging to the flank of the mountain. We'll go around, without going through, Najac, an ancient town with mud walls, the first floor garnished with trellis-work and uniformly equipped with projections forming balconies. We'll go past an immense blockhouse decorated by the natives with the name of the château, to which opulent tradesmen and shareholders in big stores will come throughout the summer, to yawn, show off and gossip in the platitudinous fashion that characterizes them, Another steep rise, which we'll take in our stride, and here were are on the narrow road where the only passers-by, at long intervals, are herds of castle with coats as ruddy as the soil of the Rouergue land, peasants and carts. A bridge over the Sereine, an adorable trout river refreshing a verdant valley. Another hill. A village: Saint-André. Then, in front of us, rushing down in zigzags for more than three kilometers, the redoubtable hill that leads down to the Viaur.

The Viaur can be seen down below, exposing the twist and tours of the gorge in which it is captive: a stream of dark emerald, set ablaze in places attained by the sun, presently very hot. About a quarter of an hour before arriving at the mill we will leave the highway, and take a sandy avenue bordered by box trees and shaded by acacias and magnolias. With a sound of ripped gravel, birdsong and barking, after having described a complex curve in front of the perron, we shall stop.

On the threshold, like a Lady in fine clothes, Alexandrine-Ysolde will make signals to us with her hand. She will embrace our dear Antoine tenderly. And while the dogs leap

215

around us, and Julia, the chambermaid, and Justin, my old manservant, take care of the luggage and the car, we'll go inside, our hearts brimming over with delight, to the dining room, where slices of bread anointed with the butter of our little Breton cow await us, and stone pots full to the neck of frothy milk. Oh, the delectable moment the three of us will pass there—just the three of us, for Alexandrine-Ysolde will serve us herself, having given orders to Julia not to disturb us. How good it will be to find ourselves together again after such a long absence!

More emotional that I would be at the return of a beloved brother, I will contemplate Antoine. Always the same! Tall, blond, rather strong, a trifle massive, his physiognomy open, his moustache turned up musketeer-fashion beneath a Bourbonian nose, the cavalier imperial beard, the hair as bushy as the fleece of a vigorous and healthy animal. He ha! Is the maestro getting a thick waist? I shall point it ought to him, smiling at my discovery. But far from excusing it, he will agree lightly to that nascent obesity. He will explain it to me in his manner—and in any case, he will affirm, the annoyance will only be temporary. A few weeks of obstinate physical culture, and we'll see him become a slender as a young willow. He'll count on me, of course, to extract him from his idleness, to oblige him to take long solitary walks in the country, to constrain him to hunt rabbits and hares over fallow land, and even wild boar rooting in the fields and devastating the crops.

Between two pipes, we'll build charming and puerile projects. When I tell him about my resolution not to fish any longer, he'll burst out laughing, and immediately extract the promise from me that we'll go down to the Viaur after lunch to dip our feet, while chatting, in the shiny water. He'll tell me about his successes and his commissions. The time of proofs is past, for him. All the lyric theaters beg him to give them his new works. Stars swear to give themselves to the roles at no matter what price. Foreigners offer him huge sum to stage his latest opera. The great symphonic orchestras all add his works to their repertoires.

And after having listed his triumphs, he'll remind me of the distant years when hunger clawed him, and those who now come to boost him refused his compositions with an insulting disdain. He'll talk about the poverty of old without bitterness or rancor. His heart contains so much indulgence, so much good will that he doesn't hold a grudge against anyone for having caused him harm or damage. He doesn't hate his detractors. He shakes hands, with no hidden agenda, with those who were his most disloyal and perfidious enemies in the course of his dolorous ascension. He only likes the joy of being useful, of doing good and cherishing his friends. Lost in the epoch of cynical egotism and hypocrisy, he advances boldly into the melee, like a knight above reproach among ruffians and mercenaries.

And my heart will swell with pride in seeing him there, close to us, in finding him as I have always known him, and for myself alone, I shall murmur as I gaze at him: "He's my friend!"

Well, Justin, is everything ready? What are you waiting for to give me the sign? Don't you know that I'm going to meet Antoine myself?

Myself! Oh, wretch, ever prey to chimerical desires, have you forgotten, then, that you never go out, that you never cross the gates of your park under any pretext, that for six years you haven't traveled the road to Najac or to Saint-André, or any other road or path along which normal humans go? Why still dream, then, about all these impossible things? Do you want travelers, manual laborers and shepherds to recoil in fright, to turn their eyes away, on seeing the black headband that hides your monstrous face so poorly? Let your chauffeur go, then. Let him devour space and born the dust of the road with the hysterical roar of the engine! The man whom you're expecting, the man for whom you're lying in wait at the top of your white terrace, he will soon bring back, without you having exposed your face to the mockery or the disgust of those you encounter.

Why, then, am I still lingering over these dreams when I hear, on the road, a few hundred meters from my dwelling, the reiterated appeals of a car-horn demanding that the guardian open the gate?

II

Antoine has been with us for three days, and I cannot get enough of seeing him and listening to him.

I don't know whether he finds Alexandrine-Ysolde and me changed, but I've observed that he still remains the same, and that my prognostications regarding his slight hint of obesity, the graying of his hair and the wrinkles on his forehead, were completely erroneous. I'm glad of that, moreover, for I don't know of anything sadder than discovering the stigmata of approaching old age in the face of another, telling oneself that with every day that passes is curbing his body, once so noble, rounding out his broad shoulders, and weakening the assemblage of his faculties, making, in brief, what was once energy and determination into debility and unconsciousness.

None of that is evident in Antoine. In full bloom, in full strength, an intense joy emanates from him, a feverish gladness in being alive; and he communicates that joy, that gladness, to his entire entourage, as a magnetizer communicates to a dazzled public the fluids without which they would not experience either surprise or pleasure in confrontation with their fallacious experiences.

A few hours after his arrival he wanted to play his piano.

Beneath his wiry fingers, the soul of the ebony box was suddenly resuscitated. From the floor to the ceiling, the vast room vibrated like a sounding board; and from the first bars, Sahib, Antoine Lux's favorite dog, stood up abruptly. He placed his forepaws on the maestro's knees, and, growling contentedly, like a veritable melomaniac, he listened from beginning to end to the prelude executed by the man who is not only a composer of genius but also a first-rate soloist.

What a strange canine nature that Sahib has! Ferocious and redoubtable to the entire domesticity, including Justin, devoid of all affection for my sister, only manifesting a disdainful indifference to me, in spite of my petting and stroking, he was seized instantaneously by a reckless passion for Antoine. Every time he is on guard in the corridor cutting my spacious dwelling in two—for my three wolfhounds take turns ensuring the security of the house from the exterior, the ground floor and the first floor—he installs himself on the carpet garnishing Antoine's threshold, and that's where he spends the night. Anyone who attempted, at any hour of the evening, afternoon or morning to introduce himself into my friend's room would infallibly be devoured. From the moment when Antoine appears and comes to find us, Sahib no longer quits him. He accompanies him in all his walks, and escorts him in his slightest comings and goings around the house and along the banks of the Viaur—everywhere.

Sometimes, Antoine, exasperated by such fidelity, wants to get away from him, or wants to drive him away. Wasted effort; the dog remains beside him. He could strike him with the utmost brutality, but he would not succeed in driving him away. The dog's instinct enables him to divine the returns to Lagarde-Viaur of the man he has chosen for his master. Scarcely has Justin opened the gray Venetian blinds in order to let some air into my companion's room than Sahib bounds on to the carpet, barks at length while agitating his flexible tail, and delivers himself to such joyful manifestations that no one could be mistaken regarding the significance of that unusual exuberance.

In truth, although Brutus and Porthos[10] gave evidence of a remarkable intelligence in all circumstances in which their sense of smell was obliged to become manifest, I am forced to acknowledge the superiority of Sahib over my other two dogs.

This morning, Antoine, Alexandrine-Ysolde and I went down to the bank of the Viaur at about ten o'clock.

The end of autumn is inexpressible mild. Not the slightest trace of frost blanches the grass or the last flowers in the garden. A warm sunlight extends playfully between the leaves

---

[10] The author appears to have forgotten that his narrator's third wolfhound was previously called César.

that are almost attached. One respires delightedly and air not weighed down by estival dust. We leave footprints in the gravel of the avenue as we go, glad to find ourselves together, avoiding talking in order not to insult the magnificence of the surrounding landscape with the banality of our words. And ahead of us, bounding in great leaps toward everything that flies or panics, Sahib utters prolonged barks.

In ten minutes, we reach the river. Moored to a pontoon that extends for several meters above the green-black water, my fishing dinghy is swaying to the impacts of the wind. How many times, in translucent June dawns, we departed for long excursions, to the purr of the engine guiding the little boat against the current! On the banks to either side, high walls of blond granite regulate the tumultuous progress of the waters. In the polished flanks of those walls, dark holes that one reaches via unequal and perilous steps attest that, thousands of years before our arrival in this miserable terrain, humans lived in those cavities, and inscribed there, in drawings and sculptures of a gripping clarity, the story of their adventurous lives and their embryonic civilization.

Today, though, nothing tempts us, neither the speed of the boat cutting through the sly waves with its prow, nor the ascension of those stairways eroded by the millennia, nor the attraction of the discoveries that can be made in the depths of grottoes unknown to archeologists and iconoclastic prehistorians. We sit down on the bench disposed in the middle of the oak pontoon and, with Sahib at Antoine's feet, we articulate in low voices the initial phrases of a conversation that will be prolonged until the chiming of the manor clock rings for lunch.

Alexandrine-Ysolde interrogates my friend.

Prodigiously endowed for music, his pianistic talent is such that the virtuoso Antoine Lux does not disdain to play the most difficult works for us, and he deplores, after each of their executions for four hands, that my sister has always refused to perform in public.

Without the slightest difficulty, Antoine responds to Alexandrine-Ysolde's multiple questions. He tells her briefly about the confection of his next lyrical drama, and promises to let her hear from beginning to end the score that he is bringing to its conclusion in our house, and we talk about the performance that the director of the Opéra has proposed to him, and illustrious names, some of which enchant him, while others unleash simultaneously his anger and his bitterness. With darts that always strike accurately, he punctures balloons of the lyrical art, dissects tenors, baritones and chanteuses whose incomprehension is only equaled by their pretention and ignorance. Above all, he deplores the conceit of the principal interpreter, a sonorous goose protected by a major shareholder, whose stupid performance and nasty voice he rightly fears, but whom he cannot persuade the director to dismiss, in spite of all his efforts.

"Oh," he says, sadly, "Why can't I find in Paris, in some official theater, the cantatrice I'm seeking? With what pleasure I'd take my four acts to The Académie Nationale to perform. But alas, the dramatic contralto of whom I dream can't be encountered anywhere."

Anywhere!

That word suddenly made me shudder. Why did I suddenly remember both the crazy letter that I had the stupidity of writing and sending, and the incomparable voice of the artiste whose voice I shall soon not have heard for a fortnight. She could translate the composer's rhythms as he desires! Better than anyone else, more perfectly than all the others, she would be able to realize the character he had created. But what would be the point of mentioning her to him? What good would it do to cause my friend further disenchantments and further difficulties, since Claudia Pichet has not replied to me, and never will!

And slyly, I nudge he conversation toward other subjects. I no longer want any talk in my presence about music or the theater, because, music, art and the theater are Claudia Pichet, and Claudia Pichet has nothing to do with the amity that unites me with Lux, his work or his projects—or my grim and retired life. That woman, who has certainly forgotten my ridiculous confidences, I hate; and if I could, I would do her all possible harm at this moment. It is about her that I am thinking as we go back up to the house, while the summons of the clock becomes more urgent as our steps slow down further.

Hold on! Two silhouettes on the perron. Visitors? Less than that: two domestics, a man and a woman, who, docile to their orders, draw away precipitately as soon as they perceive us.

What poverty! And I would like Claudia Pichet...

As we sit down at table Justin hands me the periodicals, and adds: "There's also a letter for Monsieur."

A letter? For me, who never receives any, except for those from Antoine and my rare suppliers. I decipher the address. Unknown handwriting, but undoubtedly feminine. Postmarked Paris.

Quivering with an inexplicable emotion, I tear the gray paper, turn the five pages and skip to the signature.

It's her, replying to me.

Trembling to submit to my sister's interrogation, like schoolboy who fears being caught at fault by his teacher and strives to conceal a forbidden object, I put the letter, which I dare not read, into the inside pocket of my jacket. In order to hide from Antoine and Alexandrine the disturbance by which I'm invaded, I open a newspaper at random, and without being able to explain how, I fall upon the page on which the evening's radio programs are printed in full.

What irresistible force guides my eyes and obliges me to pose them, without pausing on those of the provinces or abroad, to the transmission from the Eiffel Tower? What irresistible force rivets them to number seven? Two melodies by Gabriel Fauré, inserted between *The Ride of the Valkyries* and a defecation of the monster of German music responding to the confused pseudonym of Mendelssohn-Bartholdy. As soon as the titles of the two melodies are read I guess their interpreter. This evening, between five and six, I shall therefore experience once again, but increased by reading the letter that I am crumpling with my every movement, a joy of incomparable artistry

How long the time seems!

Devoured by impatience, I am no longer paying the slightest attention either to the menu, which is nevertheless exquisite, or to the conversation. I would like to be able to quit my chair, race to the tall pendulum clock that is distilling the seconds with the parsimony of a usurer, turn its hands brutally and immobilize them on the dial at the whim of my desires. Gradually, carried away by my galloping imagination, I forget the presence of Alexandrine-Ysolde and Antoine at my sides, and I do not even hear the maestro announcing an event so sensational and so grave that it draws a loud exclamation from the dear woman.

But as I have not flinched, and my physiognomy does not reflect any surprise, my sister abuses me with an affectionate malice.

"So, Patrice, you remain mute before such a declaration?"

"Me?" I say starting. "What is it about?"

"You didn't hear Antoine announcing his imminent marriage to us?"

Antoine is getting married?

No, I hadn't heard. But then, what does Antoine's imminent marriage matter to me, after all, since I have there, upon my breast, Claudia's response, which I am going to read shortly in my room, far from indiscreet gazes? And yet, I can't dispense with asking him a few questions, congratulating him, not to say teasing him slightly.

"Compliments, my dear."

Entirely inclined to confidences, he narrates his adventure to us briefly. A marriage of amour? Perhaps. But in any case, a marriage by which he is amazed himself., and of which he cannot explain the genesis.

"We were introduced at the Clermonts, where I was dining. She had admired my works for a long time, it appears. At any rate, a beautiful young woman, very sympathetic and very artistic. Not pretty, but charming, which is better. My forty years haven't frightened her. I've found her thirty flavorsome. And that's it."

"Rich?"

"Fairly. Quite sufficiently, in my opinion."

"A musician?"

"Enough."

"And when is the wedding?"

"No date set. We'll fix the details when I get back. Here, look."

He hands us a photograph of a woman."

Alexandrine-Ysolde waxes ecstatic over the delicacy of the features, the profundity of the eyes, the seduction emanating from the physiology, so regular and so pleasing. Personally, I examine the portrait, out of politeness, which I would have admired passionately in normal times; and, without experiencing the slightest envy, I ask to be introduced to her as soon as possible."

"You can take it for granted," Antoine ripostes, "that your sister and you will be the first to know her. Furthermore, if you want to give me the greatest joy in my life, you'll accept to be my witness."

Suffocated by that extraordinary request, I consider Antoine with wide eyes.

"What are you saying, wretch?"

"If you want to give me the greatest joy of my life, you'll agree to be my witness," he repeats, in a firm voice.

Without replying to him, I stand up and move around the table. Having arrived beside him, I take his hand and force him to get up in his turn; and, still mute, I conduct him to the immense Louis XVI mirror occupying the middle of the chimney-breast.

With my finger, I indicate the image that the crystal oblong sends back to me.

"Have you suddenly gone blind, then? You suppose that I would dare to show myself in public with such a face? Have you forgotten the reason for which I came to bury myself here, the reason for which I haven't seen anyone for six years, except for you, Alexandrine and Justin? The prospect of your union with that buxom young woman renders you so jovial that you believe yourself constrained to deliver such macabre jokes?"

With his hand on my forearm, in a tremulous voice, Antoine ripostes: "You are the individual whom I cherish most in all the world, after my fiancée. I know your anguish, your suffering and your revolt. We'll get married here, in this country church, if you wish. We'll get married by night, if you request it. Why would you refuse to serve as my witness?"

"And your wife?" I say to him, with a dolorous laugh. "Have you thought about the fright that will invade her at the sight of me? Do you believe, then, that I haven't suffered enough from the horror of the indifferent, to want to risk suffering again via those I cherish? Don't count on me, my poor fried. Dead-alive I am; dead-alive I shall stay. You'll easily find, at the Institut, among your social relationships or your colleagues, an advantageous replacement for me."

"She's agreed to it," murmurs my friend, in a bleak voice. "She knows how you have been tested; but she also knows how much we love one another, and that is why she wants as much as I do to see you beside us on that day."

Moved by those affectionate words, I shake my dear Antoine's hands. But while affirming to him, in a long hug, the intensity of my amity, I shake my head.

"Write to her that I'm touched more deeply than I can say, but advise her to see me through the prism of your fraternal devotion, and not in the flesh and bone. She'd experience too complete a disillusionment. Come on, Antoine, come and sit down and eat without thinking about anything else this bavarois with strawberries."

The lunch, commenced so joyfully, has ended in sadness.

Antoine's disappointment is legible in his anxious physiognomy. Alexandrine-Ysolde, heartbroken by that disastrous incident, no longer dares to break the silence. And with my head bowed and my brows furrowed, I sense reawakening in the depths of my being the distress that I believed to be in lethargy for such a long time. It reawakens, that distress. It stabs my entire flesh without interruption, not only because my fried has solicited me in such an unfortunate fashion, but also because I am thinking about Claudia: because I am telling myself that I shall never see her, even if her letter, which I shall read shortly, opens upon to me, against all probability, unexpected perspectives.

My God, is it possible? Can human beings be reduced by the One who plays with us as a tempest plays with wreckage, such atrocious conjunctures? More lamentable than the least of convicts, I shall always drag this cannonball behind me, then, and no science, no wealth, can ever rid me of it? What point is there, truly, in opening the letter that rustles between my fingers with a sight silky sound, since I know that the delight that is brings me will be broken immediately by the collapse that will follow its reading? Would I not show more wisdom by tearing it up and scattering the pieces in the wind that is bites the walls with that funereal leprosy, than in tearing it up with anxiety? Come on, Patrice! A little will-power! Throw those sheets away. They can only bring you dolor, only dolor!

For a long moment, I hesitate to carry out my prudent resolution. But the thirst to learn prevails. So much the worse if I suffer, provided that I read it, provided that I know.

Monsieur.

As you can imagine, your letter is not the only one that I have received since my debut at the Eiffel Tower wireless broadcasting station. All the artists and all the lecturers, from the humblest to the best-known, in communicating with the public, expose themselves to criticism, praise and insults. Although I was ignorant until today of injurious epithets—my repertoire and the obscurity of my name protected me from them better than a buckler—a few of my listeners have thought that they ought to compliment me or to mark their reservations as to my value. But I confess, not without pleasure, that I have not yet read any letter similar to yours, and I thank you for the evidence of sympathy that you have given me from so far away. Allow me forget voluntarily all the kindness you have in regard to my voice. Allow me only to retain from your long pages your appeal to a camaraderie to which I will subscribe very gladly. To exchange impressions, observations and confidences with a person whom one will never see and whom one will never know seems particularly seductive to me. I love your spontaneous enthusiasm for my effort. It touches me all the more because I am, not rich, but sufficiently favored by fate to organize me life in accordance with my caprice, and I have been able by virtue of that superiority, rather rare among debutantes, to dismiss after the first lessons the so-called masters who symbolize, in my eyes, pretention, incompetence and stupidity, and to work on my own. Undoubtedly, my scorn for established precepts, for the School, has conferred on me the personality of interpretation that you emphasize. Original, you say? So much the better. Is not originality what one seeks above all in art?

That point established, allow me to scold you amicably for the false idea of me that you have forged. I am not, alas, as pale or delicate as an apparition in church. I am more often accorded an Oriental appearance, and I won't contradict that judgment, for my mother was Egyptian and I carry in my veins defects inherited from my African origins. I believe them to be somewhat corrected, however by the French blood that mingles, in my eccentric and paradoxical being, with that of the late Gasmiliah Nour-Eddin, to whom I owe breath and song, for the pleasure of some and the annoyance of not a few others. My father, who offered me in the gift of joyous birth the prosaic name of Pichet, was a worthy band-leader born on the heights of Belleville. You see how unromantic all that is.

Since you wanted to tell me about your existence as a recluse and a misanthrope, allow me, in order that I can form a more complete idea of you, to interrogate you in my turn. Doubtless, being a country gentleman, you prosper in a manor restored by an architect, as dour as the noble lines that Monsieur Viollet-le-Duc enabled while alive? And you have been able to isolate yourself thus for six years without the desire having come to you to see Paris again and hear its tumult again, to mingle in this battle, in which the weak always succumb under the assaults of the powerful and the audacious? That denotes a firmness of character that I admire and envy, for I am reckoned, rightly, to be indecisive and I am frightened by trivia.

Do you not have with you, unlike me, who was orphaned a long time ago, and whose unique sentimental adventure goes back a long way—don't smile!—a wife whose tenderness softens your well-to-do existence, enchants your long winter evenings as is fitting, and pours into your nostalgic heart an interior light that I divine to be intense and comforting? Have no fear of talking to me about her. I know of nothing better than frankness between comrades. I have sketched a silhouette of myself, in broad strokes. Describe for me in detail the woman who bears your name and who must know—for lack of which I will interrupt these exchanges immediately—that we are corresponding and that we shall correspond regularly, in the spirit that you desire.

That is why I am asking you, in this first letter, doubtless too long and too masculine, not to make the slightest allusion to the inclination "that might bear us"—I am quoting you— "to a perfect knowledge of our two sister-mentalities, from which a kind of good fortune might emerge that is known to you." There are better things that that good fortune, believe me. And for my part, I put nothing above a solid and sure amity , as logical and as normal between a man and a woman as between two individuals of the same sex. Write to me that you share that opinion. Identify the lacunae that my next perfor-

229

*mances comport, in your opinion, and find here all the cordi-
ality of*

Claudia Pichet

I read.

I read leading on the balcony of my bedroom, and, as I read, a great discouragement takes hold of me.

That letter was not what I expected. I was expecting a response in harmony with my passionate appeal. The one I have received is intelligent, certainly, and with a style that surprises me, but it is too casual, too cheerful. My soul requires something other than banal considerations of amity between man and woman and the nullity of music teachers.

First of all, why does that stranger believe that I am married? Why reproduce, while commenting on it ironically, the phrase in which all my tenderness and fervor are summarized? Can one mock such an impulse toward amour, turn to derision that piteous prayer? I understand! That daughter of a Bellevillois and an Egyptian must possess some lover chosen from among third-rate hams, and she is defending herself in advance against any attempt to extract her from her liaison. As if I wanted to snatch her away from someone! As if I did not know that any adventure is henceforth forbidden to me.

And yet, on rereading from beginning to end what disappointed me so completely at first, do I not find there a little less criticism, a little less irony and a little less whimsy? Let's see; let's take it phrase by phrase and try to discover exactly what its author wanted to put into it. Let's search for what might have motivated my suspicions and ruffled my feathers.

This is what I find now: that, on the contrary, from each of those lines there emanates a spontaneity, a frankness and an honesty by which I find myself alternately moved and wonderstruck. That woman, whom I mistook for a mediocre mind, suddenly appears to me as an exceptional intelligence, and, after a prolonged reflection, I agree that she is doing me a great honor by replying thus to my letter instead of serving me with idle chatter or lies.

Cease, after that epistle, a correspondence of a value so rare for me? Decidedly, I ought to mistrust my first impressions. This evening, when I find myself alone in my room again, I shall make her party to the joy I have felt, and I shall invite her to continue, to renew her letters as often as she wishes, instead of cutting this inestimable dialogue short, as I had decided to do in the first minutes.

But before then, it's necessary that I reveal to my dear Antoine the magnificent voice of the woman I consider already and henceforth as a friend. Five o'clock is chiming. Let Justin go in search of the maestro immediately. Let him even snatch him away from his work if he is engrossed at present, as is probable, in the third act of his drama, and bring him to me dead or alive.

Here he is.

Disturbed by the insistence of my domestic, he fears that I am ill. I reassure him, and, without revealing to him what I hold as a secret, I hand him the headset.

"Stick that instrument on your cranium, and listen."

Antoine starts to smile, and gently pushes away my hand.

"What's the point," he says, "in extolling the virtue of an audition that can only exasperate me? I know your infatuation, O wireless enthusiast, for the marvelous discovery. But you'll permit me, I suppose, not to share it, and to refuse with a light heart the pleasure that you have so generously thought of offering me. I'm not one of those who spend their time cheerfully discussing detectors, receivers, long waves, coils, condensers and microphones. For us, performers, ebonite and grenadilla only count in metamorphosis into oboes or clarinets, brass into trombones or Turkish cymbals. We deny energetically the artistic value of these ridiculous auditions; and, I say loudly, the programs that friends or enemies have arrived, by force of perfidy or insistence, have succeeded in imposing upon me until the end, have only brought me disappointment after disappointment. Not one artiste. Not one voice. So, old friend, I'll let it drop."

And with a decisive gesture, Antoine puts down on the table the earphone that I hold out to him again. But I want him to listen, and I implore him, in such a tormented voice that he considers me with surprise, to grant me a satisfaction that I hold above everything.

"I really can't persist in a refusal that desolates you," he replies. "Since that's all it requires to make you happy, pass me the frightful object."

And, with a smile of commiseration, he puts on the head-set. I imitate him. And we stay there, motionless, him ready to mock, me gripped by an inexpressible anguish—for the pianist has just attacked the prelude to the first melody sung by Claudia.

And the voice rises, more ample, more magnificent and more serene than ever. Richepin's poetry, set to music by the adorable master, the woman about whom I think night and day, details with such perfection that we do not lose a single word or syllable. From the corner of my eye, as the strophes reach us, I look at Antoine. His physiognomy, hostile at first, gradually relaxes. An increasing astonishment brightens his features, and when the pianist has struck the final chord, Antoine stands up."

Two words, to express his amazement: "My God!"

"Well?" I say, in a triumphant fashion.

"I can't find words to translate my emotion," my friend continues. "There's a cantatrice so prodigiously endowed in Paris? And I don't know her?"

"No one knows her," I articulate, in a grave tone. "Her name is Claudia Pichet. It's the third time that she has sung at the Eiffel Tower. Pick up your headset, Antoine Lux; the woman you have just heard is going to enable us to hear a second melody.

This time, I have no need to repeat myself. Antoine is helmeted; and, his eyes half-closed, as if in ecstasy, he collects, note by note, the hymn launched into the microphone to listeners in France, England, America, Austria, Spain, Japan, Hindustan and the entire world, by the interpreter of genius.

During dinner, and throughout the evening, there has only been question of her. My friend's enthusiasm is reaching paroxysm. He is talking about taking the train to Paris, going to find her, giving her the role of Rosalinde to play, and having her hired on crazy conditions by the director of the Lyrique-Mondial—at which I smile, not being unaware of that Austrian, who was naturalized as an Italian at the beginning of the war and suddenly became French the day after the victory.

"In order to have that unique interpreter," he assures us, "I would sacrifice half my rights to his profit. There is no more Opéra. There is only the theater that I shall choose, with Claudia Pichet as protagonist."

I like that ardor, that unreason in admiration. That is Antoine Lux all over.

And while he is swearing to cede to his future star a part of the author's rights in order to attach her to the establishment to which he has decided to take his work, I know that he is a man to carry out such a promise.

I listen to his discourse, seeking his phrases, trying to include all of his thinking in precise words and images. And, far from feeling, as I listen to him, the slightest jealousy or pain, on the contrary, I encourage him to put himself in communication with Claudia, to ask her to interpret some of his melodies some day, and to propose a role to her for which he has been seeking an exceptional collaborator for such a long time. He follows my reasoning, objects, approves, provokes my suggestions and my advice...

And while conversing thus, passionately, we hear midnight chime.

One extraordinary thing that strikes me is that there has been no mention, throughout the evening, of Antoine's fiancée.

Alexandrine-Ysolde, who has participated in the discussion no less approvingly and no less feverishly, but is more sensate than us, gets up quietly, lamp in hand.

"Let's go to bed, my lads," she says. "We'll resume this conversation tomorrow."

Docile, Antoine Lux heads for the corridor landing to his room. In the middle of the doormat, curled up in a ball, Sahib is already mounting guard on the maestro's threshold.

We give my sister a long kiss. She disappears into the main staircase with the sculpted wood banisters, for her room is on the first floor. We listen to the sound of her footsteps diminishing progressively and then fading away. Antoine extends his hand to me. But instead of letting him depart, as I habitually do after having wished him a good night, I keep that hand in mine; and in a low voice, which resonates strangely in the silent surroundings, I murmur to him: "Come into my room. I want to talk to you."

My friend looks at me in surprise. "You couldn't put off the conversation until tomorrow? I'm falling asleep."

"No. What I want to say to you is of capital importance for you. The prospect of languishing in front of me in an armchair irritates you, I know, but come in anyway. You'll thank me when you leave."

Antoine takes the seat that I offer him, lights his pipe, and crosses his legs. Sahib, who got to his feet as we approached, having stretched himself and yawned, comes in after him to the oval room in which I sleep, and, sitting down on his backside, places his muzzle gently on my friend's knees.

Then, rapidly, without pausing at his astonishment or his disapproval, and then his delight, I tell him about my initial surprise, my impatience, my desire to know the woman whose admirable voice gave me such unexpected and perfect artistic sensations. I tell him the story of the letter written in the curse of a hallucination that I still can't explain, my regret at having sent it, my feverish expectation during the days that followed its departure and my surprise at receiving, that very morning, a few hours before the wireless transmission in which she was to participate, the response for which I was no longer hoping.

And without him having asked me, I hand Claudia's letter to him.

He reads it, returns it to me, and remains mute.

"Well?" I say. "What do you think?"

"That woman is quite someone," he declares. "You're going to reply"

"Certainly. And I'll tell her about you, have no doubt of it."

"What will you say to her?"

"That you admire her as much as I do, and that you hope to have her as an interpreter."

"Perhaps that's going a little too fast. Before confiding a leading role to her, it's necessary to know what she can bring to it. I need a peerless artiste, but I also need a beautiful woman. One won't work without the other. You've never seen her."

"And I never shall; you know why."

"How can you, in that case, propose a collaboration to her that I might be obliged to decline subsequently, if she doesn't fulfill all the requisite conditions?"

"What prevents me, in exposing your request to her, requesting her portrait? I'm convinced that she'll find that desire quite natural on your part."

"One can always try. Prepare your epistle and permit me to withdraw, after having wished you a good night for a second time.

A vigorous handshake; and, still escorted by Sahib, Antoine returns to his room.

I close my door again and sit down again, slowly.

The letter that I have to write on my own behalf and that of the illustrious master, I am going to draft immediately. Could I sleep, in any case, now that I am certain of obtaining, as I wished in the utmost depths of my heart, Claudia's amity?

For more than an hour, my eyes fixed on the piece of paper that they do not see, I seek the phrases susceptible of translating exactly, my friend Antoine's state of mind, and mine. In spite of exhausting efforts, I have to admit that I am incapable of tracing more than ten lines; and those lines seem to me to be so flat, so nondescript and stupid that I tear them up immediately. Until two o'clock in the morning I consume myself in vain attempts; and I go to bed in a foul mood, overwhelmed by lassitude and curing my impotence.

For two days I exhaust myself trying to put something on a reasonable footing: wasted time. I make a pressing appeal to Antoine's kindness, but he recuses himself, invoking the urgency of concluding his third act. Does he really consider that as important as securing our relationship with Claudia?

Finally, at the moment when I am beginning to despair, a great light illuminates me. A word suddenly found, which puts me on the right path. And without stopping, without a single erasure, I improvise what I had been trying to write for forty-eight hours without being able to do it.

Disdaining the labor in which the master must be plunged, I launch myself into the drawing room. Antoine Lux, poring over his score, is marking notes in pencil and then checking them on the piano. I hold out the large sheets of paper covered with violet lines.

"Read"

Without exhibiting and annoyance, he reads my letter. I wait for a gesture of emotion, a mark of satisfaction. He hands it back to me, as calmly as if I had not submitted anything to him. No criticism. He contents himself with saying: "Send it."

Then, forgetting my presence beside him, he begins to play chords again, singing in his fine warm voice, picking up the verses of his drama.

I withdraw, and, sealing the envelope, I have it taken by auto to station at Najac.

She will receive it tomorrow afternoon.

III

This time, the response does not take as long to come.

Scarcely five days between the departure of my letter and the arrival of a large envelope containing, as well as sheets covered in tightly packed lines, the portrait that Antoine Lux had charged me with soliciting from her.

I was alone in the house when Justin handed me that mail, so I have therefore been able, without fear of the indiscreet questions of my sister and the ironic appreciations of the master, to decipher the former and contemplate the latter.

The letter?

Disappointing, since there is question from beginning to end of Antoine, and almost none of me, only a few very amiable remakes in which my correspondent confirms her resolution to grant me her full and entire sympathy, and thanks me for the surprise that I have been kind enough to have in store for her.

Then, immediately after that amorphous preamble, the Lux affair!

I write "affair" because I divine at every word the frantic ambition of the woman I took to be a sincere and disinterested artiste. Her desire to make use of me, to utilize for the ends of renown and success the influence I might have over my friend, is transparent, with a clarity about which I am initially indignant. But at which I smile thereafter.

What, you possess in your abode of exile the composer that the most eminent critics have recently compared to Richard Wagner? All the way out there, in the depths of your Rouergue, you have been living with him, in his company, for weeks, and he will be your guest until the end of winter? And the man we all admire here, whose new works we await with an impatience and a fervor that each of his triumphs only augments, is your best friend? What a surprise! And what joy I

237

shall experience in knowing him one day, thanks to you! I have on my piano, while I am writing to you, fluid verses by Albert Samain, which he set to music a long time ago, and which inspired one of his most perfect melodies. I'll sing it for you on Sunday; and I'll also sing you other things of his that I love: La Chanson du Cavalier blond, *Baudelaire's* Invitation au voyage. *I would like, but would not dare to take it upon myself to organize without his preliminary consent, to give an Antoine Lux festival one of these days. What an honor it would be for me if the master would authorize me to talk about it to the director of the radio station! Ask him on my behalf, and transmit his opinion to me, unless he prefers to transmit it himself. Thus, it would be possible for him to hear me in his works and judge me in complete independence. I believe that I am presently in good form. Will my voice, which enchanted him the other day, appear as moving to him on Sunday? I will make every effort not to cause him a disappointment from which I would suffer indescribably myself. To become the interpreter of his next lyric drama! What artiste truly worthy of the name would not feel herself shivering with pride at that thought?*

Help me, since you claim to be my friend. I would like so much for you to be proud of your distant comrade, and for you to be able to say to yourself, if everything for which we hope is realized: "I did that!"

No, I shan't continue reading. A cantatrice of genius who writes such things to a man like me? Get away! A ham, nothing more. Oh, how many of those I knew while I was living like everyone else! Always the same, always the same! I'll give this letter to Antoine without comment, and even less praise. He can make of it what he will. And I'll also give him this portrait, this portrait aggravated by a dedication in which flattery is allied with baseness.

But before then, how I gaze at it! How I examine that elongated face, those almond-shaped eyes in which the shadow of the eyelashes places a softness and a languor by which I am stirred in all my flesh; that cleavage, those slightly rounded shoulders, such pale shoulders, unprofaned by a single jewel.

The woman is veritably splendid. But for the falsity, the duplicity, that I divine in that theatrical gaze, she would appear to me as one of the most harmonious images that I have ever been permitted to admire.

I have tried to put it down again on my table, to replace that rectangular piece of cardboard in its chromed leather sheath, but I no longer have the determination. Those eyes bewitch me. I seem to be able to respire the perfume of that hair, to brush those regal shoulders with my hand. I caress them; I refresh my burning fingers. I no longer recall the bright moments that I owe to the artiste; I only retain her beauty. And I'm certain of it now: it's isn't her voice that I love, it's her body.

Invaded by an insurmountable fear, I begin to tremble.

Why am I engaged in this grotesque adventure? What am I expecting in writing to her? Do I not have the courage, then, to free myself, to save myself, while there is still time?

"Here, my dear Antoine. Take it, my fraternal friend. This portrait and this letter belong to you, and if I kept them I'd be stealing them from you. Don't ever return them to me; tear them up. Do me the charity of not mentioning her to me again, since she no longer speaks to me any longer about anything but you."

As if dazzled by that unexpected vision, Antoine remains mute momentarily. He brings Claudia's portrait closer to his eyes, then moves it away, and then moves it closer again.

I wait for a word, an appreciation.

Nothing.

Only, after a few minutes: "Truly, then? You're giving it to me?"

"I can't give it to you, since it belongs to you. I'm making restitution." And, as he makes as if to return to his room: "Don't forget the letter. They're both your property. But before you take them away, I have a request to make of you."

"I grant it in advance," my friend says, turning round.

"Who knows? You hate writing, and I'm going to ask you to replace me henceforth in a correspondence that I ought not to continue."

"Replace you?" he replies, weakly. "Is it me that has engaged in these negotiations, which have testified to this magnificent individual the homage that her talent merits?"

"How could you have done? You hadn't heard her yet."

"Even if I had heard her, I believed that I would have abstained. I'm so afraid of writing, and I write so badly."

"You?"

Yes, me, my dear Patrice. I know myself. Like the majority of musicians, I'm uncultivated. I was taught well, in Paris and Rome, musical style and composition, but they neglected to inculcate me with the rudiments of orthography. You've seen it! And you know full well, you who are exhorting me to pick up a pen, that I'm incapable of it. What kind of ignoramus would I seem, with regard to a woman who, every indication proves to me, had received a complete education, and who handles our language like a veritable writer? But you, Patrice, that you continue to exchange ideas with her, and exchange impressions, I find quite natural. You have no reason to refuse yourself that, and I summon you to persevere in that amiable labor, as much for me as for you."

"I'll write and you'll love her? Christian and Cyrano?"[11]

"Why pronounce the word love in this regard? How could I love a woman of whom I was not only aware of the name, but also the existence, before setting foot in Lagarde-Viaur? Christian and Cyrano? What a joke! No, Patrice, don't fear a tentative idyll on my part. I love Geneviève Servais, my fiancée; and, more fortunate than you, long habitude has immunized me totally against the seduction of women of the

---

[11] The reference is to Edmond Rostand's play *Cyrano de Bergerac* (1897), in which the ugly Cyrano feeds lines to the handsome but inarticulate Christian de Neuvillette and writes letters on his behalf in order to permit him to woo the lovely Roxane. It does not end well.

theater. But you, formidable dissimulator, who forbid yourself with so much energy the defects and vices of your contemporaries, are you not in love with our contralto? Come on, admit it, quickly. I bear within me, as you know very well, treasures of indulgence, and I won't punish you if you break your word to yourself."

Antoine Lux's affectionate irony strikes me like a sword-thrust in the breast. I recoil on hearing his last remark, and as my eyes, at that moment, encounter the Louis XVI mirror in which my disgrace is so often affirmed, I see my face gradually acquire a livid pallor.

Antoine, too, has taken account of the abrupt change that has overtaken me. He places his hands gently on my shoulders, and speaks in a voice that emotion renders tremulous: "Come on, of chap, calm down. In teasing you thus about an amour of which you probably haven't dreamed, I didn't think I was doing you any harm. I was grossly mistaken. The contraction of your face, the frown of your eyebrows, reveal to me an interior suffering that I'm heart-broken to have provoked. Forgive me, my great, my only friend."

Incapable of responding, I let my forehead fall on to his shoulder, and like a desperate child, I begin to sob.

"Stop weeping, I implore you!" Antoine continues. But each of his exhortations increases the intensity of my crisis.

Disconcerted by that explosion of tears in a man as hardened as me, as seemingly impassive, Antoine falls silent. And gradually, as a violent storm eases, the lurches of my breast are progressively attenuated.

"What must you think of me?" I say to Lux. "I've given you the spectacle of a scene that is both pitiful and risible."

"Suffering is never risible, yours far less than anyone else's, my good Patrice, since I know the reasons for it. I should have been able to constrain myself, to avoid the idiotic pleasantry from which all your dolor issues. Believe me, I won't do it again."

I sketch an evasive gesture with my hand. Then, suddenly drawing him toward the drawing room, I say to him, while trying to smile: "Come! If you want to redeem your enormous gaffe, play me the andante of Beethoven's *Sonata in F*. At that price, but only at that price, I'll absolve you.

Sinking into a Louis XV armchair, I listen to the moving passage. And while Antoine's fingers brush the bicolored ivory of the keyboard, it seems to me that I can see, far away, in a modern studio illuminated in black and gold, also listening, the incomparable virtuoso, the woman for whom I have just wept, the woman who will never know that I love her recklessly, more than anything in the world...

IV

Today, Sunday, we have listened to Claudia Pichet, in Paris, singing us five melodies by Antoine Lux.

As I anticipated, my friend's enthusiasm has been boundless since that further audition. He no longer talks to us about anything but her, about her comprehension, about her knowledge, her talent, her future, her heart and her physical perfections.

In listening to her, he has become fond of the wireless, and I don't despair of seeing him, within a few months, counting among the most ardent apostles of radio broadcasting.

Every evening, at five o'clock, he circles his cranium with the steel arc to which the receivers are bolted, and, while smoking his long pipe of brown clay. He collects with an indefatigable ear insipidities that for my own part, I can no longer support for ten minutes without going into a mad rage. And one day, I saw him bursting into laughter as he digested—his term—a joke that I hold myself to be unspeakable. I'm witnessing a veritable obliteration of his taste, determined by manifestations of base scatology or the ingestion of quips whose vulgarity in only matched by their platitude. He has arrived at the point of envisaging as probable, as soon as he returns to the capital, the execution of his sonatas by himself before the microphone at the Tower.

He cites me, by way of excuse, a number of stupid or heavily-indebted poets, perverse balladeers and slippery composers who do not disdain to enter into communication with the masses by means of the prodigious transmitter, and to give them the first fruit of their most recent stupidities.

At his exposure of what I take to be aberrations, an immense pain invades me. Antoine Lux, joining banjo-players, reciters of monologues and music hall comedians! Could I have foreseen that when I begged him to pay attention to the voice of the woman who now passes for a divinity in his eyes?

From that unexpected interior revolution and that posses-sion of an exceptionally elevated mind by the most sordid his-trionics, Geneviève Servais appears to have suffered. Antoine Lux scarcely mentions her any more. I know that he writes to her regularly, but I suspect that the tone of his letters must be becoming less passionate from day to day, and that distresses me, on behalf of the young woman for whom the inconstant humor of my friend is storing up painful hours.

Alexandrine-Ysolde, like me, is astonished by the bizarre attitude of her guest. She has said a few words to me about it, supposing that his confidences have enlightened me as to the reasons that have provoked it, but I had to admit that I am in-capable of explaining it. Lux has never made the slightest con-fession to me.

But the portrait of the cantatrice is always on his table, the hypocritical dedication covered up.

Since Sunday, I have corresponded with my distant com-rade twice. Naturally, the subject of our letters remain invaria-ble: Antoine. Exasperated by the diminished role that he is making me play, I have implored him to write to her himself, but he refuses to do so with the utmost energy.

But I'm at the end of my tether. As I hand him the letter that Justin brought me this morning, I signify my irrevocable decision to him: I shall not write again.

That resolution affects him all the more because it will put an end to his charming idleness and will oblige him to devote himself to a task that is more repugnant to him than any other; that of letter-writing. None of his arguments, none of his pleas, can prevail, can disrupt the unshakable determina-tion in which I am anchored to stop what I take to be an chal-lenge too long prolonged.

A week has gone by since I last traced a line addressed to Claudia Pichet.

The latter, alarmed by a silence that might presage the ruination of her ambitious projects, has sent me two anxious pages. Instead of reassuring her, as I would have done in nor-mal times, I transmit those pages to Lux. They are so pressing, so anguished, that before my further refusal to serve as his secretary, he decides to reply to her briefly, not without reproaching me with an unaccustomed bitterness for what he holds to be shirking, in bad taste. Antoine is the only person whose ill humor I accept without flinching; so, far from becoming irritated when he manifests his chagrin of a spoiled child, in terms that are often discourteous, I smile gently and abstain from interrupting.

My slightly ironic silence exasperates him far more than justifications or replies. Forgetting that he is in my house, he suddenly enters into a fit of anger impossible to describe. Certainly, he does not insult me, but he avenges himself for my mute obstinacy on everything that he finds within range, And—a coincidence that is at least strange—it is the portrait of Claudia that becomes the first victim of his overexcitement. Torn from the easel on which it is enthroned like the arrogant face of a usurper, hurled by Antoine's blind hand against the wall facing him, it collides with a marble bust by Bourdelle, and rebounds because of the violence of the impact on to the table from which it was expelled, and, in its fall, tips the contents of the maestro's inkwell over the score for the third act.

Instantly, Antoine's fury disappears. Maddened by the stupidity that he has just committed, he falls upon the polluted sheets and begs me to help him, to indicate a means of effacing the enormous black stain that in striping the tenor's grand aria. Moved to pity by his despair, I sit down next to him and, without making any observation, I strive to make the wet ink disappear that is dishonoring the most pathetic passage in the work. Wasted effort: half of the grand aria remains illegible; nothing and no one will be able to purify it of its pollution. With his head in his hands, the poor fellow considers with a plaintive gaze the result of his fit of temper. What heartbreak! Everything has to be done again! Everything!

Will he ever rediscover the motif of which he was so proud, the poignant phrase in which the sousaphone underlined the melody with its funereal moan, and the entire passage modulated by the instruments of the new string decet, those surprising and novel instruments assembled with so much tenderness, patience and piety by their spiritual father, the upright cellist André Laurent, the instruments from which he hoped to draw such great effects, and for the utilization of which it will be necessary for him to work night and day?

I rack my brains in vain in the hope of being able to help him, in spite of my initial failure. To see him thus, in distress, his face contracted, a sudden indulgence for that abnormal individual, attained, like all minds of genius, by an incurable hyperesthesia, rises to my heart. And I suddenly remember that Alexandrine-Ysolde possesses a book of recipes, attentively consulted every time she finds herself at grips with a difficulty of interior order. What if I were to ask to consult it? Perhaps, on one of those pages, we'll discover the formula that I'm striving to exhume from my memory.

I make Antoine party to my project. He turns wide eyes toward me, as transparent as the gray dusk. And in a voice muffled by confusion, he replies: "I've just behaved like a boor. I beg you to excuse me."

At that phrase, in which I rediscover all the generosity of his spontaneous and genuine soul, I get up and walk toward him.

"We're not perfect, Antoine. You bear within you the sin of wrath. I bear others just as grave, which you've often pardoned. Let's go in search of my sister."

Without explaining the reasons for the deplorable accident, we beg her to open the miraculous notebook. She does so with a good grace, and, rummaging in the third drawer of her writing-desk, and pulls into the light a pamphlet covered in red paper, on which she inscribed in beautiful handwriting, a long time age—a very long time ago, alas—her name, her address at the time, and the nature of the information contained in its hundred and twenty pages.

A few minutes of waiting. A smile. A bookmark, in order for us to be able to recover the inestimable procedure without wasting time, and Alexandrine-Ysolde holds the notebook out to our friend.

"Go, and weep no more," she says, in her grave voice. "When you've made use of it, don't fail to bring those yellowed leaves back to me. I value them more than I can say."

Clutching the precious collection to his bosom, Antoine rushes into his room. I'm trembling with anticipation at the thought that we might be able to repair the damage, and already tucking up my sleeves in order to crush or boil, if that is required, the ingredients necessary to the cleaning of the stained staves.

Half an hour of effort, and the black stain has disappeared. The notations, the chords and the words written in pencil by Antoine reappear gradually, with only a relative clarity, but, in sum, everything that he has sketched or harmonized can be reconstituted, or very nearly. Lux's joy is indescribable. He gives Sahib a formidable slap on the rump, and the dog, instead of biting him, starts circling the table, barking, as if he were participating in the general delight, rejoicing with us for the fact that the most important passages of the work have been resuscitated, thanks to his mastery.

During the operation of the musical refection, neither he nor I pay attention for an instant to the misfortune suffered by the portrait. It is only when we have completed the operation that I point my finger at the photograph, the dedication of which is now indecipherable.

"What about this?"

"Bah!" he says, after having considered it for a few seconds. "Let's leave it. We can ask for another copy later."

"And the dedication?"

"Don't worry about that she only has to rewrite it. And then, is one flattery more or less worth the trouble of pausing over it?"

So he too has seen clearly? Before knowing her, he has already made up his mind about Claudia Pichet's sincerity.

"I thought," I risk, insidiously, "that the loss of that face might plunge you into affliction."

"Man devoid of perspicacity," Antoine replies, "I'll dispense with adding new stupidities to those I've just proffered, to my shame."

But I understand that my friend, in trying to joke, is striving to conceal his thoughts from me. It is only necessary to see him contemplating those shoulders splashed by ink, those arms where two long unequal lines are writhing like disproportionate serpents to be immediately certain that his second misadventure afflicts him as much as the first.

Well, so much the better. If he wants another portrait of her, let him write to her. My role has finished. It is up to him to sort it out—and I know that, within forty-eight hours, Claudia Pichet will have received a letter.

My prognostications have not been deceived. Antoine now possesses a second photograph of the cantatrice. In the first, she appears at an angle of forty-five degree. In this one, she is seen in profile; and I find her even more beautiful in profile.

The dedication has remained the same. And while Antoine examines those noble features, I perceive, beneath Claudia's letter, an unopened envelope. I recognize the handwriting and paper of Geneviève Servais.

Oh, how that one will be suffering soon!

V

What, then, has happened between Lux and Claudia? What might the present nature of their correspondence be? Doubtless their relationship has become gradually more familiar, increasingly tender, since they write to one another every two days.

For myself, I no longer count. Antoine is keeping me out of it. He not only avoids showing me her letters, but also pronouncing her name in front of me. So, I shall have been the artisan of their closeness; and just at the moment when I felt sympathy blossoming in the person for whom my heart is gradually being torn apart, the two individuals that I cherish most in the world are drawing away from me disdainfully.

And there it is. I do not experience any revolt or hatred against them, but an infinite sadness has invaded me. It seems to me that everything around me is crumbling. I no longer occupy the first place in Antoine's heart, and for Claudia I am already the stranger of whom one hardly ever thinks.

Do I merit such torments being inflicted upon me? Were the old dolors not enough, the dolors of which I thought myself radically cured? Must I moan again at the bleeding of other wounds, cry out again at the laceration of other cuts?

Since yesterday, I have been living like a brute. I have used the pretext of unbearable migraines in order to have myself served in my room, in order no longer to see Antoine, in order no longer to have the temptation to put my headphones on at times of transmissions, to listen to her, to admire her and desire her. Alexandrine-Ysolde, whom nothing escapes that afflicts me, refuses to accept the pretexts that I give her. She is searching for the true reason for this sudden isolation and this mysterious flight, but she cannot reach the point of discovering it. Far from thinking that the cantatrice, with whom no one in the manor appears to be occupied any longer, might be the pivot and the motor of my rancor and my chagrin, she is try-

249

ing, moving from one deduction to another, to succeed in solving the dolorous problem, but cannot do it.

Withdrawn into myself like a hunted malefactor, I have condemned myself to a silence all the more atrocious because I am haunted day and night by the desire to confess everything to her, to cry out and to implore her consolations, as always. But what Antoine Lux takes for a crisis of aggravated neurasthenia does not prevent him from pursuing his sentimental labor. The time he would spend with me, if I were fit and well, he employs in covering lined paper, the mere sight of which puts me in a fury, with his awkward handwriting. And from the depths of the room in which I am secluded, I try to divine the ascendant march of their amity, the growing confidence that they are granting one another, the increasingly familiar aspect of their rapport, and the incomplete birth of their amour.

Their amour? What authorizes me to make use of that word? Did Antoine not rebuke me the other day because I employed that term in speaking of her? Did he not affirm that his only amour was Geneviève Servais, and that, apart from his fiancée, no other woman could pretend to his tenderness? I know my friend's honesty, and although all appearances are in league against him, I know him to be incapable of a treason or a turpitude toward individuals that he cherishes. In consequence, all my anguish and all my dread are vain, and even odious. Bound by a formal engagement to the young woman who will soon bear his name, he will not go back on his word, and the commerce in which he is taking pleasure with the artiste whom we all celebrate here has nothing that can make me anxious or draw me into a stupid jealousy.

The argument I have put to myself several times, and I have ended up persuading myself that my duty is to reappear n the dining room, to become once again the companion of the person I have wrongly suspected of a felony, and who has never shown me anything but affection.

That same evening I take my place again at the extremity of the table. Returned suddenly to joy and health, I eat, drink and joke as if I had never suffered from anything, as if I had not retired for several days from the sight and the company of Alexandrine-Ysolde and Antoine.

In honor of what she took to be a cure, my sister has had the gardener collect enormous sheaves of chrysanthemums and decorate the table with them, filling the urns, the vases and the silver buckets on top of the various items of furniture in the room. In her eyes, this dinner is not just any dinner, but a veritable resurrection feast, and my dear friend, as well as my aged sister, is radiant with delight at finding me beside him again.

In order to demonstrate that nothing of my illness subsists, I spur the conversation myself. I ask whether there has been any interesting transmission during my indisposition, and whether he programs have revealed any new star. With a cunning in which I rejoice internally, and which gives me an elevated idea of my skill in dissimulation, I bring them, without having pronounced it myself, to pronounce Claudia's name. I learn that, in spite of their expectation, she has not sung during the week, and, delighted by the contretemps, I display an insolent satisfaction, which I do not experience in reality, but which I want to oppose anyway to the disappointment they manifest in revealing it to me.

Then I interrogate Antoine about the employment of his hours during the course of my temporary disappearance. He details his quotidian labor obligingly, extending himself regarding his prelude to the third act, in which the double bass of the string decet sings throughout, as a soloist. Vertiginously, for he is orchestrating it as he composes, he has completed that prelude, and offers to let me hear it after dinner, an offer that I accept immediately. But when I try to draw him on to epistolary terrain, I understand that some of my questions indispose him. Pretending not to comprehend his reticence, I change the subject immediately.

That evasion shocks me. The good humor that I thought I had recovered after a week of meditation vanishes suddenly. And yet, I find the energy not to allow the anxiety that has just invaded me to show, and we arrive without encumbrance at the end of the celebratory feast, in which succulent dishes succeeded one another that my beloved sister had prepared in order to please me.

Prodigiously on form this evening Antoine has played me his prelude. While he played, Sahib, attracted by the music and by his desire always to remain beside him, resumed scratching on the other side of the door. Alexandrine-Ysolde went on tiptoe to open it for him. Then he lay down next to the piano, his forepaws wide apart and his ears pricked toward the artiste, as if he did not want to miss a note that vibrated in the baby grand; and from time to time, he passed his red tongue over his iron-gray muzzle, as he does when he is presented with a choice morsel and licks it before swallowing it.

Then we get up, and, as happens every evening when we prepare to go to our bedrooms, Alexandrine-Ysolde to shut herself in hers, I offer my friend a cigarette. He refuses.

"Are you ill?"

"No, but I prefer the pipe. And since you seem disposed to chat before going to bed, would you like to come into my lair for a few minutes."

"What's happening?"

"Events that will surprise you, I fear. Patrice, I'm going to quit you."

"You're quitting me? But you promised to stay here for the greater part of the winter, if not all of it."

"When I promised you that, Patrice," said Lux, in a voice that I divine to be hesitant, "I didn't anticipate the changes that have taken place in my life and my ideas since my arrival here."

I get up, my heart constricted. "Claudia...?"

"Yes," Antoine confesses. "It's because of her that I'm leaving."

"Because of her," I repeat, downcast.

"But not for reasons that will make you shudder, in your incorrigible jealousy. I affirmed to you that I didn't love Claudia, that I loved Geneviève Servais, uniquely and exclusively; and you've tried hard to believe me, but you can't do it. Why? Am I capable, then, of seeking to destroy or diminish the affection she has for you, the sympathy that you value even more than mine?"

I shake my head, too emotional to respond.

"Then rid yourself of the suspicion and bitterness that are gnawing you. You can know the reasons for my departure: here they are. Claudia is going to interpret the role of Rosalinde at the Lyrique. The directors have accepted it; the contract was signed yesterday. But our friend—I say *our* friend intentionally—insists in an absolute fashion that I teach her the role myself. She begs me to do that in each of her letters. Can I refuse her that? Let me leave, to assist in the preparation of my work, and I promise to return here in a few days."

"I know that kind of promise, Antoine. You won't come back."

Antoine sketches a gesture of protest.

"Don't protest. My reproach is utterly fraternal. There's nether anger not offense in it. But I know that when Paris grips you again, it grips you for the whole season, Paris with Claudia all the more so."

"You're reasoning like a child. I repeat to you that I'll come back."

At that new assertion, a sudden chagrin rises to my heart. In a humble voice, I reply to him: "Don't leave, Antoine. What will become of me if you both abandon me?"

"Abandon you! What a big word! For an absence that might last two months, perhaps much less!" he says, trying to make a joke of it.

I repeat, my voice even humbler: "Don't leave, Antoine. You can't understand how much I'll suffer from your being so far away."

"We'll write to you."

"You won't have time to do it, and if you had, you wouldn't get around to it, for the concern of realizing your work will dominate you to the point that you'll forget everything else. And you, who know the most secret depths of my soul, know that I couldn't live now, if I ceased to live with the two of you."

"But how do you expect me to arrange things?" he asked, raising his arms toward the ceiling.

Then, without knowing why, without reflection, without being able to stop myself, I launch the insensate phrase that stupefies him, that freezes him.

"It's quite simple. Invite her to come here."

"To this house?"

"Why not? You can teach her the role here. And when everything's ready, you can leave—but at that point, you'll only leave for a few weeks." And I add, effortfully, my lips dry: "And if you don't come back again, at least I'll have seen her. I'll know her."

"It's not possible!" Lux attests.

"Because of this?" I stammer, pointing at the mask of black cloth.

"It's not a matter of your mask or your face. Our mentalities permit us to place intellectual merit and the beauty of the heart above accidental imperfections. Have no fear of any horror on Claudia Pichet's part; I can guarantee that."

"Then it's because you've written to her…what have you revealed to her?"

"Nothing! I swear to you, my dear Patrice, that she knows nothing about your accident and its consequences."

"And by what right, in those conditions, do you dare to affirm that the mere sight of me won't put her in flight?"

"The right that I have to tell you that her soul is worth as much as ours, and that I can answer for her as I would for the two of us."

A long silence falls between us. Outside, nothing is moving, nothing vibrating, nothing quivering.

I take up the thread of my idea again. "Well, what have you decided?"

"I don't know. I'm so bewildered, so suffocated. Have you talked to your sister about this?"

"How could I have? The project dates from a few minutes ago. It's my fear of seeing you leave that suggested it to me. But I'll explain it to her, and I'm sure that she'll immediately endorse my opinion."

Antoine Lux shook his head several times. "You're deluding yourself, Patrice."

"What makes you anticipate a refusal?"

"How do I know? In any case, I might be mistaken. In sum, talk to her anyway. But Claudia? Would she come? Would she dare to come to an abode where she'll only encounter strangers?"

"Strangers, us?"

"Certainly. Strangers who call themselves friends on paper, but strangers in the full meaning of the term. And I declare to you frankly, Patrice, that I won't transit such a proposition. That offer has to come from you, or no one."

I look at him, stupefied.

Me, ask her that? But in soliciting that favor from her, would it not be necessary for me to reveal what I could hide from her if I allowed Antoine to leave? Would it not be necessary to declare to her that I'm a man eliminated from the remainder of the living, and that the day when she sees me for the first time, she won't be able to repress, any more than all those who see me, the movement of disgust and repulsion that distances me from all my fellows.

To recommence ascending, for the insensate pleasure of putting into execution an absurd idea, a Calvary even more dolorous than all the preceding Calvaries? Evidently, that would be atrocious, and I would reawaken, pointlessly, suffering that I thought I could avoid henceforth. To receive Claudia here, as I've proposed to Lux, would be bordering on dementia. Certainly, I could hide from her the sentiment that her beauty has inspired in me, since I'm certain that she could never respond to it; but, that point settled, what attitude could I adopt with regard to her? That of a sometimes inconvenient comrade whom she dare not drive away for very comprehensible reasons, but whose frequent or absolute effacement she could not weary of desiring, alone or in petty committee?

The best thing to do, if I felt that I had the courage, would be to remain as I was at the beginning of our relationship: a music-lover. That the music-lover in question, being rich enough, should have the whim to shelter and aid an artiste, by means of the collaboration and support of an illustrious composer numbered among his friends, to conquer the glory of which she seems worthy, is perfectly plausible.

I accept, with a certain complaisance, that amelioration of my original idea, and even linger over it without posing the definitive objections that my previous plans presented. Those Maecenean perspectives wouldn't fail to cheer me up if I were better disposed than I am at present. For, to the preoccupation caused by a design whose dangers I recognize, and which I would like, at the same time, to be able to reject and to realize, is added the equally grave preoccupation of opening myself to my sister, of asking for her opinion, and deploying sufficient skill to bring her to share my views if, as everything suggests, she opposes them bitterly, at least to begin with.

For forty-eight hours I hesitate between the desire I have to let Antoine go and the obsessive idea of retaining him by means of the irresistible lure that I extended to him to days before.

Then, one morning when I find myself alone with him. I ask him point-blank: "Are you still disposed to leave if she doesn't come?"

"It's indispensable," Antoine replies "And as she truly has no worthwhile reason for nesting herself here, I anticipate that my departure will take place next Sunday."

"Next Sunday?"

"And even then I'm delaying it slightly because I'm no happier anywhere than with the two of you, and I always experience a sharp chagrin in quitting Alexandrine-Ysolde and you."

"That's your final word?"

"Can I conduct myself in any other fashion?"

Without replying to him directly, I place my hand on his forearm, and, looking him in the eye: "In a week, Claudia Pichet will disembark here."

Antoine shrugs his shoulders. "Childishness!"

"Today, after dinner, I'll talk to my sister."

"That's what I feared!" says my friend. "We've been living so tranquilly. Why strive to destroy the peace of the hearth?"

"I won't destroy it. I'll introduce a new element of charm into it, and you'll be the first to thank me for it."

"I accept the augury," the master replies, "but I hope, in spite of everything, that your sister resists with all her might the proposition that you're going to submit to her."

He gives me an affectionate slap between the shoulder-blades. The he heads for the exit, but turns round as he is about to disappear. "What a simultaneously admirable and puerile heart you possess, my dear Patrice!"

"Is that a reproach?"

"No, a regret. I would have preferred you to be less good, less impulsive."

"It's too late to remake me. And then, if I had that power, I'd commence by recreating myself physically. The rest would come later—but much later."

Two o'clock was chiming on the clock in the hall to which we usually retired for a while after lunch when I communicated to my sister, at the same time as the news of Antoine's impending departure, the decision I had made in order to retain him in our midst for longer.

I had anticipated the effect that a discourse as stupefying as it as unexpected would produce in her unprepared mind. That was why I had, before starting, implored her to listen to me until the end without interruption, even if what she heard irritated her or astounded her. While talking to her, I observed her. And, successively, I saw reflected in her beautiful wrinkled face all the sentiments that agitated her.

To begin with, pain. Antoine was quitting us; and for her, that imminent disappearance was like the flight of a second brother. Afterwards, surprise and anger. To have envisaged the advent in this retreat of a living being other than the one from whom we would soon be separated was a hypothesis she could not admit. Her revolt against a project so contrary to our resolution not to see anyone except Antoine, until our last breath, was increased further by the fact that the possible visitor was a stranger and an actress. Finally, jealousy! For, since the catastrophe in the course of which her devotion had attained the immolation of all her desires and all her dreams, no figure had been interposed between us, and the thought that the intruder would live the same life as us, would sit down at our table, would be associated with our joys, mingling with the intimacy in which she and I were egotistically confined, became so intolerable to her that she could not help weeping and moaning.

But, entirely devoted to my story, to the picture I was painting of an incomparable and unhoped-for happiness, I did not hear her. It was necessary for her to rise to her feet, at the moment when I finished my long speech, march toward me and place her trembling hands on my shoulders for me to sense the recall to reality. I saw her red eyelids, the tears that were striping the whiteness of the crumpled nacre of her cheeks—and that spectacle moved me so profoundly that I uttered a dolorous exclamation.

She made no response to that. But, after a moment of silence, when the crisis of sobbing had calmed down somewhat, she murmured: "You, my Patrice! You want to impose such a thing on me!"

"It's necessary," I replied. "It's the only means to conserve Antoine."

"Oh, let him go," she advised. "You know very well that he'll come back to us. And we'll remain alone here, as we swore to one another."

"He'll only ask to remain, if you accept the plan that I've just proposed. He'll affirm it himself. And between us, in what way would the presence of Claudia Pichet at Lagarde-Viaur be inconvenient? Wouldn't you be content, wouldn't you experience some pride in having contributed to the propagation of her talent, to her ascent toward renown? What a light in our life of darkness! Personally, I consider that we've never accomplished anything so noble."

"It's not for me that I'm afraid, Patrice."

"It's for me? What can you fear? I'll warn her honesty. I'll tell her what I am. I'll explain to her by what accident a young man with the harmonious and regular features of old became a scarecrow that everyone in the world avoids. I'll ask her, if she doesn't feel that she has the courage to confront the frightful sight of me without paling, to stay in Paris, to write to Antoine without replying directly to me, to spare herself a journey from which she might bring back an insupportable heartbreak, and we'll break there. You see, Alexandrine-Ysolde, that I've prepared for a defeat in advance."

My sister-mama's large eyes looked down into mine.

"How you must love her!" she pronounced, slowly.

At that remark, in which there was simultaneously so much dolor, so much anguish and so much dread, a shudder runs through me from head to toe. I open my mouth to reply to her, but my seizure is such that the words refuse to emerge and I remain mute and quasi-petrified before her.

"How you must love her!" Alexandrine-Ysolde repeats.

Now, I understand that I have to speak, in order not to leave such an affirmation without a reply, without a protest. I cannot find the courage. I can scarcely articulate, by assembling the little energy that still remains in me, a feeble negation.

"You're mistaken. I don't love her." Then, almost immediately, a little more loudly: "Have I the right to love anyone, as you mean it?"

"Doesn't the heart believe that it has every right, my poor boy?"

"Other hearts, but not mine."

"By virtue of what do you pretend to escape the common rule? Do you believe, then, because your face has been tortured, that your heart hasn't remained the same? No, my child. You have to love, and nothing can prevent you from doing so. And it's necessary that you love to a degree that I can't envisage without shivering, since you've settled, in order to get closer to her, on the most foolish and most reprehensible resolution that a man could invent."

"You don't approve of me, then?"

"I disapprove of you with all my strength, Patrice. And while I'm alive, Claudia Pichet will never enter here."

On hearing those words of defiance—the first bad words that Alexandrine-Ysolde had pronounced since we had been making our way through life side by side—I straighten up, moved by a sudden revolt. I must be livid, for my sister recoils instinctively before me, and collides as she retreats with the back of a chair, which she tips over. As if the anger that has been seething within me since the beginning of the conversation were only waiting for that noise to explode, I march toward her, fist raised.

"So," I cry, "I shall remain under your domination until the last breath? As a child, your despotic authority slowly annihilated my good instincts, As an adolescent, your perfidious advice turned me away from the paths I would have taken and transformed me into a young man with a larval mentality As a man, finally ready to escape the deadly law under which you curbed me, the adversity that had pursued me since birth returned me entirely and definitively to your unhealthy yoke, the day after the fall from which I emerged transformed into a monster. Incapable of a reaction, I accepted everything: the renunciation of pleasure, happiness and independence. I became once again the child that one leads in a harness, whose passive obedience, affection and credulity one is certain of conserving. You have imposed exile on me in this sinister corner, and, with the ferocity of a hunter lying in ambush, you have forced me to cut off all contact with the exterior world.

And I shall grow old, condemned without attenuating circumstances to the prison of which you constitute the odious jailer, now that the horizon has suddenly illuminated for me with such magnificence that I remain dazzled? Don't count on it!

"From this evening, Alexandrine-Ysolde, old spinster with a tyrannical and obsolete soul, I am liberating myself. Your authority usurped, I shall sweep it aside, as one draws away a curtain that hides the dawn, and before you, in spite of you, in spite of everyone, I proclaim my absolute right to liberty. The burden of your jesuitical tenderness I am finally allowing to fall, with clamors of joy. I am becoming human again! I am becoming the master here! Know this well, Alexandrine-Ysolde: it is only me, in this house, who will give orders henceforth. And the first of those orders is the following: Claudia Pichet will come to my house."

Alexandrine-Ysolde listened to me and looked at me.

Too overexcited to be able to observe the successive transformations of her physiognomy, I did not take account either of her pallor, the convulsive tremor that was agitating her, or the fear that was gradually painted on her poor tortured face. I went on, and on, more carried away as I continued my execrable tirade. And when I had belched it all, when the exacerbation alienating my judgment, my conscience, my justice and my honesty died away for lack of fuel, I collapsed into an armchair; and, like a judge awaiting the response of the accused that he believes he has confounded, I awaited my sister's reply.

It was instantaneous.

Vibrant with indignation, her black mantilla falling over her hollow temples, she extended her emaciated hands toward me.

"Patrice," she said, "You have just pronounced irreparable words. I shall not point out your insults, your infamies or your lies. I shall simply say this: when a brother who owes his sister all that you owe me forgets his sacred debt to that degree, and debases himself in a crisis of sadism and dementia like the one that has dishonored you forever, relegated to the level of the worst of ingrates and the worst of boors, that brother and that sister can no longer have anything in common. This night will be the last that I shall spend here. Tomorrow, at dawn, I shall quit, never to return, the prison where I have sequestered you for six years. Free, in accordance with your wish, master of giving the orders that come to your mind, you can finally organize life far from me. You can organize it in your own way. You can receive whoever you wish, Claudia Pichet first of all. But know this, Patrice: you will soon attain the apogee of your dolor, a dolor compared to which the bitterest of your past torments will be nonexistent. Don't appeal to me then. Don't implore me. I will not respond either to your pleas or your supplications. From this moment on, the person you named, in taking refuge in her arms, your sister-mama, ceases to know you."

And, without turning round to dart a supreme glance at me, Alexandrine-Ysolde left the room.

The sound of the door closing behind her, caused me to start. Like a subject in a hypnotic trance, I could not see or hear anything around me. But an impression of solitude, such that I thought I could feel a glacial cold falling over my shoulders, enveloped me suddenly. In a few seconds, my fury dissipated and gave way to an immeasurable depression. Then, as reason returned to me, an exact notion of my ignoble conduct became precise in my consciousness with a frightful clarity.

In the course of a quarrel unworthy of me I had insulted the person whose soul was so elevated and clement. For a remark that had disappointed me, jolted me and thwarted a dubitable design hatched in a feverish brain, I had insulted the person who loved me more than anything and who had consecrated the best and purest of herself—her heart—to me since my childhood. Were the motives I had invoked sufficient to justify my shameful reproaches, to legitimate the cynicism with which I had thrown the bloodiest insults into the face of that unfortunate woman? No, truly. Nothing could excuse me. And my sister was within her rights in quitting, without seeing me again, a house where she had been subjected to such an affront.

For she was quitting it! While I came back to myself, while I evaluated my villainy in her regard, her heart torn by the greatest chagrin of her existence, she was packing her bags, and in a few hours, I would never see her again. With her gone, what would I become? An inert thing, incapable of a decision or an initiative; and nothing and no one would be able to console me for the departure of my sister-mama. Yes, I was mad when fury had stood me up in confrontation with her, and all my life would not be sufficient to absolve myself and try to lead her to a progressive forgetfulness of that tragic afternoon.

So, what was I waiting for, to run to her, to force the door of the bedroom where she was sobbing, crushed in some armchair, to part the hands clenched in front of her eyes, to kneel before her and to ask for mercy, like an irresponsible child, for my inexcusable attitude?

I ran, hanging on to the heavy iron rail in order to be able to climb the stairs two by two, up to the first floor. Having arrived on the landing, advancing on tiptoe, so great was my fear that she might hear me, I reached her door.

For several seconds, I listened, thinking that I might perceive through the thick oak door the sound of her footsteps or her muffled groans. Nothing was moving. Everything remained mute. Frightened by that silence, I knocked on the waxed wood with my folded index finger, and as I knocked I called to my sister in a low voice: "Alexandrine-Ysolde?"

No reply.

With more violence, I knocked on the door again. and in a firmer voice I reiterated my appeal: "Alexandrine-Ysolde! Open the door, I beg you."

No movement, not a breath inside.

Invaded by an abrupt fear, I tried to release the latch, to seize the key, to open the ancient lock. The latch was blocked. The key had been removed and taken inside.

I returned to the charge for a third time, with the same lack of success.

What is happening, then? Has my sister wanted to forbid me, by locking herself in her room, any attempt at reconciliation, or is she lying inanimate on a carpet without me being able to hasten to her aid? My anguish is untranslatable. All suppositions collide in my brain, fermenting there, seething there as if to make my skull explode, digging into it with such violence that, under their mysterious impulsion, I start launching great blows of the first against the entrance.

This time, someone budges inside. I hear a chair being displaced. Muffled footsteps sound on the carpet. A key turns; and, as white as a cadaver, Alexandrine-Ysolde appears in the embrasure of the door.

Motionless and dry-eyed, she considers me for a moment. Then, in a voice so low that it is more akin to breathing than speech, she asks: "What are you doing here?"

Those five words, departing form that discolored mouth, impress me to such a point that, without finding the means to articulate a response, I fall to my knees before her. But my sister, insensible to that unforeseen repentance, does not budge. That fixity, that impassivity, ends up frightening me, unhinging me. Like a man bewildered by too heavy and intoxication, I raise my atonal eyes toward her. However, after a superhuman effort, I become capable of stammering her name again: "Alexandrine-Ysolde!"

That stifled appeal stiffens her further, if possible. The gleam of her eyes, ordinarily so tender and benevolent, has become as hard as a metallic reflection. I have never seen that gleam before! What sudden cruelty, what unshakable firmness, does it denote in a woman whose propensity for indulgence and forbearance I know so well? What metamorphosis has taken place in her, that she can look at me without tenderness and conserve in confrontation with me the silence that frightens me?

And like a plaint, I repeat: "Alexandrine-Ysolde forgive me."

Twice, in response to my imploration, my sister shakes her head. She takes a step back. Then, leaning on the open batten of the double door, this time turning her gaze away from mine, as if she feared weakening, she repeats, without changing a single word, the sentence by means of which, a little while ago, she launched anathema upon me:

"When a brother who owes his sister all that you owe me forgets his sacred debt to that degree, and debases himself in a crisis of sadism and dementia like the one that has dishonored you forever, to the level of the worst of ingrates and the worst of boors, that brother and that sister can no longer have anything in common. Go back to your room, Patrice. Everything is finished between us."

A sob shakes me. I extend my arms to her, in an infinite supplication.

"Tomorrow, at eight-thirty, I shall embark for Paris. Please give orders for the auto to be ready, and for Justin or Max, as you choose, to take me to the station at Najac or Villefranche."

"You shan't go!"

"Tomorrow, at eight-thirty," my sister says, emphatically. "I dare to hope that you will not disobey my last wish."

With a push, she closes the door again. Then she blocks the latch and turns the key in the lock. For a second, her footsteps brush the cart.

And nothing else.

Tottering, my heart horribly constricted, I return to my room. I let myself fall on to my bed, and, my head buried in the down of the pillow, I start to reflect dolorously.

I know the entire character of my sister sufficiently to know that she will not go back on her decision. Henceforth, and for a time that I cannot calculate, I am all alone in this house.

But in the midst of my affliction and my despair, a thought rises from the ulcerated depths of my despair, and like an invisible balm, it soothes the wounds where the most secret corners of my soul have been bleeding for an hour. With Alexandrine-Ysolde departed, even if I never see her again,

Claudia can come freely! Nothing more opposes my writing the letter in which I will offer her hospitality.

Perhaps...

But what shall I reply to my friend when he interrogates me about the disappearance of my sister? What story can I invent in order to explain that flight, without saying a word about my odious attack and the mortal blow that I dealt to the person he cherishes as much as me? And this evening, when the dinner bell rings, and the middle place is empty, and the usual flowers are not decorating the table where we love so much to gather, what pretext could possibly sound plausible to him? I try to invent with his intention a thousand arguments, which I reject one by one.

And night falls without my being able to find anything remotely acceptable or remotely logical.

Oh, the mealtime carillon that resonates in my ears, how it exasperates me! I haven't seen Antoine since the end of lunch. I fear finding myself alone with him, for he sees though me like a sheet of crystal and he will divine, in a matter of minutes, what I want to hide from him at all costs.

"What is your sister doing?" he asks, as he sits down. "It's the first time she's been late like this."

"She's indisposed," I proffer, in a weak voice. "I don't think she'll come down."

Justin, who serves us to the exclusion of all the other domestics, and who has just heard the end of my speech, approaches us.

"Mademoiselle telephoned me a little while ago," he said. "She begs the messieurs to excuse her, but she is suffering from a migraine so intense that she has been obliged to go to bed, and is incapable of absorbing any aliment."

As Justin speaks, the anguish that grips my throat to the point of preventing me from breathing disappears. All the trouble I have given myself in order to discover an argument susceptible of convincing Antoine Lux becomes unnecessary, since my sister has anticipated my most ardent desires by justifying her absence thus.

266

"What a pity!" Antoine sighs. "Such a fine dinner!" and, with a formidable noise of mandibles, he dissects the half-grouse that Justin has just place on his plate.

Installed facing him, I try to do the same. Wasted effort. I try to wash down each mouthful with a swig of Burgundy, but the game will not pass. Antoine, who observes my gastronomic inferiority, teases me affectionately

"Word of honor," he affirms, with a smile, "I'd swear that you're in love"

"In love, me? With whom?"

"I don't know. But you, whose appetite everyone usually venerates, are so poorly convivial this evening that it seems extraordinary to me. What's up?"

"I'm upset because of my sister." I explain to my friend.

"It isn't serious! A headache? I know that; when we wake up tomorrow it will be gone."

Tomorrow, when we wake up.

What unfortunate words my poor Antoine has just pronounced! All my anxieties are suddenly resuscitated, and, with a desolate gesture, I push away my plate, still full. Then, suddenly getting up, without a word of excuse or explanation, I leave the dining room and take refuge in my bedroom.

Antoine, amazed by that inexplicable departure, follows me there, and, brandishing his napkin, strives to obtain some enlightenment from me. I refuse him any. Bewildered by my attitude, by the dejection painted on my physiognomy, by my mutism, he leaves without having been able to get anything out of me. Even Justin, who has come to enquire about my condition, is no more fortunate, and, after half a hour of solicitations and vain pleas, he returns to his parlor.

I find myself alone, in complete darkness, in the immense room.

It was in the course of that period of isolation that I made a second attempt with regard to my sister. A failure even more pitiful that that of the afternoon awaited me. Alexandrine-Ysolde did not even deign to open her door to me, and I went back to my room after a series of fruitless appeals. I lay down without being able to close an eye, and, up at first light. I stationed myself at the threshold by through which my sister-mama would soon emerge for the last time.

Successively, with an increasing anguish, I heard her cuckoo-clock chirp the hours through the thick wall. As it sighed seven-thirty, rapid footsteps going up the staircase made me shudder; and Justin, who was coming to fetch my sister's luggage in order to stow it in the auto, appeared at the height of the landing.

At the sight of him, I stand up straight, putting a finger over my mouth to suppress the clamor of surprise that is already rising to his lips.

"Monsieur here!" he says, in a low voice.

"Shut up, Justin!" I order. "Go into Mademoiselle's room, and don't tell her that you've seen me."

"Yes, Monsieur."

I hide in the gloom of the corridor. Justin knocks on the door three times, and Alexandrine-Ysolde, in traveling costume, comes to open it.

I let the valet de chambre go in. I let him come out again a few minutes later. In his left hand he is carrying a heavy valise, and in the right a hat box that I know well. I let him disappear down the broad staircase; then, without ringing or knocking and without pronouncing a word, I penetrate into the room, where the bed is made and all the furniture covered by dust-sheets, and collapse at Alexandrine-Ysolde's knees.

My sister, nonplussed by seeing me before her in such an attitude, cannot help recoiling, uttering a stifled cry.

With two hands, I seize the hem of her dress. I veil my face with it; and in that posture of humility I implore her pardon for a third time. I do so in terms so spontaneous, so honest; my repentance of the odious incident that I provoked and from which she is suffering so much, I recognize with such frankness, with such desolation, that Alexandrine-Ysolde, gripped by a sudden tremor, leans on the back of an armchair, and replies to me in a dull voice:

"Get up, Patrice, and close the door."

While I carry out her order, she sits down in the chair on which she was bracing herself a moment before. She drops the overnight bag that she was carrying beside her. She considers me with a visible pity, but, contrary to my prognostications, she does not weep.

I stay there, understanding that she is going to speak, awaiting with an inconceivable avidity the definitive sentence that will emerge from her mouth, or the absolution that will conclude her statement.

"I believe," she commences, "in the sincerity of your regret. You know my heart well enough to know that I absolved you from the first moment that you begged me to pardon you. At the present moment, after my voluntary retreat for a day and a night, al the anger that rose in me has subsided. I am therefore speaking to you without rancor, if not without sadness, and I want you to hear me out, without interruption."

"I'll listen," I promise her.

"Our last conversation will, in any case, be brief," she continues. "It did not take me long to comprehend the irresistible passion into which you were plunged, first by the talent and then by the beauty of the artiste whose lover you are dreaming of becoming, and whom you are seeking, in order to arrive at your goal, to invite to stay here. Don't protest. Don't interrupt; you've promised. You're the master of arranging your life as you wish, and not for anything in the world would I want to retain you under my tutelage, as you reproached me for doing yesterday. Welcome her, since it pleases you. I no longer oppose it. I forgive you for everything you have made me suffer. I forgive you from the utmost depths of my soul, my poor boy. But as I do not want to be the witness of what will happen in this house after the advent of Claudia Pichet, I ask you for the authorization to absent myself for a few weeks. You will not be alone, in the company of your friend and the woman you love. You know what a gift of divination I bear within me, when it is a matter of things that concern you or the misfortunes that threaten you."

"Misfortunes?"

"Have I not always foreseen them? At this moment, in any case, there can be no question of pain or joy. It is sufficient that you are simply assured on one point: on the day when my presence here becomes necessary, I will leave. Don't call me. You will find me beside you, and you will see, whatever happens then, that you can count on the reckless tenderness of your sister-mama. Embrace me, Patrice; embrace me forcefully. And now let me go."

"Stay!"

"I'll come back, I swear to you. Believe me: it's better that I go away for the time being. Savor a little independence, and re-enter into life, as you desire so much. You still have need of further proofs, since those of old are not sufficient for your heart hungry for mourning and suffering."

Alexandrine-Ysolde stands up.

"Accompany me to the auto, my boy. You can do that. Justin will drive me."

Incapable of reiterating my plea, indescribably moved by the thought of the pardon that I have just obtained, and—why hide it from myself—the thought that I shall see Claudia in a few days, I pick up the overnight bag, and, my arm under that of my sister-mama, I go down the stone stairway. And while we go down, I risk questioning her.

"May I know where you're going?"

"Certainly. To Paris, to our town house. I've kept it, you know. Don't be sad any longer, my child. I no longer hold anything against you. I'll send you my news often, very often. And I'll come back when it's necessary."

As a sign of gratitude, I squeeze the fragile hand that is placed in mine, as if to seek a refuge there from my wickedness.

Before the perron, the engine of my Voisin is purring joyously. My sister's luggage is attached to the back of the 40CV. And Justin, the chinstrap of his helmet fastened, awaits the order to set forth.

One last long, long embrace...

My sister leaps into the back seat. The chauffeur-valet closes the door, takes hold of the steering-wheel and puts his foot on the clutch. A few grunts, a few explosions, and, panting like a delirious beast, the steel hippogriff bounds over the gravel of the driveway.

I watch it disappear. Then, my head empty, forsaken, I go back up to Alexandrine-Ysolde's room and I lie down on the bed in which she has slept so often.

I'm alone. I'm all alone, for the first time in my life, in this accursed dwelling.

I have never experienced such a sensation of abandonment. It seems to me that everything around me is extinct, and the sunlight that is filtering between the blinds, instead of calming me down, frightens me. Alexandrine-Ysolde has left me. She has left me by my own fault, by the fault of my pride, my stupidity and my cruelty. She has stepped aside before a stranger who might never set foot here; and today, I am losing, with my surest friend, my most loyal and powerful support.

Why have I let her depart? Why have I shown myself, in her regard, so weak, so irresolute and so cowardly? Ought I not to have retained her, to have demonstrated to her that her departure would bring about the total annihilation of my will-power, my intellect and my intelligence? Do I not know her well enough to know that she would have yielded to my supplications, if I had taken her in my arms, if I had placed my poor desolate head on her shoulder, as of old?

And beneath me, in the drawing room, Antoine Lux begins to play the piano.

At first very slow, like a whisper, and then more assured as the musical fever takes possession of the virtuoso, the melodic phrases unfurl around my distress, enveloping it with their softness, their caresses, their nostalgia. I recognize the refrain, Schubert's *Adieu!* The *Adieu* that Alexandrine-Ysolde loved so much...

And, sensing around me the infallible affection of my friend, a serenity, at first insensible, then warmer, and then more penetrating, rises within me. It takes away, gradually, effortlessly, the heartsickness that is tearing me. It dissipates, as a gentle breeze dissipates autumnal drizzle, the ennui in which my entire being is dying.

Propping myself up on the bed, ears pricked, I listen to him. I listen to him, resuscitated by the beauty that he pours over me with a profusion all the more impetuous because he believes himself to be alone on the ground floor. And in order to hear him at closer range, I leap off the bed on which I am languishing. Without him having heard me coming, I sit down beside him on a black wooden stool, and I stay there, my head in my hands, thinking about my sister, my misfortunes, and Claudia...

And mentally, I repeat, underlined by the harmonies of the piano, still muffled by the soft pedal, the words that Alexandrine-Ysolde pronounced at the moment of her departure:

"You're the master of arranging your life as you wish. Welcome her, since it pleases you."

VI

My letter was dispatched this morning.

It seemed to me to be so difficult to write that I spent all day rewriting it. I reread it more than three times before sealing the envelope, and now that a train is carrying it away, buried in a sack with hundreds of others, I suddenly perceive that I know it by heart and that I could reconstitute it, if necessary from the first page to the last.

It is necessary to come, Friend. It is necessary because we want to know one another, and because you could not work in conditions as favorable anywhere but here. You will come to see us, but more in order to undertake your important labor than to obey your curiosity, will you not? And I like it thus. For if other motives dominated you than the desire to learn beside my friend of genius the work of which you will be the creator this winter, you would be hastening to the greatest disappointment that a woman can experience. My dwelling only counts two inhabitants: the master and me. The master? You know who he is, artistically and physically. I have no need, therefore, to talk about him. With regard to myself, it is not the same. And it is while quivering with anguish and shivering with fear that I begin this terrible confession.

You think of me—and you have written it with the most amiable malice in the world—as a kind of gentleman farmer striding over his lands from dawn to dusk, costumed in velvet, gaitered in sheepskin, followed by a pack of hounds. You suppose that my sole occupation consists of supervising the labor of my servants, of reprimanding them, of running after hares and wild boar in the company of other local castellans, amid the bare mountains of the Rouergue. You imagine me riding astride a long-haired horse, incessantly smoking an enormous briar pipe, face illuminated, speech truculent, ever ready for gallant assaults, drinking and feasting—and that rejoices you in advance, you once confessed to me.

How far you are from the truth, my friend, and how reluctant I am to dispel with a word all the illusions that you nourish and which charm you. But I must, under penalty of lying and dishonesty. And that is why, brutally, I am warning you. The man that you see in such favorable colors was, not a stout country squire, but one of those sportsmen who, poor fools, put above the merits of intellect and intelligence, the slimness of the figure and the development of the pectorals, and care very little about their mental atrophy and their ignorance. He belonged to Parisian high society, and as he was, in addition to his corporeal advantages, rich enough to satisfy their whims and caprices, women competed for his favors and rarely refused him the most agreeable concessions.

That man, sought-after by reason of the attractions he was just listed for you, also nourished the passion of the auto. He piloted personally the vertiginous monsters that obsess you, growling with lassitude and revolt, until the day when, profiting from your inattention, your clumsiness or your ill luck, they avenge themselves in an instant for what they have endured from us for years. The horrible accident with which the entire capital and the Côte d'Azur resounded seven years ago, overtook me near Ventimiglia. One day, when you're here, I'll tell you the story in detail. Then you'll have seen me, and you'll understand, in looking at the monster that I became after my crash, my fear of being encountered by my fellows, my distress and my tragic solitude,

But don't worry. I shall not importune you. My abode will become yours. You can stay here as long as you think it appropriate, and in exchange for the luminous beauty with which you will dazzle us for a few weeks, I promise only to impose my presence and the sight of me upon you as rarely as possible. If you manifest the desire, I will even turn away from you when you pass along the pathways of the park or the terraces of my house. You will understand, in any case, how much I dread finding myself face to face with my fellows, on

learning that my servants, with only one exception, have or-
ders, under pain of instant dismissal, never to appear before
me.

Lux affirms that you will not attach any importance to
my disfigurement. I do not share his opinion. Whatever your
strength of character might be, and the nobility of your heart,
you will close your eyes on seeing me for the first time, and
you will close them often subsequently, if you are able, more
hardened than the common run, to tolerate my proximity.

Come anyway, my friend. We shall reserve for you, in
this remote manor, a welcome worthy of the legendary prin-
cess that you are; and if you grant me the favor of sometimes
singing for me, I shall not ask for anything more of the person
for whose arrival I hope with an inconceivable impatience...

A week of waiting: a week during which I watch from
my window for Justin's approach.

In the mail, newspapers, periodicals, letters from Alexandrine-Ysolde—whose absence I am amazed to support so
easily—but not a word from Claudia.

Antoine Lux, more philosophical than me, contents himself with laughing and mocking me. For myself, I suffer. I
read, as a matter of duty, the correspondence in which my
sister keeps me up to date with Paris, the people she has found
again there, and those who have disappeared—everything I
once loved and now hate, with all my might. And I arrive at
such a degree of enervation and impatience that I sometimes
let five or six days go by without replying to her.

She is afflicted by that, but not irritated by it.

All this, she writes to me, *I foresaw. But I don't attach*
any importance to it. When the time comes, you'll see me re-
turn. Until then, my dear child, count on my faithful tender-
ness, and be good.

Be good!

That recommendation, in which I divine so much apprehension, so much mysterious dread, she reiterates to me in
every letter. And it appears to me to be so ridiculous and so

aggravating, the continuous jet of that exhortation, that I cannot bear it. I heap my sister with reproaches. Docile to my slightest desires, Alexandrine-Ysolde suppresses the phrase that exasperated me.

But that gives me no more pleasure than before in reading her prose. And, obsessed by my waiting to the point of being unable to eat and drink, I soon neglect to open her poor missives, and let them pile upon my table in a pitiful little heap.

This morning, at quarter to ten, I finally received *her* response. Hiding myself away, like a wild beast carrying a royal prey to its air, I took refuge in my study; and there, poring over the paper striped with fly-specks, I devoured the lines that brought me the realization of my dearest wish.

I love paradoxical situations, my dear friend, Claudia writes. *And on that authority, it was sufficient for you to prophesy the malaise and repugnance into which the spectacle of your so-called ugliness would plunge me for me to reply to you: I'll come. I've sung twenty times over in halls where the most horrible wrecks of the war were gathered. And before those broken muzzles, not only have I never flinched, but I have never lowered my eyes. Send an auto, therefore, on Thursday morning, to meet the eight-fifty train. I'll disembark at Najac, since you advise it. And if you want to push temerity to the point of coming to wait for me yourself, nothing would cause me more satisfaction.*

Without finishing reading the other page, I rushed into the drawing room where Lux is working and hold out the sheets to him. Placidly, he read them from the first line to the last. And, as he handed them back to me, he looked at me.

"You're content, Patrice?"

"I'm exultant. Can't you see that? Aren't you?"

"Me? Not at all. That young woman is going to trouble our intimacy. And I wonder whether I haven't made a mistake, whether I haven't committed a gross stupidity, in accepting the proposition you made me in the course of an inexplicable fit of enthusiasm. Anyway, since the champagne is uncorked, let's drink it. But truly, I would have liked to have a greater pleasure than this."

"You're talking seriously?" I remarked.

"For once, yes."

"To bad, for my happiness is inconceivable, and I'd give a great deal to bring you to share it."

"Thursday is three days hence?"

"Exactly."

"Then summon Justin as quickly as possible. You'll scarcely have time to prepare everything in honor of this princess."

"Aren't you going to help us?"

"No, Patrice. I too have preparations to make. It's necessary for me to put my fingers to work, or resign myself to losing in her eyes my reputation as a virtuoso. To each his task, my dear, and mine isn't the least ingrate."

"As you wish. Justin and I will arrange her room, then," I riposted, in a dry tone.

"Now you're sulking, big baby? For such inoffensive words? Come on, calm down. I'll help you."

My heart full of joy, I ring for Justin immediately. I announce to him the imminent arrival of a lady from Paris, who is Antoine Lux's best friend. While listening to me, Justin smiled softly. I know that disillusioned smile of my old friend Justin, for Justin is more than a valet de chambre to me—and I know what it signifies

Yes, yes, my good man, you can talk! Antoine Lux's best friend? And the rest!

But as he is both discreet and respectful, my servant has progressively repressed the smile that once gave rose to rather sharp observation, and it is with an impenetrable visage that he receives my instructions and orders.

We will give Claudia Pichet a large room overlooking the park, situated alongside my sister's room: a vast room illuminated in the modern style by the painter Geo Gyaniny, of which the furniture alone, all authentic Louis XV, represents a fortune. In a corner, between the double-glazed window and the cupboard, there is a Pleyel harpsichord, a marvel of both cabinet-making and instrument-making, permitting her to work while accompanying herself on the role that my dear Antoine has reserved for her. Beyond the centenarian trees of the avenue, Claudia will be able to contemplate the aerie of the local peasants, an aerie as sinister and stony as their souls; Lagarde-Viaur. A maid designated by Justin will be specifically attached to her service, and everything leads me to suppose that the daughter of the Egyptian woman and the baton-wielder Casimir Pichet will find sufficient comfort in my abode to make her forget the paltriness and discomfort of Parisian lodgings.

In accord with Antoine, we have settled the details of our existence during her sojourn with us. Everything has been anticipated, from the majority of the menus that our old cook, Clotilde, excels at preparing for us, to the flowers with which we shall garnish the coppers of the dining room, the pewters of the drawing room and the flame-colored sandstones of her bedroom.

As a sign of rejoicing, before going to bed, I opened the letters from my sister that I had piled up pell-mell on my desk; and I found a poignant charm in that reading. On rereading them, however a slight remorse invaded me at having neglected for a fortnight that worthy woman, who is so full of affection for me that she has succeeded in having herself introduced to Claudia Pichet, in order to be better able to talk to me about her.

Yes, she writes to me, *I wanted to see her. I took advantage of my old friend d'Arbois, the former conductor, who is, as you're not unaware, and unrepentant melomaniac. From melomania to wireless enthusiasm there is only one step, in this epoch when everyone is pursuing the discovery of the unprecedented sensation and the miraculous pleasure. Naturally, when I led the conversation on to the terrain of the wireless, my interlocutor replied to me with fervor, and as he follows in preference to all the others the transmissions of the Eiffel Tower, he immediately spoke to me about Claudia Pichet, of whom the aficionados of* bel canto *declare unanimously that she will surpass the most illustrious cantatrices. He knows her; and, on hearing me express the desire that I had to be introduced to her, he offered to take me to the Tower on the evening of the first concert in which she was to figure.*

Yesterday I found myself face to face with the artiste for the first time. I consider her as a physical perfection, and I dread that the inclination into which you fell for her merely at the slight of her portrait might become mad when she is your guest. Tell me what you think as soon as she arrives. Don't content yourself with praising her and finding her incomparable. Observe her. Study her, and don't be afraid of confiding your sentiment to me on the subject of her character. I believe her to be egotistical and hard, but perhaps a little of the prejudice that still remains against that splendid usurpatrix bears me to grant her less indulgence than she really merits. You will appreciate her better than I can. Above all, my Patrice, no imprudence. You know women, and you have evaluated their duplicity several times...

With an angry impulse, I tear the evil epistle into little pieces, and I throw them into the log fire that is crackling in front of me. I watch them blacken, and then twist, as they are consumed. My study is purified of all the perfidy and all the calumny that I divine between each of the lines written by my sister.

She can come. I know her generous soul, and I have no fear of her...

VII

If I live a hundred years, not one of the details of *her* arrival will be lost to my memory.

To begin with, the appeals of the horn requesting the park warden to open the entrance gate. Then the apparition of the Farman, the fastest and most beautiful of my cars, at the extremity of the drive. And, under the supple and sure guidance of Justin, its swerves before the terrace, where Antoine and I are waiting for her, caps in hand.

Scarcely has the auto come to a stop at the foot of the broad white stairway than Lux and I are already hurrying forward to met her. Lux seizes her valise. I extend my hand to Claudia to help her descend. And, quivering with fear, paler with anguish than the cold—for the morning is glacial—I make the introductions.

"Antoine Lux. Patrice de Beaumont."

Claudia shakes my friend's hand. She smiles, glad to be alive, whipped by the wind that lashes her thick veil as if to intimate the orders to her to lift it without delay. Then, turning toward me, she boldly looks me in the eyes. I divine rather that really perceive her eyes through the gauze. Not a muscle in her face twitches. Her fingers grip mine firmly. And, precipitating myself toward the terrible proof, I launch the phrase that I try to articulate with detachment:

"Well, am I not ugly?"

"Don't be silly," she replies, in a voice that I shall hear until my dying breath. "Come closer, so that I can embrace you."

And, with her arms around my shoulders, the traveler gives the recluse a double accolade, which Antoine applauds with all his might.

"That's my response, Patrice. And now, be kind. I'm falling asleep. Show me to my room and let me sleep, if you're gallant, until lunch time."

It seems to me that I'm going mad

That woman, more beautiful than can be imagined, has embraced me! She has placed her lips on the withered cheek that has only received, for six years, the chaste kiss of Alexandrine-Ysolde. And, in giving me that caress, she has not recoiled either from my toothless mouth, or my chinless jaw, or before the cloth mask dissimulating the other side of my face, even more frightful and repulsive than the visible part, and I have not fallen over, rigid with shock and joy!

What miracle have I witnessed, then, this morning? Am I less hideous than I imagine, or does that unknown woman bear in the utmost depths of her soul such generosity that all human horrors disappear from her gaze? My heart, like a stallion seeking to escape from the paddock where it has been imprisoned, leaps in my breast with great bounds. If I dared, I would sing, I would shout, I would howl, I am so happy. I, who cursed everything that breathed, have now begun to love life superhumanly, because a woman has just kissed me! I, who only knew how to weep and lament, have now learned to laugh, and have suddenly forgotten the distress that was still crushing me not a quarter of an hour ago. Claudia! Claudia! Your name is like the clapper of a bell that is striking my heart with redoubled blows, as if it wanted to break it.

More reserved than me, Antoine does not allow himself to be disquieted by the spectacle of my abnormal excitement. But he does not furnish me, except for a few counsels of moderation, any personal impression regarding the person who has just arrived. One might think that he mistrusted her.

It is midday. The bell for lunch rings. And one after another, the three guests of the hermitage enter the dining room: me first, intent on casting a glance over the table, to see whether the places are laid in a harmonious manner, and whether the hothouse flowers that I have sacrificed without regret in honor of the beautiful woman are filing the amphorae. Yes; I recognize them. They are there, all those I go to contemplate on snowy days, in their overheated temple of glass: Tibetan abutilons, with pale orange flowers spotted with pale brown; aristolochias with bizarre flowers and concave leaves like jade receptacles; azaleas; aristocratic cacti with clusters of amaranth flowers; fuchsias with violet thyrsi from which florets fall like purple tubes on to the immaculate table-cloth; hibiscus; white myrtles; blue-red veronicas, odorous vervains and Brazilian caladiums. I find them all. And it is not too much to have pillaged the large hothouse into which no one goes except myself, my sister and my friend, in order to magnify and deify appropriately the person who is presently making us the gift of her talent and her grace,

I go around the antique extendable table, and, from time to time, I modify the arrangement of the decoration. I want everything to be perfect, like her. And in order to pay better homage I have the cases opened in which the sculpted gold cutlery has lain dormant for decades with which the noble and powerful Comtes de Beaumont, my ancestors, once ate.

Ah, here's Antoine. Not without apprehension, for he criticizes judiciously and severely everything that shocks him, I ask him to give me his opinion. He examines, and judges me work in a brief comment, which delights me: "It's charming; I congratulate you."

But while we are exchanging opinions in low voices, the two battens of the door open, and, braced in his coat with silver buttons; his calves protruding from the livery culottes, motionless against the wall of the gallery, Justin announces: "Mademoiselle Claudia Pichet."

Sheathed in a black dress with adherent sleeves whose cuffs are outlined like the extremity of an arrow over the diaphaneity of her skin, shod in high-heeled cothurnes, helmed with blue-black hair whose long wavy tresses crown her forehead and her temples, the person for whom we are waiting tremulously advances toward us.

After a few minutes of amicable conversation, she goes to sit down at the top of the table, in the Flemish chair with the trapezoidal back that I designate to her. Immediately, I notice her hands. Slightly bronzed, like the face whose oval and general rhythm reveal Oriental origins, the hands with henna-tinted fingernails evoke for me the long hands of the Saracen women on whom my ancestors forced themselves without preamble on entering conquered cities, some of whom preferred to kill themselves rather than submit. No ring or jewel dishonors her fingers, and I am grateful to her, internally, for the simplicity with which she seems to be content.

While eating with and appetite that enchants us, she tells us about her journey, and her astonishment, on disembarking from the train, to find herself in such a curious and picturesque region. She tell us about her admiration for the savage grandeur of the village perched at the top of the mountain, for the manner, set ablaze with rose by the rising sun, which overwhelms the surroundings with its prodigious silhouette and seems to howl at the Present, via the stony mouths of its towers, crenellations and loopholes, the immortality of the Past.

At every moment she turns toward me, and, no more than at the moment of her arrival, is there any reflection of antipathy or repulsion in her gaze. Over coffee, while smoking an opiate cigarette, she asks me about the details of my accident; and when I have finished the piteous narrative, she murmurs, while placing her tapering fingers on my forearm: "Poor boy! How you must have suffered!"

Poor boy!

Those two words pour an inexpressible delight into me. I have the impression of something melting inside me, and I fill my heart with Claudia's words as a gourmet fills his mouth with the flavorsome flesh of a fruit what he has desired to eat for a very long time.

After having talked about me, Claudia talks about herself.

Without boasting and without pride, she tells us about her adventurous life. She evokes the times when, as a little girl, she traveled the world with her mother Gasmiliah, the directress of the Cirque-Franco-Egyptien, and her father, initially a simple band-leader in the maternal establishment, then the lover, and finally the husband of the "patronne." With words as sonorous as the ringing of little bells, she describes the long caravans of wheeled vehicles, traveling at the pace of Arab horses, stallions trained in dressage and employees outside hours of performance, drawing the carriages in which the personnel piled up after every session the seven hundred chairs and the enormous green tent. She evokes that nomadic existence with an affection that moves us. She tells us how her worthy father, perceiving her penchant for music, taught her scales on an old Rodolphe, which has never quit her, and which she promises to show us.

And there it is: that worthy father was an artiste incapable of standing out but perspicacious enough to divine his daughter's gifts by her fifteenth year and to strive to develop them in her. Not content with revealing the vocal art to her, he persisted, in spite of his pupil's resistance, in teaching her the piano and inculcating her with an almost complete harmonic knowledge, with the result that the cantatrice can not only discuss singing but is, in addition, ignorant of almost nothing of counterpoint and fugue.

Astounded by such a confession, Antoine Lux immediately leads the conversation to subjects unknown to me. And there they are, arguing with an incessantly increasing animation, citing examples, inscribing on the ruled pad, from which the composer is never separated, cryptic bass-lines and acquired songs. At first I try to interest myself in their discussion, but I am gradually invaded by an invincible ennui, and although I strive to dissimulate it I cannot suppress a yawn. Antoine perceives it and closes his notebook.

"We're boring him," he says to Claudia. "Let's go for a walk. Today, I'll give myself leave in your honor, my dear interpreter. But tomorrow morning, between ten and eleven, I condemn you to hear my first act."

"A mild condemnation!" said Gasmiliah's daughter, smiling.

We get up. I offer my guests an iron tipped cane, and, desirous of putting her in contact with our redoubtable guard corps, I whistle for my dogs.

All three of them arrive, barking. I approach their muzzles to the perfumed hand, which strokes them, and, acquaintance having been made, Brutus and Porthos launch themselves toward the avenue of lindens that leads down to the bank of the Viaur. But Sahib, instead of following his companions, goes to place himself between Claudia and Antoine. Gripped by a sudden affection for the woman whom we are welcoming so wholeheartedly, he brushes against our guest's dress while walking, and in order to seek her caresses, licks the gloved hand that dangles beside her.

"You too!" I remark. "Until now, that dog has only had affection for Antoine Lux. He's never been able to accustom himself to the presence of the domestics. He'd devour mercilessly any marauder imprudent enough to risk himself in the vicinity of my dwelling by day or night. I only speak to him and chain him up prudently myself. But you, who have just arrived, have conquered him in a matter of seconds. What strange power of seduction do you have, then?"

"I like animals," Claudia Pichet replies, simply. "And I try to understand their souls."

"We like them too," I reply. "My three wolfhounds lead an existence here that many men would envy. But although Brutus and Porthos testify a great fidelity to me, I can't say as much with regard to Sahib. If I struck him, I'm sure he'd pounce on me."

"I congratulate myself for having awakened his sympathy," my friend concludes. "Well, my old Sahib, I won't neglect you. You can count on my solicitude. Come on, comrade, give me a good paw-shake!"

And Sahib, as if he understood human language, stands up on his hind legs, places his forepaws on Claudia's shoulders and passes his rough tongue twice over the bright face, which does not turn away. Then, very gravely, after that accolade, he resumes his place beside her.

Our walk lasts for two hours.

By the time we have returned to the house and all three of us are sitting around the large fireplace in which an entire oak trunk is burning, we know everything about her that we need to know. While walking, she has manifested her liking for the abode where I have spent six dismal years, and the manner in which we have furnished it. I attribute all the merit of my sister, and I take the opportunity to remind Claudia that she knows her, that she has been introduced to her at the Tower by the conductor d'Arbois a few days before her departure for Lagarde-Viaur.

"What!" exclaims Claudia. "That old demoiselle, so polite and of such noble bearing, was your sister? Why didn't she tell me? I would have been so glad to know that!"

"My sister detests talking about herself," I explain, not without a hint of embarrassment, which does not escape Claudia.

"Have you quarreled?" she hazards.

"Not at all."

"Then why has she quit you?"

"For a very simple reason. She wanted to see Paris again, which she left at the same time as me."

"I can understand that. If it were necessary for me no longer to breathe the creosote-soaked atmosphere of the capital and go to earth, as you have done heroically, in a deserted corner, I believe that I would lose my mind. What about you, Master?" she asks, turning to Antoine.

"Me? If it were a matter of staying with a friend as loyal and sure as Patrice, I'd consent to it without regret."

"Oh," Claudia hastens to correct herself, "I share your opinion absolutely. In any case, our friend has given us reasons that I admit, alas. But I only envisaged, in talking about exile to the country, an exile by caprice, on a whim, and without distractions."

"Do we not have the talented wireless?" I say, in jest. "Without it, would you be here today?"

"No, and I'd regret it, for I haven't been as happy for a long time as I am this evening with the two of you. Yes," she adds, in a grave voice, "life is sweet when friendly hearts beat close to your own. I lacked that joy. I owe it to you, my dear Patrice, and I thank you for it."

We fall silent, all three of use certainly very emotional. Nothing can be heard in the rectangular room but the crackling of the wood being consumed in the grate and the regular respiration of Sahib, curled up at Claudia's feet, asleep while warming himself.

"Five o'clock," I remark, on hearing the clock chime. "Would you like to listen to the Tower?"

"I'm out of range," the cantatrice relies, with charming good humor. "But if you'd like to hear me more closely than through an antenna, I'll gladly sing you a few melodies by Antoine Lux—on condition, of course, that the Master will be kind enough to accompany me. He won't refuse, I'm sure; it will serve as my audition."

For two hours, Antoine and Claudia have caused me to marvel. How is it that there are beings so exceptionally endowed down here? Whence come their magnificent gifts? Why are they superior to us? What do they bear within them that impels us to applaud, admire and envy them?

I ask myself those questions while listening to the poignant voice of the contralto and savoring the playing of the virtuoso. Who, having sustained the surprising harmony of the voice of the cantatrice, has begun to play, as if for himself alone, a rhapsody by Franz Liszt.

Not without a constriction of the heart, I compare my mediocre mentality to Antoine's genius, and suddenly, I measure the full extent of my folly. How can I believe, how can I suppose for an instant, that this beautiful woman, standing like a harmonious statue behind that powerful male, behind that illustrious man whom kings and princes have received at their table, whom the most venerated masters are honored to call their friend, could ever have anything for me but sympathy or pity?

What have I done, wretch that I am? Why have I been stubborn in bringing them together, when nothing and no one, without me, would ever have facilitated their closeness? Am I obstinate, then, in remaining blind? Can I not understand that everything is pushing them toward one another, and that one day soon he will become for her, inevitably, what I dreamed of becoming myself in a stupid temerity?

And yet, that kiss that she gave me on the terrace, the warm tenderness that she seems to show toward me, when she only shows for Antoine a respectful deference, is all that not a serious indication? No: that woman will not love my friend. And he, who has divined, who now knows, why my sister went away; he to whom I confided the insensate hope that is capsizing me, even if he felt amour surging within him, I swear that he would defend himself against it, that he would not commit such a wretched action.

And suddenly, the resolution that I hesitated to make is anchored within me. That woman is necessary to me. She is as beautiful as I am ugly, but she is also as devoid of fortune as I am rich. Make her my mistress? I doubt, discerning all the duplicity and all the frantic ambition that pierces her slightest eulogies when she addresses herself to Lux, that she would accept to become that, even if I offered to make her one of the most envied women in Paris. But what if I propose my name to her? What if I propose to enable her, a daughter born to an Egyptian woman and a circus band-leader, to become the Comtesse de Beaumont—to become my wife? Might not such a prospect dazzle her, might it not overcome her repugnance and her resistance?

Today, more than ever, everything is for sale: bodies, souls, consciences, minds, wills, intelligences. I know, for having approached them when I belonged to All Paris what incorruptible politicians are worth, artistes uniquely concerned with their art, wives celebrated everywhere for their disinterest and their fidelity. Everything is for sale! Everyone is for sale! Nothing and no one, in this rotten post-war society, can resist the power of money, and no more than the others, Claudia Pichet will not disdain that unhoped-for homage.

That woman, I shall remove from the tarnished milieu in which she trails; I shall transplant her, as one transplants into a miraculous park the flower that is wilting in a suburban garden, into a world new for her. And everyone, because she will be mine, and I can do anything because of my wealth, will bow down respectfully before her.

What director, with or without active partners, even without hearing or seeing her, would dare to refuse, on the presentation of a check signed by me, to engage her as a star and lead her, between dusk and dawn, to glory? None of them. Not one of them. Yes, that will be, because I wish it, because I can pay, and nothing will appear to me to be too dear to buy her...to obtain her...

And, without bitterness this time, I listen to them.

She quit us at an early hour, almost immediately after dinner.

Sahib, who has attached himself to her footsteps, who follows her like a shadow, accompanied her to the first floor. Without hesitation, he lay down before her door. It is her, from this evening onwards, whom he will go to guard.

Antoine observes that defection of the wolfhound with a certain melancholy.

"I should have expected it," he admits. "That woman is a charmer."

Without responding, I consider him at length.

Surprised and disconcerted by the insistence of my gaze, he turns his head away progressively. And on seeing him flee my gaze like that, my heart constricts.

VIII

Claudia slept all the way through to dawn. And when the winter sun, so pale and so cold, launched its white rays at interstices of her steel Venetian blinds, she leapt out of bed.

Scarcely half an hour for her toilette and, without making any noise, in order not to wake anyone, she went out through the servants' quarters. Escorted by Sahib, she wanted to retrace the previous day's walk. And, well wrapped up in her cloak, shod in long boots, she launched herself into the park, where frost fossilized the vegetation curiously.

At eight-thirty she had not yet returned. As we were waiting for her to have breakfast, Justin approached me.

"Before going out, the demoiselle asked me for a large bowl of milky coffee, into which she dipped more than five slices of toast. As she drew away she asked me to tell the messieurs not to wait for her, for she never knows, when she departs thus at hazard, when her fantasy will bring her back."

"Then we have only to proceed as if she weren't here," I said to Lux.

We sat down before our fuming cups. But appetite did not come. She was lacking.

She only reappeared on the terrace at ten twenty-five

"Don't hold it against me!" she cried, as soon as she saw us. "In the country, I'm incapable of observing any discipline whatsoever. Get used to seeing me depart often on my own, and live as if I didn't exist. I don't want to be a hindrance to anyone, and I don't admit that anyone should be to me, in return."

Naturally, we applauded those words, since the person who articulated them possesses the most beautiful voice in the world. And after a rather anodyne exchange of words, I went back to my study while Antoine and Claudia headed for the drawing room, where the master was to enable his future interpreter to hear the principal passages of his work.

She has been in my home for ten days, and the passion that I felt for her before knowing her features has increased to such a point that I am terrified by it.

It often happened to me once, in the course of my amorous existence, to conceive for women of various merit and beauty, passions all the more ephemeral because they began with such violence, I arrived at losing sleep and appetite in consequence, committing, because of those often insignificant persons, the worst stupidities. The slightest obstacles encountered, if I had taken it into my head to reduce them, irritated me to such a degree that I flew into made rages and made it a point of honor, even if it was only out of self-esteem, not to fail in my enterprise, whatever sums and annoyances it cost me.

But this time the matter appears to me to be quite different.

There can no longer be any question of ephemeral passion; I discern that very clearly. The beauty of that woman, her talent, bowls me over, subjugates me. The desire for her flesh growls within me increasingly. But our time is so regulated that I never, or hardly ever, see her alone!

On awakening, a walk with Sahib. On her return, breakfast with Antoine and me. Afterwards, and until midday, lyrical labor. At twelve twenty-five, a meal *à trois*, in which our reserve contrasts with the cordiality of the morning, since my valet de chambre ensures the service and circulates around us from beginning to end.

The afternoon? Perhaps: but I have made another enormous mistake in putting at the disposal of Antoine and Claudia the superb Farman of which have only made use personally twice in six years. Yes, an enormous mistake; I take account of it in measuring from day to day the increasing intensity of my amour; for, instead of seeking to retain Claudia near to me, I have incited her since her arrival to travel the harsh gorges of the Viaur and the Aveyron in company with my friend, a pilot as skillful and as prudent as I am.

What was I thinking, then, in making that absurd proposition? Of bringing them closer together, or arranging things so as to remain alone, as before her arrival? But then, why summon her? Why accept her presence with a joy that I strove to deny to begin with, but of which I was obliged to admit, two days after the embarkation of Alexandrine-Ysolde, that it delighted me and fulfilled my wishes? What an illogical being am I, then, eternally in contradiction with myself?

I would like never to quit that woman, to live in her shadow, to abdicate, at a sign from her bronzed fingers, all dignity, all will, all pride. Merely in thinking about the harmonious curve of her breasts, the marmoreal fall of her shoulders, the sway of her hips, all my impetuous blood flows to me forehead and I stagger like a drunkard. Merely in hearing her, through the partition separating the drawing room from the dining room, repeat under Antoine's direction the most moving passages of his work, I feel faint. Sometimes, veritably going mad, I drag myself on my knees, my arms extended, gasping with carnal overexcitement. At night, I can't close an eye . And when, harassed by fatigue, I succeed in falling asleep at the first light of day, it is to see her passing through horrible nightmares, to dream about her, to call out to her during my unconscious divagations.

Her presence troubles me so much that I have to deploy prodigies of will-power not to allow the anguish and dolor excited in me by that inconceivable passion to appear. Does she brush my hand? I shiver suddenly from head to foot. A glacial chill paralyzes me, to the extent that she asked, one Sunday when we found ourselves alone with one another, whether I was in pain. Did she read then, in my drowned eyes, a response that my dry lips would have been incapable of articulating? Perhaps, for she shuddered at the shock of my gaze; and under a pretext discovered after a few minutes of a silence as disconcerting and as painful for her as it was for me, she got up, and without a word of excuse or explanation, quit the vast study into which I had introduced her, ostensibly in order to showing her an original Baudelaire manuscript.

Will I, then, remain thus in confrontation with her, without declaring anything of the agony that is gnawing at me? Will I let her depart without having attempted to vanquish her by any means whatever? Will I not have the courage to cry out to her, whatever might result from my confession, all my suffering, all my insomnia, all my fury?

Why also conceal from her the frightful jealousy that grips me when I watch her depart beside Antoine in the 40CV that is carrying her away I know not where, far from the sight of me, and certainly far from the thought of me? What do they say to one another as they fly over the deserted roads, visiting the old manors and old churches with which every village in the region is provided, as if by order, the curious old houses, one of which an American has just bought not far from here in Bruniquel, and which he is dispatching in numbered pieces to New York, where he will rebuild it in the suburbs? Divinely beautiful, both of them, what do they feel when, pushed together by the somersaults of the vehicle, their bodies collide, their hands brush one another, and their faces come so close that it would suffice for them to extend their lips to exchange a long kiss, from which they would emerge panting with desire and confusion?

And yet, when I pronounce the word *jealousy*, do not all their attitudes belie my unjust suspicions? With an absolute correction in their slightest communications, they give evidence of a cordial camaraderie, but in which there seems to be, especially in regard to Claudia, les sympathy and less affection than when she and I chat and joke together. Their conversations, necessarily a trifle restrictive because, nine times out of then, professional discussions invariable revolve around art, music and harmony, to such a point that I am sometimes aggravated, and I beg them, at those times, to broach another subject.

It is something extraordinary, that empire of the métier over the minds of those who practice it, to whatever intellectual or manual category they belong. In the times when I was still a man of the world, people deemed to be remarkable regularly frequented my home. There were litterateurs unable to talk about anything but books or the theater; painters in whose eyes only perspective, thick paste, colors and drawing existed; scientists who did not admit anything except for their experiments; country gentlemen whose ideas were limited to the breeding of pigs and veal calves; industrialists closed to everything except the tumult of steam-hammers and heavy oil engines; women whose sole occupation consisted of not missing tomorrow's rendezvous with their lover of dressmaker; and spongers uniquely anxious about encircling their dupes and possible victims in their hermetic nets of cunning. And that particularity, which had struck me so many times, I find again in the two individuals I love most in all the world, under different titles.

Come on, I'm wrong to be suspicious of them. Everything proves it to me. Let them go freely, then, as their whim takes them, those who press me so often and so affectionately to accompany them in their picturesque excursions. I don't want to be anxious about them, to do myself harm on their account. What do their technical dissertations matter to a profane individual like me, since they appear to me to be insupportable? I even experience—why hide it?—a certain chagrin in observing that my friend showing a perfect politeness toward her, and nothing more, when I would be so happy to see them brought closer by a warm amity.

It's necessary that I make the observation to Lux, one evening, not to say scold him and urge him to unfreeze slightly during meals; for it often happens that he does not say a word for a hour, and scarcely responds to the questions that I ask him.

Claudia, by contrast, is much more expansive. She never misses an opportunity to proclaim her penchant for the somber region in which I live.

"If my art didn't grip me entirely," she often repeats to us, "I'd gladly accept to live here, with the two of you and Mademoiselle Alexandrine-Ysolde, of whom I conserve such an affectionate memory. And you, Master, wouldn't you also consent to that without effort?"

"Evidently, since you're here, but only if all three of you were to remain with me," replies Antoine, evasively.

Then he recommences talking about music or musicians.

This morning, Claudia didn't have breakfast with us.

"Mademoiselle rang for me at seven-thirty," Justin explained. "She shouted through the door that she doesn't feel very well, and that she sends all her apologies to the messieurs, and that she will do the impossible to come down at midday. She also added that her condition ought not to alarm anyone, since it is a matter of simple fatigue."

"I prefer that," I declared. "What about you, my dear?"

"Me too, naturally, although I suspect that the so-called indisposition is a fit of vulgar idleness. Fundamentally, I rejoice in having a little more liberty than usual this morning. Perhaps I can finish in peace the melody on which I've been working for a month."

And on that conclusion, denuded of indulgence, Antoine stuffed his pipe. Then he headed for the drawing room. Until midday he inflicted his chords, attempted phrases and singing on us. I say "inflicted" because, for the first time since I have known him, my friend pained me by treating Claudia with so much indifference, and throughout the duration of his labor, for that reason, I detested his music.

I am anxious at not having seen her this morning. Unlike Lux, I suspect this vulgar fatigue to be a serious malaise, if not a veritable malady, and until the moment when the lunch bell rang I experienced an anguish, and indescribable enervation. Twenty times I consulted the hands of the clock. And while the master, placidly sitting at the table, waits while reading a newspaper, I stand on the threshold of the door, looking out for her approach, trembling with fear.

Oh! How exact my prognostications were.

Merely on seeing her, merely on seeing the rings around her eyes, the almost lived pallor of her complexion and the anxiety of her gaze, I understand that Claudia is concealing the seriousness of her condition from us. And with an irresistible impulsion, I hasten toward her. I take her hands, which suffering is coloring with a gray tint, and kissing them for a long time, I ask her: "What's the matter, then? How distraught your face is! Would you like me to send for a doctor?

"No, thank you!" she replies, escaping from my grip with a jerky movement and looking at Lux, who is methodically folding his daily before getting up to salute her "It's a matter of half a day. Tomorrow, it will have cleared up."

Having exchanged a few words with Antoine, the almost hostile insignificance of which does not fail to strike me, Claudia Pichet takes her place at the head of the table.

The conversation drag, and drags... Between two remarks we observe silences of several minutes, after which, in my capacity as host, I have to deploy prodigies of will-power to revive the dying flame and find other subjects capable of keeping us breathing. I succeed in that, after heroic efforts, but Antoine and Claudia only listen to me with a distracted ear. Claudia's indifference I deem to be logical by reason of her morbid nervousness, but where does my friend's come from? What could have motivated it?

In vain I propose to them in a persuasive voice an excursion by auto to Saint-Antonin Noble-Val. I praise with an archeological erudition the marvels that can be admired there, the pleasant stories that the hoteliers and the peasants narrate. As if they had given one another the word, Antoine and Claudia decline my invitation to the voyage. Claudia desires to repose for a part of the afternoon; Antoine has asked the gardener to bait a spot for him on the bank of the Viaur, and, while soliciting me to accompany him, he announces that his half-day will be devoted to fishing. I refuse to go with him; and, exasperated by the singular attitude of my two guests, I retire to my bedroom.

All three of us leave the dining room. Lux goes first. Claudia follows behind. I have scarcely reached the threshold of the gallery when I suddenly recall that my cigarettes and newspapers have remained on a side-table next to the entrance.

I retrace my steps, without having taken the precaution to inform my friends, and I penetrate into the room from which we have just emerged. While taking from the side-table the objects that I had forgotten, I raise my eyes mechanically toward the large mirror above the monumental mantelpiece facing me.

And I see something incredible.

Antoine has turned abruptly toward Claudia. He has seized one of her hands in his; he has raised it to his lips, without the woman sketching a movement of resistance, and, passionately, gluttonously, he covers his companion's slender fingers with kisses. Then, at the sound of my footsteps on the threshold, he releases the imprisoned hand, places his finger over his mouth to recommend prudence to the other. And, following one another, as at the moment of their departure, they resume their march.

I remain on the threshold, bewildered by the spectacle that I have just witnessed, unknown to them. My heart is beating so forcefully that it seems to be about to escape from my breast, along with my life. A cold sweat inundates me, and a weakness that necessitates my holding on to the wall in order not to fall grips me to the point of cutting off my respiration.

Meanwhile, they go to their respective rooms, and I am still motionless in the middle of the gallery when Claudia reaches the first floor landing and Lux has closed the door to the servant's parlor, where the gardener is waiting for him, noisily.

Of what odious scene-setting, of what hypocrisy, am I the dupe? I try to convince myself that I have made a mistake, that I have not seen what I have seen, by reason of the position I occupied, but the implacable certainty which my reflections bring back to me effaces my obliging hypotheses Nothing remains of my research, of all my subtle deductions, except one brutal, undeniable fact: Antoine kissing Claudia's hand amorously, in secret.

What to think, then? That the individuals in whom I put so much confidence are betraying me? Or one of them, at least, is betraying me, since he knows, the wretch, how much I love Claudia and how much I am suffering from bearing that desperate passion within me. The man whom I cherished like an elder brother, the man for whom I risked my life thirty times over at Douaumont, at Hartmanswillerkopff, on hill 104 and at Verdun, carries such duplicity within him? It isn't true! All my loyal heart, all my intelligence, all my tenderness and all my soul, the secret recesses of which he knows so well, refuse to admit such turpitude. And I return, in spite of all appearances, in spite of the inexorable attestation of the mirror, to the initial opportunism. I did not see correctly. I am mistaken.

For if I am not mistaken, I find myself facing the most painful dilemma that can be posed for me. Either Antoine is Claudia's lover, in which case my entire plan of conquest, so laboriously constructed, collapses without hope, or they are at the prelude: a simple flirtation...and nothing, nor anyone, can prevent them, in a more or less imminent future, from belonging to one another recklessly, individuals who correspond to one another so completely. And I, poor imbecile, poor simpleton, will have been the artisan of their association and their ecstasy.

And it is almost before my eyes that they will seek one another, that they will embrace one another, that they will exchange their caresses. And I, who would give everything I possess to feel that marvelous body quivering in my arms, will watch, an impotent and unsuspected witness, that indescribable forfeiture, that larceny, that spoliation, without being able to do anything but weep and lament?

Now, as I become excited, an interior voice exhorts me to calmness, to effacement, to pardon. Can I ask of that woman anything but what she gave me spontaneously and honestly: her affection? Ought I not to deem myself fortunate, when everyone, from the humblest to the most powerful and the most arrogant turn away from me with repugnance, that that

298

superb individual can support the sight of me without paling, and even seem to find some pleasure in my commerce? To pretend to desire, to passion, on her part is pure folly. And since it pleases them, well, let them love one another freely. What is happening had to happen. I, being intellectually sterile and physically a pariah, must give way to that man, whose magnificent brain can create so much incomparable beauty. I should have foreseen it. I should have followed the advice of Alexandrine-Ysolde instead of insulting her and forcing her to go away.

Come on, Patrice, take your cane and your cap and go to the river bank to find the man who, among all the others, remained faithful to you during the days of adversity. And when you have arrived by his side, don't show him your suffering. Hide your new lacerations well, with all your might. Pretend not to know anything; for a veritably amity like his is rarer and more precious than the amour of which you dream.

I perceive him down there on the pontoon. And Sahib, who has seen me coming, races in my direction, barking. Why is that dog, Claudia's incessant guardian, with Antoine, when the person whose protector he has appointed himself, is shut in her room, prey to the most annoying of neuralgias.

But no! Claudia is sitting beside Antoine. Her indisposition was simulated, then? She has deserted her room because she supposes me to be shut up in my study and because I declined my friend's offer? In what atmosphere of deceit and falsity must I live henceforth? Will the cowardice induced by the terror of seeing them depart force me to support all insults and all humiliations without jibbing?

"Oh!" I say to Claudia, as I approach her. "You're not asleep on your chaise-longue then?"

"No," she replies, blushing. "I felt better. I wanted to get some air. And I've come to the pontoon, where I'm going to fish for half an hour in the company of the master."

"My compliments! I admire these unexpected cures, and yours, more than any other, delights me. The company of Antoine will certainly be more favorable to you than an afternoon of repose. I rejoice in that, and I'll leave you to your catch-es…and your pleasant intimacy." The smile with which I ac-company that reply must, alas, resemble some frightful gri-mace.

Deaf to Antoine's voice, which begs me to stay, I turn on my heel and, my heart constricted by jealousy, return to my room.

They are lovers!

It has sufficed for me to find them on the bank, so close to one another, so well protected by Sahib from indiscretions and surprises of any kind, to bring the assurance of it. And what will become of me, who rolls in my bed, biting my pil-low for fear of screaming in rage? I no longer have anyone here to comfort and console me, Alexandrine-Ysolde has gone, and the others are so dazzled by their passion that they will soon forget even the name and the features of the man from whom they obtained, to begin with, so much tenderness and devotion.

This evening, I shall not appear at table. Justin will bring me my dinner in my room. I no longer want to impose my presence on them. Let them enjoy their nascent amour in peace, for no one can foresee the ordeals that future has in store for them. I want them not to think of anything in con-templating one another, not even me, who is standing aside before their happiness, not even the woman whose name has not been pronounced here for a long time—Geneviève Servais, the fiancée who should have come here, like the oth-er, to spend her first weeks of ecstasy with my sister and me.

What can they be saying to one another at this moment, while I am suffering? What are they doing in this solitude created so egotistically for my sole usage? By my fault, the dwelling of dolor has now become the house of tenderness! What derision! Are they, at least, not mocking me, not heaping with their sarcasm or disgust the man they ought to be thank-ing and blessing? What would I not give to hear them, to sur-prise on the wing the words they are exchanging, the confessions underlining their passionate enlacements, like supernatural harmonies.

Listen to them?

But if I wanted to, nothing would be easier for me! Have I not at my disposal a collection of apparatus the perfection and fidelity of which surpasses everything invented to date? Can I not, without the help of anyone, install it in each of their rooms, and, at any hour, capture the slightest sighs and words sprung from their ardent mouths?

To begin with, I reject that idea scornfully. Accomplish the work of a spy, me, whom my friend Lux takes for the most honest and upright man in the world? Lower myself to the point of stealing, like a low-class burglar, what only belongs to them, in the greatest intimacy of their hearts and their thoughts? But if I did such a thing, I would feel dishonored in my own eyes, and I would be ashamed of myself until the last breath. How can I even envisage the possibility of such an ugly treason? And then, if I yielded to that detestable desire, would I not augment even further the jealousy that is undermining me? Have I not endured enough, that I want to exacerbate my torture voluntarily? No, Patrice, you won't fall to that degree of debasement. Everything forbids it. Your past, the esteem in which you are held by the last living beings who still know you, the fraternal affection that Antoine has for you....

The fraternal affection...

And has he not betrayed it, the musician? Has he not betrayed it under my own roof, when he is not unaware of anything that motivated my imprudent invitation? Does he not know that I covet and cherish that woman as much as he can cherish and covet her himself? Does his treason not surpass in baseness the action that I dare not decide to accomplish, retained by grotesque scruples? Would not everything in his conduct excuse my procedure: the feigned coldness that he manifests to Claudia: the care that he takes to dissimulate his penchant for her; the hypocrisy with which they attempt to take advantage of my hours of claustration in order to meet under the false pretext of fishing? Is there not an overwhelming accumulation of dissimulation there? Am I not absolved in advance for my underhand attempt merely by establishing grievances as indisputable as those?

How simple it would be, if I dared...

Faithful to my resolution, I dined in my room.

I gave the pretext of the necessity in which I found myself of taking off my mask in order to subject my ravaged face, to my eyeless orbit and what was once an ear with a perfect lobe, to the massage and biweekly treatment with which Antoine Lux is very familiar.

They did not insist, glad to be isolated again, and I know, personally, that I shall not sleep for a minute tonight, because I bear within me an amour stronger than death and a jealousy even stronger, if possible, than the amour of which I am dying...

IX

This morning, I succeeded in avoiding the eight o'clock breakfast.

Antoine tried to force my door, but I had him informed by Justin that I would remain invisible until midday and that I begged him not to worry about me. Claudia contented herself with addressing to me via my domestic her hopes for a prompt reappearance. I know what that is worth, and it is with a shrug of the shoulders at which Justin did not allow himself to appear surprised that I welcome his propitiatory message.

Half an hour later, at any rate, I heard the two afflicted individuals rehearing, with vocal sonorities so explosive that they seemed to by storming the walls to reach me, the finale of the second act. Five times in succession they recommenced the superb lyrical declamation. And I must confess, truth be told, that the beauty of the song and the magnificence of the work stifled within me, for three consecutive hours, any whim of vengeance or desire to spy on their amorous conversation.

Scarcely had the music stopped, however, when the hateful obsession gripped me and dominated me again; and every time, I felt hesitant, weak and impotent to combat it. When noon chimed, I was almost completely acquired by my future felony. And when, sitting opposite Antoine at to Claudia's left, I heard them reveal their intention to visit by auto the canyons imprisoning the Aveyron between Cazals and Saint-Antonin Noble-Val, my decision was made. It asserted itself so irrevocably that I complimented the two cheats on their initiative, and even indicated to them, in order to hinder and delay their return, and old road that no one uses any longer, and from which it is difficult, if not dangerous, to emerge when rain or black ice renders it even worse, as today.

With a cunning equal to theirs I wished them *bon voyage*. I saw all three of them disappear—for Sahib, naturally,

303

escorted them—and, without wasting a second, I put my perfidious plan into execution.

I possess such dexterity in matters of wireless technology, and my equipment is so improved and modern, that three hours sufficed for me to install in the obscure cupboards of their habitations the generators necessary to the efficient functioning of the transmission. The microphones I dissimulated on the front of the mantelpiece. That way, they had only to speak, while warming themselves, for me to capture their dialogues or soliloquies instantly, if they are accustomed to pay one another passionate visits before going to bed.

From now on, they can feign indifference or hostility before me, but nothing of what is said or murmured in their rooms can escape me any longer.

And it was with an open face that I welcomed them from the top of the terrace and questioned them about the incidents of their excursion. They replied to me with a perfect good grace, and did not cease, throughout the duration of dinner, to praise the wild grandeur of the verdant canyons and thank me for having revealed such a fine corner to them.

I receive their congratulations modestly. I took the most active part in their prattle. Contrary to my habit, I smoked a gold-ringed Corona in their company.

Then, as ten o'clock chimed, I shook their hands, recommending them not to be inhibited if the sudden desire for music took them, and I returned to my room. And, breathless with anguish, earphones on my head, I waited.

Suddenly, I perceived a slight sound in the receiver. Antoine went into his room. He opened the door, took a few steps, and closed it again. Then silence. Doubtless he has sat down in order to read or work by the lighted fire.

It became pointless to persist. I would not hear anything.

Determined to surprise their secret, I lay down on the bed, keeping the earphones on. The lassitude occasioned by my mental tension became such that I became drowsy; and in the semi-sleep into which I was plunged I heard two raps on my friend's door: two discreet, sly raps to which a "Come in!" whispered by the master replied immediately.

Claudia is going into his room!

As if lifted by an electric shock, I sit up. And, with my torso folded, and my fists clenched over the hollows of my ears, my entire being intent on what I am about to surprise, I listen...

Nothing escapes me, neither the rustle of the pointed shoes that Claudia wears inside the house nor the painting of her breast, nor the two words whispered as she enters: "My darling!"

And, trembling with rage, bitten by a jealousy that surpasses all imagination and all acuity, I reconstitute the scene.

Her, in Antoine's arms, or her head inclined on his shoulder. Their lips united. Their avid hands gripping one another, like little wild beasts. The ecstasy irradiating their dilated eyes; and, at intervals, the anxious glances darted at the exit, where Sahib is on watch. And, when they are assured that no one had heard it, not suspecting its clandestine descent from the first floor to the ground floor, the dialogue resumes.

It is Claudia who speaks.

"You see, my love, "she murmurs to him in a low voice, "I was dying of the desire to find you again. Since I fell in love with you, I only breathe for you. The thought of you does not desert for a minute my superhumanized soul, and your name obsesses me as if it were the most beautiful and most moving of your works. Do you recall our excursion today? Have you kept a faithful memory of our demented communion, the rustle of the poplars that lulled us like organs, the scarcely perceptible whisper of the Aveyron, which sent us our images with the exactitude of a mirror?"

"Yes," Antoine replies. "I too, since I have fallen in love with you and you have made me the gift of your divine body, forget everything else. I am dazzled by possessing you, and when your mouth dies on mine, like a great flower extenuated for having exhaled too much perfume, everything is abolished in my heart, in my memory and in my brain. My name obsesses you, you say? But are your perfect shoulders and your arched loins not rhythms nobler than symphonies for me? All your strange splendor appears to me as a music of lines, curves and living chords. And because the beauty of your soul even surpasses, if possible, the perfection of your body, I bow down very humbly before you, my mistress!"

Each of their phrases, each of their confessions, tears me more atrociously than a sharp blade. I remain there, on my bed, as if moribund. And as if I were taking an insane pleasure in multiplying the unhealthy dolor that is oppressing me tenfold, I find the courage to follow their conversation to the end.

But at the moment when the double groan of lust fulfilled sprung from their lips reaches my terrified ears, all my strength suddenly abandons me. And, vanquished by an ordeal that breaks my capacity for resistance, I collapse in a faint on my bedclothes.

How long did I remain in that lamentable coma? How long did that annihilation of my mind, my thought and my carcass last? I no longer know. In any case, when I recovered my senses, when I perceived the shiny headphones beside me, the demi-paralysis in which I found myself did not permit me to reassemble my memories. Al that I recall is that five o'clock had chimed a few minutes after my resurrection and that I fell into a heavy slumber until the moment when Justin, anxious at not seeing me come downstairs, came to knock on my door.

Will I have the energy to recommence living as we were living before my tragic discovery? Will I have sufficient self-mastery to accept their dissimulation without revolt, and not unmask them with a word when they adopt indifferent or hostile attitudes before me? Not today, certainly, but tomorrow, I want to try. I shall be able to control myself. I shall be able to keep quiet, because I must know everything about them and their passion.

This evening again, and all the following evenings, I shall capture their slightest sighs, their slightest murmurs. And when, finally hardened, drawn to that suffering like a runner to the harassing trajectory that leaves him half-dead at the finishing post, I am able to listen to them and see them without losing breath, without blanching, without bleeding from all my poor heard and poor stabbed body, I shall expel them, with a broad gesture, as one sweeps away pestilences brought into one's dwelling by a corrupt sirocco.

But before then, it's necessary that I complete the incredible machination that emerged from my brain this morning. It's not enough for me to spy on them, to listen to them when they meet by night. It's necessary for me to be able to follow them wherever they are, wherever they go, for me to be able to listen to them at no matter what distance, and that whatever they say, whatever they do, will never be hidden from me.

This afternoon, I shall confide my Voisin to them for the habitual excursion. I shall pretext a breakdown of the engine perceived by Justin in the course of greasing it, and kept the Farman here, of which Antoine Lux is fondest of all. And the day after tomorrow, when they launch forth to assault the sinuous roads, I will have placed a microphone between the chronometer and the speedometer. I will have screwed a generator to the bodywork of the auto powerful enough to send me their conversations at a distance surpassing a thousand kilometers.

They departed at two-fifty. Even before the car had gone through the gates of the park, I was at my work-station.

But this time, it was no longer a matter of headphones. With the headphones, one loses phrases. A second of emotion or inattention, and the capital words of a dialogue escape you and one doesn't grasp the whole. Now, I want to hear everything, and it's by means of my loudspeaker, without batteries, without electric current, and without a frame, that I shall surprise their sighs and their confidences.

I place it on my table, that loudspeaker whose new Neutrodyne montage,[12] invented by me, constitutes an extraordinary marvel. I put the graduated moderator in front of the apparatus and I listen.

"Where are you taking me?" Claudia asks.

"Wherever you like, my love," Antoine replies, in a soft voice. "You know very well that I have no other will than yours."

"Then let's go back to where we made love yesterday. It was so nice in that gorge, so isolated from the rest of the world!"

For a week they have selected as a domicile the place fixed by the lover, the place of which they have never pronounced the name, as if they feared profaning it by designating it.

Not once has their conversation deviated from the unique subject: their amour. To what summits of tenderness have they acceded, then, to be able to talk about nothing but themselves, and not to gaze, lost as they are in the contemplation of their radiant faces, either the landscapes traversed, or the river skirted or the sky? Such a faculty of passion disconcerts me as much as it exasperates me. I wonder whether, in their place, I would be capable of accomplishing such a prodigy and isolating myself thus from the exterior world.

The result of that monotony of transmissions, the confessions that always revert to the same epithets, the same oaths, is a sort of insurmountable torpor. I sense jealousy and rage gradually dissolving within me and giving way to a satiation that I do not know whether to call indifference or ennui. Incapable of paying attention for more than a quarter of an hour to what I now consider to be divagations, I become drowsy on that table next to which I counted on experiencing so many

---

[12] The Neutrodyne radio receiver was invented in 1922 by Louis Hazeltine. Because of its feedback-neutralizing reception it sold in millions, but was superseded within a decade.

violent sensations. The ignorance in which they seem to remain voluntarily of my name, my presence and my actions, the care that they devote to never talking about me in eulogistic or disobliging terms is what surprises me and irritates me the most.

Do they hate me? Do they disdain me? Does Antoine not feel any affection for me? Does that woman who will owe her happiness and, probably, her glory—unless the master's passion suddenly vanishes—to me have so much ingratitude and egotism in the depths of her being? Already she no longer recalls, then, what I have done for her by summoning her to this retreat?

But yes!

Today, Friday the sixth of December, they are talking about me.

My name reached my ears. At that unusual sonority, I shivered, and, abruptly woken up, I concentrated my attention in order to hear better, while the 40CV carried them in gentle bounds toward Villefranche-de-Rouergue, where Claudia has long been nourishing the desire to spend a few hours.

They are talking about me, at first in amorphous phrases that praise my benevolence, my frankness, my proverbial cordiality. The banality of the words ends up exasperating me, and I wonder whether it would not be better, instead of wasting my time catching their sentimental stupidities, to go down to the Viaur or to read my newspaper. And just at the moment when I pick up a daily, still folded in front of me since the mailman called, I stop, stupefied.

And this is what I perceive:

Antoine: "No, my love, I assure you that you're mistaken on his account. And then, I'll confess to you something that you doubtless don't suspect. Patrice is in love with you."

Claudia: "You're joking!"

Antoine: "Not at all. When he wrote inviting you to come, do you think that it was for the sole joy of feeding you, the sole pleasure of seeing you, three times a day, sit down at his table with us? Haven't you read his letters? Haven't you understood that every one of them, under its appearance of correspondence exchanged between comrades, was nothing but a long cry of passion exhaled by that poor devil?"

Claudia: "No, my Antoine, I haven't discovered that. But if I had discovered it, if I had found it written in capital letters, it would not have prevented me from coming, since it was for you, my love, and for you alone that I came. Now you'll reproach me for my absence of subtlety when you've lacked it yourself, in this instance, more than me. I came here because I love you. I'm staying here because I love you. And I'll leave when you order me to go, on condition that you accompany me."

Antoine: "And if I hadn't been Patrice's guest?"

Claudia: "Perhaps I would have risked the journey. But I would have left the same evening. There are impossible courages."

Antoine: "But you embraced him, on the morning of your arrival."

Claudia: "In embracing him, my love, it was you that I was embracing. For, I can confess it to you now, I had been madly in love with you for a long time—much longer than you suppose."

Antoine: "What are you saying?"

Claudia: "I've loved you since the evening when I saw the performance of your *Pannychis* at Gaveau's, sitting in a modest seat in the upper galley. I can still see you, dragged by Chevillard on to the proscenium, pale with emotion under the acclamations of a delirious multitude. Oh, how I belonged to you that evening! What superhuman efforts of will I had to make not to wait for you at the exit, not to write to you!"

Antoine: "You should have done that."

Claudia: "What would you have thought of my letter? A declaration such as you receive so many in the course of a year? A declaration emanating from an unknown woman, an artiste at the beginning of her career! Never!" (A silence.) "You see, my darling, it's for you that I'm here. But Patrice...how do you know?"

310

Antoine: "From him, naturally. We have no secrets from one another."

Claudia: "Really?"

Antoine: "Except this one, of course. For this one only belongs to the two of us."

Claudia: "And it will die with the two of us."

Antoine: "Yes. With us..." (A silence.) "If he knew! What heartbreak! What are you thinking about, Claudia?"

Claudia: "About the incredible thing that you've just revealed to me."

Antoine: "Incredible? Why?"

Claudia: "Because that man was able to believe me capable...he's rich, isn't he, immensely rich?"

Antoine: "Immensely."

Claudia: "Ah! That's it. Did he imagine then, that, for all the money in the world, I could....? Oh, even if he offered to marry me...! Never talk to me about him again. God! What horror!"

Her too!

I horrify Claudia, as I horrify everyone who sees me! This time, the chagrin is too much, too much, too much!

But, hysterically, morbidly, instead of breaking the contact, instead of tearing from my table the loudspeaker of which every sound burns me now like a red-hot iron, I listen obstinately. What does it matter what they are saying, what they are going to say? I have to hear them.

Antoine: "Patrice is too noble a soul to suppose that his fortune would be sufficient to reduce you. I can answer for that. And in any case, nothing in his attitude or in his speech, since you've been living in his house, has revealed the sad passion with which he's bleeding."

Claudia: "Fortunately!" (A silence.) "To think that I had the courage to look that man in the face, to brave his nose devoid of nostrils, his mouth devoid of teeth and lips, his fissured cheek. Now that you've spoken, Antoine, I won't be able to see him again. Take me, quickly, to the little railway station we can see from here. Let me jump on to the train that's fuming and whistling. Go pack our bags and join me tomorrow. I can't go back there! I can't see that thing, that human wreck, that monster, again!"

Antoine: "That's impossible Claudia. I promised Patrice that I'd stay with him until mid-January."

Claudia: "Then I'll leave on my own. Drop me here. You'll make my apologies. You'll say that you want..."

Antoine: "I won't let you go."

Claudia: "I beg you, stop the car!"

Antoine. "No, not today. A little later. Let me prepare him. Let me spare him a disappointment all the more cruel because he doesn't have his sister with him."

Claudia: "I want to leave."

Antoine: "Have pity on me! I've already sacrificed Geneviève to you. Don't force me to sacrifice the man I love like a brother, the man next to whom I suffered, shivered and trembled with hunger, cold and fear for five years in the trenches, the man whose only friend I am—the only friend, do you understand that?"

Claudia: "I want to leave. And I want to leave with you...what are you doing? Why are you taking the road to Lagarde-Viaur? Why are you taking me back to that man...the man who is stealing your affection from me and who dares to aspire, in spite of his hideousness, to possess me as you possess me?"

Antoine: "That man has been handsome, Claudia, more handsome than me. We swore to one another, in the face of death, to remain friends until the last breath. Nothing will make me commit such a sin in his regard."

Claudia: "Then I'll leave on my own. I'll leave tomorrow morning. And it will be over. You'll never see me again."

I hear a kind of gasp. Then the purr of the engine reaches me to the exclusion of any other sound.

And, after about a minute:

Antoine: "I'll do what you order me to do, since I can no longer live without you. But let's not leave tomorrow. Give me a few days."

Claudia: "All right: two days. But no more. Swear."

Antoine: "On our tenderness. On my cowardice."

Claudia: "Yes, on your cowardice, isn't it? For next to me, you no longer have any dignity, any will, any energy. And you're going to confess to me, now that we're on the eve of our departure...you detest him!"

Antoine: "Who?"

Claudia: "Patrice, of course. Your Patrice. I want you to say it to me. You detest him!"

Antoine: "No, Claudia. You know very well that it isn't true."

Claudia: "You detest him! Tel me that you detest him!"

Antoine, in a stifled sob: "Well, yes, I detest him. I detest him. I detest him as I detest everyone who loves you and everyone who dares to covet you."

Claudia: "And he horrifies you, as he does me, doesn't he? Come on, I divined it a long time ago. You can no longer look at him. You can no longer stand the sight of him."

Antoine: "It's true. He horrifies me." (A silence.) "What malevolent power do you have within you then, that you force me to say such infamous things...?"

Quivering, my hands riveted to the cornet of the loudspeaker, without being able to distinguish any of the sounds that succeed Antoine's denial, I remain there for nearly an hour...

They have just returned. And, as if he were only waiting for their return, the gardener, at the extremity of the kitchens, agitates the dinner bell joyfully.

What a meal!

They haven't dared say anything to me. I haven't said anything to them. When will they announce their departure?

It's this morning that I was told. With reticences and embarrassed pauses, the friend who has betrayed me, the companion of gehenna who is abandoning me, made me party to his decision.

I tried to retain him. I proclaimed my distress, my frightful fear of solitude. I begged him to postpone his departure until the arrival of Alexandrine-Ysolde, whom I'll recall by telegram. Nothing was able to bend him.

"Give me a few weeks," he said, doubtless to attenuate my chagrin. "Immediately after the premiere, I promise I'll come back to spend a fortnight here."

A fortnight! It's Antoine who is lowering himself to such lies!

"Well then, it's understood. But, since you're going to come back in a month's time, go by auto. I have two here. Take one of them—your choice. You'll accomplish your journey more agreeably than if you were huddled in a railway carriage, even first class. Claudia doesn't know France very well; it's a good opportunity to show it to her in passing."

"If she wants to!" Lux replied, illuminated with joy by my proposition "I'll talk to her about it. Or rather, mention it to her yourself."

As I anticipated, the woman that I hate more than anything, accepted my offer enthusiastically. She raised her great lying eyes toward me, and thanked me, in a voice as warm as a sirocco.

"I owe you a great deal, Patrice. Believe me, I'll never forget what you've done for me."

"Me neither; I won't forget anything," I replied, in a hollow voice. Anything!

And, holding my handkerchief to my face in order to dissimulate the atrocious dolor that is contorting it, I retired to my rom.

That night, she spent in his arms. It is the last night of amour she will give him here.

I wanted to capture their supreme dialogue. She forbade him to come back after the first performance.

Thus, I shall never see Antoine again. I shall never see him again...

Come on! It's necessary that the irreparable is accomplished.

X

They are leaving this morning at nine o'clock.

I wanted, to Justin's great surprise, to visit the auto that is to transport them myself. It's me who checked the engine, regulated the carburetor, greased the spring and filled the tank with fuel. It's me who took the wheel in order to conduct the roadster to the terrace where *she* arrived, exactly a month ago today, when we were waiting for her, hearts oppressed by the same anguish, the same desire that has made us enemies, whose latent hatred can no longer be put to sleep by anything.

Enemies, we who loved one another so much! That, by the fault of that woman, is what we have become. Everything—the long nights in the trenches where we were floundering waist-deep; the confidences of the encampments where we ran aground on days of rest; the attacks in which, changed into ferocious beasts by sambuca and wine, we went forth under the avalanche of shells, grenades and shrapnel; the livid evening when, crawling like a feline through bloody barbed wire, I went to look for the man that a bullet had laid low in the muddy earth—all that disappeared, abolished, effaced because it pleased a woman to order it!

Our fraternal tenderness, our confidence, our life together, devoid of collisions, devoid of quarrels devoid of discontents, all of that, she has destroyed with a kiss. Is that possible? Is it possible that I have been the involuntary cause of such a treason, such a denial, and that, as a punishment for my generosity, for my desire for amour, I remain alone in this funereal manor, without even having the person beside me who always consoles me in terrible hours?

A tragic breakfast, ours! Neither he nor I dared say a word. She alone, her spirit as free as if she were departing for the quotidian excursion, was able to joke, to laugh and eat. To laugh, above all. The joy of going away with him choked her.

And he, on hearing those triumphant explosions, lowered his head like a malefactor overwhelmed by shame.

The clock in the dining room chimed nine times. Antoine embraced me for a long time, silently. Then I raised my eyes toward his, and I saw him weeping. But at the moment when I was about to address my ultimate prayer to him, to implore him in a low voice to come back, not to abandon me entirely, she summoned him.

Submissive to that magical voice, the man who was my friend tore himself from my arms and leapt into the driving seat. And while he checked the functioning of the levers and pedals, Claudia advanced toward me. As on the morning of her arrival, she held out her arms to me. Just as I looked at Antoine at the moment when she called to him, I looked at her. Her eyes were closed.

I understood.

I pushed her away, gently. And in a low voice, certain that her lover couldn't hear, I said to her: "What's the point? I know that I horrify you."

Scarcely had I said those words, the exact range of which she couldn't grasp, than her face suddenly took on a sickly tint.

She started to tremble. And, without even extending her hand to me this time, she replied: "*Au revoir.*"

I shook my head. "There's no longer an *au revoir* between us. Adieu."

"As you wish!" she launched at me, with an astonished smile. "But I don't understand."

"You will."

And then, just at the moment when Antoine places his finger on the starter motor, Sahib emerges from the house, leaps into the seat and, barking frantically, starts licking Lux's face.

"Here, Sahib!" I order, in a loud voice

Sahib doesn't budge.

"Leave him to me," says Antoine. "We'll bring him back with the car."

Give him Sahib? I'd rather kill him.

"Here, Sahib!"

All my orders are futile. The wolfhound doesn't obey. Antoine has to muzzle him and put him on a lead himself, in order that Justin, without the risk of being bitten, can take him down and drag him to his kennel.

Like us, tugging at his chain with all the strength of his supple body, Sahib watches the vehicle draw away, and then disappear.

And when it is all over, when nothing can any longer be seen on the horizon, nothing at all, not even a little back dot traveling along the road, the dog starts to howl, dolorously, sinisterly.

God, those howls that reach me, while, rigid next to the loudspeaker, I want to capture for the last time....

"Shut up, Sahib!"

Gripped by a terrible fit of rage, I ring for Justin.

"Make Sahib shut up."

"I can't, Monsieur."

"Take him to the end of the park, the edge of the water, wherever you like!"

Yes, no matter where, as long as I obtain silence, can no longer hear that plaint, the effect of which is indescribable, that moan, which chills me, penetrates me and maddens me!

Sahib is far away. I've replaced the loudspeaker on the table in my study. And again, I'm on watch.

First kisses. Then confessions—always the same. Finally, orders: orders intimated by Claudia.

"Faster my love! May I never see this lugubrious place again! Let me live again in a blue frame, alone with you, a life as blue as my soul. Faster, my love. Faster!"

"It's not prudent, it seems to me that something's wrong with the steering!"

"It's a pebble. Here...I'm putting my foot on the accelerator!"

I no longer have a drop of saliva on my lips. My hands cling on to the corners of the table that supports my apparatus; and as the seconds go by, my hair stands on end.

Ah!

Screams! Cries of pain! And at the same time, a loud noise of broken glass, metallic collisions; the engine turning over in the void with a vertiginous rapidity, yapping like a human being.

Two more screams...

A man's cry: "I'm dying!"

A woman's cry: "Antoine! Help!"

Then the man's voice falls silent. And increasingly feeble, the woman's voice stammers, at widely-spaced intervals: "Help....help!"

I bound on to the terrace. I open my mouth to scream. Down below, at the far end of the park, Sahib's howling, more prolonged and more anguished, immobilizes me.

"Shut up, Sahib! Shut up! It's too late!"

XI

They were brought back at four o'clock. A motorist passing by, who saw them, recoiled in fright at the spectacle:

My roadster with its wheels in the air. Between the steering-wheel and the seat, his chest caved in by the violence of the impact, Antoine, dead. And on the edge of the ditch, horribly disfigured by the shards of the windscreen, Claudia, unconscious and covered in blood.

The silver plate on which my name is engraved informed him. With the help of two peasants, he loaded the inanimate victims into his Ford. And now, with dry eyes, without a tremor, I help Justin and the unknown rescuer to transport the dead man and the unconscious woman.

While we put the woman to bed, my chauffeur flies toward Villefranche-de-Rouergue in search of a doctor or a surgeon, at top speed. She is moaning softly, like a bruised child. And in every one of her plaints there is Antoine's name. Then, suddenly, she becomes delirious.

"Faster, darling! Faster!"

While awaiting the arrival of the doctor who will treat Claudia, we lay her lover on his funeral bed. On his face, the nobility of which death seems to accentuate, there is nothing but pallor. One might think him a wax statue like those the English and provincials come to admire for a few francs in the Musée Grevin. All the vigor of that man of genius, all the blood that was beating recklessly in his arteries, has escaped through the horrible wound in his chest: a hole as large as the depths of a hat, where the entire steering wheel was embedded.

It is necessary for us to deploy considerable strength to straighten the forearms folded over the wound. At each of our efforts we hear the joints creaking, already stiffened, and that sinister task takes more than half an hour.

When it is over, Justin, white with fear and emotion, begs me to let him leave. I refuse, because I don't feel that I have the courage to remain alone with him. And my old servant hides his head in his hands, incapable of looking at the man he loved as much as me, and whose open eyes, widened by horror and suffering, are staring at us without seeing us.

This, my friend, my beloved brother, has just died! He is dead: not the peaceful end for which he was ambitious, but an atrocious and banal end that nothing presaged this morning. He died at the moment of abandoning me, and it's to my home that he has returned, in spite of his desire, in spite of the will of the other; and it is beside me that he will spend his final slumber, in the great crypt constructed by my care at the extremity of the park, a few meters from the river. It's there that we'll come to find him again, Alexandrine-Ysolde and I, and we will all decompose progressively, far from people, far from the humankind from which we separated ourselves voluntarily six years ago.

And we will keep him, who liked crowds, tumult, the ardent life of cities and capitals, in the depths of that silent and deserted retreat; no one but us will file past his coffin, and no one but us will ever come to pray before his granite tomb. Death, the redoubtable death that we brushed so many times in Argonne, in Alsace, in Belgium and the Ardennes, everywhere that the hazard of battles took us, will soon reunite us...

Yes, this is better, Antoine. The dolor that you've just experienced is very little, compared to what the future had in store for you. I, at least, will conserve your memory until the final moment of my agony. I, at least, will weep for you as your exceptional soul and your incomparable heart merit being mourned. Did the other truly love you? Was she not playing in your regard the base comedy of tenderness? Was I not correct when I discerned in her first letters a tone of duplicity that frightened and revolted me? And even if I'm mistaken, if her passion for you was neither exaggerated nor feigned, I have no regrets. You betrayed the man who had put all his confidence in you, and I had the right to hate that treason.

This evening and tomorrow I shall pass your last two terrestrial nights at your bedside. The other will not be able to trouble my meditations and my tears, and you will finish your glorious route under my guard, in my dwelling, forbidden to the profane and the wicked.

In a few hours, the aggregate of black-clad functionaries, conservers of the obsolete formulae and hypocritical ceremonial of the Law will come to certify your decease officially. In phrases that will aim at the eloquence of a public meeting they will pour over your impassive remains syrupy regrets and rancid eulogies. How you would smile if you were able to see them! All the notable people of the principal town of the canton will be there. A young deputy mayor, a junior magistrate, a commissaire, perhaps even a clerk, who will argue, prophesy, appreciate and decree in consequence of what clumsiness, what distraction or what weakness you permitted your vehicle to crash and kill you.

I had to accompany them myself.

The catastrophe happened a few kilometers from here. We recovered the auto. It was lying at the bottom of a ditch, with no windows and no windscreen. The hood of ultramarine sheet metal was ripped open in two places. Nothing but formless debris any longer exists of the small generator screwed between the two axle-trees, in the middle of the bodywork signed Labourdette. The chronometer, speedometers and microphone are all smashed, broken and pulverized. On the seat occupied by Antoine Lux the messieurs found traces of blood. They were devoured by such a fever to conduct that sensational investigation thoroughly that they envisaged with the most perfect seriousness the necessity of taking the dead man's fingerprints.

After an hour of palaver and hypotheses, they concluded that the death was caused by the rupture of the steering column, and the junior magistrate, apologizing with a delightful urbanity, asked me several questions that he certainly took to be insidious.

Since I had checked the roadster myself that morning, had I noticed anything abnormal in the mechanism? No crack in the thin steel rod commanding the front wheels of the 40CV? No? Then it was necessary to put it down to a false maneuver on Antoine's part, an excessively abrupt jolt on a road rich in fissures and potholes, or to a malfunction of the brakes that cause the lurch that had precipitated my poor friend into the ditch where he had died.

On returning to Lagarde-Viaur, I had to sign the official report drawn up by the clerk who completed the procession of magistrates. Before retiring, the messieurs manifested the desire to salute one last time the man whom France entre, all the way to and including Villefranche-de-Rouergue, held to be one of the illustrious figures in modern music.

After that homage, they slipped into the room where Claudia, her head swathed in bandages, like a mummy destined to sleep in some hypogeum on the banks of the Nile, continued divagating softy. They listened to her attentively, murmuring inconsequential words: always the same; words that I knew so well.

"Faster! He horrifies me! Let's get away! Let's quit that monster!"

But, incapable of discovering in those divagations the slightest indication appropriate to enlighten them, they took their leave of me, piled into an old taxi and left, preparing *in petto* the revelations that they deemed themselves bound to make as soon as they arrived to their friends, their relatives and acquaintances regarding the dead man, the injured woman and the mysterious individual who had gone to ground in the depths of that somber gorge, and whose frightful face no one but them was permitted to consider.

Left alone, I interrogated Justin regarding the diagnosis of the doctor who had come to examine Claudia and had left again during my absence.

Profound disturbance: cerebral commotion such that the injured woman would probably be divagating for days yet. No danger of death, since the body bore no trace of internal le-sions, but total, incurable, irremediable disfiguration of the face. The eyes could probably be saved. The nose might perhaps be narrowed, the partition having been crushed. It would be relatively easy to replace the broken teeth with dentures. As for reestablishing the harmony of the features, it was necessary not to think of it. The woman whose strange beauty we admired would remain hideous for as long as she lived—as hideous and repulsive as the man from whom she had begged her lover to deliver her.

At about ten o'clock I attempted to eat something, without succeeding.

After the absorption of a cup of very strong coffee, I headed for the mortuary chamber where I was to replace my servant until five o'clock in the morning

On my orders, the domestics had improvised a chapel of rest around Lux's bed. Four lighted candles at the corners of the table projected a flickering light into the immense room. In the midst of that penumbra, Antoine, enveloped in an immaculate sheet, seemed to be reposing.

I approached him.

Without shivering at the contact of his icy flesh, I touched his prominent forehead, and, as if he could hear me, I whispered to him: "Rest in peace, my brother. I won't quit you again."

And, having sat down in a wing-chair in front of the incandescent hearth, I attempted to analyze my suffering.

It's infinite. I didn't love anyone, except for Antoine and my sister. My sister is no longer here. Lux is dead. I ought, logically, to be sobbing, but since he was brought back I haven't shed a tear. But a malaise increasing by the minute is annihilating my thought, my lucidity and my respiration. It seems to me that I am going to expire momentarily, like him, if I don't succeed in expelling from my body what is stifling and asphyxiating me.

I see again, point by point, all the phases of his sojourn in Lagarde-Viaur, lingering most particularly over the instants when Claudia appeared in his existence, as she appeared in mine, I rediscover in my memory, as if I had noted those things on a pad, his changes of attitude, his dissimulations, his lies—and above all, the progressive disappearance of his affection for me.

Moving from one deduction to another, I end up concluding that Antoine, when he departed this morning, hated me. Did I hate him, for my part? I don't believe so. The jealousy that was devouring me was not, could not be, a generator of hatred. All my hostility, all my rancor, all my desire for vengeance, only *the other* had provoked. Whatever my heartbreak, whatever my decay and distress might be from now on, what happened *had to happen*...

Eleven o'clock chimes. A candle has just gone out. I get up in order to go and plant another on the copper spike of the holder. What to do until two o'clock? I can't do anything. Then I head in the direction of the bookshelves and I take down a book at random.

Victor Hugo, *La Légende des Siècles*.

I open it, or, rather, the book opens of its own accord, *Cain!*

Why that title rather than another? No, no! Not this volume! Wildly, I throw the octavo volume into the hearth, as if to burn, at the same time as the accursed pages, the execrable poem that Antoine reread with so much fervor when he was alive, when he called me his brother.

And suddenly, without being able to master it or retain it, the torrent of my tears, which was growling within me, which was about to choke me, breaks through the walls of my brain and bursts from my eyes.

Oh, how I'm suffering, this time! How I feel all that I forbade myself desperately to feel since the minute when, in the inexorable apparatus, I perceived the sound of the accident and the first cries of pain.

Antoine, Antoine! It's true, then! It's you that I see in front of me, rigid, eyes closed, a strap under the jaw? Never again will I hear your powerful laughter, your truculent pleasantries, your voice, so warm and so beautiful, intoning the arias that we both loved? You'll no longer animate these cold corridors these funeral halls and that crypt-like park with your impetuosity, your exuberance, your verve and your fantasy, the genius of a man-child? And all that for a woman who lured you, I remain convinced, who was playing a comedy of passion for you, who saw nothing more in you than the man who would take her out of the shadow in which she was etiolating, who would bring her into the light, and of whom she would have rid herself, after obtaining her goal, as one gets rid of a hindrance or an indiscreet individual. It's her, not you, whose disappearance I wanted. And by a cruel trick of destiny, she's alive, and it's in my house that she's watched over, cared for and will heal? Why that anomaly? Why has Providence imposed such a punishment on me? Why do I not have the energy to follow you, as I had sworn to do so many times when jealousy was crushing me and I envisaged, in order to remain alone with Claudia, artifices of neurosis?

And now, she remains...she's moaning in a room a few meters away from us...

But I suddenly think, in an explosion of joy that dilates my breast as if to make it burst, that her beauty no longer exists, that she is like me, as repulsive as me, that no one will ever desire her again; that no one will ever dare look at her again; and that we form, from today onwards, an abnormal and accursed couple.

Five o'clock!

The door opens quietly. Justin reappears. And while he moves the heavy oak batten in order to slide alongside me, a long moan reaches me, as poignant as a hymn of lament. Sahib! Until midnight, he did not cease howling mortally. He interrupted himself when fatigue wore him out and closed his eyes. Now that the icy gray-green light of dawn is tinting the Venetian blinds of the small pavilion where I've ordered that he be shut away, his canine courage has revived. He's recommencing! What redoubtable instinct possesses that animal, then, that he sensed before they were accomplished the catastrophes of which his friend, his master of election, was to die?

Justin leans toward me.

"I beg monsieur," he says to me in a low voice, "to re-place me at half past seven. I have to go down to Najac station in the auto."

To Najac? For what reason has my heart suddenly begun to beat so forcefully?

He explains to me, and I listen stupefied.

Yesterday, a few hours after the reception of the agents of the Law, a man on a bicycle handed a telegram to the park warden. That telegram, addressed to Justin Naudier, which he holds out to me, came from Paris. It bears the signature of Alexandrine-Ysolde. A few words, which petrify me, which fill me with an insurmountable fear:

Arriving tomorrow Najac station. Come for me eight thirty. Inform monsieur. Beaumont.

My sister in Lagarde-Viaur! Why?

And suddenly, I remember. She prophesied it at the mo-ment of her departure. And, emerging one by one from the mysterious coverts of my memory, reanimating like resusci-tated entities, her words return to me. I can hear them all...

"On the day when my presence here becomes necessary, I will leave without calling me. You will find me beside you; and you will see, whatever happens then, that you can count on the reckless tenderness of your sister-mama."

But if she is coming back, she has divined! She knows! What extrahuman power has revealed to her what I have been able to hide from everyone else, has suggested to her the idea of coming to find me, to protect me?

I dared not run to the car when I heard the creaking of the gravel under the attack of the tires. White with fear, I sank into the wing-chair, as if I wanted to take refuge there. And, my head bowed, my eyes blurred by fear, I waited for her.

She's here, white under her gauze veil, her eyed circled by the fatigues of the journey and by the dolor that grips her. Without speaking to me, she heads for the bed on which An-toine is lying. She leans over. A prolonged, immensely tender maternal kiss on that cold skin, which death has already marbled with yellow patches.

Two words: "Poor boy!"

Then silence. A silence of a few minutes, in the course of which I hear nothing but the disordered beating of my heart. I would like, on seeing her approach me, to get up, to throw myself into her arms, to huddle against her shoulder, as of old. Something retains me, rivets me to the seat in which I have been incrusted since the arrival of the auto. I would like to speak to her, but I can't find the strength to articulate a syllable. It's her who comes slowly to my side. It's her who encourages me, and who sympathizes with me.

"Don't stay like this, Patrice. It's necessary to overcome your prostration. It's necessary to free your mind from all the anguish that is torturing it, and robbing you of the lucidity of which you have so much need. Get up, Patrice, and come with me."

I followed her.

My heads in my hands, I listened to her talking to me. Not a word of reproach. Not a gesture of malediction or accusation. An infinite pity, and above all, a passionate desire to avoid our name being sullied in the course of the torment that might perhaps fall upon us.

"This, I order you to do. And all those who are asleep out there, in the great marble crypt with the gold armories, order you to do it, as I do. What has just happened, I foresaw. No one, in your place, would have been able to resist the frightful thoughts that dissected you day and night. No one, save perhaps for the man who is lying not far away from us, in whose hatred you believed unjustly. Don't weep like that, Patrice. I won't leave you again. When everything is over, and we've deposited Antoine in the tomb to which, I sense, we shall not be long delayed in joining him, when the person from whom all our woes emerged has returned to Paris, we shall strive never to speak again about any of it, never to evoke these atrocious hours. But it will be necessary to pray often, to pray for him, who can perhaps see you, and who is absolving you, as I am myself, at this tragic moment.

Shaken by sobs, I knelt down before my sister. She lifted me up. She opened her arms to me. Then she took me by the hand and, silently, we returned to the room from which the man will soon emerge on whose account I am perhaps so frightfully mistaken.

XII

The burial will take place tomorrow at two o'clock.

The second mortuary vigil we spend together, Alexandrine-Ysolde and I: a vigil already less heart-rending than the other, but perhaps leaving a deeper impression. Antoine's body is decomposing gradually. The perimeter of his fingernails is already violet. In the morning, a slight odor floats in the air, which is compounded out of burnt incense, stuffiness and all the imprecise odors that compose the atmosphere of a supersaturated chapel of the faithful.

Alexandrine-Ysolde has given orders to cut all the flowers and all the plants still blooming in the hothouses. She knows Antoine's passion for the perfumes of their calices, and she spreads armfuls of them herself on his couch.

At ten o'clock we laid him in his bier. How heavy he is, and how tall! Three of us can scarcely lift him. And there he is, his hands folded over his staved-in breast, immobile forever between the walls of the oblong box. My sister has transported to his rigid body the odorous sheaves that were strewn over his bed just now. One last glance. One last grip of the hand; and Justin advances to screw down the lid, while the chambermaid appears on the threshold and calls to my sister in a low voice.

A few seconds later, very upset, Alexandrine-Ysolde reappears. She stops Justin's arm. and draws me to one side.

"Geneviève Servais is here. She's just arrived by auto. She's been traveling for more than half the night. She wants to see him."

We stand aside to make way for the young woman, who loved him to the extent of quitting everything in order to contemplate him before his definitive effacement from the earth. She too is beautiful, although dolor and lassitude have hollowed out her face and deformed her features—less beautiful than the other, however, and above all less enigmatic.

As we make as if to leave, she retains us.

"We already know one another," she says, in a broken voice, "since it's here that I was to come with him to hide the first days of my happiness. I want to see him again next to you, because you loved him, and you are, for that reason, a little of him."

She kneels before the bier and weeps silently. Then she takes a ring out of her handbag, a simple and slender gold band. She deposits it between Antoine Lux's fingers, and gets up.

"I owed him that restitution," she explains. "He gave it to me when we were engaged." Then, gazing at him: "I don't hold anything against you, my poor boy. We're poor things, impotent and weak, and we know nothing of what regulates us and makes us act. Sleep in peace. I shall remember. I shall remember the bright hours, for I've already forgotten the others, and I forgive you for everything that you made me suffer, in favor of the untranslatable joys that our amour revealed to me."

I listen to Geneviève speaking. I listen to her, astounded, and each of her phrases causes to raise a kind of horror of myself from the remotest recesses of my being. What a lesson! She suffered as much as me, and more than me, and the words that emerge from her mouth are nothing but words of absolution and forbearance.

She followed the body next to Alexandrine-Ysolde. For myself, I walked alone, with a thick kerchief over my face, in order not to be seen either by the officiant or the altar-boys carrying the censer and the cross.

And when the cortege passed in front of the pavilion where I ordered Sahib to be locked up, a howl that made us all tremble emerge from the interior.

Sahib sensed his master passing, and he was mourning him!

On returning, we interrogated Geneviève. We asked her how she had known...

"It was by wireless that I learned the terrible news," she replied. "Since his departure, since the letters had become rarer, I had had a receiver installed in my bureau. Thus, deprived of his news, I could nevertheless hear his works executed. Yesterday, at four o'clock, the announcer informed his listeners of the death of the master, and the disfigurement of the woman for whom he had denied and abandoned everything. Truly, the punishment is too frightful for the crime!"

Geneviève asked us for news of Claudia. We showed her the room in which the sick woman, prey to a fit of fever that becomes more intense as time passes, continues her delirium.

"What irony," she murmurs. "The forsaken and the mistress under the same roof."

We insist, in view of the excessive fatigue to which the double excursion has plunged her, that she dine here and stay overnight.

"You can leave tomorrow," proposes my sister.

"Thank you," the young woman replies, "but I'll stay in Villefranche tonight, and I'll be in Paris before midnight tomorrow. Here, everything would remind me too much of him, and it's necessary that I strive to forget him, since he forgot me."

"Will you be able to do that?" asks Alexandrine-Ysolde.

"Perhaps, in a few years, if I'm still alive." Then, abruptly: "I know that Antoine's score is still in your hands. Can you and will you return it to me? It's necessary, more than ever, that that masterpiece sees the light of day. Antoine is dead. His drama ought to live. I knew him. I loved him. It's up to me to prevent it being removed from the stage that was being prepared, while he was alive, to welcome it and to display it worthily."

I handed her the large sheets on which, in his large, firm handwriting and his imperious script, he had noted the orchestration and the lyrical declamation of the three acts. She buried the work at the bottom of the trunk of her cabriolet. Then, without wanting to accept anything from us but a slice of toast and two cups of black coffee, she climbed back into the car that she drove herself, and boldly, at high speed, entered into the penumbra that the falling night was spreading around the mountains and over the whiteness of the roads.

XIII

This morning, before nine and ten, I went down to the Viaur.

I wanted to go as far as him, to bow down before his tomb, to pray for him if I could. From the umbrella stand at the entrance I had taken a stout ash-wood walking-stick destined, in my thinking, to sustain me on pathways varnished with ice.

A quarter of an hour of walking.

I perceive, a few meters in front of me, the somber mass of the burial vault. And as I approach the mausoleum, a sudden roar rips through the air. Something black bounds toward me. Teeth, sharper than the teeth of a saw, close on the collar of my sheepskin, puncture it frantically, seeking my throat, while two clawed paws collide with my shoulders and knock me over with the violence of their unexpected impact.

I fall alongside the vault. I try to defend myself, to turn the iron tip of my stick against the slavering jaws. The enormous weight of the dark gray body paralyzes me. I shout for help, desperately. Letting go of my useless weapon, I try to seize the maw of the aggressor, to close it enough to stifle it, or at least to make it let go. A sudden weakness prevents me.

And, vanquished by the ferocious beast that had just planted its fangs in my wrist, I fainted.

Justin and the chauffeur, who were coming back up from the river, and who heard me, saved me.

My wound is deep, but not serious.

Sahib who had just attacked me, was taken back to his cell. He too, then, must know everything, in order to hate me to that degree and to want to kill me.

My sister bandages me. After dinner, I ring for Justin.

"Have Sahib put down," I order him.

"Impossible, Monsieur," the valet de chambre replied. "He ran away when the gardener took him his mincemeat, and in spite of searching everywhere, no one can find him.

I'm afraid.

A week has gone by since the wolfhound's aggression. No one was able to pick up his trail, and it was supposed that he had leapt over the wall surrounding the property in a single bound and then fled across country.

After that moment, my fear was so great that I didn't risk myself outside the house. I understood that if I encountered him again, the administrator of justice would not show me any mercy.

Sahib was found at seven o'clock yesterday, dead of starvation and cold in front of the burial vault. Having doubtless gone to earth in the thickets during the day, he rejoined his master when darkness fell and the living were shut away in their shelters, and the space belonged to free wild beasts until the following dawn.

That one truly loved Antoine Lux!

XIV

After a convalescence of a month, during which Alexandrine-Ysolde has never ceased to lavish the most devoted and tender care upon her, Claudia Pichet went outside for the first time this afternoon.

Still very weak, but sustained by an inflexible will, she went down all the way to the tomb of black stone that extends like an inanimate monster over Antoine's coffin.

She knelt down on the white flagstones and, her head between her hands, she prayed for a long time. Then, standing up with the aid of the woman who had guided her and accompanied her, she resumed the route to the house, mute and hostile to any question and any gaze on the part of her protectress.

What I discerned, what I believed I understood, though the lacerations of my jealousy, is exact.

Claudia had no passion for my friend. She did not cherish him. Everything in her was resolved in implacable calculations, in cold schemes.

The man who is asleep between the heavy planks of oak, she considered as an instrument of success, as a stepping-stone thanks to which she could accede to renown, a servant whom she would have rejected disdainfully on the day when the accomplishment of her design was realized.

Neither in going nor returning, nor during her prolonged station over the tomb, has she shed a single tear. It is with an atonal gaze, and dry eyes, that she has considered the portrait of the dead man, a copy of which occupies the Louis XIV table in her room. It is in a weary voice which is not pierced by any tremor of dolor, that she has talked to my sister about the deceased, either at meal times or in the course of sessions on the chaise-longue during which her indefatigable nurse neglected all her domestic occupations in order to distract her and care for her at the times fixed by the surgeon.

Face striped with suture points; eyebrows burned by the backlash of the flame that determined the burning of the auto; nose devoid of proportions, devoid of symmetry; nostrils pierced like two unequal holes above the lips, which now affect the appearance of a hare-lip: that is what remains of the resplendent daughter issued from the Egyptian Gasmiliah and the band-leader Pichet.

And it is that alone, her own misfortune, that she laments. On the disappearance of the other, not a word, not a single cry of despair or regret.

Poor Antoine! How fortunate he is not to see anything, to think anything, or to hear anything!

XV

She left this morning at eight o'clock

Alexandrine-Ysolde, who wanted to embark her, took her with Justine as far as the Lexos station, where she manifested the desire to wait for the Paris-Orsay express.

At the moment of departure she asked to see me, to say goodbye. I sent the response via my sister that I held that formality to be superfluous. Did she understand that the reply comported hatred, scorn and rancor? I don't think so, for Alexandrine-Ysolde affirmed to me that she seemed greatly affected by my decision. That's better, all things considered. Would I have been able, in facing her, to master myself, to repress the tumultuous upsurge of my heart? Would I have been able to prevent my clenched hands gripping her throat and squeezing it until her last vital breath escaped from its execrable envelope?

All the quivering of my revolted being suggests not.

Now we're alone, as we were two months ago, between the thick walls of the dwelling where I have gone through the most terrible crisis of my existence. We're alone—with Antoine. He is still here. We have conserved him in spite of himself. And long after she would have lost the memory of his features, the wonderstruck face of our friend will survive for us. Not one of his attitudes, not one of his gestures will fade away from our memories. And every day, my sister or I will go to find him, outside his stone retreat.

I had Sahib buried beside him.

It is good that beasts, equal to humans, superior to humans in their instincts, their prescience, their devotion and their sensibility, share the repose of those they loved and for love of whom they push sacrifice as far as death.

XVI

While rummaging in the drawer of the table at which Lux worked, I found the portrait of the cantatrice. It's here, in front of me, regal, arrogant and enigmatic.

What will become of her, the witch with the mask disemboweled by destiny? In what city is she parading her nostalgia, her disgrace and her rancor?

I shall doubtless never see her again. That photograph is all that remains to me of her. And one day, when my hatred, attenuated by the omnipotent hand of the years, has given way to the indifference for everything that swarms around us in which I make my way, I shall tear it up and scatter its odious debris in the fire.

But how long the cure will be in coming, as I contemplate her often, in silence, evoking all the phases of the drama of which she was the promoter, and of which no one will ever know the final word.

The days go by. April is reborn in the park. The flowers are risking themselves outside the white morning frosts. The trees are gradually dressing themselves in jade and Veronese green again.

At about three o'clock, Alexandrine-Ysolde asked me to accompany her to the tomb. Where she wants to deposit a wreath of newly opened flowers. How she has aged, my sister-mama, and how stooped her entire restless body is over the stone that she is flowering. What evil secret is undermining her thus? What evil secret, extending its mysterious ramifications over me, has blanched my hair, curbed my once proud stature, withered my horrible features and made a human rag of a man once admired or his slimness, elegance and strength, in the space of six months?

I too, I sense, will not take long to rejoin him. I await the great moment with an impatience that is increasing by the hour. Nothing any longer keeps me here but my sister; and when she is laid down next to Antoine, I shall doubtless say at the same time, extended on my bed in advance, my eyes already closed, a definitive adieu to all terrestrial things.

We chatted as we left the table.

Mechanically, I picked up one of the receivers immobilized since the accident next to my improved apparatus. For how many days have I heard nothing, know nothing, of exterior events? All the dailies received, all the periodicals, all those attestations that, everywhere apart from here, people are acting, brains are creating, envies are fermenting, I disdain and reject. What would they bring me except things of which I know too much?

And seeing me this, handling the accursed headphones, an idea occurs to Alexandrine-Ysolde. "It's five o'clock," she says. "Would you like to catch the Eiffel Tower? You have so much need for distraction, my poor boy."

"Never!" I reply. "It's finished. Everything came from that!"

"What had to happen, Patrice, nothing could have prevented. Go on, put them on..."

I obey. And as I put them on, I evoke the splendor of Claudia. Unable to prevent myself, I take her portrait from the depths of the drawer where I have hidden it. And I receive, and we receive, shivering, the unexpected announcement

"The Tower invites you to listen to two fragments of *Rosalinde*. It is the posthumous work of the illustrious composer Antoine Lux, who died six months ago in Rouergue after an automobile accident. The woman who was with him at the time and who has remained, although irremediably disfigured by the crash, the master's companion, the cantatrice Claudia Pichet, will enable to you hear them..."

The master's companion!

Out there, hundreds of kilometers away, the jingling piano ritornelle reaches us on the invisible vibration of the waves. By wireless! And while she sings, I contemplate her.

A little while ago, after that ultimate audition, I destroyed my headphones, my antennae and my loudspeakers.

And I shall remain alone at Lagarde-Viaur, alone in my old funereal manor, with my sister Alexandrine-Ysolde and the tomb of Antoine Lux...

Alone? Who knows?

Now that we are both monsters, why should she not return one day? Later...much later...

At Mas de Libande, in Quercy, February 1926.